"I just want what's best for you," Parker said.

And he meant it. Maybe she wasn't concerned that the trail rides couldn't guarantee a steady income, but he was.

"Yeah, I'm a lucky girl," Hailey said. "Everyone wants what's best for me." She laughed and then half smiled. "So. Tell me, Parker, how much do you *really* know about horses and stables and barns?"

It was a fair question.

"I think we both know the answer," he said.

And just like that, he was back to being *Parker* again instead of *Parks*. His suggestion to tear down the barn seemed to have put him back at square one. Fortunately, *square one* was very familiar territory. He wasn't scared of it.

It was only after he'd left Sunrise Stables shortly thereafter that he realized the subtext of what she'd asked. What she really meant was, *how much do you really know about me?* There was only one honest answer for that.

Not nearly enough.

Dear Reader,

Sometimes it seems the harder we try to shape our journey, the more our journey is determined to shape us. That's how I felt while telling Hailey and Parker's story in *Her Kind of Cowboy*—the second book in my Destiny Springs, Wyoming series.

Hailey Goodwin's future is as open as the trail rides she offers through her new business. Finally, a chance to find her footing and convince her mom and sisters that she's no longer a child. By contrast, Parker Donnelly grew up fast, having been raised by a single mom who struggled. He knows where his life is headed...until he's thrust into the unlikely role of "cowboy" for the cowgirl who stole his heart twenty years earlier.

But Hailey's heart was broken once by a big-city boy. She doesn't want to go back down that trail. Now, they must navigate this unexpected situation, as their hearts take the reins.

I hope you enjoy finding out where their journeys ultimately lead them, and the happiness that awaits.

Warmest wishes,

Susan Breeden

HEARTWARMING

Her Kind of Cowboy

—

Susan Breeden

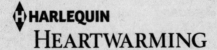

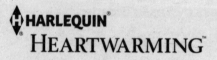

HARLEQUIN®

HEARTWARMING™

ISBN-13: 978-1-335-58500-4

Recycling programs
for this product may
not exist in your area.

Her Kind of Cowboy

Harlequin Enterprises ULC
22 Adelaide St. West, 41st Floor
Toronto, Ontario M5H 4E3, Canada
www.Harlequin.com

Printed in U.S.A.

Susan Breeden is a native Texan who currently lives in Houston, where she works as a technical writer/editor for the aerospace industry. In the wee hours of morning and again at night, you will find her playing matchmaker for the heroes and heroines in her novels. She also enjoys walks with her bossy German shepherd, decluttering and organizing her closet, and trying out new chili con queso recipes. For information on Susan's upcoming books, visit susanbreeden.com.

Books by Susan Breeden

Harlequin Heartwarming

Destiny Springs, Wyoming

The Bull Rider's Secret Son

Visit the Author Profile page
at Harlequin.com for more titles.

For Martha and Bobby.

CHAPTER ONE

HAILEY GOODWIN WAS an awesome babysitter, if she did say so herself.

Sure, she could have microwaved some instant oatmeal for the kiddos. But Pop-Tarts were *so* much more fun. In fact, *fun* was the goal of the day because for the next week, she'd be walking a proverbial tightrope without a net. Her Sunrise Stables business partner and "brother from another mother," Cody Sayers, was abandoning her.

And she couldn't be happier for him.

In her opinion, a month was way too long to postpone a honeymoon. Yet, Cody had refused to leave until he'd helped to get Hailey's rescue horses trained, fixed up her stables and used his celebrity bull rider name to help spread the word about the return of a Destiny Springs tradition: trail rides.

They had succeeded, with behind-the-scenes help from Parker Donnelly.

Parks. She was rather glad he'd be going

back to Chicago in a week or so, after having come here to help his grandfather Vern with Fraser Ranch's bookkeeping for the past four months. Then agreeing to help Hailey with the financial side of her trail-ride reboot. Big-city, suit-and-tie types were too much of a distraction.

Then again, Parks had always been a bit of a distraction even when they were kids, visiting their respective grandparents in town. Who knew they'd end up in a working relationship? However, with the soft opening of the trail rides fully underway, and the official launch scheduled for three weeks after Cody's return, Parker's work here was done.

Hailey leaned against the kitchen counter, wrapped both hands around the warm mug of instant coffee and observed the three little ones. Six-year-old Max was looking more and more like his famous dad, Cody, with each passing day. Except for the red hair, which he'd inherited from his mom and Hailey's BFF, Becca. The twin girls favored their own father—her dear friend and local rancher Nash Buchanan— all the way down to the tips of their long eyelashes. Hailey had never met their mother, but she must have been pretty.

She took a sip of coffee. It tasted bitter when

paired with the reminder that there would never be any little kiddos running around that looked like her.

"Can we play dress-up now? I want to be Cinderella," Elizabeth Anne said while continuing to chew. The strawberry filling smeared across her lips resembled lip gloss.

"No talking with your mouth full, Lizzy. Besides, where would we ever find glass slippers and a ball gown?"

The little girl pointed at the most obvious splash of color in Hailey's otherwise neutral living room.

Of course. The maid-of-honor dress from the Sayers' wedding. Sweetheart neckline, full skirt. The most *romance-y* dress Hailey owned. But Cinderella? It looked more like something Juliet Capulet would have worn. It was still hanging from a nail in the living room. Getting Sunrise Stables up and running had been like the Belmont Stakes on a continuous loop. Less important tasks like putting away clothing had to be relegated to the back burner.

"Cinderella's dress is blue," Katherine Claire insisted, which set the pendulum in motion.

"Is *not*!" Lizzy argued.

"Is too!"

"Is *not*!"

Max quietly collected the pieces of his disassembled Pop-Tart and headed toward the hall as the disagreement escalated. Hailey's black cat, Sergeant, who didn't suffer humans or situations that chafed, took his favorite little person's cue but quickly surpassed him and disappeared.

"Stay in here where I can see you, kiddo," Hailey called out to Max.

As unpleasant as that might be.

Max returned but sat at the farthest end of the table.

Hailey could relate to Max's impulse to flee. They both hated confrontations.

"No dress-up today. We're doing yoga, remember?" Hailey said, switching the topic to something the girls could agree on. "Finish your breakfast and drink your milk, then it's off to the barn."

Lizzy finished her tart first and licked her fingers clean, while Katherine Claire took her time to chew every bite before reaching for a napkin. Max reassembled what was left of his Pop-Tart and polished it off in a few ginormous bites.

Hailey turned on the kitchen faucet and let the water get warm while she retrieved a footstool.

"Up," she said as she pointed to it.

Everyone knew the drill. Lizzy took the lead. She darted her hands into the stream for all of two seconds, then held them out for Hailey to dry.

"No, ma'am. Soap."

Her words played tricks on her ears. She sounded exactly like her own mom. Same words, same tone.

Of course, her mom's words played like a broken record in her head anyway. The chorus of questions regarding her life choices and future, of which her sister Georgina had recently taken over as lead vocalist. The hovering. The unwarranted concern. The unsolicited advice.

That was why the trail rides had to succeed. If reinstating the tradition that her great-grandparents began and that the whole town was rallying around didn't convince her family that she knew what she was doing and could take care of herself, nothing would.

It wouldn't hurt if she could convince herself, as well.

Lizzy pumped some liquid soap into her palm and slathered it all over her hands, then rinsed. Hailey dried them and helped the little girl safely to the floor.

"Your turn, Kat. Let's see you wash them paws." That nickname tickled the little girl to pieces. Hailey didn't have to tell this one to use soap. Kat was so methodical and thorough, it was scary.

Max politely waited for the young ladies to finish. To no surprise, he did an exemplary job. Becca and Cody clearly worked in lockstep to teach their son how to be a cowboy *and* a gentleman.

Once all hands were clean and dry, it occurred to her the washing was pointless, considering what they were about to do. Except for Max. The cleaner his hands, the better.

"Okay, kiddo," she said to him. "I need some help. You know how you like telling stories on the trail rides? I'd love for you to make up one about the goats and record everything with my phone. But you have to hold it as still as possible. And be careful not to drop it." She switched her cell phone to video mode, walked him through the steps a few times, then proceeded to question her judgment.

He seemed beyond delighted with the responsibility. It *would* keep him busy and less likely to wander off while she wasn't looking. Better to worry about her phone's safety than about his.

For practice, he pointed the lens at the girls. Or, sort of pointed. Kat slinked off to a corner, avoiding the spotlight, while Lizzy performed some sort of crazy banshee dance.

"Remember our deal?" she said, leading them to the back door but stopping short of opening it.

They nodded in unison, although Hailey knew they couldn't keep the Pop-Tarts a secret for long. Even if they didn't confess to ingesting a million grams of sugar, the inevitable energy explosion would give it away. They were like cuddly little time bombs. Becca had given her the sugary breakfast treats for Max in the first place, so she couldn't hold Hailey completely liable. But Nash wouldn't know what hit him. As a single dad, he doted on the girls, but his plate was otherwise full. Too much ranch and not enough hands.

Cody and Nash would be by soon to pick up their respective kids. In exchange for the favor of babysitting their little angels, maybe she'd ask them about introducing her to some friends. Born-and-bred cowboys, like themselves. Only less brotherly and more...*romance-y*.

As if she had the time.

"Last one there has to clean up goat poop!" Max declared as he launched into a sprint. Lizzy stayed hot on his heels, never one to let a boy take first place in anything.

"Hey, kiddo, real cowboys don't talk like that. And do *not* drop that phone!" Hailey called out, to no avail.

Kat slipped her tiny hand into Hailey's and tugged as they neared the barn. Her grandparents had used it for storage. For Hailey, it had been a haven from her mom and sisters. Her safe place.

Still was. Sliding that door open always filled her with a peaceful feeling. Seeing the goats was icing on the proverbial Pop-Tart. Max and the twins ran directly to the pen and let themselves in.

Hailey joined the motley crew, retrieved three yoga mats and unfurled them on the ground, even though two of them were nothing more than a formality. Although the girls liked the concept of yoga, they weren't interested in actually *doing* it. Similarly, Max couldn't have cared less. They were there for one thing: the goats.

Not that she blamed them. Such cute, fun, silly creatures.

Speaking of fun, silly creatures, Max had already launched into some crazy story about how the goats were superheroes in disguise. At least he was holding the phone with both hands. Perhaps part of the video would be salvageable.

After wrangling her long ponytail into a messy bun, Hailey positioned herself on the yoga mat and laid flat on her stomach, arms bent, palms positioned beneath her shoulders.

"Kat, will you grab some treats and do the honors?" Lizzy couldn't be trusted with the task, but her twin knew exactly where to place the pellets. "Max, get this on video, please, sir." Her friends were going to get a kick out of it. No one believed goat yoga was actually a *thing*.

Moments later, one of the flat-surface-loving babies climbed aboard Hailey's back and began grazing. The kiddos all giggled as Hailey transitioned from the cobra position to a modified cat. The furry, four-legged kid of another variety wobbled but kept his balance. Another baby goat brushed back and forth beneath her chin before bouncing away with random, spastic jerks as if he were being controlled by an inebriated puppeteer.

It was Hailey's turn to giggle. These little bundles of energy always de-stressed her, no matter what was happening in her life. Like now, as the thought of flying solo for an entire week began to sink in. At least Cody and Becca were closing the Hideaway while they were gone. Their B and B was the source of most of Hailey's business, to date, so trail-ride bookings would be down. Less chance of some-thing happening that she couldn't handle. There was no room for any glitches in advance of the official launch.

Lizzy ran over and sprinkled some pellets on Hailey's neck. Right where she wasn't sup-posed to, because the goat would decide Hai-ley's hair should be dessert.

"Elizabeth Anne Buchanan, what did I tell you about doing that?"

The little girl giggled, then skipped away in search of some other kind of mischief, no doubt.

"Stay inside the pen, Lizzy. That goes for all of you," she admonished.

The barn door slid open, then closed. She craned her neck to see that Cody had come in. He was early, which ordinarily wouldn't have been a big deal, but did he have to bring Parker with him?

As they approached, Hailey wiggled to gently coax the critter off her back, since her current configuration couldn't have been flat-tering. But the little guy didn't budge. Instead, he began sampling her updo.

How embarrassing. Not to mention, a bit painful.

She was rather hoping Parker would remember the maid-of-honor version of her when he left. Or even the jeans and T-shirt version, which he'd seen a few times, although not much lately. He'd been busy wrapping up his stay at his grandpa's ranch. Not that she imagined he'd been much help to Vern, aside from the bookkeeping. Couldn't exactly deliver a calf or feed chickens in a button-down and tie, like he was currently wearing, as though he were en route to a business meeting. He usually wore more practical clothing. At least today's formality was offset by jeans and sensible boots.

The goat finally had enough of Hailey's movement and jumped off. She stood and brushed the remaining feed off her back.

"You still have some corn in your hair. But it's a good look for you," Cody said, adding a wink.

And to think she complained about having two older sisters when Bro here was such a tease. Parker, on the other hand, politely walked away. In fact, he intervened to rescue a baby goat that Lizzy had taken hostage and was trying to carry like a child. He eased the squirmy little thing out of her arms and set it on the ground, where it bounced away.

Hailey took advantage of the semiprivate moment with Cody. "Seems I have a smart aleck in my hair, as well. Did you stop by to make fun of me, or are you picking up Max super early? And why did you bring you-know-who?"

Cody served up his trademark mischievous grin, which meant he had something up those flannel sleeves of his. "In the order you asked, why not, no, and I told you I was going to hire someone to help you while I was gone."

"I know you mentioned it, but I told you not to go to the trouble and expense. I don't need any help. Go be a newlywed. Focus on your beautiful wife instead of worrying about me. That's my mother's and sisters' job, and they're convinced they know what's best. But I'm mature, reliable and can take care of myself."

"I can see that," he said. "I intend to focus my attention on Becca, which is why I don't want to worry about our business while I'm gone. Besides, I owe you for getting me and the love of my life back together."

The *worrying* comment stung a little. Did he doubt her ability to manage the business alone for a week? But the last part caused the skin on her arms to goose bump, although she wasn't sure why. Truth be told, having some assistance might be a good thing. She could delegate the duties she least enjoyed to the temporary help.

"If the person you've hired is a handsome,

single, hometown cowboy who can pick up the slack around here, consider the favor paid in full," she teased.

Cody pursed his lips. "How about two out of four?"

While she was trying to decide which two qualities Cody might mean, Parker rejoined them. This time, however, he was looking at her the way he had at Cody and Becca's reception. Like she was too pretty to look anywhere else.

She didn't need this. Come to think of it, *cute* and *single* might end up being a similar distraction in someone else. She couldn't let anything jeopardize the momentum they had going at the stables.

No, a hometown cowboy would work just fine. Hardworking and humble. Someone who knew the area and might be willing to pick up more work later down the line or could be available in a pinch.

"So, when do I get to meet the lucky guy or gal who you've hired to save the day?" she asked.

Parker cleared his throat and lifted his index finger.

Was he asking permission to speak? This wasn't a business meeting. She could picture him in some fancy boardroom with floor-to-ceiling glass windows. Surrounded by female coworkers who wanted to date him. Near-movie-star looks but with a few rough edges. As if success and the good life hadn't been handed to him on a gilded platter. He'd earned it the hard way.

When no other words or gestures were forthcoming, she looked to Cody.

"You already have," he said, then looked to Parker, who simply smiled with confidence.

"Wait. You mean…?" *Noooo!*

Parker was a hard worker, and he'd been indispensable in helping with the numbers side of the reboot, but he knew nothing about leading the trail rides.

The goats started bleating in the background. Animals always did sense danger, but this was ridiculous. Everything about this scenario was wrong.

So much for this day being fun. So much for having some help this week. Now, she'd not only be walking a tightrope without a net, she'd also have to train and supervise someone.

Make that a handsome, single someone who was already way too much of a distraction.

PARKER DONNELLY DIDN'T think it was possible for Hailey to look any prettier than she had a month ago at the wedding. Or more confident than she did in jeans and tees. But this version of her? Fearless came to mind. And understandably shocked.

He was determined to make a good impression this week because once he returned to Chicago, it might be a while before he'd see Hailey again.

"I know I'm not your typical ranch hand, but I'm a quick study," he said, putting an end to the awkward silence. It was true. For example, Parker quickly figured out Hailey wasn't onboard with this arrangement.

He'd had his doubts, as well. But Cody wouldn't take *no* for an answer. Not that Parker had needed persuading. The little boy in him was elated at the prospect of playing cowboy for a week, while the adult in him embraced the challenge.

As of this morning, however, a new and very welcome challenge had been added to the mix. He was still reeling from his online meeting with his boss. Despite the fact that Parker was on a leave of absence, he was up for a promotion to senior consultant. The caveat: he had to provide a proposal that demonstrated his range and diversity, and he had a week to do it. Talk about a tight deadline. But there was no way he was backing out of his commitment to Hailey and Cody. He'd find a way to do both. The effort would be worth it. More stability. Greater financial security. He'd be well on his way to the place he always wanted to be.

Maybe he didn't know the difference between a trot and a cantor, but he understood money. He and his mom knew how it felt to have none. This promotion would assure that he and those he loved would never return to *that* place ever again.

"You're in good hands, Hailey," Cody said, driving home the declaration with a slap on Parker's back. "In case you weren't aware, he's the only consultant in his firm with a one hundred percent customer satisfaction rating."

"Client satisfaction would actually be the correct verbiage," Parker said. *Oh, Parks, no you didn't.*

Was his face as red as it felt? The accomplishment read beautifully on paper, but the spoken version sounded like a car commercial or late-night television twofer sale on cutlery. Not that he wasn't proud of it. His clients' successes were his successes. He'd never let one down before, and he wasn't going to start with Hailey. Although this was a business relationship and nothing but, she was also a friend.

"That's very impressive, Parks, but this is a whole 'nother animal," she said. "I've spent my life around horses. It's not as easy as it looks."

"I understand your concern. If it helps, I've been around my grandpa's horses quite a bit, and I've pitched in."

Hailey cocked her head and smiled. "Okay. For instance…?"

"I've fed them," Parker said.

She squinted.

He winced. "And stuff."

Cody cleared his throat.

Stop talking. Although he could talk circles around other consultants, Hailey had a way of tongue-tying him with a single gesture. He'd been much more articulate throughout this entire trail-ride reboot when going over things with her by phone or text. She and Cody handled all the hands-on tasks. But the CliffsNotes version of horsemanship that Cody tutored him on ahead of time had flown out the barn door the minute they'd opened it and he saw her.

Cody clapped his hands together and clasped his fingers, as if it could somehow bring this whole awkward exchange to a tidy close. Either that, or he was praying that it would, which would make at least two of them.

"I've filled him in on the basics, Hailey. Thought you could show him the actual ropes."

"You thought what?" she asked.

Before either Cody or Parker were forced to elaborate, Max cuteness-bombed them. He pointed the phone at Cody. "Daddy! Daddy! You're in my video! Tell 'em what sound bulls make when you ride 'em!"

Cody seemed to contemplate it. "Tell 'em? How about we show 'em?" He whisked Max up into his arms and blew a raspberry on his neck.

Parker nearly lost it. What he wouldn't have given to have had a father like Cody. Or a father at all.

Max shrieked and giggled uncontrollably until Cody set him back down. Miraculously enough, the little boy didn't drop the phone. Meanwhile, Hailey released her long brown hair from its confines, causing Parker's traitorous heart to skip a beat.

All the while, four tiny goats bounced around them, chased by Nash's five-year-old twins. The whole menagerie had to be the most adorable thing Parker had ever seen. Add two or three more children to the mix, and it would resemble the type of family he imagined having someday. He would fill his six-bedroom dream house with love and laughter, assuming the seller accepted his offer. Best school district in the Chicago area.

"I need to scoot," Cody called out. "Becca's waiting on me to finish packing. We'll be back over later. You kids play fair but have fun." He tipped his Stetson to Parker and winked at Hailey, as if the last sentence pertained to them instead of the children.

Hailey crossed her arms and slowly shook her head. But Parker would show her he *could* do this.

He loved a challenge. Let the helping commence.

CHAPTER TWO

PARKER WATCHED AS Hailey sidestepped him, picked up one of the yoga mats and shook it off, then rolled it up and tossed it in the corner.

He knelt beside one of the remaining mats, but when he started to roll it up, a baby goat grabbed his dangling tie with its teeth and proceeded to tug. "Oh, no, you don't. Not the only one I brought." But the more Parker tried to pull away, the more the little creature dug in. If he hadn't just wrapped up that pivotal meeting with his boss when Cody came knocking and was in such a hurry to get over here, he would have changed back into his polo shirt.

Within seconds, Lizzy, Kat and Max had caught on to his predicament, which must've looked even more ridiculous than it felt. Hailey was quick to intervene. She promptly extracted the tie by prying the goat's mouth open with her fingers, then redirecting the little critter with a loving shove toward the others.

Parker stood and dusted off his knees. She

stood, as well. So much for that good impression he'd intended to make. Not all was lost, however. He simply needed to also prop up his ego.

"Thanks for saving me from death by humiliation," he said. Might as well call it like it was. Although the indignity was horrifying, he'd suffered much worse in his life. Besides, the whole crazy thing made Hailey smile for the first time this morning.

"Goats rarely bite. Their palate structure makes it difficult. But if they do, you could lose a finger. I mean, look what it did to your tie." She moved closer and examined the damage.

He gulped. He hadn't seen her this up close since the wedding. She'd been all made up and picture-perfect then. No makeup today, though. Nothing to skew those green-and-gold eyes, thick lashes and heartbreaker cheekbones.

Her proximity started making his nose itch. Only one thing had that effect.

"How many barn cats do you have?" he asked, realizing he'd never even been inside the barn. Nor had he ever been inside her home. Cody, Hailey and himself had conducted all in-person meetings on this project at the B and B.

She straightened his tie with both hands and adjusted his lapels, then quickly stepped back as if the whole sequence suddenly felt like something a wife or serious girlfriend would do. Or perhaps he was simply projecting.

"None that I know of. Only a domesticated house cat. Why do you ask?"

"Just curious." He wasn't about to discuss his allergies. She must have some dander on her clothing.

Hailey finished rolling up the mat he'd started and placed it beside the first. He tossed his tie over his shoulder for safekeeping and rolled up the remaining mat, setting it against the wall beside the other two.

He turned his attention to the structure around them, if only to avoid getting pulled deeper into something that would never work—the two of them.

Speaking of things that didn't work. This barn certainly didn't. Not from a financial standpoint, much less an aesthetic or functional one. Although her trail rides were already generating some revenue, she couldn't weather too many ups and downs, much less enjoy a comfortable margin of security.

Yet...this barn was perfect for one thing. Seems he'd literally walked right into the perfect solution to his proposal dilemma. This was unlike any other project in his portfolio.

"What would you think of tearing this down, building an arena and offering riding lessons? I could put some numbers together for you."

"Tear it down? What do you mean?" she asked.

What else could it mean?

"Raze? Level?" *Put it out of its misery?*

Her pause seemed more like a brick wall than an open mind. "But where would the goats live?"

Was she being serious? Fortunately, Kat provided a nice distraction, because he had no idea how to answer that, thus leaving his slam-dunk idea in midair. She ran over and wrapped her little arms around Hailey's waist.

"Can I come live with you?" Kat asked. "Lizzy's being mean."

"Aww, is she?" Hailey swooped the girl up into her arms and gave her a quick kiss on the cheek.

The whole of Parker's insides melted like butter on a hot biscuit…for only the second time in his life. He'd gotten one of those kisses from Hailey when he was around ten. Its healing power wasn't to be underestimated.

He didn't know whether she remembered the pony party, but he'd never forget. Her, struggling with some tangled ropes. Him, the only boy to jump in and help even though the body brace felt like a prison—one in which he'd served only three years out of a six-year sentence. He was the only child there who couldn't ride a horse, but he wasn't going to sit back and watch her struggle. Yet, that cowgirl in blue jeans ended up helping him.

Then something occurred to him. The kiss on the cheek that she'd given him after failing to negotiate a payment for his unsolicited help—was it because she felt sorry for him?

"You'll have to ask your daddy when he gets here," Hailey explained to Kat. "Until then, let's show Parks the ropes. Hey, kiddos! Onward to the stables!"

She set Kat down, and the little girl took her hand. Lizzy and Max exited the pen and raced to the barn door, where they competed to be the first to open it.

"Last one there has to clean up the horse—"

"Maximillian Albert Sayers!" Hailey called out in a forceful voice that belied her petite stature. "You've already spent your one and only freebie. Don't push it, or I'll have to tickle you silly!" She looked over her shoulder and nodded for Parker to follow.

He wasn't about to disobey.

Parker could easily picture her as a mom.

She'd be the one whose reprimands were covered in sweetness and easy to digest.

"Max has a love-hate relationship with tickling. I only threaten him when he forces me to," she said as they walked. "Whereas Kat loves to be tickled. Don't you?"

"Nooo!" The little girl squealed and jerked and giggled as if Hailey had actually touched her.

"You're great with kids," he said.

"That's the rumor. I'm not the most requested babysitter in Destiny Springs for nothing, although I suspect it comes down to availability. But the kids are the ones who are great."

Her semimodesty was quite endearing.

"They certainly are. I bet you'll be one of those fun mommies who all the other kids wished they had," he couldn't help but add.

This time, she looked straight ahead and quickened her gait. Had he touched on something? With Hailey, it was sometimes hard to tell. She could speak volumes without saying a word. And when she did speak, there was often subtext lodged between the lines.

Once they got to the stables, he walked up to the horses. They both thrilled and terrified him in a good way. Kind of like Hailey did.

"You probably already know that horses do

bite, since you've spent time feeding Vern's. And *stuff.*" She embellished the last word with a smile and a wink.

Not a word he usually laid claim to, but he was happy to own it, if it got that reaction.

"That said," she continued, "aside from a few affectionate nips, my older rescues won't bite. Unless you make them mad."

He petted one of them on the nose with all the confidence he could muster, hoping to convince her that the *stuff* he'd bragged about included basics like this.

"Or if you rub them the wrong way," she added. "Soft touches can tickle. Hence, Charmed's pinned-back ears."

Was this strike two, or three? He was beginning to lose count. And he never lost count of anything. He withdrew his hand immediately.

Okay, so he didn't know squat. He followed Hailey to the next stall. Max and the girls flitted from one horse to the next. He envied their comfort level. Parker watched and learned how Hailey patted and petted each horse. He observed the kids, as well, and mimicked the moves. *Maybe I won't make such a bad cowboy after all.*

Hailey reached into a paper bag that was on

the ground, pulled out a couple of small apples and handed him one.

"Thanks, but I'm not hungry."

"Good, because I can't cook. Show me how you earn that one hundred percent client satisfaction rating. Charmed is your customer. She wants an apple. But she'll settle for a finger or two."

Parker forced a laugh while resisting the urge to shove his hands into his pockets. He did a quick evaluation of what he'd learned so far about these magnificent creatures. Like his clients, they were all different.

"I need to get to know Charmed a little better first. Find out how she likes her apples."

Hailey's smirk indicated she was on to him but proceeded to demonstrate anyway. She placed the apple on her palm, keeping her hand flat. Parker took copious mental notes. Charmed bit off half the apple first, then gently took the rest.

"I was giving some thought as to where your goats could live," he said. After all, time was of the essence, although he wasn't going to mention that he had only a week to come up with something. Last thing he wanted was for her to feel pressured. "You could build a separate structure next to the arena or convert one of the paddocks."

She shook her head and looked at the ground. "Seriously, that isn't necessary. My goats are happy there, and I'm perfectly happy with focusing on the trail rides."

Again, was she joking about the goats? She certainly seemed serious. So much for his promotion-securing idea.

"I just want what's best for you," he said. And he meant it. Maybe she wasn't concerned that the trail rides couldn't guarantee a steady income, but he was. Promotion or no promotion.

"Yeah, I'm a lucky girl. Everyone wants what's best for me." She laughed, and then half smiled. "So. Tell me, Parker, how much do you *really* know about horses and stables and barns?"

It was a fair question.

"I think we both know the answer," he said.

And just like that, he was back to being *Parker* again instead of *Parks*. In the last few months, he'd noticed she gave nicknames only to the people in her inner circle. He'd earned his within a week of their working on the trail-ride reboot together. This whole arena recommendation seemed to have put him back at square one. Fortunately, *square one* was very familiar territory. He wasn't scared of it.

It was only after he left Sunrise Stables shortly thereafter that he realized the subtext of what she'd asked. What she really meant to point out was, *how much do you really know about* me? There was only one honest answer for that.

Not nearly enough.

HAILEY TOOK A sip of piping hot coffee and pursed her lips.

Heaven? Not one she wanted to visit. Way too thick and bitter. That's what she got for switching brands. She picked up the canister and reread the label.

Directions: Bring water to a boil and pour into your favorite eight-ounce mug. Add one teaspoon of granules and stir until completely dissolved. To avoid burns, allow to cool slightly before enjoying a taste of pure coffee heaven.

"Oh. A *teaspoon*. Duh. User error."
As usual.
Hopefully, this wouldn't end up being a tablespoon-by-mistake kind of afternoon. Not

after the day's rocky start. She rinsed off the utensil and set it in the drainer, then poured out a third of the sludge and added milk.

Her real idea of heaven was a few hours away: a bubble bath, a house full of nothing but quiet and a long, uninterrupted nap. Nash would be over any minute to pick up the twins. Becca and Cody would stop by shortly thereafter to collect Max.

With Cody being gone, she could relax in the knowledge that certain rides were put on hold. He led the most extreme ride, which they'd named Rascal's High-Ridge Ramble. It was a once-a-month, experienced-adults-only advanced trail with plenty of switchbacks and narrow backbones, and ample opportunity for elk and moose sightings. Usually booked by people interested in the novelty of rubbing elbows with a celebrity former bull rider while being capable of handling a horse and navigating the landscape without assistance.

He'd also step in to help with other rides, including their intermediate trail. Rocks and Rolling Hills was currently a half-day-minimum excursion, but they were still cutting the trail to include creek or river crossings. Possibly explore fishing and camping options at some point in the future.

For all the rides, Cody helped with matching the horses to the riders and saddling, going over safety instructions and posing for photos.

Parker wouldn't be able to step into that role, unless folks wanted their photo taken with a truly rare sighting in these parts: the city slicker. Even her flexible one-to-three-hour Plains and Simple trail ride, which stuck primarily to grassy open fields and meadows with colorful wildflowers and assorted wildlife, would be too advanced for him.

She'd have to come up with some other ways Parker could help. Otherwise, his being here would accomplish the opposite. Not that it was his fault. Cody got full credit for this one.

In the meantime, she stood sentinel while the kiddos napped. Lizzy hogged most of the sofa, leaving less than a third of it for her twin to curl up on. Max shared his usual spot on the recliner with Sergeant. Sometimes Hailey was convinced the feline loved that little boy more than he loved her. Not that she could blame him.

The coffee wasn't doing a good enough job of keeping her awake. Her head kept bobbing, even while standing. Fortunately, a tap at the door forced her eyes open. On the other side stood Nash, looking like he needed a nap more than she did.

"Your little angels are sleeping," she whispered as she ushered him in.

Nash gave her the side-eye. "Uh-huh. What did Lizzy get into this time?"

Hailey shut the door quietly behind them. "Actually, I can't think of anything. Except offering up my hair to the goats as dessert. Can I make you some coffee? Maybe a Pop-Tart to go with? I've mastered the toaster settings."

"Tempting, but I'll take a rain check." He walked over to the sofa. The twins stirred, then opened their eyes.

"Daddy!" they said in unison. Kat jumped up first and gave him a hug, then proceeded to collect the Breyer horse she'd brought to show off. Lizzy wrapped herself around her daddy's legs and squeezed.

"What's Hailey been feeding you today, Katherine? I think you've gotten stronger since I've seen you."

Lizzy looked up, then pouted. "I'm not Katherine. I'm Elizabeth."

He gave her a quick kiss on the top of the head. "I know, sweetheart. Just teasing."

Nash looked to Hailey and shrugged. Didn't seem like he was kidding. Probably just exhausted. She could only imagine how his days must be, trying to take care of a ranch while corralling two little ones. He'd get a bit of a break when school started, but that also meant a whole new set of challenges.

Max woke up but otherwise barely stirred. Sergeant leaped off his lap and darted down the hall to his new favorite hiding place. Wherever that was. With that solid black fur, he'd disappear into dark corners and beneath furniture. Until the light found him, and those emerald eyes gave him away.

"Thanks again, Hailey. I owe you one," Nash said.

There was one form of payment she could think of. "Before you go, I could use some advice. How well do you know Parker Donnelly?"

Nash thought about it for all of three seconds. "Not well. We didn't hang out when we were kids, and we have nothing in common now. But he went out of his way to help his grandfather, and I hear he takes excellent care of his ailin' momma, which makes him good as gold in my book. Why do you ask?"

Funny, but she remembered Parker's mother from the pony party. Most of the moms didn't know what to make of the little tomboy who was bossing their sons around. But Mrs. Donnelly had given her the sweetest smile.

"Parker is Cody's replacement while he's gone."

Those soft-and-easy brown eyes of Nash's widened, then he burst out laughing.

"Wish I could find something funny about it," she said.

Nash shook his head. "Boy howdy, that's a stretch. Unless he has some superpower I don't know about. If you get in a bind, promise you'll give me a call."

That was the nicest, most helpful offer she'd gotten so far. At least one of her brothers from another mother had her best interest at heart.

"Same extends to you. If you need for me to look after the girls, I'll find a way to make it happen."

Just not this afternoon. I need some Hailey time.

Nash nodded, then led his girls to his truck. Maybe she should introduce him to some of *her* friends. Except, wait, she didn't have any single female friends. All she had nearby—and temporarily, at that—was Georgina. And she wouldn't do that to her worst enemy. Not that her sister was horrible. Just a little on the high-maintenance side.

Hailey snorted at the understatement. Max bolted upright.

"What's so funny, Miss Hailey?"

She sat on the arm of the recliner and brushed the hair out of his eyes. "You have a third eye on your forehead. That's what's funny."

Max jumped out of the chair, ran to the nearest mirror and studied his face.

"No, I don't!" he shouted.

"Oh, wait, it moved to the back of your head."

Max felt the back of his scalp.

"Did not!" he huffed.

Before he started running back, she took off down the hall. The chase was on, and he was *it*. They'd barely finished one lap through the house when Becca tapped on the door while balancing a large tray of food.

Hailey rushed to open it. "You didn't have to do that, Mom," she teased, although she wasn't joking. Becca already knew Hailey couldn't cook. Her friend never lost sleep over it before, so why was it an issue now?

She stepped aside to let Becca by and stuck her head out the door. She'd come alone.

"Tell Cody I'm crushed that he didn't want to say goodbye to me," Hailey said.

"He wanted to, but he had to drive Mom to the airport."

Confusion swirled. "I hope you don't mean *your* mom. Isn't Rose supposed to be taking care of Max while y'all are gone?"

"Her dearest friend is having major surgery in the morning. The woman lives alone and doesn't have anyone else. Mom is the only solution."

"But what about your honeymoon? And Max?"

Becca took a deep breath and set down the tray. Hailey studied it closer. Two large, foil-covered plates, a couple of Tupperware containers with diced fruit and two boxes of Pop-Tarts.

Oh, no.

Hailey shook her head. "Becs—"

"Please. I know it's a lot to ask."

She looked at Max, who was pretending to ride a horse while Sergeant, who had reappeared as soon as Max started running around, observed the little boy as he galloped circles around him. Then the perfect solution sprang to mind. Georgina was housesitting the B and B while it was closed for the week, which had worked out nicely since her wedding-planning career was in a slump. Knowing her sister, she'd probably love some company. Why couldn't she babysit Max, as well?

"I know I haven't spoken that highly of my

sister in the past," Hailey began, "but I'd totally trust Georgina with Max. He'd get to stay at home with his puppy and sleep in his own bed with all his stuffed animals and that cute little night-light with all the circling stars."

"Oh! Thanks for reminding me. I have his night-light in the truck. And his stuffed horse. Of course, he can go back over and spend as much time as he wants with Penny. I know the pup is going to miss their playtime. And your sister offered to bring more toys whenever he asks," Becca said.

"She wouldn't have to if Max—"

"I don't wanna stay with her. She makes me eat vegetables." Max pretended to throw up.

Although his gesture was for effect, Hailey could have used some Dramamine herself about now. That was her sister, all right. Bossy didn't begin to describe Georgina. Her intentions were good, but still.

"He eats veggies for you," Hailey said to Becca. "I've witnessed it. Besides, they're good for him."

"So are you," Becca said. "I mean, Georgina has been *really* great. Don't get me wrong. I don't know how I've been managing without her."

Hailey could have done without the last part.

The whole thing dredged up the past, where Georgina would hijack Hailey's friendships, being the most fun and social of the three Goodwin sisters. At least Becca hadn't completely switched to Team Georgina if she trusted Hailey with her precious little boy instead.

Even though Hailey had watched over Max when she worked at the Hideaway, it was never for an extended period. And never overnight. Hailey's unspoken rule. That much responsibility for someone else's child stressed her out.

Maybe it's a good thing I can't have kids.

Hailey quietly reprimanded herself for that thought. Advanced endometriosis at a young age had chosen her, not the other way around.

Becca and Max stared at her with those matching copper-colored eyes, and her resistance melted. Max already spent part of his days at her house as the unofficial coleader and spinner of tales on the Plains and Simple rides. Having him stay wasn't unreasonable.

"Okay. But under one condition, kiddo. You have to help Parker with your daddy's duties around here."

"Okey dokey!" He wrapped himself around her.

"I told Cody I didn't think that was the best idea, but he has it in his head that both of you will do fine with the setup," Becca said, then whispered to Hailey, "And I already know you're crushing on Parker."

Max looked up. "Why are you crushing him?"

Hailey cringed. The kiddo must have super-hero hearing. Last thing she needed was for Max to blurt that out to Parker. Truth was, she wasn't sure how she felt, except that she intended to keep their relationship strictly professional.

Hailey didn't answer. Instead, she hoisted Max up on her hip, even though he was almost too big for her small-boned frame. She carried him all the way to the kitchen counter where she peeled back the foil to reveal two of Cody's signature dishes—Rascal's Rodeo Scramble, which was his own *migas* recipe they served at their B and B, and his chicken enchilada casserole.

She replaced the foil and turned to Becca. "Your kiddo here will lose weight because after we devour all this, he'll turn up his nose at whatever I make for him."

Instead of disagreeing, Becca offered up a sheepish grin. "Actually, I have some great news. Georgina will be doing some cooking and bringing by meals every once in a while."

Great news? Not for her. And perhaps not for Max either. But the debate wasn't over yet.

"So what you're saying is this kiddo will be eating vegetables anyway." Hailey playfully poked Max in the side.

"But *you* won't make me eat 'em," he said.

"Just the peas." Hailey knew those were his least favorite. "In fact, we're gonna have pea soup for dinner tonight instead of this lovely casserole. If any peas are left over, we'll add them to the *migas* for breakfast. Sure you don't want to stay with Georgina instead?"

Max scrunched his adorable face and shook his head as if being forced to choose between the two evils and choosing Hailey. His willingness to eat pea soup was a testament to how much he didn't want to stay with her sister.

Of course, she was kidding about the peas. Just like she'd been kidding about him having a third eye on the back on his head. Too bad she didn't have one on the back of hers because she was going to need it to keep watch over the most precious little boy in her life.

Goodbye long, luxurious bubble baths. Goodbye quiet, empty house.

Hello sleepless nights.

CHAPTER THREE

IF PARKER HAD a tail, it would be tucked between his legs. His client-satisfaction score for today with Hailey? A big fat zero. And that was a combination tally that included his horse skills—or lack thereof—and his idea for her property.

When days like this happened, there was no better place to retreat than his grandfather's house. Fraser Ranch had been his safe place when he and his mom would visit. A place where the little boy with scoliosis had been the go-to resource for a doting grandpa who would give Parker fun math problems to solve. Like: *If a chicken is walking home from town at two miles per hour, how long will it take if she doesn't cross any roads?* And Vern was always impressed when Parker not only came up with an answer, he'd provide supporting evidence.

Hopefully, this place would have the same ego-building powers today.

Once inside, he closed his eyes and did a

slow neck roll to work out the tension. He raised his arms toward the ceiling to stretch out his shoulders and back. Stepping into Cody's role wasn't going to be as simple as the rodeo star turned business entrepreneur had made it look or sound. Then again, the man made riding a bull for eight seconds look as easy as staying on top of a carousel pony.

Maybe Hailey could do without his ideas for her property, but she had every right to expect a certain level of support, now that he was back to working for her in a paid, professional capacity for the week. If Parker hadn't spent the better part of the last four months helping his grand-father with nothing but the books, he might've learned something that could add value to this newest job.

But he hadn't. Now, any free time would be dedicated to developing a proposal she would love. He'd make the goats' living arrangements and comfort a centerpiece, based on what little input he could glean from her rejection. Along with recommendations for plenty of support personnel so that she could focus on the trail rides but still make a profit off the arena. And he had to do this in a hurry. His presence was needed at Mason, Shumway and Pinkerton

Consulting. Besides, he'd left something even more important behind in the Windy City.

Make that, someone.

He checked his phone and text messages again. Nothing. His mom always responded in a reasonable amount of time. The past couple of weeks, however, her responses had been sketchy.

Then again, what was reasonable? He expected her to call him back within four hours. After what they went through to get her cancer into remission, any longer of a delay put his senses on high alert because she was the absolute worst at asking for help. Even her own father didn't know how much his daughter had struggled to feed and shelter the two of them.

Except, Vern had suspected. He'd even invited the two of them to move to Destiny Springs. But his mom had wanted Parker to have the best specialist she could find, and that woman was in Chicago.

"Anybody home?" he called out after realizing he hadn't heard so much as a footstep, even though his grandpa's truck was there.

No sign of his cousin Vanessa, and her crossover SUV wasn't in the drive.

He walked to the kitchen window. In the distance, he could make out Vanessa's six-year-old son, Perry, and Vern entering the chicken hutch. He had to keep reminding himself that Perry insisted everyone call him by his first and middle initials now: PJ. Apparently, a little girl with the same name—and with a serious case of *cooties*—had moved to town and was going to be in his class at school. As if the worst thing in the world was having to share his name with a girl.

Parker knew an opportunity when he saw it. No reason he couldn't pitch in with the chickens or hens or roosters, or whatever the critters were technically considered. Maybe even learn a new skill and help Hailey in the process. Which begged the question: Did she even own chickens? She didn't have a hutch on her property, but maybe she kept them someplace less conventional. After all, she had goats living in her barn.

He had to laugh at how much he didn't know about her. Except that she still made his heart race like no one else.

Parker crossed the property and let himself into the chicken run. Vern and PJ were inside collecting eggs. Vern retrieved one from a nesting box and handed it to his little assistant.

"Could you gentlemen use any help?" Parker

asked, which must have startled PJ, because he dropped the egg and it shattered.

"Oops! Looks like that one tried to escape. But he didn't get very far, did he?" Vern cackled at his own joke.

"I'm sorry, Pawpaw," PJ said.

"No, it was my fault. I snuck up on you," Parker said.

"Nonsense, to the both of you." Vern swatted his hand in the air as if batting the apologies away. "Lucy'll lay us new ones, won't cha, girl?" He then attempted to lift the hen, but she wanted none of it. Lucy ran out the open door with the old man hot on her heels.

Parker reached into one of the nesting boxes, retrieved an egg and handed it to PJ, who cradled it with both hands and gingerly placed it in the crate.

"Nice work!" Parker held up his hand to initiate their high-five ritual. PJ's smile made all the trauma of the day completely fade away. Children had a magical way of doing that.

Vern ventured back inside with a balking Lucy in his arms. "By the way, who are you, and what have you done with my grandson?"

"Just trying to help."

"Like you always do. But this is uncharted

territory. Were you also trying to help the fella or gal who did that number on your tie?"

He'd all but forgotten. Why hadn't he changed before coming out here? *Oh, yeah.* Because those eyes of Hailey's had put him in a trance, and he'd yet to fully snap out of it. Wasn't entirely sure he wanted to either.

"You're right. This is uncharted terrain, and I don't know what I'm doing," he said. And he wasn't talking about the chickens.

Today was the first time he'd been that close to horses for an extended length of time. Or with Hailey. Not even at Cody and Becca's wedding reception. The closeness reminded him of that kiss on the cheek. He could swear he still felt its warmth, as if she'd branded him like Vern did his cattle. Or did Vern even brand them?

Turned out, he didn't know much about his own grandpa either. Not that he'd spent all that much time at Fraser Ranch. Sporadic visits when he was young and weekly phone calls ever since. Until recently, when he and Vanessa were both commissioned to check on their senior-most relative to make sure he was doing okay and to help him get caught up on housework and finances. Which reminded him…

"Where's Vanessa?" he asked.

"Mommy went home to see Mr. Bill," PJ said.

Parker remembered the name. Bill was Vanessa's favorite ninety-five-year-old client. As a professional caregiver, she had a few in that age range. The fact that she drove three-plus hours to visit this one made him wonder if something was wrong, because another caretaker had otherwise stepped in during Vanessa's absence.

At the same time, it was reassuring. She wouldn't have left her only child alone with Vern if she felt the man wasn't capable of such responsibility. Parker had reached the same conclusion. He and Vanessa could both report that Vern was fine, and everyone could go back to their own lives.

He knew exactly what his would look like: business suits and briefcases, client lunches and working happy hours, black-tie galas at grand openings. And hopefully a new job title.

Vanessa's absence did have an upside, however. It created an opening for Parker to help in another way.

"I'll make dinner tonight. You gentlemen have earned it," he said. "Crown roast of pork with mushroom dressing, perhaps. Or, better yet—"

"Skettie and meatballs!" PJ said as Parker handed him the last egg.

PJ was a young man of few words, so when he did speak, everyone listened. Skettie it would be.

"With grated parmesan and fresh basil," Parker added. Might as well elevate the dish. Although he was more than satisfied with the cuisine in Destiny Springs and a fan of good home cooking, he missed his favorite restaurants in Chicago. Besides, a good meal nourished the soul. And his soul needed some nourishment today.

"You never did say what happened to that fancy tie of yours," Vern said.

And he didn't intend to. What happened in that barn would stay in that barn. Hopefully by tomorrow, the whole goat incident will have been long forgotten.

Parker grabbed the crate before anyone else had the chance.

"I wanna carry it," PJ said.

Parker sized up the little boy, then the crate. The proportions weren't in PJ's favor.

"I'm getting all sorts of help today," Vern said. "I think it's a splendid idea."

I beg to differ.

Parker relinquished the crate. But when PJ wobbled a little, Parker steadied him by reclaiming one side.

"How about I carry it this time?" He gently tugged.

PJ shook his head in defiance and gripped tighter. "I can do it."

Whoa! Where did that come from?

"Well, you'll do a better job than I would, that's for sure," he said to defuse the situation.

"I'll second that," Vern chimed in, giving Parker a discreet wink and nod.

A tentative smile replaced PJ's scowl. Parker concluded that being thrown under the bus by his own grandfather was worth it in this case.

"Then it's unanimous," Parker said. "Just let me know if you need anything."

"Can I wear the tie?" PJ asked.

"You certainly may." Parker gave PJ the royal treatment, complete with walking him through the Windsor knot, which seemed to have scored some points back.

As they walked to the house, Vern asked, "Are you any good at making popcorn?"

Strange question. Was there even a way to mess that up?

"The good old-fashioned kind, popped in oil on the stovetop and drenched in salt and butter," Vern added.

"I think I can manage. Why? You want that instead of skettie?"

"Oh, I want it all. Just don't tell my cardiologist. Or Vanessa. No, Mr. PJ and I are gonna slip into our pajamas, put our feet up and watch a movie. He's earned it for all his hard work today. We'd love for you to join us. Plenty of room on the sofa."

Another thing on Parker's bucket list: a huge sectional with room enough to accommodate him and a wife, more beautiful children than any couple deserved and a lovable rescue dog or two. All watching a movie together on a lazy Saturday afternoon.

"If it's a comedy, count me in." His day could use some levity. The upcoming week was looking quite serious, if today was any indication.

"Oh, I hear this one's hilarious," Vern said, adding his signature cackle at the end. "Hailey sent it to my phone. Said it was about goats. PJ and I already figured out how to get it to magically appear on the big screen in the den. It's all queued up and ready to go."

A sense of dread slogged through Parker's veins. So much for putting the day's horrors behind him. Once inside, he headed directly for the kitchen, where he located the popping kernels and oil and fired up the stove. The excited murmurings between PJ and Vern coming from the other room were drowned out by the popping.

Parker had barely reached the sofa with the huge butter-and-salt-soaked popcorn when his grandpa pressed *play*.

He handed the bowl to PJ since he did such a good job carrying the crate. In fact, the little boy looked quite confident. Not to mention, all grown up in that tie.

By contrast, Parker's esteem had sprouted a new leak. Judging by the goings on in the video, he figured he had about two minutes until the close-up of him and his four-legged nemesis appeared. Had he screamed in terror, or had it just felt that way? And didn't Max have that phone in his face? They were all about to find out.

He checked his phone again. Good news. A text from his mom. Late lunch with a friend.

One other text.

Hailey: Check to see whether we have any bookings for tomorrow, like Cody showed you. If none, wrangle up some riders (kidding, sort of). Be at Sunrise Stables by eight to help with the horses. And stuff.

He opened his mouth to ask Vern for some pointers, but he'd have to wait for a break in the cackling. His *Mr. DeMille* moment had arrived.

How had Max jumped around throughout most of the video but held the camera reasonably steady for those ten-or-so miserable seconds?

I can't watch this.

Instead, he accessed Sunrise Stables reservations on his phone using the credentials Cody had provided. No bookings, largely thanks to the Hideaway B and B being temporarily closed. At least the trail rides were almost fully booked for the official launch week. Only a few openings left on the last day.

But he had a great idea. And a distraction. "How would you like to go on the trail ride tomorrow, Grandpa?"

Vern looked his way. "Now you're really trying to make me laugh."

Parker simply shook his head. For someone who was the most lovable octogenarian in Destiny Springs, his grandpa shied away from all group activities.

"I wanna go," PJ said.

Parker and Vern exchanged cautious glances. The little guy had never expressed much interest in horses before. PJ seemed to be wanting to try a lot of things today.

"We'll have to check with your mommy first." With that, an easy victory fell right into Parker's lap. That led to an idea for at least two more possible bookings: the Buchanan twins.

From what he knew about Nash, which admittedly wasn't a lot, the cowboy had the girls on horses practically while they were still in onesies.

Maybe Hailey had been sort of kidding about wrangling up some riders, but he took his duties very seriously.

Just as he was about to text the best babysitter in Destiny Springs with the good news, Vern let out his loudest cackle so far. Either they'd gone back to the beginning of the embarrassing part, or the goat's reign of terror had lasted longer than Parker remembered.

Admittedly, he saw the humor in it. At the same time, he was convinced that folks wouldn't be laughing much longer, because he was committed to having at least a reasonable understanding of everything that needed to be done.

He had no choice. Not if he wanted to show Hailey that he respected her world and understood it enough to turn out a proposal that would assure success for both of them.

And, with a little extra luck, the term *stuff* would be replaced by real cowboy words.

MORE THAN A few men had let Hailey down in her lifetime, but Orville Redenbacher wasn't one of them.

She wasn't going to let him down either this time. Wasn't going burn him again by leaving the popcorn bag in the microwave too long. She'd made that mistake once. Okay, maybe twice.

Three times, tops.

Max was turning into a wild child, even though they hadn't had room for dessert after only one helping of the chicken enchilada casserole. She'd managed to throw together a salad with some romaine lettuce and tomatoes to round off their late dinner. But even after she doused the salad with Max's favorite ranch dressing, he wouldn't finish it. Her argument that a tomato was more of a fruit than a vegetable resulted in a couple of skeptical bites, which felt like a victory in itself.

One thing was for sure: if Max had been left in Georgina's hands, he wouldn't have gotten any popcorn without cleaning his plate first.

Hailey poured the perfectly popped treat into a large bowl and joined Max on the sofa. With a walk-through from Vern earlier over the phone, they'd managed to stream the video from her cell to the television.

Once the movie started, she realized that it had probably been a mistake to trust Max with the phone. The movements were jerky, to put it mildly. But what it lacked in smoothness, it made up for in cuteness. The best part was Max's narrative.

"The animals you see here look like goats. But they're not. They're superheroes and they're gonna save planet Earth from the horrible Lizzy Lizard Breath."

Max stuck the camera in his first victim's face. Lizzy did what any lady would do under such circumstances and stuck out her tongue.

Hailey nearly choked on a kernel.

Max then pointed the phone toward the tiniest baby goat and whispered, *"This is Wonder Woman but don't tell anyone!"*

In the background, Hailey heard herself call out for Max to tape the goat-balancing pose, and he complied. For this so-called scene, she rather appreciated his unsteady hand. Did she really look that awkward? Was that what Parker had seen when he first walked in? Her face suddenly felt warm.

Thankfully, Max got distracted again and started chasing Kat, who wanted nothing to do with the chance at stardom he was offering.

The jerkiness was starting to make Hailey queasy. Then it happened. Max ran over to Parker, who was on the losing end of the tug-of-war with the goat. Finally, the little boy held the phone reasonably still. Max giggled so hard at Parker, he tipped to the side, nearly knocking over the bowl of popcorn.

After an initial snort, Hailey had a very different reaction. How could he look so good under those circumstances? Then, after she rescued him—while educating him about goat bites—he was clearly listening. When she wasn't looking, he smiled and dropped his chin to his chest, then looked back up at her. Max had somehow captured it all with reasonable clarity.

Then came the moment where she straightened his tie.

She swallowed the popcorn just in time. Her breath hitched at the impulse she'd almost acted on in that moment: to kiss his cheek like she'd done so long ago.

Still giggling, Max hoisted himself back up to a sitting position and proceeded to put a huge handful of popcorn in his mouth.

"Be careful, kiddo. Wouldn't want you to choke. Your mom would kill me, and I'm not quite ready to die." Not after all the work she'd put into this property and business. "So, Mr. Movie Director, I didn't hear a story behind the goat incident on the video."

He gave it a good minute of thought. "Parker

is really Clock Kent, and he's fighting the evil Goatzilla."

Now, *that* made Hailey laugh out loud. Parker did look a little like "Clock" in that button-down and tie. Even more so when he'd wear reading glasses, which he'd wisely left behind this morning. But she did have one question. "Why didn't he turn into Superman instead of letting Goatzilla win?"

"Because he doesn't want Lois to know. Cuz he likes her."

There was that, except who was his love interest in this crazy scenario? "Is Lois the pretty little goat jumping around in the background?"

Max shook his head. "No. *You're* Lois. So y'all have to get *married*." At that, he started that uncontrollable giggle again.

Was she really having this conversation with a six-year-old? Instead of saying what she was thinking—as in, *Don't even joke about that!*—she decided the best way to change the subject was to flip it.

"And the cameraman has to marry Lizzy Lizard Breath!" she said.

"Ewww!" Max scrunched his nose and added a dry heave. Interesting response, because she was pretty sure he'd had a crush on that particular little girl at Becca's wedding.

Hailey grabbed a handful of popcorn. Max followed suit. They looked at each other and chewed. And she contemplated. She and Parker *were* working together now, like Lois and Clark. They were also going to be spending a lot of time together, so he'd need to stop speaking in numbers and turn into Superman instead.

Specifically, he needed to stay away from the subject he'd brought up out of the blue. Making property recommendations wasn't on Parker's list of assigned tasks.

No, he'd need to help around the stables—a scenario that was even more unlikely than the two of them getting married. Besides, she didn't want to marry Superman or even need his help.

What she needed was a cowboy.

For now, she needed to focus on the little cowboy in her care. It didn't take long for the excitement of the day to make Max sleepy. So much so, he didn't put up a fuss and beg to stay up late when it was time for bed. But there was still one more thing they needed to discuss.

"So, kiddo. I need your help in coming up with tasks for Parker," Hailey said as she tucked Max beneath the covers and turned on his night-light, which flooded the walls and ceiling with animated stars that spilled into the hallway.

"I know! He can clean up the horse—" Max yanked the comforter over his mouth, his eyes suddenly as big as those holiday serving platters that were collecting dust in her grandparents' china cabinet. Another area she'd yet to go through.

Hailey slowly raised both hands until they hovered over him in the full-on tickling position.

He started squirming. "I didn't *say* it!"

"You thought it. And you know what that means."

Max stared intently, as if trying to formulate a defense for which one did not exist. Although, in thinking about it, Max's suggestion was quite logical.

Hailey remained poised. "It means I get to think about tickling you." She lunged for his side as he shrieked and begged for mercy, even though she hadn't so much as touched him.

She stopped and reached for his purple stuffed horse instead. It had been a gift from his dad, from one of the last bull-riding events he'd participated in before giving up the rodeo circuit to become a full-time father.

Hailey would totally ask him to fix her up

with one of his brothers if she didn't know for a fact that they were hyper-ambitious, big-city, suit-and-tie types. She was already trying to resist one of those now. No use asking for more trouble when she'd already concluded that a cowboy would be a better fit.

"Let's go over the house rules one more time," Hailey said.

Max's eyes were still wide open enough to be of concern. The pretend-tickling session wasn't the best idea. Got him all worked up.

"Wake me up if you need anything. And don't go outside for any reason."

Max nodded. "What if the goats need help?"

"Then you come and get me, and we'll go outside together. Understood?"

"Okey dokey."

She arranged the blankets and tucked him in tight. He nestled his head into the pillow as his eyelids started to get heavy. She gave him a kiss on the forehead, leaving only the animated stars to guide his dreams.

Unfortunately, dreams of any kind weren't in her immediate future. Two hours later, tossing and turning, Hailey conceded defeat. She couldn't stop thinking, in horror, that she'd come so close to kissing Parker on the cheek again.

She grabbed a pillow and covered her face, as if she could belatedly hide from the near miss. That sort of thing could not happen again. Hopefully, there were enough tasks to keep him occupied and out of her field of vision.

A written list. That's what she needed. She'd text it to Parker tonight.

Tossing the pillow aside, she untangled herself from the twisted mess of blankets and sheets, rolled out of bed and followed the animated stars to the guest room.

Max hadn't budged since she'd put him to bed. She checked her phone for the umpteenth time to make sure Becca and Cody hadn't contacted her with any kind of emergency. As she did, the text message alert chimed.

She blinked. "Parker?" She read his text.

I've booked one rider for the trails tomorrow. Two more are a solid maybe.

Shouldn't you be asleep instead of drumming up business? Busy day tomorrow. Especially for you. Oh, and leave the tie at home.

Hailey snickered at her own response, blaming the casual tone on lack of sleep. She bit her lip and waited for his response. And waited. Was he writing a novel? Then finally...

Oh, I plan to! That was the only one I brought, and PJ has taken ownership. I'll be there by eight to help with the horses and collect eggs from the chickens. Just please don't make me feed the goats. I need to prepare, emotionally, before facing them again.

Hailey snorted so loud she could have awakened Max. Sergeant, who'd been sleeping on the pillow next to her, jumped off the bed and scurried down the hall to sleep with Max.

I don't have any chickens.

She stopped short of promising anything as far as the goats.

He seemed so different over text. Less uptight. Arguably less professional, even more so than their previous text conversations. Possibly even a bit...*romance-y?*

That's unfortunate. It's my area of expertise. In fact, I'll bring over some of the eggs I helped procure.

Can you procure one of your grandpa's home-grown tomatoes? I'm going to attempt a BLT for the little one.

You must mean tomahto. Let's call the whole thing off.

Hailey reread the last sentence. Super weird. And oddly disappointing.

If that's the way you feel. But I'm confused.

It's the name of a song. Gershwin.

Now she got it. Sort of.

I'll Google it when I'm not so sleepy. Good night, Parks. Zzzzz.

She turned off the phone and stared at the animated stars that were spilling into the hallway. Right now, they felt like a comforting tether to the little boy in her care. Which was good because she had a new thing to worry about. Was this a business relationship or a friendship with Parker? Or something entirely different?

Whatever it was, it needed to stop. That road was a short one, less than two weeks in length.

Furthermore, it had a big, fat Dead End sign at the end of it.

CHAPTER FOUR

HAILEY ASKED. Parker delivered. At least, when it came to his Cody duties. Sure, it was a smaller package than she was likely hoping for. PJ must have weighed all of forty pounds.

He was now second-guessing the risk/benefit of pursuing the topic of building an arena. Although he still wasn't sure whether Hailey was serious about the goats, she seemed honestly content with where her business was at the moment. He could let her get the launch out of the way, then bring up the subject again down the road.

Not to mention, it might be too risky to waste time on something that had such a little chance, when he had so little time to submit the proposal to his boss. He had two less-risky ideas he could pursue instead.

Parker managed to get PJ into the car seat the next morning and pointed Vern's truck in the direction of Sunrise Stables.

The Dodge was old, but it drove like a dream.

He loved manual transmissions. Like his vintage Porsche that was waiting for him in Chicago. Not so long ago, he was raring to get back and blow out the cobwebs. Yet, lately he'd been thinking more about four-door sedans, like his rental, and soccer-mom crossovers, like Vanessa's. Being around PJ and Max and the twins was making him itch to get started on the next season of his life.

"Horses!" PJ called out as they passed Nash's Buck Stops Ranch where a couple of the majestic beasts were out grazing.

"Are you excited about riding?" Parker asked as he shifted the truck into second gear. If he'd been alone, he would have kicked up some serious dust. But the cargo was too precious to take chances, even on a deserted road like this.

He'd already kicked up enough dust, so to speak, by joking around with Hailey over texts. Might need to do some damage control if he'd come across too casual and familiar, even though it hadn't felt that way in the moment. It felt completely natural.

"I wish Mommy could see me ride my first time," PJ said.

First? The word prodded his conscience. Parker assumed PJ had at least a little experience, although he wasn't sure what had given him that impression. Thankfully, he'd called Vanessa for permission. She said it was fine as long as Hailey was in charge instead of him.

The truth stung, even though he was in complete agreement. He had no plans of riding a horse or doing anything that could wreck his back unless the benefits outweighed the risks. He loved taking chances, but only calculated ones.

"We'll take pictures for her."

PJ pouted. "It's not the same."

Parker was tempted to explain how tough Vanessa's job as a single mom was. But PJ shouldn't have to worry about the adults who were supposed to take care of him, and especially not at such a young age. Besides, riding a horse for the first time had to be one of the most exciting days of a child's life. It would have been for him.

One thing was for sure. Whenever Parker became a dad, he'd be at every event for every child. That would take lots of time and money, but he didn't plan to be at the mercy of his job forever. Just long enough to amass enough for those interest-bearing accounts to replace his current income without having to touch the golden goose. That, and he planned to leave it as a legacy for his children so that they would never have to struggle.

He smiled at the thought. No one could accuse him of lacking ambition when it came to family and finance.

Hailey and Max were already working around the stables when Parker pulled in. She stopped what she was doing and watched as they approached.

PJ made a beeline to Max, who was brushing one of the horses.

"This is a nice surprise," Hailey said. "They can play after Max's ride."

"After *their* ride."

"What do you mean?"

"I booked and paid for PJ. But the good news doesn't end there. The Buchanan twins are riding. You're welcome." Parker couldn't help but grin.

However, his proud announcement didn't so much as earn him a smile.

"Is Nash coming with us?" she asked.

Parker shrugged. "He mentioned needing to take care of some things at the ranch instead."

She exhaled what sure did sound like pure anxiety.

"Is something wrong?" he asked.

Hailey leveled her shoulders and smiled.

"No! Just walking through the trail in my head. Four kiddos. Whew! Doesn't get any more fun than that."

He would have otherwise agreed wholeheartedly, but something about the way she said it made him suspect there was some subtext there. He simply wasn't fluent enough to know for sure.

She turned her attention to the horses. Moments later, Nash's truck turned into the drive. The girls jumped out and joined Max and PJ, and they immediately began arguing over who would get to ride which horse.

Hailey called out, "I'm doing the matching, kiddos."

Nash gave Hailey a big bear hug, his muscular physique nearly swallowing her strong yet lithe one. "Thanks so much for doing this, Hailey. The girls are excited about this little adventure. Maybe I can knock out a chore or two at the ranch while they're gone."

Even though Parker knew they were just friends—more like siblings—he felt a pang of jealousy over their lingering embrace.

"What's on your plate?" she asked as she broke free.

Nash put his hands on his hips. "Where to begin? I'm late checking the waters. I'm also keeping a close eye on a couple of springers. My horses haven't gotten worked a lot this week, so there's that too."

Parker nodded as if he'd understood every word. Not that anyone even remembered he was standing there.

"How many you up to?" Hailey asked.

"Three. Recently added an Appaloosa as a favor for a friend. Still have one quarter and the paint-draft mix."

"One quarter is better than twenty-four pennies," Parker said, immediately regretting his attempt at accounting humor.

Nash and Hailey simply looked at him for a few seconds before resuming their one-on-one.

"I feel your pain. You know I'll help in any way I can," Hailey said.

"What you're about to do helps a lot," Nash responded.

Hailey tucked her hands deep in her back pockets. "I know the girls have ridden plenty. Max has a number of rides under his belt now. I guess the wild card is PJ," she said, directing the last part to Parker.

"First time," he said.

Hailey nodded slowly. "Well, okay then. I'll give him a tutorial along with some lunge work. Nash, if you don't mind helping with the horses while I'm doing that, I'd greatly appreciate it. Just give me a minute."

She turned on her heel and walked away with a determined gait.

"What can I do to help?" Parker called out.

He halfway expected her to say *nothing*. Instead, she retrieved a utensil, then walked back over and handed it to him.

"Start with No Regrets, even though he's staying behind. Still has a fear of boulders. Last stall." She waited for what they both must've known would be the inevitable question.

He studied the utensil. The brush side was clearly for cleaning something. He wasn't sure about the purpose of the pointy side, but logic suggested it was used to get into tight corners. He resisted shifting from one foot to the other. He was afraid to make eye contact with Nash, who was offering no support whatsoever.

Not that Parker expected it. He and Nash had barely crossed paths growing up.

After Hailey and Nash both left, he'd seek guidance on the internet or from Vern. He certainly wasn't going to interrupt Cody on his honeymoon. But Hailey clearly wasn't going anywhere until he gave some indication that he'd understood her directive.

"And after I finish cleaning the stalls?" he asked. Seemed generic enough.

She cocked her head and squinted, like before.

Nash laughed, then covered his mouth to stifle the worst of it.

Uh-oh.

Hailey cast Nash a shame-on-you-for-laughing look, then turned to Parker. "Right attitude. Wrong tool. But no worries. I'll walk you through it in a sec."

She turned back to Nash. "Max has been riding Star. Let's pair Kat with Whiskey. Lizzy should get the super-tolerant Blaze, since she's super wiggly. And PJ would be a good fit with the unflappable Gabby. She follows so well and loves kids. I'll take Bad Boy and a chill pill. If you don't mind making sure their hooves are clean while I work with PJ, I'd appreciate it."

Parker stood at a safe distance and took copious notes as Hailey gave PJ some basic training. Meanwhile, the girls fought over the only pink riding helmet.

Once Hailey finished, she walked back over to Parker and eased the strange tool from his hand.

"I have to admit, you would've been able to get into those corners. This is a hoof pick. It gets the rocks and dirt out of their hooves. The brush side finishes the job. I always do this before and after a ride."

"And they let you?"

"If you ask nicely. C'mon. I'll show you." Hailey headed toward No Regrets's stall and confidently strolled inside.

"First, never surprise them. Make sure they know you're there. Line up with the leg and face the opposite direction," she explained as she demonstrated. "Then run your hand down the inside of the leg like this. Most times they'll lift their hoof."

Looked easy enough. "And if they don't?"

"You can try gently squeezing the chestnut, right here, or tug at the hairs on their fetlock."

"Ah yes. The old chestnut squeeze. That would have been my guess," Parker said.

Hailey sighed and shook her head.

"Sorry. I crack jokes when I'm nervous."

"Nothing to be nervous about. Give it a try," she said.

Parker took a deep breath and positioned himself. He tried to copy the whole run-the-hand-down-the-leg move, but No Regrets wouldn't budge.

"You may not have used enough pressure. Try the fetlock since you're already down there,"

Hailey said, then pointed to the horse's ankle area. When it worked, Parker felt victorious. Until he got a closer look at the task before him. In fact, he wasn't sure where to start. Didn't want to somehow hurt the big guy.

"Clean around both sides of the frog with the sharp end," she instructed.

Frog? Parker studied the bottom of the hoof. Was Hailey messing with him? Her expression offered no clues.

"I'm at a loss."

She reached down and traced the center part. "You mean they didn't teach you that at Harvard?"

"Columbia Business School," he said.

"So you say. Well, I suppose they would have horses in Bogotá."

Parker bit his lip, but he had to say it anyway. "Different Colombia."

Hailey stood up straight and put one hand confidently on her hip. "No doubt. I know it's in New York. I tend to crack jokes when I'm *not* nervous."

"Touché."

"You'll remember what it's called next time." She gifted him with a tentative smile, then lost it and looked away. Hopefully, she was focusing again on the ride ahead.

Strange thing was, he hoped there would be a next time. This, he had to admit, was something he never imagined doing. Much less enjoying. There was something quite gratifying about being this close to a thousand-pound creature and helping him be more comfortable.

Parker's confidence increased with each subsequent hoof until No Regrets was all taken care of. His back felt a little sore from the bending and twisting and picking, and his hands got a bit of a workout, but in a way it felt good. Made him feel alive.

Everything for the trail ride played out so beautifully. He felt a bit envious as Hailey and the children headed out of the back gate of her property, single file.

Nash stood nearby, watching, as well. Parker stated the obvious. "Hailey seemed nervous about something."

"Probably about leaving you alone to tend to the stables," Nash said with a straight face. Thankfully, a smile cracked through the facade, although there was truth to what he'd said. She didn't feel comfortable with it. But probably not nearly as uncomfortable as he felt. He scanned the property. The word *daunting* summed it up nicely.

"Since I've mastered the hoof pick, I'd be happy to stop by your ranch before I go back to Chicago and lend my expertise," Parker teased.

"I'd take you up on it, but I don't need a ranch hand as much as I need someone to help look after the girls," Nash said.

"If you want to head back now, I'll babysit them for a few hours when they get back from riding. Give you a chance to take care of some of those tasks you'd mentioned."

Even though he wouldn't be able to get on the computer, maybe he and the girls could hang around the stables and he could look for further inspiration and run some numbers in his head for the proposal.

"That's a mighty tempting offer, but I'm going to stay put. My chores can wait."

"Because you're afraid to leave me unsupervised?"

Nash shook his head. "No. Because Hailey needs some help around here. And you could use a little more too. Especially since you're trying to impress her."

Was it that obvious?

Nash continued. "Then again, I'm sure she was quite impressed with how you handled that goat."

"You saw the video?"

Nash nodded. "Me and the girls were able to stream it to the television. Had to shut my eyes through a lot of it, but your scene turned out good."

All Parker could see was that horrified look on his face, captured in excruciating detail. There was only one thing to do: own it. "I've been nominated for an Oscar for my performance. Hoping to play an equally convincing role as a cowboy."

Thankfully, Nash once again got Parker's sense of humor and laughed under his breath.

"I hope so too, for Hailey's sake," Nash said. "You might be in luck. As much as anything else, being a cowboy is about what's in your soul. And you seem to have one of those. But it doesn't hurt to know what you're doin', and I can help. Maybe we can even scratch a few other tasks off your list today."

That was so much more than Parker had even dreamed of asking for.

"Name your price. I'll sell some stocks if I have to."

The stock-selling part was meant as hyperbole, but Nash didn't even crack a smile this time. Instead, he gave Parker a long, hard look and named a price that Parker wasn't sure that even he could deliver.

"The only thing I ask is that you don't break Hailey's heart."

CHAPTER FIVE

"A ZILLION YEARS AGO, people rode on this trail. And they never came back," Max said, with such a high degree of confidence that Hailey almost believed him.

And to think Becca hadn't wanted her son to ride horses at all. The adorable little boy's embellishments were always well received on the Plains and Simple trail ride.

It would be a while before he'd be ready for the Rocks and Rolling Hills trail. Four years, to be specific. No riders under ten for that one.

The day couldn't have been clearer and crisper. So far, the ride couldn't be smoother. She'd had her reservations about the child-to-adult ratio but was able to reason with that self-doubt. It hadn't bothered Nash. He would have spoken up. And a couple of weeks ago, Cody had successfully led a ride with six children under the age of ten.

The kiddos were listening to Max but still doing as they were told. Hailey's horses were being saints and walking single file. All that ground training had paid off. They now knew to stand patiently in cross ties and a single rope and while being groomed. They all stood calmly when being tacked and learned to lower their heads to be haltered and bridled.

"A zillion years ago, there were dinosaurs," Lizzy argued.

"That was *two* zillion years ago," Max insisted.

Hailey laughed under her breath. Every story began with "a zillion years ago" but immediately cut a different path.

"What happened to the horses?" PJ asked.

"I'm glad you asked," Max said. "The superheroes took them so that they could save planet Earth."

"What happened to the people?" Kat asked.

"They're still out there cuz they can't find their way home. We'll probably see some today," Max said, which prompted all the kiddos to start looking around.

"You're lying. Superheroes are only in the movies," Lizzy said.

"Are not! Just ask Clock Kent," Max countered.

"Who's hungry?" Hailey interrupted. Not her usual stopping place, but this was going to be a shorter trip than normal, she'd already decided. "Peanut butter and jelly sandwiches and chips. But only one cupcake."

"Why only one?" Kat asked.

Because I wasn't told in advance that there would be four children on this ride and didn't have time to pick up more.

"It's for whoever is the sweetest during this ride," she said.

Lizzy waved her hand in the air. "That's me!"

"Both hands on the reins and resting in front of the saddle horn," Hailey admonished.

They reached the shaded spot she had in mind, and she helped everyone safely dismount. While the kiddos unfolded the blanket and retrieved the thermal pouches from the saddlebags, she slipped the halters over the bridles for each horse, then snapped on the lead ropes she'd stashed. She wrapped the loose ends around a tree and secured the horses.

Once situated on the blanket, Hailey pulled the sandwiches out of the pouch. One for each of the kiddos. She made a bigger production of handing out the chips by pretending names were attached.

"Lizzy, you get potato chips. The puffed cheese balls are for Kat. PJ, I heard that corn chips are your fave." She held back on the last item. "Max. You wanted a superhero snack, right?"

The look on his face was priceless. He nodded enthusiastically.

"I hear this is one of Popeye's favorites," she said.

"Spinach!" the twins yelled out in unison.

Max looked crestfallen. Hailey hadn't even known whether Popeye was considered a superhero or was even popular with kids anymore.

"Oh, is it spinach? I guess I heard wrong. I thought it was tortilla chips, so that's what I brought." She shrugged and handed the bag to Max. That put a superhero-sized grin on his face.

Of all the kids, she knew PJ the least. Put him in a tie, and he'd strongly favor Parker with that killer combination of dark hair and light blue eyes. They both obviously inherited the good-looking gene. *And someday, so will Parker's children.*

Hailey's breath hitched at the thought, which had come out of nowhere. A strange feeling rushed through her. Envy? Sadness?

No. More like loneliness, even though she was far from being alone. Max, Lizzie and Kat were bouncing and talking over each other with their mouths full, while PJ sat there so quiet and refined.

"So tell me something. I know the *P* stands for Perry. What's the *J* stand for?" she asked.

"Jackson," he said.

"Oh, I like that name," she said.

He rewarded her with the sweetest smile.

"I bet you've enjoyed spending so much time with Parker, huh? You gonna miss him?"

PJ nodded and finished chewing a bite of the sandwich. After a thick, peanut-buttery swallow, he said, "Yeah. But he said I could visit his new house. And I can have any bedroom I want."

New house?

"Must be nice to have a choice. How many bedrooms does it have?" she asked. Her log cabin bungalow had two, which made for interesting sleep arrangements when her mom and dad and sisters used to visit.

PJ had taken another bite of sandwich but set the rest of it down and held up six fingers.

That wasn't a house. That was a mansion. Becca and Cody's B and B didn't have many more than that.

"Not six rooms overall? Six bedrooms?" she asked.

He nodded.

Another blow, although she wasn't surprised. Parker seemed to thrive in the goat pen with all the children running around. No doubt he wanted a house full.

"How does his girlfriend like it?" she asked, feeling a little tricky. But if it turned out that he had one back home, it would make resisting him a no-brainer.

"I dunno. He liked Debbie Taunt, but she's not his girlfriend anymore."

Debbie Taunt? "Debutante?"

PJ shrugged. "I think so."

Hailey picked at the frazzled edges of the gaping hole in the knee of her jeans.

"He's actually Superman," Max interjected.

"Who's Superman?" Lizzy asked.

Max rolled his eyes in an exaggerated fashion. "He's a superhero. Duh."

"Duh, I know who Superman is," Lizzy countered.

"Max thinks Parker is Superman," Hailey said, clarifying, before the disagreement escalated into a *duh* war.

"Let's finish up here and get home, where I'll award the cupcake." No way she was going to put more sugar in any of them now. They were animated enough. The calmer everyone stayed, the safer they'd all be.

Hailey helped all the kiddos mount their respective horses, and they headed back the way they came. Single file.

Along the way, Max resumed his story about the trails while the kiddos took turns claiming to spot one of the lost riders. But after PJ shouted his trail-rider sighting, Hailey heard an uncharacteristic shuffling of hooves, followed by a blood-curdling scream. The girls both shrieked.

She twisted around to see PJ on the ground, curled up in ball. A shock of pain raked down her spine, as if she'd been dragged over broken glass.

"Everyone stop! Hold as still as possible," she ordered. She dismounted and knelt next to PJ. "Where does it hurt?"

"My arm," he managed to say through the tears.

She contemplated removing his coat and checking out the injury but thought better of it. They needed to get back ASAP. She tried her cell. No service bars. She couldn't exactly send Max galloping for help.

"I'm sorry to do this. Bear with me." She gingerly lifted him, keeping his hurt arm away from any unnecessary pressure against her body.

He whimpered, and her heart bottomed out

with such force she had to pause to catch her breath.

"You're doing great. Such a brave man, Mr. Perry Jackson. Hold on to me as best you can." She positioned his chest against her shoulder and secured his uninjured arm around her neck. Not ideal. She quickly attached the lead line to PJ's horse and handed it to Max. "Please hold this until I get situated. But let go if Gabby starts to pull too much. Okay? Just let her go."

The kids remained deathly quiet as she attempted to slowly hoist herself and her precious cargo on top of Bad Boy. After putting all the options through a swift mental triage, she figured the best thing to do was to hold PJ with him facing her while using her spare arm to secure him. His tears and breath warmed her neck as she took it nice and slow, but it was his heartbreaking shriek that made her step back down to the ground without completing the mount.

"It'll be okay," she said, trying to reassure him. Yet, when she put her boot in the stirrup once again, he began shaking and sobbing and shrieking uncontrollably.

"Shh," she whispered, to little avail. Anything sterner would likely upset him even more. But she had to do something.

Even though Bad Boy was steady and dependable, she couldn't risk stressing him out and putting them all in danger. That left only one viable solution. Walking. Thankfully, they were only about a mile out. She attached the lead line to Bad Boy, as well, and eased the line to Gabby from Max's hand.

"Okay, everyone. Follow me." She periodically checked her phone for service along the way. Fifteen minutes in, she got a signal. Neither Parker nor Nash answered their phone, but she left voice mails anyway. By the time she composed a way to direct 911 to find them, the signal went dead again.

So much for taking the shortest, safest route. Without a cellular lifeline in certain stretches, she was left vulnerable. Especially so, being the only adult on the ride. If she hadn't been balancing a precious little boy on her hip, she would have made it a point to kick herself in the pants. Why didn't she trust her instincts about this to begin with? Why did she not think of checking the cellular issue sooner and more thoroughly? Yet, even the best cellular service in the universe wouldn't have kept PJ safe today.

When it came to caring for children, there was no such thing. It wasn't the horse's fault. PJ had probably been twisting around and pointing and lost his balance. The girls should be able to confirm.

Max didn't continue with his story on the trek back, but she had a theory of her own. Perhaps someone got hurt on the original trail rides. Even worse than PJ. Perhaps a child. She might not ever know whether that was the case. Not that it mattered.

Even one hurt child was one too many.

PARKER FINISHED MUCKING the stalls while Nash supervised and occasionally pitched in. Parker's back was now giving him fits, but he wasn't about to complain.

"I think you've found your niche," Nash teased.

Parker would have thought it funny if it weren't true. If there was one thing he could do well and took pride in, it was tidying up and decluttering a space. In fact, the vacant stall he just finished cleaning would make an outstanding home for the goats, once modified and expanded. The little critters would get a room with a view of the sparkling arena, rather than being holed up in a dark barn. Now, that, he could relate to. His current office was windowless, but if Hailey loved this proposal, he'd be looking out over Lake Michigan instead.

"I hope I've further redeemed myself in the boss's eyes for the whole hoof pick misunderstanding," he said. *And the goat incident. And the apple incident.*

"I guess you'll find out soon enough," Nash said, shielding his eyes from the sun and pointing toward the approaching group.

Now, that was a beautiful sight. Except something didn't look right, even to a novice like himself. Two horses were missing their riders. Hailey was on foot, carrying one of the children. Max launched into a trot, his tiny voice piercing the gentle breeze.

He and Nash had the same inclination at the same time and started running toward the group. Parker took the lead—a feat he could only blame on pure adrenaline, because if he learned anything today, it was that he wasn't as physically fit as he'd thought himself to be. Certainly not as fit as Nash.

Max could be heard more clearly now. "PJ fell off his horse!"

An overwhelming ache coursed through Parker's own body, as if he'd been the one to fall. He kept running until he reached Hailey.

Nash caught up and took the leads from her grip, while Parker eased PJ from her embrace.

"Where does it hurt?" he asked.

"My arm," PJ said, although his words were blurred by the tears flowing freely down his cheeks.

Hailey retrieved a backpack from inside one of the larger saddlebags and pulled out her keys. "He lost his balance. I didn't try to take off his jacket. Considering his pain level, I bet it's broken," she explained as they speed-walked toward the vehicles.

Parker planted a kiss on the brave little boy's cheek.

"I'm so sorry," Hailey said. "I... I don't know how—"

"It's not your fault." Parker didn't need to know what happened to be certain that it had nothing to do with Hailey. The girls remained quiet. Even Lizzy. And that little firecracker always had something to say.

"Let me drive. You can navigate," Parker said to Hailey once they got to the vehicles. "Max can come along for moral support. Nash can stay behind with the girls and remove the tack, then groom and put up the horses."

Hailey looked at him as though she didn't recognize him. He barely recognized himself.

Sure, he probably left out a few steps and didn't quite nail the verbiage. But some of what Nash had taught him over the past couple of hours must have sunk in.

But showing off his newfound knowledge had plummeted to the rock bottom of his priority list. Taking care of PJ was all that mattered.

Parker opened the door to the extended cab of Vern's truck and gently secured PJ in the car seat. Hailey slid in next to him, buckled up and cradled him best she could. Max claimed the front passenger seat, and Parker got him all buckled in, as well.

Didn't take more than fifteen minutes to reach the nearest emergency clinic, but it felt like the longest quarter hour of Parker's life. Once at the clinic, he went back to the exam room with PJ. He texted Vern but wanted to wait until he knew more before texting Vanessa. No use worrying her at this point when she was too far away to do anything about it.

The staff was quick to take X-rays and address PJ's pain level with some medicine, which he did not want to take. The nurse insisted and ultimately got her way.

"You're going to have quite a story to tell your friends when you get back to Cheyenne," Parker said as they waited for the results.

PJ nodded. At least the crying had stopped, but Parker was more than a little concerned over his reluctance to take medicine.

The doctor came in the room in short order, pulled up the X-rays on his computer and pointed to the injury.

"You've got what's called a buckle fracture, young man. You picked a good kind to have, because it's stable." The doctor then directed his attention to Parker. "The bones haven't been displaced, and it doesn't involve the growth plate. Often happens when a child tries to break a fall with an outstretched arm."

Parker exhaled. "That sounds like good news, overall."

"He'll need to wear a splint for a couple of days until the swelling goes down. Then we'll put him in a cast for a few weeks. Sometimes, the splint is enough, but the younger kids tend to take them off when they're not supposed to if they get uncomfortable. I'd rather err on the side of caution."

"I appreciate that."

"Besides, casts are fun these days. More fun than this temporary contraption because you'll get to pick your color, so be thinking about it," the doctor said to the patient as one of the assistants worked on fitting and adjusting the splint.

"Can I get blue?" PJ asked.

"Sure can. We have light blue and dark blue."

That produced a smile, although Parker suspected there was still work to be done in the cheering-up department. By the time they got back to the lobby, Max was busy playing with some action figures in an area set up for children but looked up and ran over to his friend.

"Wow! Can I have one too?" Max asked.

"I'm afraid that's something you have to earn," Parker said. "You two play over there while we wait on the paperwork and instructions."

PJ followed Max back over to the play table, and they started rearranging the figurines. Parker tried to call Vanessa but got her voice mail instead. He'd try again later.

Meanwhile, Hailey had barely shifted positions since they got there. She was still in that hard, wooden chair even though a comfy-looking sofa was vacant. It was almost as if she were punishing herself, not even making eye contact as he sat beside her.

"Buckle fracture. A couple days in a splint, then a few weeks in a cast," he said.

She simply nodded and tucked a lose strand of hair behind her ear. She was holding a smashed-up cupcake. Must have been in that backpack. That's when he noticed that her hands were trembling. Her breathing seemed shallow, as well. Maybe PJ wasn't the only one he should be concerned about.

"Is that for me?" He knew it wasn't but figured it might get a smile out of her. No luck.

"It's for Perry. But he deserves a prettier one."

Even her voice was trembling, and her eyes had dampened. He eased the cupcake out of her grip, set it on a side table and placed his hands over hers to still them. "Are you okay?"

She nodded. "A little anxious. It'll pass."

"Has this happened before?"

She closed her eyes and managed to say a barely audible, "No."

"Breathe in through your nose, slowly, to the count of five. As much air as your lungs will hold," he instructed. "Then exhale slowly through your mouth."

She did exactly what he recommended. Three times. No change. Time to take it up a level, which meant doing what no one in this room would prefer him to do. Himself included.

Parker cleared his throat, hummed a couple of bars and began to sing. Hailey opened her eyes. Her expression fell somewhere between pained and curious. Another couple sitting across the room turned to look. Max and PJ stopped playing to watch but didn't seem sure what to make of it. The receptionist simply looked down her glasses at him, as if having fun wasn't allowed here.

Hailey's beautiful features contorted. "What are you doing?"

He stopped, midstanza. "I think it's obvious. I'm singing 'My Heart Will Go On.' Celine Dion."

She let her head fall back and hit the wall behind her. "Ella Fitzgerald would've been a better choice for your vocal range. No offense."

"None taken." His purpose hadn't been to impress her with his vocal stylings. It had been to distract her and get her to breathe again without overthinking it. And make her laugh, even though a smile and sarcasm would do for now.

"I'm quite pleased you listened to the tune I mentioned," he added.

"I couldn't sleep after we texted. I thought it would help."

"Did it?"

"Honestly? No." She began inhaling and exhaling normally and sat up straight. "Okay, I see what you did. Thank you for that, although I don't think you should hold your breath waiting for praise from anyone else in here."

"None required. And you're welcome. Now that you're back in the land of the living, let's clear the air about something. The accident wasn't your fault," he said.

"You weren't there. How can you say that?"

"Because you're a professional."

She let out a nervous laugh and looked away. "I wasn't watching him closely enough."

"And if you had, all you would have seen was him fall. Accidents happen. To everyone, eventually."

She nodded, unconvincingly.

"Have you ever fallen off a horse?" he asked.

"More than once."

"And whose fault was it? Your mom's? The horse's?"

"Oh, please. It was my fault more than anyone else's."

"So what you're telling me is that the fall was PJ's fault. More than anyone else's. Glad we cleared that up. Case closed." Parker brushed his hands together.

That got her to finally look at him. "I did *not* say that! It wasn't his fault."

"That's not what I heard you imply."

Hailey gave him a long, hard look, then rolled her eyes. At this rate, they'd roll right out of her head. "I think he was pointing at what he thought were the lost trail riders."

"Lost *what*?"

"Max's latest theory about why the trail rides ended. Some superheroes hijacked the ride because they needed to use the horses to save the world. And folks are still trying to find their way home. Or something like that."

Parker looked to Max. Thankfully, the little boy hadn't been traumatized. Then again, he'd probably heard all kinds of near-death stories from his daddy. Being thrown from an angry bull was more dramatic than falling off a horse.

"Does anyone know what really happened to the rides?" He'd pretty much stayed on the outskirts of that topic.

"No. My grandparents never mentioned it, and now they're gone. My mom didn't seem all that interested, so she never knew, and us girls were too wrapped up in our own lives to care. Lately I've done plenty of asking. No one in town has a clue. My theory is that someone got hurt."

"I don't know. Max's superhero angle sounds more plausible."

Hailey smiled, then shook her head. "Well, it won't be a mystery why they shut down this time."

"What do you mean?"

"I can't go through this again. Not with a child."

"That would be a big mistake, Hailey."

Especially after all the work she'd put into it. They all knew this was a high-risk venture. Hence the liability wavers. The insurance company sure saw it that way.

She cast him a stern look. "Okay, first of all, I was being dramatic. Of *course* I wouldn't shut it down. Second of all, I'm sure you know what's best for my business. But how about what's best for me?"

"I didn't mean for it to come out that way. Just trying to help."

This was beginning to feel like the weird crate incident with PJ when Parker had tried to help but got scolded instead. Was there something in the Wyoming air?

She crossed her arms and looked straight ahead.

"Just ignore me," he added.

After a few minutes of silence and no eye contact on her part, he concluded that of all the advice he'd given her, that was the piece she was going to take.

CHAPTER SIX

HAILEY UNCROSSED HER ARMS, but couldn't bring herself to look at Parker. Not after telling him a blatant lie then snapping at him.

The possibility of shutting down the rides did briefly cross her mind when it occurred to her that her mom and sisters might have been right all along. Maybe she couldn't handle responsibility. Maybe she needed someone to swoop in and save her. By telling her it would be a mistake to shut them down, Parker made her question herself even more.

Yet, her conscience kept reminding her that she was the only one who'd had reservations about the child-to-adult ratio. And she'd been correct. *So there.*

She should shut the rides down for a few days, however. Do some reevaluating before the official launch week. Word of this accident likely wouldn't get around, but another one would raise a red flag in people's minds.

Parker would likely feel relieved, as well,

once she told him that his cowboy services wouldn't be needed for the rest of the week. However, the clinic wasn't the best place for it.

The doctor came out to the waiting room and approached them. She and Parker stood.

"PJ can take children's formula over-the-counter acetaminophen for the pain. If that doesn't help, please call me. Darla has the paperwork and instructions for at-home care. You can make an appointment with her for the cast."

"Thank you, Doctor," Parker said.

Hailey headed to the checkout desk. Parker was promptly at her side. "What are you doing?"

"I'm taking care of the charges," she said.

"No, you're not. I'll run this through the insurance company after I get specifics from Vanessa. How about you go wrangle those two little cowboys into the truck." Parker handed her his keys.

Her first inclination was to insist on paying, if only to ease her conscience a little. Until she realized that her guilt couldn't be paid off. Besides, she was too exhausted and deflated to argue.

Hailey kept PJ practically glued to her side until they got to the truck. As they waited inside, the boys chatted. Make that, Max chatted and PJ listened.

Parker finally emerged. As he approached, she couldn't help but notice that his posture was immaculate, as was his cool confidence through this whole ordeal. Her dad had handled her broken bones with the same ease. As if clinic visits were as commonplace as running into the grocery store for a gallon of milk. Versus her mom and sisters, who were one step away from making funeral arrangements if she so much as sprained an ankle.

Parker climbed in the truck and started it. "Ice cream for everyone. My treat, if PJ is up to it. We need to pick up some pain medicine while we're out anyway, in case Vern doesn't have any at the house." He looked at Hailey. "Do you mind navigating again?"

In her opinion, stopping somewhere was the worst idea. The poor little guy had been through a nightmare. But breaking her news to Parker in public wasn't a bad idea. And ice cream was always a good one.

"I know a place that has amazing root beer ice cream floats," she said.

"Perfect!" He put the truck in gear. Two left turns and one right one later, and they'd arrived.

The drugstore was quiet. She led the way to the old-fashioned soda fountain counter. Max somehow climbed on top of one of the stools and started spinning himself around. PJ tried to do the same, but Hailey swooped in, took his hand and led him to the nearest booth instead. Max eased off the stool and followed.

"You kiddos stay put. I'll be right back," she said, once they were safely seated.

Parker had claimed a barstool and was on his phone, probably trying to get ahold of Vanessa and updating Vern on the situation.

She walked back over and tapped him on the shoulder. "Order a float for me, please, and keep an eye on the boys. I'll be right back." Parker gave her the thumbs-up. He set his phone down and swiveled toward PJ and Max.

Hailey zigzagged down a couple of aisles and located the permanent markers. Next, she asked the pharmacist to recommend the best OTC pain medicine for a child. By the time she paid for the items and returned to the soda fountain area, Parker had joined Max and PJ in the booth. They were yakking it up about something, as if this were a typical day in the life.

She eased in next to Parker. "What's so funny?"

Parker bit his lip. Had they been making fun of her?

"Spill it," she said.

"Anything you say, Lois."

Although she'd expected the whole "Clock Kent" comparison to get back to Parker, she didn't think it would happen so soon. "I'm not a Lois, nor have I ever been. But you really are Superman. You certainly saved the day today."

And she meant it. That anxiety attack, or whatever it was, could have been a lot worse had he not been there.

Hailey pulled out the medicine and handed it to Parker.

"Don't even offer to pay me back for this. You can pick up the tab for the floats, if your conscience bothers you."

"You won't be able to deduct it as a business expense. These things add up," Parker said.

Seriously? "I'll skip lunch tomorrow to make up for it."

Parker simply shook his head.

She retrieved the markers from the sack and handed them to PJ. "These are for when you get your cast. You can have all your favorite people sign it. That's what I did whenever I had mine."

"Cool! Can I be first?" Max asked.

"If it's okay with PJ."

"Awesome idea, Mom," Parker said.

"That's Lois to you." At that, she stood and motioned for Parker to follow her back to the barstools where they settled in but stayed facing the kiddos.

"So PJ tells me that Superman owns a mansion with many rooms," she said.

Parker seemed to think about it. "Oh, that. Not quite. I put in an offer on a home in Chicago. Mom used to work as a housekeeper when I was young, to support us. She loved that house, so when I saw the listing, I knew it was meant to be. Now, when she visits, she'll have a master suite all to herself."

"Wow. That's quite a gift. My mom's lucky if she gets a necklace that she'll actually wear. Can you write that off as a business expense?"

Parker cast her a look she couldn't quite put a finger on. "Is that a serious inquiry, or are you making fun of me?"

"A little of both," she admitted.

"Since I'll be using one room as a home office, I can file a deduction on my taxes. Figure I can claim roughly ten percent on things such as utilities, homeowner's insurance, property taxes. That sort of thing."

Hailey managed to suppress a yawn. Fortunately, they were saved from further discussion on the topic when the server placed their root beer ice cream floats on the counter. They swiveled to retrieve them, then turned back around to face the boys.

Parker removed the spoon and straw, sipped directly from the glass, and nodded in approval. He promptly wiped the whipped cream from his upper lip before she had a chance to tease him about his mustache.

"Do you have a family in Chicago?" she asked. Bold question, but it hadn't occurred to her until now that he may have a whole 'nother life that few people here knew about. She certainly kept some things to herself, as well.

He'd taken another sip and nearly choked on it. "As in a wife and kids? No. Only my mom. Why?"

"Six bedrooms," she said, dipping the spoon into the float and retrieving a huge scoop of ice cream.

"That's for someday," he answered.

It was her turn to nearly choke. "You want that many kids? Someday?"

He nodded. "Give or take one or two."

Although every fiber in her being admonished her to change the subject, she couldn't seem to help herself. "Boys or girls?"

"Whatever I'm blessed with. I hope they turn out as brave and cute as those guys over there."

Parker nodded to the booth. "Or as smart and pretty as Nash's girls."

"With you as their dad, how could they be anything but?" Hailey said, even though her chest was starting to feel heavy from the weight of the issue.

She expected a smart-aleck reply. Instead, he looked her right in the eyes as if that was the first time he'd really seen them.

Definitely time to change the subject. At least this conversation made her task at hand much easier, because they had even less in common than she suspected. "I have something I need to tell you."

"Go ahead."

"You don't have to work at the stables anymore. I'm thinking about putting the rides on hold until Cody returns. Max and I can take care of everything that Cody usually handles, and the horses can rest up for the big launch."

Parker actually looked disappointed.

"I'm almost afraid to say anything, but since I'm still on the payroll, I feel obligated to give you my professional opinion. I know bookings are slow, but even one new satisfied trail rider could produce a ripple effect."

"And then I'll be wealthy beyond my wildest dreams," she added.

"You say it like it's a bad thing."

Hailey shrugged. "I'm fine with getting by. I want to be happy and love what I do. That's my definition of wealth."

"If you build some stability into it, you can have both. I'm already concerned about the projection of your revenue stream. I, personally, would feel better if you added some bread-and-butter income to your plate."

Yet another thing to worry about: the uncertainty of what she'd gotten herself into. Even though a six-figure income wasn't on her bucket list, she had to make this work. Her independence depended on it. She grudgingly admitted that he did have a point.

Parker took the final sip of his float, then swiveled until he was facing her. The stools were situated awfully close. Her heart kicked up a notch, and it wasn't from the sugar.

"I'll make you a deal," he said, glancing at his watch. "If there aren't any bookings for the next three days by the time I get PJ settled in at grandpa's and am able to check the website, let's put the rides on hiatus like you suggested and regroup. But if there's even one booking, let's make some lucky person happy. And they *are* lucky. You've created something amazing here."

The compliment was the sweetest, but didn't

go down so easily. Her thoughts went to Cody. He'd put his heart, soul and back into the venture, and even put them on the map. He'd probably give her the same advice if he were here. Besides, she hadn't received any notifications and frankly wasn't expecting any, so this was a safe agreement. Her spur-of-the-moment bookings usually came from the Hideaway. Reservations from others who'd seen the marketing were made further in advance.

"Okay, but your friends and relatives don't count this time. It has to be a legitimate booking from someone who wasn't pushed into doing it. And adults only, for now," she said.

"Ouch! No pushing, I promise. Besides, I've exhausted my resources in those areas. Unless I can talk Grandpa into going. But he's already turned me down. Hates group outings. Plus, that would count as a relative anyway."

Thankfully, they understood each other. Worst case, Parker could watch Max while she went on the trail, because she wasn't quite ready to take any chances with him. Her emotional wounds were still as fresh as PJ's physical ones.

Which meant she should be happy about their agreement, right? Relieved, even.

Not even close.

"I HEAR YOU took quite a tumble, young man," Vern said to PJ as soon as he and Parker walked through the door. "I fixed up a comfy place on the sofa with your favorite pillows and blankets so you can watch some TV or nap."

PJ immediately settled in and got comfortable. Parker pulled the blanket over him and followed Vern to the kitchen. Looked as though his grandpa had been in the middle of making fresh-squeezed orange juice.

"I tried to call Vanessa but didn't leave a message. I'll try her again," Parker said.

"No need. I got ahold of her."

"Is she upset?" Parker could only imagine how it must feel to be out of town when an injury like that happened to your child.

"She understands that accidents happen. In fact, she got into one herself. A little fender bender in Cheyenne but didn't tell us because she didn't want anyone worrying. Seems someone behind her was texting and didn't see her taillights when she stopped at a light. Could have been a lot worse, I suppose."

His family was sure running into some bad luck this week. "Did she get checked out by a doctor?"

"Claims she's fine. She was gonna get a rental and come back here tonight, but I told her to stay put and make a doctor's appointment for first thing tomorrow. Make sure she's okay and then get her car fixed. PJ's in good hands with us. Besides, I've been down the road of broken bones before. More than a few times with my kids."

"I wish I could do more to help."

Vern pulled out two glasses and a plastic cup from a cabinet. "I know you do. You can't help yourself. Get it? Can't *help* yourself, but also can't help your *self* cuz you're too busy helping others."

Parker had to smile. Yeah, he got it. In this case, it was true. Looked like he'd be pitching in to care for PJ until Vanessa returned. Less time to spend on one of the other proposals he was considering. But after everything that happened today, Parker wanted to go back to his original proposal-modification idea that focused on Hailey's property. Her impulsiveness in wanting to shut down the rides for even a few days struck fear in him.

"Any idea how it happened?" Vern asked.

Parker grabbed some oranges, sliced one in half and put it in the squeezer. Then another. "Hailey and I think our PJ was pointing at something and lost his balance. The twins must have seen what happened, but I haven't had a chance to ask. Lizzy wasn't her usual chatty self."

"Now, that's interesting," Vern said.

"I agree. It was unsettling to have her be so quiet. She could use a filter sometimes, but I like that she's got such confidence and speaks her mind."

"Me too, but that's not what I'm talking about. You said *our* PJ. As in yours and Miss Hailey's."

"Semantics. Don't read too much into it," Parker said, although he wasn't quite sure why he'd phrased it that way. Was it a Freudian slip?

"He'll be fine," Vern said. "My boys and girls are tough as nails. You certainly were. Off and on for six years."

"I think I set a record for time in a brace. PJ won't have to suffer that long, fortunately. Hailey blames herself."

Vern cocked his head. "If it's anyone's fault, it's mine. If I would've gone instead, none of this would have happened."

"Nonsense," Parker said, taking a quick break from his orange-squeezing task to swat at the air, using his grandpa's favorite word and gesture against him.

"I suppose you're right. He wanted to go, and his mama gave her blessing. Besides, a ship in the harbor is safe, but that's not what a ship's for. Just gotta make sure you have a good crew with you when the seas get rough."

Vern always did add a why-didn't-I-think-of-that twist to proverbs. PJ had a good crew in Hailey today, even though she didn't see it that way.

"Speaking of which, you're sure handy to have around. Together we've squeezed the perfect amount of juice for the three of us." Vern proceeded to pour some in PJ's plastic cup, then filled the other two glasses.

Parker downed the drink, pulled the children's pain medicine from his pocket and placed it on the counter. "I need to take care of some business upstairs, then go back to Hailey's and finish up a few things. In case I'm not here and our patient starts hurting, we can give him this."

Vern picked up the box and read the instructions. "One teaspoon every six hours, as needed. When was his last dose?"

"About an hour ago, although the nurse had quite a time trying to get him to take something. I guess if the pain gets bad enough, he won't put up a fuss."

"I'll keep an eye on him. If it looks like he's

hurtin', I'll make sure to get some down the hatch," Vern said.

Parker squeezed his grandpa's forearm. "You're a good crew to have around."

With that, he retreated to his room and logged into the Sunrise Stables admin site to check for bookings. None.

After several minutes of staring at the screen and willing that zero to change to at least one booking, he concluded it was like staring at a phone when you wanted it to ring. He entertained ideas about how he could talk Vern into going but remembered his promise: no friends or relatives.

However, every promise had a loophole. And the one that came to mind was as big as the state of Texas.

His back hurt at the thought of falling off a horse. Falling off anything, really. After spending his childhood in a brace, doing anything to risk messing up his bones was the last thing he wanted to do. But the thought of letting Hailey down hurt even more.

With a few keystrokes, Hailey had her booking for tomorrow morning. Ten o'clock. With PJ in good hands, he shut down his computer and headed back to Sunrise Stables.

Thankfully, the crew member he needed to

talk to most was still there. Nash was busy wiping down the bridles that had been used on the trails.

"I thought you'd be long gone by now." Parker grabbed a spare rag and joined him. Meanwhile, the girls kept busy trying on all the helmets and modeling them for their daddy.

"I came across a few things that needed attention. Plus everything takes twice as long when these lovely gals are underfoot. Mostly, I wanted to be here as moral support for Hailey, in case she needs it."

Parker winced. He was hoping to be that for her. "You're a good friend," he managed to say.

Nash hung one of the bridles, then started working on the next. "I suppose. Whenever she lets me be one. She says PJ has a buckle fracture."

"Yes. Didn't even want to take any pain medicine."

Nash nodded. "Tough little guy, that's for sure."

"Tougher than I ever was. But that's about to change."

"How so?"

"Because I'm going to learn how to ride a horse today," Parker said.

Nash tossed his rag on the bench and gave

him a look of disbelief. That was one thing about this particular cowboy. His expressions pretty much revealed what the man was thinking, and they didn't mince words.

"How do you plan to do that?"

"For starters, I sold some stocks so I could hire the best teacher." Parker hoped Nash would remember his previous attempt at a joke. Except this time he meant it. The man could name his price.

"Oh, no," Nash said, shaking his head. "Not gonna happen."

"I just need to know enough to get on top of the beast and stay on. Whatever basic skills a first-time trail rider needs."

"And if I refuse?"

"Then I'll google it."

Nash put his palms together and rested his fingertips against his chin, as if in prayer. "Please don't do that."

"That's where I first learned the purpose of a hoof pick," he teased.

Nash stopped pretend-praying and rested his hands on his hips. "Since you're bent on doing this, let's saddle up Charmed."

"Not here. Not in front of Hailey."

A knowing grin spread across the cowboy's face. "Uh-huh. I was right. You're not interested in horses. You're trying to impress a certain cowgirl."

Parker straightened. "Only in a professional manner. Trust me, your warning about not breaking her heart is branded in my head. I'm not about to anger a man whose belt buckle is larger than a watermelon."

"Whatever you say, smarty-pants. Before I agree, any limitations I need to know about?" Nash asked.

"I had childhood scoliosis, but that isn't a limitation now. If anything, I've probably built the strongest core of anyone you could name. Except, perhaps, Cody Sayers. And as I'm sure you know, a strong core helps with balance."

Nash looked him in the eye. "I never knew that. About the scoliosis, I mean. I knew something had happened, but the few times you were in Destiny Springs when we were kids you kept to yourself."

"I didn't exactly fit in here. The only attempt I made to socialize was going to a birthday party for a kid named Zach something or another."

"Ledbetter. I know him. He went on to compete in rodeos. Bull rider, like Cody, except didn't get as far. I was at that party. I remember you helping a certain little cowgirl untangle some ropes. I was gonna step in myself, but you beat me to it."

"Do you also remember seeing her give me a kiss on the cheek?"

Nash smiled. "I think everyone remembers that kiss."

"I'm kind of hoping Hailey doesn't, and I'm not about to remind her, so please don't say anything. It's too late for me to ever be a cowboy like you, but I want to help her as best I can. While I can." Which reminded him what he had to do at some point today. The proposal. As if he needed reminding. His boss had sent him a text, saying that he was in Parker's corner, one thousand percent. Oh, and he needs that proposal. The man had been an amazing mentor. And the definition of integrity. Parker didn't want to let him down.

"I'm inclined to believe it's never too late to pursue your interests," Nash said.

"I like the way you think. So, will you help?" Parker asked.

Nash picked up the rag and resumed polishing. "We'll finish up here, and you can follow me and the girls back to Buck Stops. In the meantime, I could give you even more valuable information if you want to impress Hailey. For business purposes." Nash winked.

Parker shook his head and looked to the

ground. No use trying to argue it. "Okay. I'm all ears."

"For starters, you'll need to get on Sergeant's good side. She trusts his judgment about people's character."

"Who's that?"

"Her cat."

"Oh, yeah." *Oh, no.* That meant an emergency plea to his doctor for an allergy prescription.

"Next, whatever you do, don't criticize her cooking. You might want to keep an energy bar or some almonds in your pocket in case she ever offers to cook."

"It can't be that bad."

Nash stopped polishing and shook his head. "I love Hailey like a sister, but you don't want to be on the receiving end of her beans and hardtack."

Parker got the message loud and clear, even though he'd be consulting Google for a definition of the last item. No criticizing. Keep emergency provisions on his person at all times.

"And finally," Nash continued, "get some proper boots and jeans. Lookin' the part might make up for a lack of expertise. Smoke and mirrors, as they say."

Parker looked down. "I understand about the boots. But these *are* jeans that I'm wearing."

Nash pointed at the crease down the front of the legs. "Did you iron 'em yourself, or did your mom help?"

"I had them professionally starched and pressed before I came here. Otherwise, the crease wouldn't have held up even this good in the wash."

Nash rubbed his chin with one hand but didn't say a word. Didn't have to.

"Okay. No crease," Parker said.

"And the shirt has to go too. You'll thank me for it."

"It's a polo, and I usually wear a jacket over it anyway." Okay, so it didn't scream *cowboy*, but it was comfortable and casual, and it did have a tiny horse embroidered on it.

"Perfect for yachting, I'm sure," Nash said.

"I wear a linen button-down for that. Cooler than cotton," Parker said, realizing a little too late how that sounded. "Not that I own a yacht. One of my clients takes me out in his. As a perk. Rarely."

Stop talking.

Nash stared as if Parker were from another planet. Kind of felt that way to him, as well. But he was being put on the defensive.

"What's the best way to make the whole extreme makeover happen?" Parker asked.

"Kavanaugh's Clothing and Whatnot. Ethan, the owner, will get you all fixed up."

Parker wasn't afraid of changing his look a little, especially for such a good cause. He thought about Vern's advice. Parker's own ship was about to leave port and venture into uncharted territory. Without a crew, which left only one logical question.

"How late do they stay open? I'll swing by after my horseback riding lesson."

Nash checked his watch. "Probably another couple of hours. He shuts down before sunset then opens again around ten."

Parker shook his head. "That's going to conflict with my trail ride."

"You could go over there now, and come over for your lesson first thing in the mornin' instead. If you don't mind starting early."

Perfect. He could go straight to Hailey's with the lesson takeaways fresh on his mind. Which reminded him: he needed to text her to let her know about the booking, and that he might be a little later than normal.

With the logical question out of the way, he was about to ask an illogical one. A question he never thought he'd ask another man.

"Want to go shopping?"

CHAPTER SEVEN

WHAT A DAY she'd had. They'd *all* had. And it wasn't over yet.

Looked like Nash and Parker had finished putting away all the tack and had left, which she appreciated. Hopefully, the rest of her afternoon would be easy because Hailey needed all the "easy" she could get.

Parker had texted earlier that one person was booked for tomorrow morning at ten. With Max asleep, she checked the website for the stats. Adult. Male. Thirty years old. Some horseback-riding experience. No name, address or phone number. She made a mental note to make all the fields on the form "required." Otherwise, she was setting herself up for no-shows or surprises.

The soft pattering of Max's bare feet against the hardwood floor grew closer. When had he gotten up?

"Look, Miss Hailey. I got a cast!"

The white towel that was loosely wrapped

around his arm made her breath hitch, even though she knew it wasn't real. She suspected he was more than a little envious of his best friend for getting so much attention.

"A broken arm, huh?" She reached down and tucked in the corners for him.

Max giggled and nodded. "It broke in half."

"I bet it hurts."

"Just a little, but I've had worse."

Hailey raised her brows and nodded. He must have picked up that phrase from his dad. At least if Max did end up breaking a bone on her watch, he would probably thank her for it. Not that she wanted to imagine such a thing.

"You know what's good for helping bones heal, don't you?" she said.

"Hot chocolate?"

"Good guess, but no. Vegetables!"

Max's face scrunched, and she felt a giggle bubbling up in her throat.

A knock on the door put an end to that, especially since the knocker was none other than the bubble-burster herself. Georgina waved from the other side of the window. Her blond hair was in a tidy French twist, as usual. The most Hailey could ever manage was a ponytail. The already long day was about to get longer.

"Speaking of food we didn't ask for," she

muttered under her breath as she walked over to let her sister in while privately admonishing herself to play nice. It was a good reminder to install a shade or curtains.

"You don't need to do this. I won't let Max starve," Hailey said as she tried to ease the tray from Georgina's hands. But her sister insisted on carrying it to the kitchen counter herself. Max was hot on her heels.

"Look, Miss G! I broke my arm!" The full name proved to be too much of a tongue twister for a six-year-old. Hailey used to have her own nickname for her sister, but for some reason she couldn't think of it now. Too many lifetimes ago.

Georgina went along with Max's game. "Oh, my! I heard that someone broke a bone. Does it hurt?"

Max adjusted the towel. "Sure does. But I can handle it."

Georgina and Hailey looked at each other. Another mature phrase that he certainly didn't pick up from Hailey. Maybe she could learn something about self-confidence from this kiddo.

"I believe you. But you do know what helps heal broken bones, don't you?" Georgina reached for one of the containers and tried to hand it to him.

Instead, Max scurried to the bedroom as fast as his little legs would transport him.

Hailey laughed under her breath. She couldn't have planned that any better.

"It's banana cream pie! I thought he'd love it. What did I do wrong?" Georgina asked.

"Nothing. What else you got there?" Not that she really wanted to know, but the sooner she got Georgina out of her hair, the happier she'd be.

A smile of pride spread across Georgina's face. The woman was an amazing cook. Unlike Hailey. And unlike Faye, their oldest sister, a successful attorney who hired people to do the cooking for her. The three sisters couldn't be more different.

"I made chicken and vegetable pasta Alfredo. My recipe. It's not spicy, so it won't upset your and Max's tummies," she said.

Yep, her sister still thought of Hailey as a child.

"I also made some pimento cheese for sandwiches or to have with crackers. Oh, and some pea salad. Mom's recipe." The way Georgina gingerly placed each container in the refrigerator and admired it was like watching a mother set her newborns in a crib.

Hailey struggled to contain a snort over the

fact that Georgina didn't have a clue about Max's serious aversion to peas. Otherwise, she privately envied her sister's cooking ability. Then again, their mom was always a little too worried that her youngest might accidentally cut herself or get burned. Instead, she got tasked with washing the celery. Eventually, she lost interest in cooking altogether.

Georgina clasped her hands, cocked her head and gave Hailey *that* look. The one that warned Hailey to brace herself for a heaping serving of unwarranted concern and unsolicited advice.

"I could take Max off your hands until Becca and Cody get back. I know you're not that fond of children."

"I shouldn't even have to say this, but I *love* children. Other people's, but what's wrong with that?"

Georgina bit her lip. Hailey should have held her tongue because she didn't want to have this conversation.

"To be honest, I want him at the B and B for selfish reasons," Georgina said. "The puppy is fun, but it's awfully lonely housesitting such a big place. And a bit scary at times. *The Shining* was on last night, and I couldn't bear to watch! It would be nice having him around."

While they were being honest, Hailey was

tempted to say that she would welcome a little alone time for herself right now. Since Georgina was such an extrovert, her excuse was believable. But that wouldn't be fair to Max, and it wasn't what Becca wanted.

"I didn't mean to snap. It's been a stressful day. I'll give it some thought," Hailey said.

Georgina nodded. "I guess I better be getting back. Do you think Max would mind if I said goodbye to him?"

The request tugged at her heartstrings, quite unexpectedly. Georgina seemed genuinely sad. Because of her and Max's reaction. Then Hailey remembered something she'd been putting off that would cheer up her sister. Another heartstring-tugging task on her long and dusty to-do list and one that she *wanted* some help with.

"Sure. But before you do that, could you spare a few minutes?" Hailey asked.

"Minutes? Try hours. Days."

"I found a box of Grandma's things and thought you might like to have them. Looks like costume jewelry, from what I can tell. For some weird reason, she put that sort of stuff in marked envelopes. I haven't opened them all, so no telling what kind of shape the items are in. Whatever you don't want, I'll give to Nash's twins so they can play dress-up."

Sure enough, Georgina's whole face brightened. "Of course. I'd be more than happy to help. And I'll leave a few things for the girls anyway. Unless there's something valuable you could sell instead. You know, make a little money for a rainy day?"

That topic again. Usually, she'd feel trapped by the question. Obligated to *try* to explain why she didn't have some emergency fund with three months of living expenses saved up. *Blah blah blah.*

"On rainy days, I prefer to stay home in bed, which doesn't cost a thing," she said.

Georgina simply shook her head. Judgment rendered. Back to the topic at hand.

"Follow me. Oh, and grab that piece of banana cream pie and a fork. I'm pretty sure Max will be your best friend once you take off the lid. Max!" Hailey shouted. "You can come out of hiding. Georgina has something for you and it isn't vegetables."

Max peeked around the corner. Georgina held out the open container with the piece of pie. Max followed them to the master bedroom like a puppy. Sergeant simply watched the human-comedy parade from his perch on top of a tall dresser. He swatted at Georgina's French twist as she walked by but missed.

Hailey retrieved the box from her closet, placed it on the floor, then sat cross-legged beside it. Georgina followed suit and immediately began pulling out envelopes and reading them one at a time before opening.

"Broaches from Aunt Virginia." She emptied the contents in her hand. "Look! One is a cameo."

Georgina opened another envelope and a beautiful strand of pearls slithered to the floor.

"Oh my. Those look real," she said, picking them up and inspecting them. Wasn't something Hailey could authenticate. They were also nothing she'd ever wear.

Max finished the pie in record time. He'd let his so-called cast pool to the floor as he reached inside the box.

"What does this one say?" he asked, handing the envelope to Hailey.

The ink was smudged, but it looked like... "'Engagement ring.'" She was tempted to drop it like a hot potato but handed it to Georgina instead. "You can definitely have this one."

Georgina squeezed the somewhat thick envelope. "She must've wrapped it in tissue or something. Shall we have a look?"

Max nodded. At this point, he was practically on top of Georgina. Personally, Hailey could have done without the preview. Engagement rings and wedding sets still gave her the heebie-jeebies.

Georgina reached into the envelope and pulled out something other than a ring, then immediately dropped it to the floor. *Like a hot potato.*

"What is that? Human hair or some kind of fur?" Georgina asked.

Max hovered over it like it was roadkill and he was making sure it wasn't still breathing. "Wow! Your grammy had *huge* fingers!" He dropped to the floor, rolled around and couldn't stop laughing.

Hailey picked up and studied the bracelet. Had their sweet grandma suffered some dementia toward the end of her life, because this wasn't a ring. She'd otherwise done a pretty good job labeling everything so far.

The thought made Hailey's heart ache, and she was reminded how much she missed her.

This piece was simply beautiful if not a bit frazzled. A blond braid intertwined with a chestnut-toned one. Clearly from two separate horses. It didn't have a clasp. Rather, it was fitted with slivers of rough-edged suede ties on each end.

Max finally stopped laughing, but Georgina hadn't stopped staring. In horror, it appeared.

"Relax. It's horsehair," Hailey said.

Max ran his little fingers over it. "Cool!"

"The hair is clipped from the tail. They don't feel a thing." Hailey tried to slip it over her hand, but it was too tight. She untied the knotted suede strands and wrapped it around her left wrist, then struggled to retie it. Georgina leaned in, took control and tied it for her.

An odd, familiar warmth swept over Hailey as she remembered her sister layering tons of jewelry on her as a little girl. She was Georgina's own dress-up doll for a short period. Until Hailey realized she didn't like all those baubles and frills and turned full-on tomboy instead.

"Thanks, sis," she said to Georgina.

"Anytime, sis."

"I don't want any sisters," Max said.

"Why not?" Georgina and Hailey asked in unison, then laughed at the same time. At least they'd reached a point where they could. The early years weren't all that funny.

"Do you think you'll ever change your mind about not having children of your own someday?" Georgina asked.

And so it begins. The pressure to have a family, even though Georgina herself had yet to marry and start one. Hailey knew exactly how to put an end to it. Tell her sister about the diagnosis. Hailey was rather surprised that their mom had respected Hailey's wishes and kept it between the two of them. If Georgina ever found out, so would the rest of the world.

There was one other way to shut down the topic.

"Ask me after I meet a man who doesn't ditch me at the altar," Hailey said.

She knew she'd shoveled salt into the wound. As her wedding planner, Georgina was still beating herself up about the whole debacle, even though Hailey had forgiven her for the role she'd played in the overall disappointment. Sort of. It wasn't her fault Hailey's fiancé bailed. But maybe it was Georgina's fault for siding with the future mother-in-law and pressuring Hailey to have a huge, elaborate ceremony when she'd wanted something small and understated.

Georgina maintained eye contact for a couple of seconds before looking away, which was fine. Hailey didn't want to go back down that aisle either.

In fact, she'd be more than happy if the subject of weddings—and having children—never came up again.

PARKER STARED AT the store sign. That last word—*Whatnot*—struck fear in him.

Nash had already waltzed right inside Kavanaugh's as if he'd been there a million times. Probably had. Parker tugged on the antler handle. The door was much heavier than it looked, although Nash made it seem light as a feather.

When Parker finally got it open, some cowbells dangled from the inside, announcing his arrival. Nash was already chatting it up with another equally handsome and rugged cowboy.

The guy set down a stack of paper he'd been holding and came out from around the counter, taking long strides in his direction.

"You must be Parker. I'm Ethan," he said, extending his hand. Ethan's grip was quite firm. His palms, calloused.

Nash joined them, and the two proceeded to size up Parker.

Why did he feel like Eliza Doolittle in *My Fair Lady*—only they were contemplating how to turn a city businessman into a country cowboy.

Even though Parker had hoped Nash would bring his girls along instead of dropping them off with Vern, he was rather glad because he didn't want any of this to get back to Hailey.

"I see what you're talkin' about, Nash."

Ethan broke away and began pulling pairs of jeans that were stacked on a shelf. Nash began perusing some circular racks. He selected a couple of plaid button-downs, then held one up against Parker's chest.

"The red looks good with your dark hair," Nash said. "What do you think, Ethan?"

"He'd have to try 'em on, but I was thinkin' yellow when he first walked in. That would make a bold statement, but he could pull it off. Red's nice but always screams *Christmas* to me. Maybe try navy to be safe."

"Safe from what? Goats?" Parker asked, throwing in the last bit to lighten the moment, because these guys were taking this more seriously than necessary. Nash would certainly get it, yet neither responded.

"I've put some jeans in the first dressing room. A couple different sizes, although you look to be the same waist and inseam as me," Ethan said, relieving Nash of the shirts. Nash headed for another rack, leaving Parker and Ethan in his dust.

"Follow me," Ethan said. "We'll save the boots for last. And speaking of goats, I don't think that little cuss was playing fair."

It took a moment to sink in. Ethan hadn't

simply heard about the incident. He'd seen the video. Was there anyone she didn't send it to?

"I'll be sure to thank Hailey for forwarding it to you," he said.

Ethan looked toward Nash as if making sure he was out of earshot. "I had a similar run-in with one of them critters. They're so sweet lookin', but boy, can they be assertive," he whispered, as if the two of them shared a secret bond over their experiences.

Unsure how to respond, Parker simply smiled.

"Holler if you need another size," Ethan said, pulling the dressing room curtain shut behind him.

"Model 'em for us," Nash called out from the other side, then snickered.

Very funny. He'd have to, anyway. The dressing room didn't have a mirror, but he'd noticed a full-length one in the common area.

The first pair of jeans fit, but what was with all the fading and tears? Was this a secondhand shop? Not secondhand prices. He paired it with the yellow-and-black flannel shirt, then pulled the curtain aside.

Nash did a quick glance and ran his index finger across his throat.

Parker's thoughts exactly, and he hadn't even gotten the full-length picture.

The next ensemble was black rinse jeans with some fraying at the knees and hem, paired with the dark gray flannel shirt.

This time, when Parker drew the curtain, Nash wasn't alone. Ethan raised his eyebrows and cocked his head. Nash crossed his arms and craned his neck for a closer look. Parker yanked the curtains shut again without even asking or bothering to look himself.

One more set. After that, he was giving up. The traditional-looking blue jeans had minimal fraying but a lived-in look. No creases. He paired them with the navy plaid button-down. He wasn't sure how it looked, but it sure felt right.

The cowboys on the other side of the curtain gave an enthusiastic thumbs-up. That was the only response that would get him to drop cash on clothes that he might not ever wear again after leaving Destiny Springs.

Next stop, boots. Ethan pulled out a black pair, as well as a brown.

"Got any ostrich?" Nash asked.

"I'll have to search in the back," Ethan said, leaving the two of them alone.

"Well? What do you think so far?" Nash asked.

"Hailey isn't going to recognize me. But I think she'll approve."

"On a business level, right? Don't worry. I won't tell her that you like her. Although, Hailey is smart as a whip. She probably already knows."

Parker believed him on both counts. But he still wasn't sure how to define how he felt. Sure, he really liked her. In all honestly, he was pretty sure he might love her in an unrequited first-crush kind of way.

Ethan came back with two more boxes, putting the private conversation about Hailey on hold. "Didn't have any ostrich but got in some gator. Two different styles. Both quite handsome, but I'll let you decide, Parker."

The guy stepped away and began tidying up one of the display tables while Parker modeled the boots for Nash. He also picked up where they left off with the previous conversation about Hailey, because he'd bet his 401(k) that the subject was going to come back around anyway. "Okay. So, yes, I like her. What's not to like? She's smart. Beautiful."

"But does she enjoy yachting?" Nash had a serious look that he seemed to be struggling to maintain.

"Of course. It's one of my requirements,"

Parker countered, then muttered, "wise guy. Hey, what do you think about these?"

Nash nodded, all but confirming Parker's good taste in boots. He liked them too. Ethan stepped back into their orbit and offered his two cents. "Now, those look really smart. Your girlfriend's gonna love 'em."

Parker was tempted to say he didn't have such a thing and that it wasn't nice to eavesdrop. But he refrained. He looked at the price on the box. *Ouch.* No wonder they looked so good.

"I think we have a winner," Nash said.

Parker had to agree. But as comfortable as they felt, he wasn't so sure he belonged in them, as though the privilege to wear boots like these had to be earned.

On their way out, Parker realized he'd only begun paying for this charade, or whatever it was. "I owe you, Nash. Like we talked about, I'll watch the girls for you. When I'm not acting as a stunt double for Cody at Sunrise Stables, that is."

Yet another thing that would distract him from finishing the proposal, but Nash really did seem to need help with the twins. Among other things.

"I thought you were joking before. You have

met my girls, haven't you? They're a handful, even on the best day," Nash said.

"It's a sacrifice I'm willing to make."

Kind of like the other sacrifice he was about to make: risking his back on a horse. Yet, it was a chance for him to get to know Hailey better, and thus tweak his barn proposal in ways that would benefit her business most. Because, yes, Nash had it all figured out. Parker was trying to impress her.

And, yes, on a personal level too.

CHAPTER EIGHT

HAILEY WASN'T SURE how to go about breaking a little boy's heart.

Even after a long, sleepless night obsessing about it, the best she could come up with was a second Pop-Tart to sweeten the news that he wouldn't get to ride today. She'd even let Max sleep in a little since Parker had mentioned that he might be a little late.

Still barefoot and in his purple flannel pajamas, Max had disassembled his first breakfast treat and looked to be constructing something with it using the two sides as walls. The second one had cooled, so she handed Max the material to complete his masterpiece.

"What are you building, kiddo?"

"A hospital."

Hailey tapped her fingers against her coffee mug. That sparked a brilliant idea. "I have a special favor to ask. I'd like for you to spend the day with PJ instead of helping with the ride. It would be a huge sacrifice on my part to not have you along, but he could really use the company."

Max seemed to mull it over. "But what about the story?" he asked.

Of course, that was the best part of the ride for Max.

"Oh, that's an excellent point because people need to know. When our client arrives, you can tell it to him while Parks and I get the horses tacked up. How does that sound?"

Then Parker and Max could go back to Fraser Ranch and stay there long enough for her to finally get some long overdue *Hailey time* after the trail ride ended. A goat yoga session topped the list.

"Okey dokey," Max said after several more seconds of contemplation.

Not bad, Hailey. She did have a good idea every so often, she had to admit.

Max disassembled the frosting-coated hospital and polished half of it off in record time, but left the other half behind.

"Nice demolition work," she said, taking the plate away before he changed his mind. "Go wash those paws, brush them fangs and put some clothes on those bones of yours, kiddo. Don't forget your jacket. Then join me at the stables."

She bundled up and ventured outside, where Parker was already in the feed room, reading her posted notes and studying the supplements. He looked so intense. And confused.

"Got it all figured out?" she asked.

He offered up an uneasy smile. "I'm guessing you already fed them. I was thinking that I could take over tomorrow morning. But frankly, it's a little intimidating."

"A little different than feeding Vern's horses, huh," she said, calling him out on his earlier claim. At the same time, he was showing some serious initiative.

"You may not believe this, but I have fed them. Only after Grandpa measured and assembled everything. I poured, though, which I hoped counted for something, since I really wanted this assignment from Cody."

The uneasiness had faded from that smile of his. It wasn't always clear when he was teasing versus when he was being serious. She concluded it was a little of both this time.

Gosh. That smile. Like a soft hug that took her breath away every time.

But there was something else about him today that made her feel awfully warm and fuzzy. Something that kept toying with her concentration. Must be that navy-blue plaid flannel shirt. He'd never worn that one before. She would have remembered.

She'd walk him through the feeding process another time. Today, she'd teach him about matching riders to horses. With only one client, this would be a good introduction. She'd ride Bad Boy, her natural leader. Gabby was on probation through no fault of her own. Star was the no-brainer choice for pretty much any rider, but she'd be respectful of Max's feelings and give her a vacation day. No Regrets was still off-limits for everyone. That left Whiskey, Blaze and Charmed.

"Max is getting dressed. I suggested he spend the day with PJ. He seems okay with it."

"Let's talk about that." Parker headed toward the tack room and nodded for her to follow. Exactly who was in charge here?

"Did you hear what I said?" she asked.

He opened the door and ushered her in first, which prompted her to visualize him opening doors for his *Debbie Taunt* at some fancy party.

"I heard. It's an excellent idea. In fact, I'll drive him over in a few, because I'd like to get the trail ride started as soon as possible." He selected a saddle pad and pulled it off the rack. Did he even know how that would be used?

"Maybe your meetings in Chicago are that

flexible, but it doesn't work that way here. The client should arrive fifteen minutes before the ride. Sometimes, they're a bit earlier. Sometimes a little late."

"The client is already here."

An hour early? Hailey stuck her head outside the tack room. No one.

When she turned back around, Parker held up one finger like he did that morning when Cody dropped the bomb that Parker would be his substitute. Except, today he was the client. That was possibly even worse.

"I said no friends or relatives."

"I didn't invite any."

Hailey struggled for a comeback, but he'd won on a technicality. And he obviously knew it, judging from that grin.

"Which saddle should I use with Gabby?" he asked.

"She's taking the day off." As Hailey was now considering doing. "My horses, my rules."

"According to the woman whom I trust completely to lead my trail-ride experience, Gabby wasn't at fault for the accident. In fact, Nash tells me the twins confessed that PJ was pointing and twisting, even after you admonished them not to."

She wished someone would have told her

that. Poor little PJ. No, Gabby wasn't at fault, which she already suspected. But if she or another adult had been watching more closely, the accident could've been avoided. The revelation made her feel worse about that ride but better about the one directly in front of her.

"Okay then. I give you permission to take Gabby."

"I was hoping Max could come with us. Since he's not, it will give me a chance for us to talk, one on one. Get to know each other better," Parker said.

Since he put it that way, maybe it would be a good idea to have Max along. Although that wasn't going to happen. She wasn't ready. Instead of arguing, she grabbed Gabby's saddle and took the lead in carrying it out the door. Max soon joined her and helped with the bridles.

"I hear you won't be riding today, but you're a super best friend for visiting PJ instead. I'll drive you over in a few minutes," Parker said to Max.

Max shrugged. "I s'pose."

"Maybe you two cowboys should do that now. Before we tack up the horses. I'll rustle up some goodies for the trail while y'all are gone." *And try to find my bearings because I desper-*

ately need them. Parker was the last person she was expecting. Oddly enough, she wasn't sure whether that was a good or bad thing.

Once Parker and Max were en route to Fraser Ranch, Hailey went back inside. She set the front burner on high and plopped the buttered sides of bread in the skillet and topped them with cheese, then assembled the rest of the snacks. Bad decision because the snack assembly took too long. The edges of the bread turned solid black, but they could eat around them. Served him right for surprising her.

By the time Parker returned, she'd not only finished preparing the food, she'd tacked up Bad Boy and Gabby. He almost seemed disappointed that he didn't get to help with the latter, but that would've prolonged the torture for all of them. Horses included.

She handed him the standard waiver. "I think you're familiar with this. I've been advised by my business consultant that I'm not liable if something awful happens to you." She added a smile to let him know she was exaggerating. Sort of.

"I'm not worried." He signed without reading it. Then again, he'd helped install this guardrail for her business in the first place.

Next, he correctly mounted Gabby. His form

wasn't the greatest, but he seemed to kind of know what he was doing.

"According to your booking information, you have some experience, even if you don't have a name. Please fill out all the fields next time. We'll still go over a few basics."

"Like pressure and release? Heels down and toes up? Keep hands in neutral position and leave a little slack in the reins unless giving a command?" he asked.

The man was full of surprises this morning. Hopefully he wasn't also full of hot air.

"Okay then. Follow me." She led them to the trailhead. Fortunately, the Plains and Simple ride didn't require a load up or transport. Unlike Rascal's High-Ridge Ramble and Rocks and Rolling Hills. Until they cut some new paths, she was perfectly content with calm meadows and chirping birds.

She was so used to Max doing all the talking, with her inserting a fact here and there, she wasn't sure what to say along the way. It wasn't as if Parker was seriously interested in this ride. She'd bet he'd done this to keep from putting the rides on hiatus. She wasn't sure whether to thank him or scold him.

Although they got off to an impressive start, he didn't look comfortable on the back of a horse. Still, she had to commend him for his fortitude. She also had to commend him for those cowboy boots. When had he gotten those, and why hadn't he worn them sooner? And those jeans! If he was trying to impress her, it was working.

"Is something wrong?" he asked.

Had she been that obvious? Might as well be honest. "I was checking out your riding outfit. Quite appropriate for the occasion."

He simply shrugged. "I grabbed a few things from my closet. No biggie."

But the way he couldn't seem to contain a smile when he looked away suggested otherwise.

No question he was trying to impress her. He deserved kudos for learning a few things on his own. Still, by the time he'd become fluent enough to be of any actual help, Cody would be back, and Parker would be on his way to Chicago.

They finally reached a good spot for lunch after a painfully awkward half hour. Parker wobbled a little on his dismount but regained his balance in time. He caught her watching, even though she'd tried to look away.

Something seemed to be shifting between them, pulling them together rather than pushing them apart. Something that being alone together like this seemed to aggravate.

With any luck, one of Max's superheroes would swoop in and take their horses, thus ending this horrible feeling that Parker would end up with a broken bone before this ride was over.

Or that she would eventually end up with a broken heart.

PARKER SPREAD OUT the blanket while Hailey secured the horses. So far, so good, even though he'd botched the dismount.

He'd blame it on the polished soles of the new boots, but the fault was his. He'd allowed himself to be distracted. By her. He could stare at her all day long and feel nothing but admiration. And attraction, to be honest. But the moment she looked at him with those green-and-gold eyes, his insides began twisting, and he had trouble forming words. Hard to come across as professional while being tongue-tied. But he hadn't spent all that money on new clothes or inconvenienced Nash to stop trying now.

Once done, she sat cross-legged opposite him on the blanket. She reached into a thermal pouch and handed him something square, then pulled out a selection of chips and a couple of sodas.

He unwrapped the foil. Inside, a slightly burned grilled cheese sandwich. Even the sight of it made his mouth water. It took only one big, warm, gooey bite to transport him back to his childhood. How quickly he had forgotten. His mom always burned the extreme edges of grilled cheese sandwiches. The few times that she didn't, he was disappointed.

Hailey took a big bite of her own sandwich and looked out over the open land, while he looked at her. The breeze caused a wisp of hair that had escaped her ponytail to get into her eyes. She nudged it away with the back of her hand. She reminded him of a Volegov painting he'd seen at an exhibition in Stockholm, only much prettier.

"This is delicious," he managed to say.

She raised an eyebrow. "Liar. I can't even make grilled cheese without burning down the house."

"Did you just call me a liar?"

"Sure did. I call it as I see it."

"Then I'll do the same. Liar. You've never burned down a house," he said.

"The carcinogens all over the crust aren't enough to convince you that it's highly likely?" she asked.

He tore off the burned edge and popped it into his mouth.

She smiled and shook her head. "Anyway, you have no idea what I'm capable of."

Parker shifted to take some pressure off his back.

"You're the one who has no idea what you're capable of. Look what you've already accomplished with Sunrise Stables. You should cook a five-course meal to prove to yourself that you *won't* set your house on fire," he said, taking another huge bite of sandwich.

"I'm fine not knowing. But if I'd known you were the one who booked the ride, I would've asked what you wanted for lunch. Oh! Maybe I should include food options on the booking site. Enhance the guests' experience and give them a chance to report any food allergies in case it isn't covered by the liability waiver. Is it, by the way?"

"Excellent point. We'll double-check that. Being proactive on such things is always a smart business decision. At this rate, you could *get by* reasonably comfortably," he teased, hoping she'd remember their previous conversation.

He was pleased she was finally thinking in those terms. Made him cautiously optimistic that she'd consider his detailed proposal, which was forthcoming unless life threw a new wrench in his path. Even then, he'd have to find a way to step around it if he wanted the promotion. And he definitely wanted it.

"What's your favorite dish? In case you book another ride with me before you leave."

Favorite? Now, that one he had to think about. There were so many.

"I'd have to say vichyssoise. Such a basic soup, yet with such depth."

She'd just taken a huge bite and seemed to struggle with swallowing for a moment. "Now, that's what I call a coincidence."

"How so?"

"Because I almost made some today. Then I realized I was fresh out of *vichy*."

He waited for the inevitable eye roll. She didn't disappoint. He took another bite of the cheese sandwich. "Actually, I'd like to change my answer."

"To something else I can't spell or pronounce, much less cook?"

Parker smiled and shook his head. His intention hadn't been to make her feel self-conscious. Quite the opposite. "This sandwich has bumped vichyssoise out of first place."

"We better get you to the clinic. Did you fall

back there and hit your noggin when I wasn't paying attention?"

"Not that I recall. Besides, clinics and hospitals don't scare me," he said.

She didn't ask why. She didn't have to. The long pause spoke volumes.

"What was it like?" she finally asked.

He sat up straighter. Felt as though he was in that brace all over again. As many times as he'd imagined this topic coming up over the past few months, he wasn't prepared to talk about it with her.

Now he was the one to look away. Hopefully, she'd admit that she'd kissed him because she'd felt sorry for him. It would give him closure and make his inevitable exit from this working partnership a lot easier when the time came. His emotions had become tied to this place. Destiny Springs felt like home, in a way. People he'd never gotten to know in his youth were beginning to feel like family.

"It was what it was, and it's not like I chose childhood scoliosis," he said.

"I hear you on that," she said. Although the sentiment was casual, her expression had a certain depth he couldn't define.

"The most difficult part was having people look at me a certain way," he said.

"What do you mean?"

"Like I was someone to be pitied."

She pinched her brows. "Why would they pity you?"

For the first time in his life, he was at a loss for an answer. To him, it seemed obvious. Although in thinking about it, pity wasn't what he would feel for someone in his predicament. Empathy, perhaps. Bravery, for certain.

"You didn't feel the least bit sorry for me?" he said.

She shook her head, swallowed her last bite of sandwich and wiped her mouth with a napkin. "Hardly! I offered to let you ride my own horse that day for helping me untangle those ropes, didn't I?"

"After I turned down your cash offer."

"Untangling the ropes wasn't your job."

"Exactly. Which is why I refused to accept payment in any form."

"Then the joke is on you, because the kiss on the cheek *was* the payment. Just so you know, I don't kiss boys I feel sorry for. Never have, never will."

If that was the case, it was the best payment ever. But the way she was looking at him and smiling suggested otherwise.

"That's not the real reason you kissed me, is it?" he asked.

Was she blushing? The bigger question had to be, was *he* blushing? Sure felt like it.

She sat up straighter. "You are correct. I kissed you because I could tell you had a huge crush on me, and I thought I'd toss you a crumb."

He had to laugh. So that's the way it was going to be. Not that he could deny it. Nor could he deny that the crush continued to this day. He took a long swig of soda, trying to formulate his next words now that the cat was out of the bag on his other childhood condition: his crush on Hailey.

"If you don't kiss boys whom you feel sorry for, then your crumb-throwing excuse doesn't hold water. You're the one who had a crush on me. Admit it."

"Because all the little girls did?"

"Only the smart ones." On impulse, he added a wink.

"Aside from my dad, no one has ever accused me of being smart."

"I'm pretty sure I just did." Even though he was saying it with humor, he was dead serious. Hailey had the kind of smarts that didn't come with a formal education. One had to be born with them.

"With those smarts, you might even become wealthy beyond your wildest dreams," he felt compelled to add. Maybe it wasn't very subtle to say that, but he'd love to see her parlay those smarts into a financially secure life.

"I don't know. Maybe I'm not all that wealthy *because* I'm smart. Did you ever think of that?" she said.

He could honestly say he hadn't. But he could practically feel his mind trying to wrap around the concept.

They finished their lunch in silence, caught somewhere between childhood fantasy and adult reality. He pulled out two hand wipe packets from his pocket. Kept one for himself and gave the other to her.

She stared at the packet before realizing what it was. Her expression could only be described as amused.

"When do you think you'll be ready to let Max colead again?" he asked.

Hailey finished cleaning her hands, then wadded the wipe into a ball and pressed it between her palms. "Right now, I don't think I can. It was stressful enough with all those kids, even before the accident. But now..."

That was news. Parker couldn't recall her

voicing any concerns. But, yes, she had seemed to be worried about something.

"I didn't know you felt that way. I apologize."

She took a deep breath. "Not your fault. I should have said something. It wasn't unsafe or anything, but the child-to-adult ratio concerned me. Ultimately, I wanted to believe that I could handle anything thrown in my path. Guess I proved myself wrong."

"You're excellent with kids. Stop second-guessing yourself on your abilities. I believe that we go through these trials for a reason. Forgive me if I'm being presumptuous, but maybe this is the universe's way of preparing you for motherhood one day. An occasional broken bone seems to be part of the standard package."

Once again, Hailey stared at something in the distance. Then she straightened.

"I love kids, and they seem to love me. But I don't have my life all planned out, like you. I'll make that decision when the time comes."

Now it was his turn to look off in the distance. That wasn't quite the direction he'd intended for her to take. But since she did, he couldn't imagine *not* wanting kids. Yet, that wasn't quite what she was saying.

"But it's not about the accident, or having kids," she continued, thankfully redirecting the conversation. "Truth is, I don't enjoy the leading part of this business as much as I thought I would."

He scooted closer. "There's no shame in not loving certain aspects of your business. I don't enjoy some aspects of mine, like trying to come up with options for housing my favorite client's goats." He added a wink. Couldn't hurt.

Little did she know he was totally serious. In fact, that's how he'd be spending this evening. Or what's left of his evening after helping Vern take care of PJ.

"Logically, I know you're right. About the trail rides, that is. *Not* the goats." Hailey sat up straighter. "I'll get Max back in the saddle soon."

"Good. Since you aren't banning children for life, may I be direct with you about something else?"

"You hated the sandwich after all?"

"Hardly!" he said, borrowing her word. "No, these rides are the resurrection of a tradition. Wasn't that the whole selling point? Since no one can confirm the origins, it helps to have a story. Even a fantastical one, like Max spins. My unsolicited advice would be to hire the best trail-ride lead you can find, and let Max go with him or her."

"You're right. You're also welcome to try to find someone with experience and maturity who I can afford."

Challenge accepted.

"If I do, will you cook something special for me?" he asked.

"Sure. As long as it doesn't have *vichy* as an ingredient. The markets around here don't carry it."

"Oh, this one's easy. Chicken noodle soup."

"If you think I can't manage to ruin it, you seriously underestimate me," she said.

She might be right, but she'd yet to ruin these growing feelings he was having for her. So much for keeping this strictly professional.

PARKER FELT LIKE the sheriff in some old Western, putting up Wanted posters all over town. Help Wanted posters, in this case. Nothing fancy—just big-and-bold type on plain white printer paper. But time was of the essence. He even added the hook about reviving a Destiny Springs tradition. Sure, he could have waited until tomorrow and designed something fancier on his laptop. But he didn't want to waste a minute.

By the time he got back to Fraser Ranch, he already had three messages on his cell. A brief phone interview eliminated two, but the third sounded promising. Sylvie Moss. Had been riding horses all her life. She even rode the original trails. The best part: she'd work for meals.

"But none of that fancy stuff I can't pronounce," she said, clarifying.

So far, she couldn't be a better fit for Hailey. "Can you come over for an interview?"

"Name the time and place. I'll be there."

"How about now?" He gave her Vern's address, and she said she could be there in fifteen or so minutes.

Vern came downstairs as Parker ended the call. "Glad you're back. Our little patient has been worried sick about you."

"Why?"

"Max told PJ you were riding horses. I told PJ he must've imagined that, which made the little fella start crying. Hailey had already picked up Max, so I couldn't confirm. I feel rotten to the core."

"He didn't imagine it. I went on Hailey's trail ride."

Vern stared as if waiting for Parker to blink. "Well, color me surprised."

"Pull out the crayons because I have another surprise. Someone is coming over for an interview. Sorry I didn't ask first, but this is an emergency," Parker said.

"My home is your home. Who are we hiring, and what for?"

"Trail-ride lead for Hailey so that she can focus on other areas of the business."

"I'll put on some coffee. You can do your interview in the kitchen if you'd like. Best lighting in the house."

"Don't go to any trouble," Parker said.

Vern simply waved off his comment and proceeded to be his usual helpful self.

Parker went upstairs and cracked open the door. PJ was sitting up in bed, eyes rubbed raw.

"What's wrong?" he asked as he eased next to him.

PJ put his uninjured arm around Parker and held him tight. "I was scared."

Now Parker was the one to feel rotten to the core.

"Honestly, I was a little scared myself. But I rode Gabby, and she was such a sweetheart. Very gentle, even when I accidently kicked her during my dismount."

"I'm never gonna ride again."

"You don't have to, but she adores you. She even told me so and wants to be friends. But what if I told you that you could sit on a horse right now, with that splint, and there's no chance you'd get hurt. Would you do it?"

"Gabby talks?"

"Sure! Fortunately, I speak horse."

PJ giggled, but in a way that sounded like he wanted to believe Parker.

"What do you say? Want to ride?" Parker asked.

"I won't fall off?"

"Zero chance of it." Parker proceeded to get down on all fours and made the most horselike neigh he could manage.

That earned an unmistakable giggle. "Horses don't make that sound."

"Sure they do. How do you think I communicated with Gabby?"

He repeated it, then nodded for PJ to climb aboard. Probably not the best thing for his own back, but this was more important in the moment. Thank goodness Max wasn't getting *this* on video.

"Careful. Use the bed for balance," Parker suggested.

PJ did as instructed, transitioning from the mattress to Parker's back. As Parker attempted a more animated neigh, Vern opened the door. "Sorry to disturb your pony ride, but your job applicant is here. I parked her in the kitchen."

"Can you do me a favor and help our rider off his trusty steed?" Parker asked.

Vern lifted PJ and placed him back on the bed.

"Can I ride you now, Pawpaw?" PJ asked.

"I have a better idea," Parker interjected, even though PJ's enthusiasm was encouraging. "How about you help me interview the nice lady, since you're an experienced horseman. If Hailey likes her too and we hire her, she can sign your cast after you get it put on to seal the deal. You'll be the most important person in the whole business transaction."

That perked him up. "Can I wear your tie?"

"For the signing, or the interview?"

"Both."

"Absolutely." Parker retrieved the accessory from the top of the dresser and helped him with the knot, then took his hand and they headed downstairs. Vern disappeared altogether.

When they reached the kitchen, the lady stood. Her long, braided silver hair and sun-stained skin told a beautiful story. So did her immaculate posture. No telling how old she was, and he wasn't going to ask. She was youth and maturity in one package. He imagined Hailey would look as strong and graceful as this woman as she aged.

She took a step forward and extended her hand to PJ first. "I'm Sylvie Moss. You must be the gentleman I spoke with about the job."

PJ giggled, then hid behind Parker's legs.

Parker adored the woman already.

She offered her hand to him, and he accepted. He'd shaken plenty in his career, but few as confident yet warm as this one.

After brief introductions, they all took a seat around the kitchen table.

"I appreciate you coming over on such short notice. As you know, we're looking for someone to lead trail rides. You mentioned that you're quite familiar with the area."

"Grew up here, then lived in Casper for several years. Moved back a few weeks ago and was hoping to find something to occupy my time. Still getting used to the role of widow."

"I'm so sorry for your loss," Parker said.

"Thank you. But Lance made me swear I wouldn't sit around feeling sorry for myself or being lonely. I did a bad job of it for a couple of years, but then I saw a sign."

"Sounds like the effort I put into posting those paid off for both of us," Parker said.

"Actually, someone else saw your poster and called me. I'm talking about a sign from the universe."

"Those can be even more powerful," Parker admitted. He'd been seeing a few of those himself lately.

"Like I mentioned, I rode the trails with the Goodwins. Been more decades ago than I care to admit. The daughter, Estella, was about ten or so years my senior. She led the rides before something happened and her parents shut everything down."

"Any idea what that was?" Perhaps the mystery could be solved in one sitting. He'd even score some points with Hailey for making that happen, although it might take the wind out of Max's creative sails.

Sylvie tapped her fingers against her lips as she thought it through.

"My best friend says some superheroes borrowed the horses to save Earth, and all the people are still trying to get home," PJ said.

Sylvie raised her brows. "That's possible. I've lost track of many years. And I just now found my way home. Maybe that's why. By the way, young man, what happened to your arm?"

"It broke when I fell off Gabby."

"Oh my! I know that hurt," she said, rubbing both of her own arms in empathy.

"A little. I guess."

"Can't say I've ever broken an arm. A broken

leg and collarbone, yes. And I have a nice scar on my tummy where I got kicked when walking too close behind a horse but forgot to let the fella know I was there. My fault, not his."

Parker thought about PJ's accident and wondered whether the little one was blaming himself. He'd absolutely hate it if that were the case. Unfortunately, some of life's lessons were best learned through such mistakes.

"Seems like broken bones go with the territory, no matter how careful a rider is," Parker offered.

"You're exactly right. All we can do is educate ourselves as much as possible. That's why I'm a firm believer in teaching horsemanship at a young age. I've got thirteen grandkids, and they're all competing in this or that at fairs and rodeos. Whenever I have a chance, I go back over the basics. Can't be reminded enough."

"Thirteen? Sounds like a lucky number to me," Parker said.

"And I've spoiled them rotten," she whispered.

"As it should be," Parker whispered back.

Vern wandered into the kitchen. How much cologne had the man spritzed? And he'd tucked in his shirt. His beard had been trimmed and his sideburns sculpted, as well, leaving him looking slightly less like Santa Claus than before.

"Coffee's ready, if anyone would like some," Vern said, directing the question to Sylvie.

"Don't mind if I do, Mr. Fraser," she said.

"Please. Call me Vern," he said as he placed a cup in front of her. "Cream and/or sugar?"

"And ruin a perfectly good cup of coffee? No, but thank you," she said.

"A woman after my own heart," Vern said. The man wasn't known for his subtlety, and this situation was no exception.

"PJ, do you have any questions for Ms. Moss?" Parker asked.

"How can you not fall off a horse?"

Sylvie finished taking a sip of coffee and set down the cup. "I've done my share of falling, so I'm no expert. But if you and Mr. Donnelly decide to hire me, perhaps we can solve that mystery together. How does that sound?"

PJ nodded.

"Then start solving," Parker said. "Of course, you'll have to make it past the owner of the stables and through a trial run. Would tomorrow morning work for you? If so, I'll confirm with Hailey."

"The sooner the better, as far as I'm concerned. Sittin' around with my thoughts isn't the best use of all this spare time."

Vern cleared his throat. "Tell Hailey I'll pick up Max first thing in the morning. He and PJ can stir up their brand of trouble around here while you adults take care of business."

Sylvie rose, and Vern scrambled to open the door for her.

"Why, thank you, Vern. Do you spoil all of your guests?"

"Only the ones I hope will come back and visit."

"Uh-huh. You should know that once I'm spoiled, there's no going back. Consider yourself warned." With that parting line, Sylvie headed for her truck.

Parker was rather surprised Vern didn't run out and open that door for her, as well. Then again, his grandpa must be a little scared of her now. Much in the way he himself was scared of Hailey. In other words, in a good way.

"Could you be more obvious, Grandpa?"

"At my age, I don't have time to waste. A strong, beautiful woman with sass doesn't come along every day. Besides, I could say the same about you."

"That I'm strong and beautiful?" Parker fluttered his eyelashes for special effect.

Vern squinted. "And a comedian too. No, I mean that you've had a crush on Hailey for, oh, twenty-somethin' years. I've had this crush for only twenty minutes. And which one of us is doing something about it?"

CHAPTER NINE

HAILEY SUMMONED HER complete focus while reading the label. She was determined to get this right.

Directions: Mix soup plus one can of water. Microwave on HIGH two and a half to three minutes.

If only other things in life came with such simple instructions.

Feelings, for instance. This playful side of Parker was putting her at ease. At the same time, he admittedly made her nervous. Especially knowing he remembered that kiss on the cheek. But they were kids, only a few years older than the one who *wasn't* sitting at her breakfast table this morning.

Vern had come by and picked up Max at the crack of dawn and insisted he spend the night.

The microwave beeped. Hailey retrieved the bowl of Campbell's Chicken Noodle soup, stirred the contents and tasted a spoonful. "Success!"

Her mom and sisters would be speechless. Hailey had to laugh at the thought because, as ridiculous as it was, it was so true.

She poured equal amounts in three separate thermoses, then grabbed a tube of saltines to go with it, along with a can of mixed nuts. Using the homemade pimento cheese spread that Georgina had brought over, she made sandwiches and put everything in thermal bags.

For the first time, Hailey was grateful her sister had been a little too helpful and insisted on bringing food.

Parker had already arrived with the prospective employee. From what Hailey could tell from her kitchen window, the woman was tallish. Slender but fit. Long, blond hair in a loose, thick braid that snaked halfway down her back.

He'd lined up a trail guide so quickly, it felt too good to be true. Hailey wasn't going to trust her clients with just anyone, no matter how solid her liability waiver had ended up being.

But kudos to Parker for not letting his bootheels cool. If they could get through this interview without a hitch, she'd make a trip into town and buy him a new tie to replace the one her goat had destroyed. Of course, she'd let him know it was a business expense for his loss so he wouldn't get the wrong idea.

Hailey locked the front door behind her. As she got closer to the woman, Hailey realized that her hair was silver. Not blond.

The woman took some long strides toward her but stopped in her tracks. "Oh my goodness," she said. "You're the spittin' image of Estella."

"You knew my grandmother?"

"I rode the trails with her a few times. She must have been around seventeen, and I was a good ten years or so younger. But you never forget a pretty face like that. I'm Sylvie Moss, by the way." The woman extended her hand. "Mr. Donnelly and I were trying to decide which horses to take, but I told him I'd rather leave that up to you."

Parker stepped in and relieved Hailey of the lunch totes.

"I appreciate that, Sylvie. Let's see. Parker, since you did so well with Gabby last time, how 'bout you take her. I'll take my Bad Boy. And Sylvie, you can meet the others and see who you connect with. I have a feeling Charmed will be perfect for you. They're all rescues that have been specifically trained for their job here. All have impeccable ground manners, except for one. No Regrets didn't make the cut. My Sunrise Stables copartner and bull rider extraordinaire, Cody Sayers, even spent extra time with him." Hailey pointed to the far stall.

Sylvie walked over to the Morgan horse. Hailey and Parker followed. When she petted him, he balked a little, but not as much as with other people.

"If you'd like to give him another chance, I'd be happy to work with him in my spare time. What's his issue?"

"Boulders," Hailey answered.

"Ah! Sometimes, it takes a woman's touch. Or, the right woman's. No offense, Mr. Donnelly," she said.

"None taken. In fact, I couldn't agree with you more. And, please, call me Parker."

When he added a generous smile, that was it. Hailey was burned toast. Those dimples were going to be the death of her. So deep, it was like she could sink right into them.

Hailey cleared her throat. "Since we're all in agreement about the power of feminine energy, let's saddle up and hit the trail." Also, she wanted to get this over with because her initial resistance to hiring Sylvie had pretty much crumbled.

And her resistance to Parker was being seriously tested.

PARKER WONDERED IF the primary goal of horseback riding was to *not* fall, because it sure felt that way. Even though this was his second ride—not counting the brief tutorial with Nash—the possibility was still foremost in his thoughts. And they'd yet to leave her property.

He figured Hailey and Sylvie would hit it off, but he'd had no idea how quickly. The two were fully engaged. They kept laughing and chatting it up.

They set out on the same path he and Hailey had taken, except Sylvie took the lead. He was in the middle and Hailey was in back, apparently open to Sylvie's instincts and whims. Every once in a while, Sylvie would nod toward a mountain peak or down a faintly marked trail and comment that it looked or felt familiar.

The farther into the ride, the more his back pain increased. Each step on uneven terrain sent a hot jolt up his spine. Between the rides and the piggyback excursion for PJ, his body was beginning to protest. Not to mention the hefting of feed bags and saddles that he'd taken on around Sunrise Stables. Oh, and mucking the stalls. But he gritted his teeth and forged ahead. No damage was being done, aside from aggravating some lazy muscles.

The only damage would be if he fell off Gabby—and the damage would arguably be more severe emotionally for PJ and Hailey than physically for him. He gave his horse a gentle kick, circled back and around to Hailey's side, and tugged the reins to cue Gabby to slow down. Exactly the way Nash had showed him.

The maneuver wasn't lost on Hailey. "Well, look at you!"

Her compliment washed over him like warm water. "Oh, that's nothing. Next, the *piaffe*."

Hailey raised both brows. "You speak dressage?"

"I'm not fluent, but yes. A little."

"Something you picked up at the Windsor Royal Horse Show, I presume?" She served up an I-dare-you-to-top-that smile.

"Close. I learned a few terms at the World Equestrian Festival in Aachen."

Hailey stared. Then squinted. That particular look of hers always squeezed information out of him when it would be wise to stop talking altogether. She'd make a great police interrogator. Or lawyer. Yet, part of him couldn't get enough of it.

"As a spectator," he explained.

"Uh-huh." The squint intensified.

"I didn't compete. Obviously. The trip was a perk from a client."

Hailey smiled and looked straight ahead.

"What?"

"Deutschland, *ja*?" she asked.

Parker nearly fell out of his saddle. "You speak German?"

"I took a year in high school for my foreign language requirement. Surprisingly, I remember a few things."

"I'm seriously impressed, Hailey. I'm guessing you said, 'Germany, yes?'"

"Ja," she said, offering up an even bigger smile.

"Now, this trail looks familiar," Sylvie said, leading them down a partially overgrown path.

"I've been this way a couple of times with Cody, but we haven't mapped it out yet," Hailey said. "Turns into more of an intermediate trail a mile or so ahead."

"I agree. I seem to remember taking a tumble while crossing some water on a horse who decided he didn't like getting his feet wet halfway through. Didn't break a bone like PJ, thankfully."

Parker was about to stop playing cowboy and speak up, thus putting his safety first. But Hailey beat him to it.

"Let's find a stopping place and refuel before we head back," Hailey said.

Parker had a smoother dismount this time. He watched both Sylvie and Hailey tie their horses to a tree, but their hand movements were quite fast.

He'd mastered a few knots in his lifetime, thanks to one of his favorite clients. The guy built yachts, and was based in the Netherlands but expanded into the States. When in Chicago, his client would take him out on Lake Michigan, where he'd educate Parker on nautical knots. A bit of an obsession for his client, to put it mildly.

But that bit of trivia wouldn't save him here. No use pretending to know what he was doing because he was certain he couldn't pull one over on these pros. And he wasn't about to do anything that might end up harming Gabby in some way.

"So, ladies. Would a Windsor knot or a bow work better?" he asked.

He expected an eye roll or squint. Instead, Hailey smiled and quickly stepped in to help.

"You'll need a quick-release knot. I'll show you." Hailey snapped on a lead line and stood next to him.

"First, wrap the rope around the tree, like this," she said. "Leave about this much slack for Gabby. Then make a cross, turn your left hand over to form a loop. Bring this other end around and through the other loop you made. Then tighten. If she starts to panic, tug on this rope."

Hailey yanked the rope and the knot deconstructed. She handed him the lead line. "You try."

Her hands had moved fast. Parker replayed her words in his head and visualized the steps. Nailed it the first time, although it took him about three times longer. He'd remained super focused but swore he heard a few words of encouragement from Hailey along the way. *That's it. Good job!*

Sylvie applauded.

Hailey put her hands together, as well, which was the greatest reward of all. This day, he concluded, could not get any better.

Parker took the initiative and spread out the

lunch blanket. Sylvie helped Hailey unpack and distribute the food.

He winced a bit as he eased to the ground but was rewarded once he unscrewed the thermos cap. He took a sip and recognized the taste and texture and balance of ingredients immediately. Campbell's Chicken Noodle. Again, like his mom used to make. She'd even tried to create the soup from scratch, but they both concluded that the canned version was better.

"I hope everyone is okay with what I brought."

"I couldn't have put together a more appetizing spread," Sylvie said.

"Everything is perfect," Parker said, even though he'd yet to sample the sandwich.

"You haven't met Max, my best friend's son, have you?" Hailey asked Sylvie. "He rides on the beginner trail. We gave him the unofficial title of colead and storyteller, and he takes his job very seriously. If we ever find out the truth about how the rides ended, he'll have quite the story to tell."

Sylvie took a swig of soup and nodded her approval. "I'm still trying to remember anything I can about it, but so many details are lost or hiding. Happens when you're seventy-four. But maybe riding again will spark something."

"How many kids and grandkids did you say you have?" Parker asked. He already knew but hoped Sylvie's answer would put Hailey at ease about letting Max or other children ride.

"Seven kids. Out of 'em, two of my sons went on to become professional bronc busters. I also have a bull rider and a barrel racer. Thirteen grandkids altogether. Hoping for even more, but I'm not gonna push. That's such a personal decision."

"I bet holidays are a blast at your house," Parker said.

Sylvie nodded. "Best times of my life." She pulled out some paper-clipped squares from her back pocket and handed Parker a photo of her with her kids and grandkids.

Parker squinted to see their faces. "Yep. Those are yours, all right. Can't make out much detail, but they inherited your smile."

Sylvie seemed to contemplate it. "I never thought about it, but I suppose you're right. They also inherited my late husband's beautiful brown eyes, although you can't tell from this photo."

"Do they all ride?" he asked.

Sylvie nodded, but Hailey looked off into

the distance. Was she still blaming herself for the accident?

"All but a couple. I taught 'em most everything they know as far as the basics. Especially when it comes to safety."

At that, Hailey rejoined the conversation. "Anything you can do to make it safer for the riders will be appreciated. Especially for the children."

Sylvie nodded and said, "If you two will excuse me for a minute, I brought some apples for these lovely horses in hopes of winning them over. They've done an amazing job, although you deserve the credit for that, Hailey." Sylvie crossed her legs and rose to a standing position without using her hands. The woman was beyond amazing. No wonder his grandpa was smitten.

Parker smiled. Hailey caught him doing it.

"I'd ask what you're so happy about, but I assume it has to do with the thought of all those kiddos under one roof."

"I won't lie. That's a fun thought. But, no, I was thinking about this delicious soup. In fact, if you don't mind making some for PJ, I'm sure he'd appreciate it. Chicken noodle has magical healing powers."

And he meant it. He hadn't given his aching back a second thought since sitting down. He unscrewed the cap on the thermos again and took a long swig.

"Tease me about my cooking at your own peril," Hailey said.

He reached over and squeezed her hand without even thinking about it. "I'm not. You knocked it out of the park."

They both looked to Sylvie, who was deep in discussion with Charmed. Hailey certainly knew her horses, he had to admit. Sylvie and Charmed seemed to have known each other in another life. Who knew Hailey was such a matchmaker?

Perhaps at least one person. Cody kept crediting her for getting him and Becca back together.

"Even if you aren't teasing, Sylvie is the shining star. Which means you're the one who knocked it out of the park. Parks. Let's offer her the job. Today." Hailey squeezed his hand in return, which revved his heart. He quickly concluded that he'd been wrong when he thought the day couldn't get any better, because it just did.

"Confession time. My goal for the day was to not like her," Hailey continued.

Oddly enough, he understood. His goal had been to not fall. Yet there he was, safe on the ground but falling all the same.

For Hailey.

CHAPTER TEN

"ARE YOU LOST, Miss Hailey?" Ethan called out from behind the register.

You could say that. Especially after that hand-squeezing session with Parker yesterday. What part about keeping her distance from that man did her brain not understand? As of this minute, it was back to business, exclusively.

At least she'd enjoyed a nice bubble bath last night and slept like a baby. She did wake up once and walked down the hall to check on Max, only to remember that he was spending the night at Vern's. With no rides booked for the day, Hailey could take care of some things before picking him up. Things like getting her new hire set up in the computer system and transferring all official launch reservations from Hailey's name to Sylvie's.

That, alone, made her feel so much more at ease, especially after witnessing the woman's level of professionalism and knowledge. In fact, she was finally getting excited about the trail-ride launch.

She did a once-around Kavanaugh's Clothing and Whatnot but didn't spot what she was looking for.

"We got some new lady tops in." He pointed to the first rack.

"Actually, I need a man's tie." Although she wasn't sure whether that would fall into the category of *clothing* or *whatnot*. Or neither here. This place was outfitted more for the working cowboy and cowgirl. Not the executive.

"Is this for someone special?" Ethan asked.

"I suppose you could say that. He's an employee of Sunrise Stables who had a run-in with one of my baby goats, and lost."

"Oh, I know who you're talking about. That little fella was as mean as the dickens. The goat, that is."

Hailey cocked her head. "Who showed you that video?"

"You sent it to me. Don't you remember?"

What she remembered was showing Max how to send it to Vern's cell phone. Come to think of it, Max had access to her entire address book. She suddenly felt sick to her stomach at the possibility that he'd accidentally group texted it.

Hailey shook it off. Nothing she could do about it now.

"Please don't share it with anyone," she said.

Ethan raised his brows. "Oops!"

"Okay, please don't share with anyone else."

He made the sign of the cross over his heart. "Promise. Oh, you were wanting to see some ties. I have a few on the whirly thing." He pointed toward a display counter near the back wall.

There they were. All three of them. And none looked remotely like that slender, red silk tie of Parker's. All of these were superwide and had some sort of bold design.

"I'll take this one," she said, grabbing the yellow tie with fat blue stripes. *Ugh*. It was the least obnoxious one. A touch more subtle than the black-and-white-cowhide print or, even worse, the one with comical-looking horses. Although the latter did resemble the whimsical horse on her entry sign at Sunrise Stables.

"Excellent choice," Ethan said. "I bet his girlfriend will love it too."

Girlfriend?

"I didn't know he had one. Then again, we don't discuss our personal lives, so..."

"I won't lie. I couldn't help but overhear when he and Nash Buchanan were talking about some lady. If it wasn't his girlfriend, it sure sounded like he wanted her to be."

"Parker and Nash were here? Together?" She had trouble even visualizing it.

"Funny, huh? They reminded me of the *Odd Couple*. Remember that old show? Granny Kavanaugh used to make me watch it with her. Anyhoo, by the time Nash and I worked our magic, the guy walked away looking like a cowboy. Almost. All the swag but none of the swagger." Ethan snickered at his clever wording.

She might have snickered too, except her mind was still stuck on his previous comment.

"Maybe I should get his girlfriend a gift, as well. What did you overhear that might help me pick out something she'd like?"

Ethan looked up at the ceiling and drummed his fingers on the counter as he recollected. "He said she was beautiful and smart. Oh! And she likes to go yachting or some such."

That definitely ruled her out. Not that she had a reason to suspect he'd been talking about her.

"Tell you what. I changed my mind about the stripes," she said. "Let's go with the horses instead. I'll switch it out."

In the meantime, Ethan hurried across the

store and back, holding something in hand. "Just a suggestion. These horse earrings almost match the tie. I'll knock twenty percent off since they've been sitting here quite a while collectin' dust."

She studied the jewelry. Big and bossy. Cute for a ten-year-old girl, but not so much for a sophisticated city gal.

"They're perfect. I'll take 'em," she said, feeling a tad bit evil in the process.

Hailey collected the gifts and headed straight to Vern's to collect Max, making only one stop to pick up a cupcake. She could hand off the tie and earrings and witness Parker's reaction. She also wanted to say hello to PJ and beg his forgiveness, and hoped the baked treat would help. After all, he *was* the sweetest rider that day. The sweetest of the sweet. However, he'd also be the most difficult person to face. She hadn't mustered up the nerve to do it yet.

Unfortunately—or possibly fortunately—Parker wasn't at Vern's, and PJ was sound asleep on the sofa when she arrived. Max was also in the middle of a nap. He looked so adorable, curled up on Vern's easy chair.

"Let me keep the little rascal awhile longer," Vern said. "We had a busy and exciting morning at the clinic, getting PJ's cast. Max came close to talking the nurse into putting him in one, as well. A few of us have already signed it."

Hailey leaned in to study the light blue cast. He'd collected three signatures so far.

"You already kept Max overnight. Are you sure?" she asked.

"I'm positive. Go home and get some rest. I'll bring him over later when I collect my babysitting fee, even though I should be paying you. Having a couple of kids in my house makes me feel like a young daddy all over again. Nothin' quite compares."

Vern's smile lit up, and the corners of his eyes crinkled. In that moment, she could see Parker saying the same thing when he got to be in his eighties, which made her feel both happy and profoundly sad.

Then there was the other part. She and Vern hadn't discussed a babysitting fee. Not that she thought he was even remotely serious. "I definitely owe you, but I'm more than a little scared. What's your price?"

"Make dinner for me."

Why was everyone wanting her to cook for them all of a sudden? "You're a lousy negotiator on your own behalf. There's a reason why I'm known as the Firestarter around here."

"I'll take my chances. And make plenty extra of whatever you decide to conjure up. I'll bring some back for our little patient, unless I can talk him into coming with us."

"I don't know. I think I've hurt PJ enough already. Hence, the cupcake," she said, handing it to Vern. She'd take Parker's gifts back with her. For now.

"And I think you're being too hard on yourself. Matter of fact, I *know* you are. Seven o'clock."

"If you get lost, follow the smoke signals."

On the way home, she thought about asking Georgina to whip something up but reconsidered. Hailey had a family-size frozen mac and cheese in the freezer and a couple cans of chili in the pantry. Whatever Vern didn't eat or take back, she and Max could munch on tomorrow.

And with Vern coming for dinner, she might also be able to get to the bottom of a brandnew mystery. One that had nothing to do with business.

Did Parker have a girlfriend, and what did Vern know about her?

TONIGHT WAS A big night. Parker was about to meet the "client" he most needed to impress: Sergeant Goodwin.

Hailey's cat.

Nash had stressed the importance of getting on Sergeant's good side. For Parker, it was also a test to see if allergy medication worked. Although he adored all animals, he was a card-holding dog person so there was never a need to try.

The extra money he paid to retain a concierge primary physician in Chicago finally paid off. One Zoom meeting was all it took to get the prescription filled in Destiny Springs.

Tonight was important for another reason. Parker brought his win-win proposal for Hailey, and he couldn't be prouder of it. Win-win-win, if you counted the goats' interest in the outcome.

But as soon as Hailey opened the door and said, "Oh. You're here too," he knew the journey to acceptance just got steeper.

He hid the proposal behind his back for now. It was a discussion best eased into since it was quite detail-intensive. That was, if Hailey would un-tongue-tie him. She'd let her hair down and traded her usual faded jeans for some black, soft-looking, understated drawstring pants and a matching tank top.

Even though it was a bone-chilling evening, a rush of warm air from inside her home washed over him. Vern took the lead and gave her a hug, which meant perhaps it wouldn't be out of line for Parker to give her one, as well. Except Max slipped between him and Vern and beat Parker to it.

"Miss Hailey! I missed you!" Max cried out.

The subsequent body slam made her beautiful smile explode. "I missed you too, kiddo! I think you've grown since I saw you yesterday. Which would make you, what, six foot two?"

Max straightened his posture, lifted his chin and grinned as if he had everyone fooled.

"So your best friend decided not to come?" she asked.

"Trent offered to babysit. He and PJ are gonna watch the goat movie instead," Vern interjected. "It'll give my ranch hand a chance to prop up his feet for a spell."

Parker felt his shoulders literally drop. Was the exposure ever going to end?

After Max released Hailey, Parker took a step forward to claim a hug. She turned away, which made him wonder if he'd imagined a connection yesterday.

No matter. He planned to be the businessman she needed tonight. No hand-squeezing, even though he'd keep the possibility of a hug on the table. Only to not feel so left out.

Yeah, right.

When he closed the door behind him, the smell of cheese and beef and spices quickly filled the room. A timer dinged, and Hailey rushed to the stove, stirred something, then replaced the lid. Meanwhile, Vern had enlisted Max's help to figure out what was wrong with a floor lamp that wouldn't switch on. With those two preoccupied, Parker took advantage of the opening to have Hailey all to himself.

"May I help?" He placed a hand on the counter next to her and leaned in to get her attention. She wouldn't even look up.

"Nope. You're a guest. Make yourself at home."

"Vern didn't tell you he was bringing me, did he?"

"Nope." She shook her head and kept stirring.

"I can go home, if you wish." For some people, there was nothing worse than having to entertain uninvited guests. His door was always open. The more, the merrier. But clearly Hailey didn't operate that way.

She set the spoon down, replaced the cover, and her stance softened. "Actually, I invited someone too. Since you were responsible for finding her, it's only right that you be here."

Talk about pleasant surprises. Before he

could formulate a response, someone knocked. Hailey walked around him to answer the door but stopped short when Vern called out, "I'll get it!"

"Thank you!" She pivoted back and pointed to the envelope before he could adjust its position. "Are you planning to get some work done while you're here?"

"It's a gift. One that you didn't ask for. Like the gift of my presence tonight. Except I'm pretty sure you'll embrace it." *Embrace* being the operative word here. He'd settle for any kind this evening.

"That's a coincidence, because I have one for you, as well. Two, actually. We'll do a gift exchange after dinner." At that, she abandoned him to greet her guest.

Why did he have a feeling that her gifts were going to be something awful?

He set the envelope on the counter next to that bracelet Hailey always seemed to be wearing lately and watched her give Sylvie a huge hug. Now he really felt left out. He was striking out on every level and didn't have a clue as to why.

Yet he wasn't striking out in the most important one. A warm sensation brushed against his ankles. He looked down to find two beautiful green eyes staring up at him. Either the kitty had a motor stuck in his throat, or he was purring. Then he did something he didn't know cats could do. Sergeant stood on his hind legs and stretched his front paws skyward as if wanting to be held.

Parker picked up the feline as one would a child. Sergeant's claws immediately hooked into his flannel shirt, their sharp points piercing his skin. His nose hadn't so much as itched, which was the most important thing. Then again, he'd been distracted by all the wonderful smells wafting from the kitchen.

Funny how Nash had all but forbade him from eating anything she made. So far, everything she'd prepared for him was delicious.

Hailey shifted into full gear, setting out dishes and utensils—buffet style—on the counter with impressive precision. No surprise. She had worked at Becca and Cody's B and B, helping set up breakfasts every morning. She finally came up for a breather long enough to notice that he and Sergeant had bonded.

"I don't believe what I'm seeing," she said, coming to a full stop.

"What do you mean?" he asked, although he knew why.

Hailey crossed her arms. Was he holding the

cat incorrectly? This was the first time he'd so much as picked one up, and he didn't even think to google it first. Never in a million years did he believe a cat would gravitate to him, much less want to hug.

At least someone wanted to.

"Sergeant has always been a man's man, but he's never warmed up to anyone this quickly. Except Max. Are you carrying sardines in your pocket?"

That tickled his heart. *So this is what it feels like to inwardly gloat.*

"Okay, everyone," Hailey called out, switching gears before he could formulate a clever comeback. "Dinner is ready. Help yourselves."

Vern had caught Sylvie's ear and wasn't letting go, while Max was busy galloping around on a broomstick, pretending to fall off his imaginary horse and break his arm. Yet everyone stopped in their tracks when Hailey gave orders. It was like her voice had a built-in megaphone for certain situations.

"Ladies first," Vern insisted, bowing to Sylvie.

Now, that was fun to watch. His grandpa treating Sunrise Stables' newest hire like a princess. Her expression suggested that she was taking his gallant-knight act with a grain of salt. Little did she know it wasn't an act at all. The royal treatment never ended for those Vern cared about.

Before Sylvie even reached the counter, Max galloped to the front of the line and reached as high as his little arms would go.

Hailey swooped in and took over. She apologized to Sylvie, then lobbed a huge spoonful of mac and cheese on a plate. She lured Max to the table, then came back and ladled some chili into a separate bowl for him. The coast was now clear for everyone else.

Parker managed to unhook Sergeant from his shirt, but the cat insisted on herding him to the table, weaving between his feet and nearly tripping him in the process. After everyone was seated, Hailey brought over a separate dish and sprinkled something black on top of Max's mac and cheese.

"What's that?" he asked, nudging a piece with his finger.

"Bacon crumbles, kiddo," she said, setting the bowl on the table for sharing and taking the empty seat next to Parker.

"But it's *black*. Bacon's supposed to be *brown*," Max said.

Parker leaned toward Hailey and whispered, "You say bacon, I say carcinogen."

She had barely looked at him the entire time, but that got her attention. The term *stink eye* came to mind. Kind of scared him, but in a fun way. He had to bite his lip to keep from laughing.

Max shrugged and took a huge bite. "Mmm. Black bacon tastes crunchy."

Hailey cracked a victory smile. Parker did his best to match it, then used his spoon to get a heaping helping of crunchy bits for himself. Vern and Sylvie politely declined.

"Anyone who doesn't eat it is a *scaredy-cat*," Max declared, punctuating it with that adorable giggle of his.

"Someone's in rare form tonight," Hailey said, then acted as though she was about to tickle him.

"The only thing that scares me, little fella, is that eye on the back of your head. Miss Hailey told me all about it, and she wasn't exaggerating," Vern said.

"I don't have one back there," Max insisted, but set his fork down and felt around anyway.

Vern and Hailey exchanged a smile and a wink. Yep, she was a natural with kids.

"Sylvie tells me that you're the spittin' image of your grandmother," Vern said to Hailey, officially kicking off the dinner conversation.

"Wish I would've known your grandparents better, but they kept to themselves. Probably why no one around here knows what happened either."

"I've been thinking about Estella practically nonstop since meeting you, Hailey, and I recall a few things that might be of interest. Like that old barn, for instance," Sylvie said.

Parker's ears perked up.

"The goats live there now," Max said, his mouth half full. A glob of cheese rested on his chin. Hailey whispered a loving reprimand that he swallow his food before speaking while wiping the glob away.

"Is that right? We'll have to go visit them after we eat," Sylvie said.

"Okey dokey!" Max shoved an even bigger spoonful of food in his mouth as if that would expedite the process.

"What do you remember about it?" Hailey asked.

Sylvie finished a bite of chili and washed it down with some water. "Your great-grandparents used to host weddings in there. Charming structure from the outside. So much character."

"Weddings, huh? I can see that. It's a beautiful space, if not in need of some TLC," Hailey said. "It used to be my safe place when I was a little girl. I could hide there and no one could find me."

"Hide from what?" Vern asked.

"Anything. Everything," Hailey said, then shrugged. "I don't know how to explain it, but it's always held a special place in my heart."

That would have been good information to have. If they ran out of firewood, they could always use Parker's thick, detailed proposal to keep the place warm. But all was not lost. In fact, an even better idea was percolating. Barn weddings could generate great publicity and revenue without additional overhead costs.

"I wish I could remember more," Sylvie said. "These senior moments happen at the most inconvenient times."

"Oh, I have plenty of those too," Vern chimed in. "But if this is a senior moment we're having right now, I'll take more of 'em." He added a huge grin for Sylvie.

She simply shook her head and softly smiled as if he were completely off his rocker but in a charming way.

The man wasn't a half-bad flirt, in Parker's opinion, although the jury was still out as to whether his charms were working on Sylvie. But that was one thing he and his grandpa had in common: neither shied away from a challenge.

"Weddings are overrated, in my opinion," Hailey said. "They aren't a measure of someone's love. Take Romeo and Juliet, for example. They never made it to the altar, but what a romance."

"Or Jenny and Oliver in *Love Story*. I cry like a baby every time I watch that movie," Vern said.

"They did get married, though," Parker said. "But, like Romeo and Juliet, they were opposites. And, as they say, opposites attract."

"Like Rose and Jack in *Titanic*. They would have married, I'm sure of it. Breaks my heart that they barely had a chance to be happy," Sylvie offered.

Vern nodded. "Yeah, that's a tough movie to watch, yet I'm drawn to it every time it pops up on the TV screen."

The table turned respectfully quiet, yet Parker felt a tickle in his throat and a song coming on. He hadn't even sang the first bar of "My Heart Will Go On" when Hailey shot him a heaping helping of stink eye and whispered, "Don't even *think* about it."

He winked at her. Vern was rubbing off on

him. But maybe the old man was on to something, because this time Hailey winked back.

The second everyone set their fork or spoon down for good, Max jumped off his chair. "Let's go see the goats!"

"You and Sylvie go with Max," Parker suggested to Vern. "I'll hang back and help Hailey with the dishes."

Vern smiled and patted him on the arm. Yep, they were speaking the same language tonight. By the time the trio headed out the back door, Hailey was next to him with presents in hand.

"These are for you, but I'd rather you go first." She nodded at the envelope he'd placed on the counter.

Parker shook his head. "I'm reconsidering the gift I brought."

"You're still trying to sell me on tearing down the barn, aren't you? But since you went to all the trouble, I'll read it. At my leisure."

"I think you may find some of it interesting, as I was proposing a higher standard of living for the goats. State-of-the-art accommodations, scenic Wyoming views. I concluded that tie-chewing incident was a plea for my help."

Hailey crossed her arms and pursed her lips.

"You get points for creativity, but my goats' standard of living is fine. As is mine. I'm not looking to make a lot of money off this property."

"If *not* making a *lot* of money is your goal, you wouldn't have to offer the full menu of changes I've proposed. That way, you'd just make *some* money," he said. It meant to come out a joke, but she wasn't amused.

"Thanks for acknowledging I have a choice. I'll make note of your recommendations."

Clearly, he wasn't getting through. He didn't want to label her as lacking ambition because that wasn't the case. However, they had wildly differing views. Hers, a seat-of-the-pants approach; his, an I-don't-want-to-wonder-where-my-next-meal-is-coming-from approach. He, for one, couldn't function her way. It was the most helpless feeling in the world. He knew from experience.

"Now that we've settled that, I'm confident you'll like my unwritten proposal," he said.

Now he was truly winging it. Nash had yet to name the Appaloosa he'd recently taken in as a favor to a friend. But he'd mentioned how it might have been a mistake, having another mouth to feed when he barely had time to feed the ones he already had.

Maybe Parker could even parlay this into the proposal he needed. Of course, it would need a lot more *oomph* and projected growth. Such as adding more stalls and horses. But she wouldn't have to sacrifice the barn, and that seemed to be the main sticking point.

"Sorry, but I'm not ready to get married," she teased.

"Good to know. I won't make a fool out of myself by asking," he teased in return. "You have an empty stall, which I originally proposed expanding and turning into luxury accommodations for your four-legged kids. But since that's off the table, what would you think about adding a horse?"

Hailey's expression brightened. "Love it! But only one, so don't even *think* about proposing an expansion. I'm limiting the number of riders on any trail. Keep it more personal and one-on-one for my clients."

So much for that bright idea. At the same time, he couldn't be more pleased that she liked this one. Most important, he was witnessing a certain enthusiasm that had been missing.

"Excellent. You have it in the budget for the extra feed and care, but you might want to shift around a few things. I'll put together some numbers, if you're interested in the breakout."

"Yes, I am interested in seeing the numbers," she said.

Had he heard that correctly? Her usual response when it came to the nickels and dimes was more along the lines of "whatever you recommend." She was full of surprises tonight.

"My turn. Open the big one first," she said, handing him both of her gifts.

Speaking of surprises...

He took the boxes to the table, sat down and looked at the knot on the ribbon. He recognized it as a quick release. With one tug of the loose end, the knot dissolved and he lifted the lid.

"Oh! A tie," he said.

Hailey was definitely irritated about something. Either that, or she had supremely bad taste in menswear. At the same time, it was charming that she thought of replacing the one that got shredded.

"The other gift is for your girlfriend," she said. That box didn't even have so much as a bow.

Girlfriend? He opened it up anyway. A pair of bossy horse-head earrings stared back.

"I didn't want her to see the tie and think I was putting the moves on her man," Hailey continued.

He didn't come right out and say it, but he had no intention of letting *anyone* see the tie.

The night kept getting stranger.

PARKER HANDED THE earrings back to Hailey.

"What?" she asked. "Not her style?"

"I don't have a girlfriend to give these to."

Hailey swallowed hard. She'd either made a colossal fool of herself or he was lying. Or both.

"What made you think that?" he asked. "I know we've never discussed such topics, aside from my clarifying that I don't have a wife and kids back in Chicago."

Hailey looked to her feet. Confession time. "When I was at Kavanaugh's picking out the tie, Ethan mentioned overhearing you and Nash talking about a woman you liked. Beautiful, smart. Enjoys yachting."

Parker blinked hard. Then again, as if awaiting further explanation.

She squirmed. Had her dining room chairs always been this uncomfortable?

"And stuff," she said.

That did it. He cracked a smile. Then he tilted his head back and looked to the ceiling. "Ah, yes. I remember the conversation now."

He paused.

She held her breath.

"Nash and I were talking about my boss," he said, looking directly at her now.

It was her turn to be confused. "I always imagined your boss to be an older man. Maybe that's stereotyping on my part. No reason why it couldn't be a woman."

"You're absolutely right. No reason at all. But think about this, Hailey. Who else do I work for? Or perhaps work *with* is a better way to phrase it."

"You weren't talking about me. I've never been yachting and am pretty sure I'd hate it. Open water totally freaks me out."

"We have that in common," he said.

Hailey paused as her heart skipped a beat. Had she heard him correctly? If so, how awesome would that be, as superficial as it was?

"Really? You're scared of open water too?" she asked.

Parker shook his head and smiled. "No. Just teasing you. I'm a scuba enthusiast. PADI certified. Working toward my master's."

She swatted at his arm. "You're awful!"

"I have my moments. But I didn't say you'd been yachting. Ethan misunderstood. The smart and beautiful part he got right."

Was Hailey the one misunderstanding now? She could think of only one way to find out.

"Truth or dare," she said.

Parker raised a brow. "Interesting pivot. I haven't played that game in years."

"Neither have I, so let's give it a go. Unless you're afraid."

"Nothing frightens me. I choose truth," he said.

"Were you talking about me at Kavanaugh's?" she asked.

"Yes." Once again, he was looking at her like he had at Becca and Cody's wedding reception. And again when Cody offered him up as a substitute cowboy for a week.

"Well, you always did have a crush on me, so I suppose that makes sense," she said.

"I'd answer, except it's my turn."

"It wasn't a question," she said.

"Truth or dare?" he asked.

Neither option was good, but she liked what she was finding out so far. "Okay. Truth."

"Is it obvious that I just learned how to ride a horse?"

"Yes."

He dropped his head in a dramatic fashion. "Ouch. You could have at least pretended to give it some thought."

Perhaps it did sound a little harsh. "Here's your chance to get even. Do you really like my cooking?"

"I love it."

"Why?" she asked.

"That's two questions. You only get one at a time," he said.

"It's an extension of the original question."

His expression turned serious. "Your cooking reminds me of my childhood. Mom used to burn the grilled cheese sandwiches too. And Campbell's Chicken Noodle was her go-to. Still is."

Hailey shifted. "I think there's a compliment in there somewhere."

"The highest," he countered.

Silence fell between them.

"So, if you had to eat your mom's cooking in the house or apartment where you grew up or the food at the swankiest restaurant in Chicago exclusively for the rest of your life, which would you choose?"

The question was meant to be playful, but Parker wasn't smiling. She'd never seen such a somber expression. The way he answered was equally serious. "No contest. My mom's."

Hailey thought her heart might melt in that moment.

"Really? But you *did* have to think about it," she pointed out.

"Actually, I didn't. But your question caught me off guard because nice restaurants have always been my kryptonite."

"So Max was right about you all along. You are Superman."

"My secret is out," he said, then smiled.

"How's your mom doing these days?" she asked.

Hailey hoped he wouldn't ask the same of her, because she didn't keep up with her own mother or her sisters. Then again, she didn't have to. They kept up with her. Checking on her constantly. By default, she knew they were okay.

"Still in remission but hasn't hit the magical five-year mark yet."

"She's lucky to have such a smart, successful son who is willing and able to take care of her," Hailey stated.

"You forgot to mention 'handsome.'" He offered up that smile again.

She couldn't argue with that. "And modest."

At that, he laughed. "You say modest, I say cautiously humble."

"I say Bluegrass. You say...?" she asked, hoping he'd catch on. Seemed to be a night of playing games.

"Opera," he countered.

"Two-step."

"Ballroom."

"Night in," she said.

"Evening out."

She was running out of ideas. In the meantime, Sergeant had gotten comfy on Parker's lap and was purring up a storm. Didn't matter to the cat what kind of music or dancing he preferred, so why should it matter to her?

"Children," he said.

Why did he have to go there? They were having so much fun with this.

"We've already discussed. Next," she said.

"Fair enough. Big, blowout weddings. Think Will and Kate, Westminster Abbey."

"Waste of money. You of all people should get that," she said.

"An investment in a special once-in-a-lifetime event. Allowed," he countered.

"More like a gamble on something dressed up in pretty satin and rhinestones that all come off after the big performance. Las Vegas drive-through makes more sense. Elvis presiding."

She'd said too much. *Game over.*

He leaned in and kissed her on the cheek as if he somehow knew her secrets. But he couldn't have. She'd been like her grandparents in that respect, keeping secrets from everyone in Destiny Springs.

She gulped. Hard. Had the kiss on the cheek she'd given him twenty years ago felt so sweet?

Without thinking, she leaned in and gently pressed her lips against his. When she pulled away, his expression was unreadable.

Hailey covered her face with her hands. "I'm sorry. I don't know why I did that."

On the lips, Hailey? Seriously? Furthermore, why did she keep moving closer when she should be stepping back? The warmth and tenderness of the kiss lingered, and she found herself wanting to kiss him again. Now.

No!

When she finally mustered the courage to look at him, he was wearing the biggest smile. Dimples included. Those should come with a warning label.

"No need to apologize," he said. "I expect nothing less of someone who's had a crush on me for two decades."

"Says the man who bought new clothes and got all dolled up for a beautiful, smart woman who hates open water," she said.

"It's the truth. What can I say?"

"You can say you'll take those shiny new boots out two-steppin' with me before you abandon all of us country folk and go back the big city."

Chicago. The elephant in the room. For both their sakes, they needed to address it.

"We'll celebrate our business collaboration when Becca and Cody get back," she said. Might as well clarify that it wasn't intended to be a date. And that the kiss wasn't intended to go any further.

"Only if you'll cook that five-course meal for us first. Unless, as Max would say, you're a *scaredy-cat*." He looked down at Sergeant. "No offense, buddy."

"You should be the scared one. But I accept. We'll go dancing as soon as the fire department leaves."

"It's a date," he said.

She had to admit, it was sure sounding like one. Hopefully, it wasn't also a mistake. They were growing closer. No doubt about it.

So was his departure date.

NEITHER VERN NOR Parker spoke a word. They didn't have to. Thank goodness it was dark on the drive home, because anyone passing them on the road would've wondered what they were up to with those silly matching grins of theirs.

Parker kept replaying that kiss, over and over in his mind, like a happily broken record. Hailey's adorable embarrassment over it made it all the better.

But reality wiped the smile off Parker's face as soon as he stepped into the house.

Trent greeted them at the door.

"PJ's hurtin.' I just know it. I asked if he wanted some of that medicine, but he refused."

Vern shook his head. "I'm at a loss on this one. I even called Vanessa. She says he always refuses medicine. Speaking of which…"

His grandpa disappeared into the kitchen and returned with a glass of water, then went over to his pill organizer, which he kept on the dining room table.

Still on the sofa, PJ was now fully awake and paying attention as Vern dumped the evening lot of medication into his palm and popped them all into his mouth at once. PJ even flinched when Vern washed the pills down.

That's it. Had to be.

Parker retrieved two forks from the kitchen. He plopped down on the sofa next to PJ with the container he'd brought home from Hailey's.

"How does that arm feel?" he asked.

"Okay." PJ pulled his teddy bear a little closer.

"Hey, I was wondering something. Does your mom ever take you along when she visits her clients?"

"Sometimes."

And her elderly clients most likely take pills, like Vern.

Parker pulled his own prescription from his pocket and read the label out loud. "Take one tablet every twelve hours, as needed. With or without food. It's been twelve hours, and I definitely need one."

He popped the top and put one in the palm of his hand. He made sure PJ was watching as he placed it on his tongue and chased it with a long swig of water. He then peeled the lid off the container, took a bite and savored it.

"Miss Hailey's food is awesome. Best mac and cheese I've ever tasted. Want some?"

PJ stared at him. "You took a pill."

"I sure did. And it's going to make me feel much better," he said, taking a huge bite of the leftovers.

"But..."

"But what?" Parker asked.

"You're gonna get old now."

Bingo. PJ associated taking medicine with getting old. He had the cause and effect all twisted around.

"I hope I get very old someday. I'm looking forward to living a long, healthy life. The medicine is helping me feel better while I'm still young."

"But…"

Parker set down the container and faced PJ. "You do know that taking pills doesn't make you older, right?"

PJ simply stared as he tried to process this new information and decide whether to believe it. Meanwhile, Vern was settling up with Trent and seeing him out the door.

"What's your pill for?" PJ asked.

"I'm allergic to cats, and I had to go to Miss Hailey's house tonight. Sure didn't want to be miserable the whole time. Not when I didn't have to be."

Vern walked over and peered into the container. "What did I miss out on? Besides the mac and cheese. What's left of it."

"We're talking about taking medicine. PJ's worried that it makes you older."

Vern sat down on the other side of PJ. "I never had to take any pills till I turned seventy. Healthy as a horse. The pills I take now don't make me older. They don't make me younger either, unfortunately, but they make me feel that way so that I can enjoy things like mac and cheese. And pecan pralines. Almost forgot about those."

Vern stood and shuffled into the kitchen.

"So, what do you think? Do you need some pain medicine?" Parker asked.

PJ nodded.

Vern came back with the pralines just as Parker was measuring out a teaspoon. PJ opened his mouth, and down the hatch it went.

That deserved a reward. Parker placed the remainder of the mac and cheese in the little boy's lap. Vern gave him an enthusiastic thumbs-up and handed him a praline.

Parker unwrapped the candy and took a big bite out of it. Sweet. Just like Hailey's gifts. Those earrings she'd bought for him to give to his girlfriend? He brought them home anyway in case he ever found one. With a little luck, he already had. If there was a chance she felt the same way, he'd give those earrings right back to her.

If she didn't feel the same, it would be a tough pill to swallow.

CHAPTER ELEVEN

"HEY, KIDDO, no running!" Hailey called out.

Max paid no attention as he jetted up the steps of the Hideaway to surprise his mommy and daddy. They were no doubt counting the seconds until they could hold their precious son again. They'd even come back two days early, likely for that reason. With the way Becca and Cody had called and sent texts for Max through Hailey's phone every day during their honeymoon, she wondered why they'd decided to take one at all.

The smell of caramel brownies filled the air as Hailey stepped inside. She headed to the kitchen to steal one, but her sister was there. Georgina had her back to the door, so Hailey quietly pivoted and headed toward Max's cries of, *"Mommy! Mommy! Daddy! Daddy!"* that had come from the direction of the master suite.

She peeked inside to find Cody balancing Max on one hip while his other arm embraced Becca.

That family made so much sense. The couple spent nearly a week together without interruption, yet their honeymoon continued. It made Hailey almost believe that any obstacle could be overcome. After all, Becca and Cody had been apart for six years, until Max had brought them back together.

With my help.

Cody hadn't been shy about trying to make Hailey's happily-ever-after happen, as well. But she regretted to inform him that their "numbers guy" Parker Donnelly didn't fit into her long-term equation.

After several seconds of being a voyeur, she decided to give this family its privacy. She could wait in Max's room next door, where Georgina wasn't likely to find her. But as soon as she turned away, she was busted.

"Hold it right there," Cody called out.

Becca rushed over and gave Hailey a hug. Meanwhile, Cody set Max down.

"Let's go find Penny," he said to his son.

Max started running and nearly tripped. He'd barely seen their three-legged rescue labradoodle the past week. Hailey would have invited the pup to stay with them rather than at the B and B with Georgina, but Sergeant wasn't a fan. And any creature spending time in her home required his approval.

"Careful there, kiddo!" Hailey called out, only to remember that she wasn't his mommy substitute anymore.

Cody leaned in as he walked by. "You and I need to talk when you're done here."

Why did she have the feeling it had something to do with Parker?

"Since when did you get so overprotective?" Becca asked.

Hailey folded her arms. The initial warm, fuzzy feeling made a quick exit, and the truth left her chilled. "Since PJ broke his arm during my trail ride."

"I hear he's doing fine. Things like that happen. And Max appears to not only be in one piece, but happy as ever. Did the two of you have fun?"

Hailey didn't even have to think twice. "Of course. But that reminds me. I forgot to pack his night-light."

"No worries. We brought back lots of souvenirs from Galveston for him to play with. I doubt he'll even realize it's missing for a while."

Hailey nodded. Truth be told, she might take advantage of having it and sleep beneath the stars tonight.

Becca sure looked *glowy*, if not entirely well rested. That's what honeymoons and true love must do to a gal. Before Hailey could ask for specifics about the trip, Cody returned with Max and Penny.

"Do you mind accompanying our children on their walk, darlin'?" he asked Becca.

"If you'll run a hot bath for me later, handsome," Becca answered.

Even though Hailey hadn't had so much as a Pop-Tart, she was about to hit sugar overload being around these two. The thought of taking a long bubble bath of her own, in her little two-bedroom log-cabin bungalow, made her feel a little glowy herself.

Becca smiled that sheepish grin of hers when she passed by, which meant she knew what Cody was about to discuss. At the same time, it was also a reminder that Hailey was now the outsider.

"How 'bout we talk over brownies in the kitchen? That smell is torturing me." Cody headed toward the door as if it was a directive instead of a question.

Hailey was in luck. Georgina was no longer there. That's when she realized how lonely her sister had been. The woman had reorganized and rearranged the entire space.

Cody pulled out a chair for Hailey and transferred the plate of warm chocolate treats from the counter to the breakfast table. He went to the fridge and poured them both a glass of ice-cold milk to wash them down.

"How's it going with Parker?" he asked, setting a glass in front of her, along with a napkin.

She shrugged. "It's okay. Of course, Parks doesn't have to help anymore, now that you'll be stepping back in, even though he did learn how to do a few things. Which begs the question, why did you recommend him in the first place? To see how much stress I could handle?"

"So he's back to being Parks, eh?"

"You didn't answer my question. But I'll answer yours anyway. We've grown a little closer. And don't read too much into this, but we're celebrating the end of our working relationship tomorrow night."

"And the beginning of a personal one?"

Hailey wasn't sure how to answer that. A personal one had begun, yet it was already on the chopping block.

"He and I have nothing in common."

"I don't buy it."

"He lives in Chicago, I live here."

"Folks have been known to move around. No law against it."

"He likes opera."

"That's hardly a deal breaker. Becca kept Max a secret for six years. If I can forgive that, you can overlook Parker's questionable taste in music."

"He wants kids. Lots of them."

Cody took a bite out of a brownie. "Mmm. Now, *this* is yummy."

"Did you hear what I said?"

"I'm pretty sure everyone in this house did. But you know what? I wasn't ready for even one. Until I met Max. I can only imagine lots more little ones like him running around. And I like what I'm imagining. You should try visualizing."

Such a comment usually deserved an eye roll, but she couldn't manage one. Nor could she visualize little ones like her running around.

"You're absolutely zero help. I already have seven kids in the barn, eight children in the stables and Sergeant to share a bed with every night," she said.

Cody started counting on his fingers.

"Comes out to sixteen. I can get Parks to confirm the total if you wish," she said, adding a smirk.

"Very funny. I was counting horses. Either

you can't count, or you adopted another one while I was gone and didn't tell me."

"Parks suggested it yesterday. Nash took in an Appaloosa that he doesn't have time to care for, and I had an extra stall. The stork made the delivery last night, although we still have some paperwork to finalize. I think the addition should result in a little income bump. He's going to put together some numbers for me, but even with the cost of additional feed and medical, I'll still make a profit."

Cody cocked his head and looked at her funny.

"What?"

"Just looking. Something's different. You're growing a head."

"Do I even want to know?"

Cody broke character and laughed. "For business. Get it? I mean, you've done so much with the reboot, but you never waded into numbers."

"Oh, I'm planning on staying in the shallow end, where the water is nice and warm and safe. Parks suggested I tear down the barn and build an arena, claiming it would result in an enormous income boost. He seems to think I'm doomed to failure otherwise. But I'm perfectly comfortable in my tax bracket, Bro."

Yet, something about what Cody said—about

having a head for business—was quite flattering, and felt like it could be a *little* her.

"Okay. I'll back off for now. Can I at least talk you into giving me a better nickname?"

"It's better than the one Parks gave me. Scaredy-Cat. He got it from Max, by the way."

"That's my pride and joy," Cody said.

"In keeping with Parker's apparent goal to expand my comfort zone, he dared me to cook a five-course meal, which is not only terrifying for me, but for the community at large."

"You're the least scaredy person I know."

"You *have* met me, right?" Then again, he hadn't witnessed her anxiety attack at the clinic. That was yet another about-Hailey secret she intended to keep.

She finally gave in, reached for a brownie and sank her teeth into it.

"You remind me of a mutton buster I used to compete against. Nothing scared that gal. We had silly nicknames for each other. Those were the days." He smiled, then took another huge bite of his brownie and closed his eyes as he chewed.

Georgina's cooking had that effect on people. It was like she'd cast a spell.

"I guess that was a thing back then. I was a mutton buster too," she said. "I even won several rodeo events, thanks to a little cowboy I called Pickle who offered the most awesome tips. Probably regretted it after I beat him by four seconds for the buckle in Reno."

Cody nearly coughed up his brownie, then looked at her as if seeing her for the first time. Kind of creeped her out. "What? Do I have brownie stuck in my teeth?"

"It wasn't four seconds. It was three," he insisted.

She had to think about it. "You're right. How on earth did you know that?"

"Because *I'm* Pickle," he said. "That means you're Pumpkin."

She could feel her jaw drop. If it had been made of glass, it would have shattered on the tabletop. Now that he pointed it out, she could totally see the resemblance. Although one of Cody's facedown bull-riding accidents as an adult had permanently altered his smile.

"So, our connection wasn't imagined after all," she said. She'd felt it immediately when he'd come to Destiny Springs four months ago. Which made her wonder, if he'd steered her in the right direction back then, could he be doing the same about Parker now?

"Can't believe I didn't make the connection sooner. Your eyes haven't changed. No one has peepers quite like yours," he said. "But your hair was a lot shorter."

"Grew that out, but never quite grew out of my tomboy phase."

Cody wiped his mouth with a napkin and tossed it on the table. "That's funny. I always saw you as this pretty little thing who happened to also be tough as nails. Still do. I suspect we would have had a connection regardless. But wow. Talk about a small world."

She sat up straighter. "We have a lot in common, so that makes sense. What doesn't make sense is that I feel a connection with Parker too. Not the brotherly vibe, like with you and Nash. It's almost as if I'm doomed to repeat the mistakes of my past by falling for someone who is so different."

"Yep. Opera and bluegrass has spelled the end of so many promising relationships," he said with an exaggerated frown.

She shook her head. "I get your point."

"Good, because Pickle has another tip for you. Differences don't have to make a difference when it's true love."

"Spoken like a true romantic. One who owes me a favor for lighting a fire under this... this—"

"Promising relationship?"

"I give up. But you do owe me a favor. Will

you keep Georgina here for the duration of her trip? I think she was planning on staying with me, now that the spare room is free. I can't deal with her right now."

"Becca wouldn't need convincing. In fact, she'd probably offer your sister a job if she lived closer."

Hailey had an odd feeling Georgina would move to Destiny Springs in a heartbeat. She could do wedding planning anywhere. Not only would her sister set up twenty-four-hour surveillance of Hailey and take over her old job as a side hustle, she'd end up replacing her as Becca's best friend, if she hadn't already. In fact, Hailey and Becca had barely spoken the past week.

"I'll let her know she's welcome here, but your sister will have to make the decision about where she'd rather stay," Cody added.

"I'll do whatever Hailey thinks is best," Georgina said.

Hailey's breath hitched. How long had she been standing in the doorway? Not that Hailey had to ask.

The hurt expression said she'd been there long enough.

CODY STOOD, put on his Stetson and grabbed a brownie to go. "If you'll excuse me, ladies, I have to finish unpacking my suitcase and catch up on some hugs from my little cowboy."

The man knew how to make an exit.

"Whatever you say, Pickle." Hailey stood and approached her sister, who now had her arms folded across her chest. "I'm sorry, Georgina. I know how that must have sounded. I just need a few days to decompress after keeping Max. That's all."

Georgina stepped around her, retrieved a dish towel and started drying a bowl as if intending to remove its pattern. "You do like your alone time. I certainly don't want to intrude on that."

It was true. Yet she always felt as though she had to apologize for it, as she did now. Still, she felt awful. But there was a way to make it up to her because there really was something she needed.

"I *could* use your help with something, though," Hailey said.

Georgina seemed to perk up at the request, although she was still playing it cool. "Go on. I'm listening."

"Will you help me accessorize an outfit for tomorrow night?" she asked, reverting once again to her childhood role as Georgina's dress-up doll. But to her sister's credit, she did have good taste, if a bit too girly.

"Is this for a date? Parker, right?"

So her sister had overheard more of the conversation than Hailey first suspected. She struggled to remember exactly what she and Cody had discussed.

"It's a celebration to mark the end of a successful working partnership, but I want to leave him with a good impression."

"Uh-huh. I feel like I have to say something about this, Hailey. But please don't take it the wrong way. I'm a little worried."

As if that was a surprise. "About what this time?"

"Parker Donnelly reminds me of you-know-who. Chasing money and success. And with those looks, probably a few women. I don't want you to get hurt."

"He's nothing like the man whose name shall never be spoken again. Not that it matters. Parker's going back to Chicago, and I'm here to stay. A relationship is out of the question. That's understood." *I think.*

"You know him better than I do. It's just that he didn't want to associate with us when we'd visit Grandma and Grandpa, like we weren't good enough. By the way, where are you two going?"

Hailey was tempted to grab Georgina by the

shoulders and speak very slowly and clearly that Parker had not only been a child at the time, he'd had scoliosis and had to wear a body brace. That might have had something to do with the fact that he hadn't been all that social.

But she refrained. Thank goodness she'd never told Georgina about the kiss on the cheek at the pony party. Or the kiss on the lips the other night.

"I'm making dinner at my house. We might go dancing after that. Hey, did you organize all those? They look terrific." Hailey pointed to the spice rack on the counter in a desperate attempt to steer the conversation in another direction, because she knew what was coming next.

"You're cooking?"

"Uh-huh. Miracles happen." At least, Hailey hoped they did. Since she wasn't getting any boots on the ground to help her, she needed wings in the air in the form of angels.

"Why don't you let me cook? That way, you and your...business partner can talk. I'll stay out of the way."

"No, thanks. I've got this covered." It came out harsher than Hailey had intended, but no.

Georgina busied herself with folding the dish towel and avoided eye contact. "Just trying to be helpful, but if you don't need my help, you don't need my help."

There it was. A first-class guilt-trip ticket with Hailey's name on it. Georgina's treat.

"His expectations are low. I wouldn't want to disappoint him by having it be too awesome," Hailey said, hoping flattery would get her out of this awkward exchange.

"Well, if you have any questions, please call or text. I can walk you through it."

She wanted to say that getting help with this would be cheating. Not to mention, she was rather looking forward to doing it herself. Besides, she'd enlisted Georgina's help in something else already. Had her sister already forgotten?

Could I be that lucky?

"So! Let's go shopping in my closet, shall we?" Georgina hung the dish towel neatly from a drawer handle and led the way to the Hideaway guest room she'd chosen for the week. The Lace Room, specifically, which was a bit too *wedding-y* for Hailey's taste. When she'd worked at the B and B, it had been the most requested room by honeymooners, with the Velvet Room coming in a close second.

Georgina opened the closet. She must have

brought a couple of trunks' worth of clothes, because the walk-in was packed.

"I already have a pair of jeans and boots picked out, but I could use help with the top and jewelry. However, this stays," Hailey said with emphasis. She held up her wrist and pointed to the horsehair bracelet, adjusting the ties so that they weren't in view. Otherwise, Georgina would notice what a shabby job Hailey had done and insist on redoing them.

"Oh, yes. Grandma's engagement ring. The woman with those *huge* fingers, as a certain adorable someone described them. You really like that thing, don't you?"

"I do."

Now, *that* was an uncomfortable choice of words. As soon as they slipped from her mouth, she felt a strange pang in her heart. A mixture not only of loss, but of hope. Admittedly, she felt a little of both when it came to Parker.

Problem was, she wasn't so sure she was prepared for either.

CHAPTER TWELVE

It ALMOST FELT as though Hailey were performing surgery, considering how meticulously she'd checked and double-checked the ingredients and required cooking utensils, and arranged them on the counter for maximum efficiency. She scrubbed her hands with soap and hot water and picked up the recipe.

Directions: Vigorously whisk egg yolks and lemon juice together until mixture doubles in volume. Place the bowl over a saucepan containing barely simmering water or use a double boiler. Do not allow the water to touch the bottom of the bowl.

"Seriously? What language is this?" Hailey set the recipe down and resisted the urge to use the lifeline that her sister had offered, but then reconsidered. "No. You've got this, Hailey."

Once she turned on the burner to get the water simmering, her thoughts turned to Georgina's concerns. Maybe Hailey should have explained that she and Parker weren't meant to be, without going into specifics. After tonight, she may never see him again. This particular man couldn't hurt and humiliate her by standing her up at the altar because she couldn't bear children. There was never going to be an altar.

Hailey plugged in the old turntable and blew off the dust, careful not to get anything on Georgina's white silk blouse, even though the dramatic bell sleeves could double as a furniture duster. Or on the multistrand faux pearls that were a bit heavy-handed.

She'd warned Georgina that the items may not come back as pristine as they left. But her sister was so giddy that her dress-up doll looked girly, she didn't seem to care.

For once, Hailey's procrastination paid off, because she would've otherwise given away all her grandparents' music albums. As luck would have it, one of them was opera. Said so right there on the cover. She set the needle down on the first song. Not appropriate for dancing. More like background-noise-while-soaking-in-a-bubble-bath music.

All that remained was finishing the five-course dinner to fulfill her part of their negotiation.

Maybe she didn't have a master's degree in business or finance—or scuba diving—but her daddy always told her she was a smart cookie. Pair that with what Parker had said about her intelligence, and she was beginning to think there might be some truth to it.

Case in point: the pork tenderloin. Didn't look exactly like the photo in the recipe, but it smelled amazing. The fact that Sergeant wasn't milling around underfoot was odd, but he was more of a seafood kind of guy anyway. Instead, he kept hanging around the door as if he wanted to go outside.

"Sorry, babe. Not tonight," she said.

The caprese salad was easy, although she needed a better knife with which to slice the mozzarella medallions. With a little creative arranging, she was able to hide the worst offenders. The dish that was being the biggest stinker was the vegetable appetizer. Hollandaise was as difficult to make as it was to spell. At least for her. She draped a towel across the front of Georgina's blouse, combined all the ingredients and was about thirty seconds into the required whisking when someone knocked.

She glanced at the clock. Parker had arrived on the minute, as usual.

"Come in. It's unlocked," she called out in

lieu of answering the door, because her hands were full, and she was *not* going to mess up this meal.

"Excuse me, ma'am. I'm looking for Miss Hailey," a man said.

What? Who?

She craned her neck while continuing to whisk. There he stood. Her unexpected cowboy. Although she'd seen Parker in blue jeans, flannel shirts and cowboy boots already, he'd topped it all off this time with a black Stetson that looked suspiciously like one of Cody's.

But it was more than that. He struck a comfortable pose after strolling into the open kitchen, leaning against the refrigerator and hooking his thumbs in his belt loops. So different from his usual perfect-postured, feet-directly-beneath-his-shoulders-and-toes-pointed-straight-ahead mannequin stance. Even more jolting, Sergeant had changed his mind about going outside and was rubbing against Parker's boots instead. Or whoever this man was.

"Does Miss Hailey's guest have a name?" she asked, playing along.

He stepped in closer. "He does, but it went right out of his head when he got a look at the chef."

Someone was being quite flirty tonight. She swiftly pivoted to stir the sauce before the edges turned dark.

"Nice selection of music. One of my favorites. *Tristan and Isolde,*" he said.

"Let me guess. You saw the opera in Aachen."

"Even better. Chicago. I took my mom."

Hailey removed the saucepan from the heat and dared herself to turn back around. "How is she doing, by the way?"

"Fine, from what I can tell. She's still difficult to get ahold of. I have some concerns."

Hailey almost stated the obvious. That those concerns would be put to rest within a few days.

While she continued with the hollandaise, he followed the music to its source. "I love these old turntables," he said. "My grandpa has one, but he never plays it. May not even work."

"If it doesn't, Vern can fix it. He can fix anything. But you already know that."

Parker returned to her side. "Speaking of that, can I help fix anything here? Not that it needs it. Everything looks as good as it smells."

She shook her head and was tempted to say that accepting help would be cheating. But that went without saying.

"Ahh, one of my favorites. Tomato caprese," he said as he stared down at the plate.

"*Tomahto* caprese," she corrected him, then giggled. "What kind of music would 'Let's Call the Whole Thing Off' be considered?"

"Jazz. Or maybe pop. Why? Are you thinking of abandoning bluegrass?"

"Not in a zillion years, as Max would say." She didn't even have to think about it, but she did have a question. "So, could two genres be more different than opera and bluegrass?"

He studied her as if he knew what she was asking. Could any two people have more different lives than the two of them? For once, he didn't offer a snappy comeback. Or *any* comeback.

"The good news is the pork loin should be done in about five minutes, the broccoli with hollandaise appetizer is complete. I need to transfer it to a plate and make it look pretty," she said. "We've discussed the *tomahto* caprese salad. I hope you like your *potahto* soup on the lumpy side. I did so intentionally because I prefer it that way, even though the recipe dictated otherwise. And for dessert, we will be having my specialty—Rice Krispies squares."

He broke out in one of those deep-dimpled smiles. "You not only did it, Hailey. You owned it. I'm proud of you."

To be honest, she was rather proud of herself.

She never would've attempted a five-course meal if not for him. But before she had fully absorbed the magnitude of her accomplishment, he leaned in and kissed her, holding his lips to hers for an extended moment.

He took a step back, shook his head and dropped his chin to his chest. "Sorry about that."

She took a deep breath and willed her heart to stop pounding. Furthermore, she could totally relate. She hadn't intended to kiss him the other day either.

"No need to apologize. My cooking has that effect on people," she teased. "But maybe you should reserve your final verdict for when you taste everything."

Seemingly relieved by the pivot, he picked up a tomato wedge and mozzarella medallion with his hands and took a bite.

"Nailed it," he said before bothering to swallow.

She was tempted to admonish him to swallow his food before speaking but was too won over by the compliment.

Just when the evening had seemed to have course-corrected, the album started skipping. Hailey rushed over to lift the needle. "Hey, cowboy. Wanna pick out another one? There's a big stack in the spare room, although this was the only opera. Maybe something else will strike your fancy."

"How about we pick one out together? Maybe we'll find something we both like."

"And ruin this incompatibility vibe we have going?" she teased, then stepped into the hallway and nodded for him to follow.

Once in the guest room, she switched on the overhead light. "Here they are." She pointed to the stack of albums on top of a dresser. Parker walked over and started thumbing through them.

"There's some great stuff here. Beethoven, Berlin Philharmonic 1963. Johnny Cash. Perry Como. None of these appeal to you?"

She shrugged. "I didn't look that closely at all of them. Perhaps I could be persuaded to at least *like* something in there."

He continued to peruse the stack. "Now, here's one you might be able to connect with. Folk ballads. Country music is rooted in folk, by the way. But you probably already knew that."

She didn't remember seeing that one. She'd been laser focused on finding something that at least remotely resembled opera and stopped short because the dust had made her nose twitch.

Like it was doing now. But there was something other than dust in the air, and it took only a few seconds to figure it out.

"Nooo!" she practically screamed.

She ran out of the room while Parker called out, "Maybe give it a chance first?"

Too late. She grabbed some mitts and pulled out the pork loin. It was already beginning to burn.

Parker was at her side in a heartbeat. "My fault. I distracted you."

He had, but not in the way he meant it. This faux pas was hers to own. The temperature gauge in her oven was wonky and it ran hot. She kept forgetting because she rarely used it.

"Look at it this way," he said. "Every great chef has a signature style. A stamp that's uniquely his or hers. Maybe this is yours."

"I should write a book. *Cooking with Hailey: Fifty Ways to Prepare Carcinogens.* Maybe it would become a bestseller and I'd be wealthy beyond my comfort zone."

Parker was doing a poor job of containing a smile. She cut off the most blackened piece, put it on a plate and handed it to him. "To your health."

He started to take a bite, but it was still practically shooting flames, so he set it back down. He walked over to the potato soup, which she'd transferred to a bowl, and fished out a lump nearly the size of a golf ball, added it to his plate, then bit into it. "Perfection." Same with the broccoli and hollandaise.

"Aren't you going to join me?" he asked. "I'd suggest we sit at the dining table, but I'm digging this casual arrangement."

"Are you saying you'd choose this over the cushiony velvet dining chairs at such-and-such steakhouse in Chicago?"

Once again, he seemed to have to think about it.

"That's exactly what I'm saying."

She fixed a small plate for herself and privately agreed that everything tasted better than she'd imagined.

He piled even more on his. While he finished up, she grabbed a peppermint from a jar, unwrapped it and popped it into her mouth.

"Is that your dessert? What about the Rice Krispies squares?" he asked.

"We need to get to Renegade before they close so you can fulfill your end of the agreement. We'll take dessert to go." She washed off her plate, put it in a drainer and wiped her hands on a dishcloth.

"Good. I don't want to leave the best course behind. In the meantime…" He reached around her and grabbed a peppermint for himself.

"Let me guess. Your mom used to make Rice Krispies squares."

"Every Saturday."

She put a few treats in a baggie and tossed it in her handbag. The way he smiled made her wonder if his mom had done the same sort of thing before they'd leave the house. But she wasn't his mom.

And, as of tonight, she was no longer his business partner.

ALTHOUGH PARKER NO longer felt like a fish out of water, he still felt as though he was getting away with something as soon as he stepped foot inside the honky-tonk and no one gave him a second look. Hailey, on the other hand, was getting all kinds of attention from appreciative cowboys, to which she seemed completely oblivious.

"Let's get something to drink." She took his hand and led him to the near side of the horseshoe bar.

They'd barely claimed their seats when the

bartender fished a soda out of a large tub of chipped ice, popped the top on the glass bottle and slid it in front of Hailey without even asking what she wanted. The guy poured some peanuts into a paper cup and placed them in front of her, as well. She selected a few and slipped them into her drink.

It didn't escape his attention that no one else at the bar was getting such favorable treatment. Was she a regular here? He wasn't sure he wanted to know.

"What can I get for you?" the bartender asked him.

"Chilled tonic water. Neat. Fever-Tree, if you have it. And dress it with lime."

Hailey snorted and nearly choked on a sip of soda.

A few moments later, the bartender placed a drink in front of him, along with a napkin weighted down with lime wedges.

Okay. So it was a do-it-yourself kind of place. No problem. Parker ran one of the limes around the rim of the glass and took a sip. Canada Dry.

Hailey eyed him while taking another long sip from her drink. The band stepped back onstage. After checking their tuning, the singer slash guitar player said, "Count it." At that, the drummer clicked his sticks together, which also signaled the crowd. The couple next to them scurried to the dance floor. He practically felt the atmosphere shift as people began to pair off.

"Sure you'll be able to two-step after drinkin' that?" Hailey teased.

"I'm not sure I'll be able to two-step under any circumstances." The music started, but he didn't recognize so much as a bar or lyric. "Is this band famous?"

Hailey shrugged. "They're popular around here. Certainly not as famous as someone like Montgomery Legend. If you remember, he played at Becca and Cody's wedding."

How could he ever forget? Hailey, in that purple maid-of-honor dress. He'd been sidelined as other wedding guests danced. She'd come to his rescue that night. They talked business instead of joining the others on the makeshift dance floor, even though cowboy after cowboy had approached and given it their best shot.

Just like this whole week had given him an opportunity to ride a horse for the first time, tonight was his chance to *not* be an outsider.

He set his drink down and eased the bottle from Hailey's hands. "Shall we dance?"

Translation: shall we get this over with? He was about to make a fool of himself. Plus everything in this place reminded him that he was a fraud. Maybe he shouldn't have let Cody gift him with one of his Stetsons. That made Parker feel even more obvious.

Apparently, Cody found out through Hailey about their business wrap-up celebration date tonight and felt compelled to help. Yeah, like the way Cody had set them up to work even more closely together while he was gone.

Set them up to be knocked down by reality was more like it.

"Are you asking me to dance, for real, or are you speaking Gershwin again?" she asked.

If he'd been holding a drink, he would have dropped it. He hadn't even been referring to the movie, *Shall We Dance?*

"Someone's been doing her research," he said as they walked to the dance floor.

"I stumbled upon the movie title when you introduced me to the tomato song."

"Oddly enough, stumbling is the best way to learn something. Either way, I'm impressed."

Getting to the center of the dance floor was like trying to walk through a cattle stampede. Not that he'd done that either. All of a sudden, he was more than a little nervous. But Hailey was a good teacher and put him at ease. Soon enough, he was two-steppin' with the best of them.

They were two-steppin'. And now he was even thinking *steppin'* instead of *stepping*. When had that happened?

"I can't believe this," she said.

He suppressed a grin. "That I haven't broken your toe yet?"

"No. That you cheated," she said, then intensified that semiuncomfortable mutual gaze they had going. His confidence took a nosedive.

"What do you mean?"

"You know exactly what I mean. Was it with Nash?"

Now he was really confused. And she seemed genuinely upset. And accusing him of cheating? They weren't even dating.

"Nash isn't really my type," he teased, hoping she'd tease back.

"Then who? Cody? Becca? If it was Becca, I'm gonna kill her."

Speaking of killing someone, Hailey spun them around, putting him in the lead. They didn't talk anymore about the cheating topic, and he nearly popped a brain vein trying to figure out what she meant. Maybe this was a good thing, because he'd been much too reckless tonight with that kiss. Even getting impulsive thoughts about finding a way to move here or suggesting that she move to Chicago. Had the bartender spiked his tonic water?

The song mercifully came to an end. They made their way back to the bar where the server put two fresh drinks in front of them. Time to stop dancing around this whole cheating topic.

"Hailey. Look at me."

She offered up an interrogative squint. "You ready to fess up, cowboy?"

"Sure, if you'll give me a clue as to what I should be fessing," he said, taking a sip of his drink and realizing too late he'd forgotten to dress the rim of the glass with lime.

"Someone gave you a crash lesson in advance of tonight. That's cheating. I pulled together the five-course meal on my own."

He placed his hand over Hailey's. "I swear, nobody helped me. And you can't honestly say that I was any good out there. I stepped on your toes at least twice."

"At first and on purpose, I strongly suspect. To throw me off."

"I meant to step on your whole foot, but I

couldn't even get that right. That's how bad of a two-stepper I am," he said, stubbornly refusing to give up on humor.

She finally cracked a semismile, paired with a shake of her head.

"I've been two-steppin' all my life and even taught for a while in my teens. If you've never had a lesson, then you're a natural. And I've never met one of those before. I'm not saying it isn't possible, but…"

He swallowed. Hard. She had no idea how much of a compliment she'd given him. He'd been feeling as though everything he'd done lately had been a misstep. Even what he got right had somehow turned out wrong. But he did have a confession.

"I've competed in ballroom dancing. Also dabbled in tango and salsa. Anything to help with my posture. I find commonality in many of the forms."

Her brows raised. "Any trophies?"

He dropped his head, unsure whether the correct answer was the best answer. He looked up again and opted for correct. "Five. Mostly local competitions."

Hailey slowly nodded. "I see. That's why you caught on so fast and were so coordinated." She took a long swig of her soda, apparently realizing too late that she'd forgotten to drop in a few peanuts. He nudged the paper cup toward her.

"Sorry I accused you of cheating," she said. "I'd say you've won, fair and square."

"I didn't realize it was a competition. But if you're determined to make it one, we haven't had the best squares of all. The ones in your handbag. I think that will put you back in the lead. Not that you ever weren't."

The band stopped playing and the overhead lights flashed. "Last call," the bartender said as he did a final sweep of the horseshoe. True, they got a late start. But had they really closed the place down? Was their evening about to come to an end?

More important, was *this* about to end?

As they walked back out to Vern's truck, Parker paused and looked up. The skies in Chicago didn't seem nearly as clear as they did here.

"What are you lookin' at?" Hailey asked.

"Cassiopeia," he answered as he opened the truck door for her.

Instead of getting in, she looked up, as well. "Andromeda's mom. I see her too."

"You like stargazing?" he asked.

"Every chance I can."

Me too. So they did have something in common after all. He wasn't sure how Hailey felt in that moment. But, for him, the stars would never look the same again.

CHAPTER THIRTEEN

Thank goodness Parker checked his email before he went to bed. His boss had called a one-on-one for first thing this morning.

He lifted the collar of his button-down and went through the motions of putting on the tie that Hailey had given him. He positioned the laptop to where the comical horse heads weren't in view. Only the knot, to suggest he was wearing a proper tie. Theodore Mason, his mentor and boss, joined him online.

"I have another meeting in ten minutes, so I'll cut to the chase, Donnelly." Mason tapped his index finger against his lips. "I'm withdrawing your name for the senior consultant position."

Parker's heart tanked. Had he misunderstood what was expected of him? It wasn't like him to get such an important detail so wrong. Yet, last night, he hadn't so much as thought about anything other than Hailey, as if the promotion of a lifetime was no longer driving him but had been relegated to the flatbed of Vern's old Dodge truck.

"I was waiting on the client's final review of my proposal. But I suppose you don't need that anymore," he said.

Hands now planted firmly in front of him, Mason nodded. "Oh, I need it more than ever. As in, before you return."

"I don't understand."

"I'm retiring at the end of the month, and I've nominated you to take my place as partner. It's a leap-frog promotion, but you can handle it. However, some of the board members are worried that you've gone AWOL. I need to convince them that you're serious. That is, if you *are* serious."

Parker hadn't seen this coming. A full partnership would give him a level of job stability he only dared to imagine. The base pay alone would be the stuff of dreams.

"I'm both humbled and flattered, sir. Who else is being considered, if I may ask?" he asked.

"A few members are backing Frank LaCroix. I'm sure I don't have to spell that out for you."

Older, more experienced, better portfolio, also a junior consultant. And with a couple of negative marks against him as far as client satisfaction was concerned. Still, that might not be enough to cancel out the fact that LaCroix's uncle was on the board.

"No, sir. I understand what I'm up against. I guess there's no chance the Capricorn franchise deal came through when I blinked," Parker said.

Even though his boss was blind cc'd on all email correspondence while Parker was on leave—to make sure nothing fell through the cracks—Parker still went in and checked his email every other day. Capricorn was the only pitch still on the table when he left. If that came through in time, it would provide the missing piece, and he could share his new idea for Hailey's property in a more personal manner.

"They contacted me directly and it's a no-go. Italy's loss," Mason said. "By the way, what's with that tie you're wearing?"

Parker had shifted during the call, thus revealing one of the most animated-looking creatures. "A gift from a client," he said, coming dangerously close to saying "girlfriend" instead.

"Nice. But it can't hold a candle to the gift my lady friend gave me." Mason proudly displayed a needlepoint sign that read, *Life Begins at Retirement*.

"That's very special. She must be crazy about

you." A few ladies at the firm had formed a needlepoint group. Which begged the question: Was Mason dating a coworker? If so, he'd be breaking his own rule about fraternizing. Unless he was retiring early to preserve his integrity, which wouldn't surprise Parker at all.

"If she's crazy for me, the feeling is mutual," Mason said.

Now, *that* was the look of happiness. Sure, the widower had four grown children and five young grandkids, but he probably got lonely when they all went to their respective homes at the end of a visit.

Mason looked down at what Parker assumed to be his phone. "Oops! Speaking of the needlepoint angel, she's waiting for me at the restaurant. I need to wrap this up."

"I thought you had a meeting."

"I do. I'm meeting someone special for breakfast," he said. "Get that proposal to me ASAP. I'll stall the board as long as I can."

Parker logged off and leaned back, admiring how Mr. Mason had his priorities straight. At the same time, he visualized the corner office he could be inheriting with a view of Lake Michigan.

He checked his own phone for messages. One from his Realtor. The seller of the six-bedroom home got another cash offer for more. The bidding battle would turn into a full-blown war unless one of the prospective buyers didn't accept a caveat: a mural in one of the children's bedrooms was never to be painted over since a well-known local artist had been commissioned to create it.

Not a deal breaker for Parker. He rather appreciated that it was part of their asking price.

He remembered the mural from when he accompanied his mom while she cleaned. He always thought every child should have a room that beautiful. It was looking as though one of his future children might make Parker's own childhood dream come true.

In the meantime, he had another kind of work to do. Vern had forgone some of the ranch duties to stay inside with PJ, who was watching cartoons in the den and refusing to take off that ragged tie. At least he'd been taking his pain medicine and seemed to feel better, physically. But when Vern would take him anywhere around the horses, PJ shied away.

In all fairness, his grandpa's horses weren't the most gentle or well-behaved, according to Vern himself, which gave Parker an idea. He could use a good-looking, tie-wearing business partner to help with his pitch to Hailey.

Maybe they could say hi to Gabby while they were there.

Parker sat next to PJ. "May I get your professional assistance with something? I need to talk to Miss Hailey about some improvements I'm recommending for her property. I thought maybe you could go to Sunrise Stables with me and help. I'll pay you in cupcakes. Of course, you'd have to wear a tie."

PJ's expression lit up at the last part.

Sure, he wanted PJ to get over his reluctance around horses and hoped that Gabby's big brown eyes would make him feel secure again. Just like he hoped PJ's big blue eyes would convince Hailey to reconsider the benefits of income stability and security over just getting by.

Of course, he ran the risk that his plan could backfire on both counts. But, like getting on the back of a horse, it was a risk worth taking.

LAST NIGHT WITH Parker seemed as far away as the stars they both admired. His time for playing cowboy had ended, and it was back to reality for both of them.

Just as well. Her life had already begun course-correcting after the strangeness of last week. She was even stepping in for Sylvie tomorrow to lead a privately booked trail ride, along with Max, because Sylvie had something personal to take care of and Cody had promised Becca he'd finish some chores at the B and B.

That ended up working out beautifully, since the adult couple specifically asked for Hailey and Max. But she didn't plan to let her trail-riding day end there. After that, she wanted to explore another route. Map out a whole new trail to add to their offerings. Eventually, maybe they could partner with area farms and ranches and offer a progressive dinner on horseback. The possibilities now seemed as endless as the clear blue sky overhead.

For today, she planned to focus on what was right in front of her. Sylvie and Cody working together, tacking up the horses for a fully booked, half-day Rocks and Rolling Hills trail ride.

Cody jogged over. "Hey, Pumpkin, you okay with everyone abandoning you? Or should I get some boots on the ground to help?"

"Like you did last time with someone who had to go out and buy a proper pair?"

He bowed his head, as if he knew his efforts to set up Hailey and Parker had failed miserably. He looked up again, his gaze intent. "But he wore them quite well, didn't he? He did try."

Ancient history.

"The only boots I need on the ground today are mine. Thanks for going with Sylvie and taking Gershwin." She'd lucked out on multiple fronts. Besides being a sweetheart, the Appaloosa Hailey purchased from Nash had been trained for trail riding. Still, she wasn't going to let anyone but Cody ride Gershwin until she was sure he wasn't too good to be true.

"Gershwin sounds like a name Parker would pick out, more than you."

"We picked out the name together."

"Like expectant parents?"

"You clearly have honeymoon brain. Ask me after you've come down from cloud nine."

Cody pursed his lips and nodded. "The view is incredible. I highly recommend it."

"You know what? I'm having second thoughts about you taking him out so soon. I'm not sure I completely trust his easygoingness."

"Can we ever be sure about anything?" Cody said.

He had a point, although she suspected he wasn't referencing horses. Or maybe it was because she hadn't stopped thinking about Parker.

When she didn't respond, he rejoined the crowd. Hailey watched as Cody and Sylvie loaded the horses.

Even though there was much to do outside,

a front had moved through overnight, and she felt uncharacteristically cold. Besides, she was inspired to tackle what she'd been putting off. Organizing her home. Storing everything she didn't use and either throwing away or giving away reminders that churned up feelings that distracted her from moving forward.

She was about to go inside when Parker's rental sedan turned into the drive. She knew this time would come because they didn't say goodbye last night. Still, her heart didn't feel prepared for it.

As if he'd never turned into a cowboy, he was halfway decked out in business attire. Button-down and tie, paired with jeans and boots. *City on the top, country on the bottom.* Her Superman was turning back into Clark Kent. He walked around and helped PJ out of a car seat.

Hailey shielded her eyes from the sun as they approached, hand in hand. That's when she realized he was wearing that goofy tie that she'd given him. She had to bite the inside of her cheek to keep from laughing. At the same time, she felt that familiar tug that only a boy in a tie could trigger. In this case, a man. More specifically, this one. But Parker wasn't the only one who was all dressed up.

"Love your tie, PJ. And that cast!"

PJ produced a marker. "Will you sign it, Miss Hailey?"

Sure, if my hands don't completely melt, because my heart just did.

She found an empty spot next to Sylvie's signature, then handed the marker back to PJ. "Are y'all on your way to a business meeting?"

Parker smiled. "We are. In fact, we just arrived. Glad we caught you at home."

"He's gonna propose, and I'm gonna help," PJ said.

Hailey felt her brows raise so high, they must have touched her hairline. She looked back to Parker. "Is that true?"

Not exactly how she'd envisioned it would happen. Not that she'd dared to.

"It's not untrue. PJ and I have an idea to help you not only *get by*, but *get by* beyond your wildest dreams. Can you talk now?" Parker held up an envelope. Like the other night, she hadn't noticed he was carrying one.

Truth was, she didn't have time to listen to another one of Parker's pitches. Her thoughts were gearing up for the launch. The press release she'd written needed Cody's review. She wanted to add more content to Sunrise Stables' social media sites. And the fun part: she wanted to take No Regrets out on all three trails—even

Rascal's High-Ridge Ramble—now that Sylvie worked her magic on desensitizing him to boulders. Hailey's dance card was full, so to speak.

But two handsome men stood before her, looking at her with those big blue eyes. She found herself leading them into the conference room of their choice: the barn.

Parker retrieved three folding chairs, with Hailey facing the two of them.

"How would you feel about bringing back another Destiny Springs tradition?" He pulled out copies of a report and handed one to her. However, they lost her at the title: *Happily Ever Rafters.*

She didn't have to read any more to know what he was proposing. But she didn't have the heart to shut him down. Not in front of PJ. The little boy seemed beyond happy and excited and proud to be helping with this business meeting.

Parker cleared his throat. "PJ and I did an internet search, and we discovered that no other farm within two hundred miles offers a wedding venue like the one that has historically graced your property. All that charm that Sylvie mentioned is built into its bones. We've proposed several options to update it, but I'll let my partner walk you through those."

PJ flipped to the second page, held it up and

pointed to a photo of a barn. A red one. Hers was brown. "This one's red, but you can paint it any color you want. I like blue."

Parker patted him on the shoulder. "Good job."

PJ beamed.

"What do you think so far?" Parker asked.

Hailey cleared her throat. She was still grappling with her heart, which was now pounding its way out of her chest. "Umm. What about the goats?"

Parker smiled. "We anticipated that question. Turn to page three. We've put together some options, but this is our recommendation. Partition off their current space and build a wall that separates their living area from the main building. To give them a view, we can add windows to the back side. I'll need to confirm numbers and consult with a contractor. But I think the concept would work."

"So do I," PJ added. Hailey could already tell he was going to be quite the salesman.

"The rest of the pages provide breakdowns of the individual elements. A menu, of sorts. You can customize this any way you want."

She wanted to ask if he could customize it to *not* hold weddings. But in skimming the pages, that concept wasn't only the thread that held it all together. It was the fabric itself.

Parker collected PJ's copy and handed her the envelope. "I know it's a lot to absorb, but promise you'll sleep on it. Let me or my partner here know your overall thoughts or concerns in the morning. Or whenever. No pressure."

Hailey put the proposal back into the envelope then stood and tucked it under her arm.

"Can I play with the goats before we leave?" PJ asked.

"I'll leave that up to Hailey," Parker said, before she had a chance to suggest that he decide.

"Since you have that cast, you'll need to stay out of the pen itself. The only other rule I have is, no ties anywhere near the goats."

"That's a brilliant rule," Parker said, jumping in to help PJ remove his.

After the accessory was safely in Parker's possession, PJ ran over to the gate of the pen but no farther.

"I want him to see Gabby too, if he's up to it," Parker said. "He's afraid of horses now and I thought if he could face her again, that might help."

"Sounds a little mean to me." Poor little PJ. So small and vulnerable.

"Mean? That isn't my intention. It's up to

him whether he ever wants to ride again. I'm proposing a simple *hello*."

"Gabby is working right now, so your evil plan has been thwarted," she said, even though it was difficult to even attempt humor. She had to get this off her chest.

"About your plan for the barn..." she continued.

"You've already made a decision?"

He'd put so much into this, she could tell. The presentation itself was achingly adorable. But this idea was worse than the first. Not that he could have known how she felt about the subject, much less why. She'd put up a front at the dinner when the subject was brought up, and shut it down without explanation later that evening. Still, this wasn't going to happen.

Now that PJ's big blue eyes weren't trained on her, and with the little executive out of earshot, she was left with another pair of blue eyes that were equally difficult to turn down. But there was no reason for either one of them to waste any more time.

"I have. No weddings. No 'happiest day of a woman's life' on full display because, for me, it was the worst. Having such celebrations in my backyard would be a constant reminder." She bit her lip. She'd said too much already.

"Hailey, I didn't—"

"And no more proposals, please. The barn stays as is."

NOTHING LIKE BEING awakened by the smell of fresh-brewed coffee. Except when it was 3:00 a.m. and his ego felt as though it had been run through a garbage disposal.

After the colossal failure of the pitch to Hailey, both on a personal and professional level, he needed all healing time he could get. It cut him to the core that he'd inadvertently brought up a painful subject. In fact, he'd literally made a presentation of it. She hadn't gone into a lot detail, but he'd gotten a clear enough picture. Someone had hurt her in the worst way.

Parker rolled out of bed, stretched his back and went downstairs to make sure Vern was okay, because the man usually didn't rise until 5:00 a.m.

But when he got to the kitchen, he stopped short. Was this some sort of crazy dream? Vanessa was sitting at the table but immediately stood. He closed the distance between them and gave her a big hug.

"I'm so sorry about what happened with PJ," he said, even though he'd already apologized a dozen times over texts and emails. He'd finally convinced Hailey the accident hadn't been her fault, but he'd began wondering if he was partially to blame for encouraging it.

"Stop it. This is part of life." She pulled away and looked at him.

She was the closest thing to a sister he'd ever had. They were often mistaken for siblings. Same dark hair, same light eyes. Only, she was a lot better looking, in Parker's humble opinion.

He checked the clock on the stove. Maybe the one in his room had stopped, and it wasn't some unfathomable hour after all. Nope. 3:00 a.m. He shook his head and gave her his best shame-on-you look.

"Don't say it. I know I should've let someone know." She sat back down and took a sip of coffee. "I started caffeinating yesterday evening as soon as I got the message that my car was fixed. I wanted to be here when PJ woke up. I've looked in on him a few times already. Couldn't help myself."

"I don't blame you. He's going to be so surprised and excited. But still, don't do that again." Parker poured a cup for himself and joined her at the table.

"I'll try. I was thinking he might be disappointed that I'm back. No doubt he loved hanging around with you so much. He loves watching when you're talking to your boss over the computer."

Parker cocked his head. "I didn't know he watches me."

Vanessa took another sip and nodded. "Oh, yeah. Your every move."

"I'm more than happy to have business meetings with him over the internet when I get back to Chicago."

In fact, the prospect of keeping in touch with PJ on a regular basis tickled him. He lifted the lid off the sugar container and retrieved two cubes.

"Sounds like someone else is eager to get home," Vanessa said.

"Not sure I'd describe it that way." He wrapped his hands around the warm mug and stared at the murky liquid.

"What's wrong?" Vanessa asked.

He didn't want to burden her with the details about Hailey or his job until there were actual details. And even then…

"I have some difficult goodbyes to take care of," he said instead. Besides, it was truth.

"Grandpa tells me that you and a certain cowgirl have gotten pretty close."

Those tender kisses they'd shared immediately came to mind. "It was a business arrangement. But the proximity did us no favors."

"Or perhaps it did you the biggest favor of all."

He hadn't thought of it that way. Didn't dare to. He sure wasn't going to find a woman like Hailey in Chicago. The scary part was, he didn't even want to try.

Vanessa gently squeezed his arm. He could tell she'd been up all night, yet she was one of those people who wore their stress well. And he'd been making this all about himself for the past several minutes. When had he become so self-absorbed?

"What about you? How are you holding up?" he asked.

"I'm much better now that I'm with my baby."

"Speaking of PJ, I'd like to borrow him for a few hours today. If that's okay with you. I need to stop by Nash's and say goodbye to him and the girls. And his horses."

"You go right ahead, because I'm not going anywhere. Except to get one of those pecan candies that keep staring at me from the kitchen counter. Want one?"

"Sure." Even though one of Hailey's Rice Krispies squares would taste even better.

"I bet you enjoyed being back in your own home, though," he said.

Vanessa handed him a praline and sat back down. "I thought it would feel good after so long. And the house sitter I hired has gone above and beyond with keeping it clean. But it was so big and empty without PJ. I found that I couldn't wait to get back here."

"I would've felt the same way." In fact, he'd be going back to an empty house in Chicago.

At that, they both bit into the sweet-and-salty treat.

They sipped on their coffee and sat in silence as the sun began to rise. He, for one, couldn't wait to hear the pattering of footsteps directly overhead, in the room where PJ was staying. He sure was going to miss that sound.

At least he wouldn't have to truly say good-bye to PJ. Maybe Vanessa was only halfway serious about him and her son having regular business meetings over the internet, but he was loving that idea.

It was all the other thoughts filling his head that he didn't love so much. Thoughts of no longer seeing Hailey for a business meeting, or a personal one.

Time heals all wounds.

Right.

Out of sight, out of mind.

Yeah, sure.

If Vern was awake, he'd likely have some words of wisdom to add to both of those sayings. Because, as it stood, neither felt possible.

CHAPTER FOURTEEN

"Thanks for coming with me," Parker said as they headed to Buck Stops Ranch.

"Are we gonna propose to someone else?"

"Not today." Or tomorrow either. Today was for saying his goodbyes, and visiting the horses.

Nash and the girls were the ones Parker really needed to see. He'd become fast friends with the cowboy rancher, so this wasn't going to be easy. Even though Nash wasn't a relative, he felt like a brother. In fact, the whole town of Destiny Springs had become family.

But as soon as he turned into the drive, he knew saying goodbye was going to be much more difficult than he had anticipated. In Parker's experience, people who needed help the most were typically the least likely to ask for it…until their situation reached a critical state.

Nash was a textbook example.

Maybe Parker hadn't become anywhere near an expert, but it was clear that the fence needed mending. Several head of cattle were grazing awfully close to the damage. And the Buck Stops Ranch sign was dangling by one chain. When had one of the supports broken?

Parker helped PJ out of the sedan and held his hand as they walked up the steps. An exhausted-looking Nash answered the door. In the background, the girls were jumping on an ottoman and sofa, and shrieking about something.

"Come on in, if you dare," Nash said, then turned to the girls. "Quiet, ladies. We have company."

The shrieking stopped, but the jumping persisted. Nash should have been more specific.

Once inside, Parker realized that this cowboy not only needed a babysitter and a ranch hand, he could also use a housekeeper.

"I know this is a bad time, but—"

"No such thing when it comes to friends," Nash assured him, which warmed Parker's heart.

The girls finally looked up from whatever game they were playing. Lizzy ran over and wrapped herself around his legs.

"Did I say friends? I meant family," Nash said.

Now his heart wasn't only warm, it was boiling

over. Such an unexpected parting gift to know that at least a few people in Destiny Springs felt the same way he did.

Kat soon joined them, not wanting to be left out. She wrapped herself around the other side, turning him into a bona fide Parker sandwich.

The girls finally let go and ran back to the sofa, where they commenced jumping. Thankfully, PJ wanted nothing to do with it. Not a good idea with that cast.

"Ladies, please stop," Nash said.

"Yes, Daddy," they said in unison. Instead of jumping, they sat on the sofa and bounced.

Nash exhaled an I'm-at-my-wit's-end sigh.

"I have a great idea. It's a beautiful day. Let's all go outside." Parker attempted to mimic that commanding voice that Hailey always used. "Lizzy, Kat, how about grabbing some bottled waters for all of us? PJ, you have a free hand, maybe you can help."

Much to Parker's delight, that voice worked, like it always did with Hailey. The kids scrambled to the kitchen, returned with the loot and distributed the bottles.

Nash took the lead and headed out the back door. "Pretty impressive what you did back there. But what's this about?" he asked under his breath. The kids lagged far enough behind to not overhear what Parker was about to say.

"PJ's afraid of horses now. I took him over to Hailey's to see if he could make friends with Gabby again, but she wasn't there. Then I thought of your gentle ones." Not the main reason why he was there, but he couldn't quite bring himself to say the "g" word just yet.

Nash rubbed his chin, seeming to give it serious thought.

"Is that mean of me?" Parker felt compelled to ask.

"Mean? Sounds like something Hailey would say. If you force it on him, I suppose it would be. But there's an easy fix for that," Nash said.

"Oh, yeah?"

"Yeah. All you gotta do is not force it on him." Nash offered up a smirk.

"Why didn't I think of that," Parker said. He did tend to push his clients past their comfort zone and for their own benefit, but that was business. This was personal.

"How are you holding up?" Parker asked. As if he needed to. Exhaustion was etched not only on his face, but on his entire being. Looked like a little hip and back pain might be involved, the way Nash's gait was stiffer and slower than it had been yesterday.

"Aside from one of my ranch hands leaving town for a family emergency, and the other quitting? Everything is terrific."

"How about I take the girls back to Grandpa's for a while?" Parker offered.

"You're family. Not the enemy. I'm not gonna do that to you," Nash said. Finally, a bit of a smile. Parker knew good and well Nash was teasing. No daddy could ever love his daughters more than that man.

"I have a selfish motive. I want to practice my fathering skills for when I have little ones of my own."

"That's not a half-bad plan. Follow me." Nash headed in the direction of the horses.

Parker lagged behind long enough for PJ to catch up. He lifted the little boy and balanced him on his hip. With a few long strides, he caught up with Nash.

PJ buried his face in Parker's neck as they reached the horses, which broke Parker's heart. It also made him feel...*mean*. What if Hailey was right? What if he traumatized the little guy even more? He wasn't a licensed psychologist.

"We can go back to the house if you want," he said to PJ. "But they're on the other side of the fence, so they can't hurt you. You're safe with me. Your call."

PJ looked up and watched as Nash and the girls petted the horses. "We can stay."

Parker angled his own body so that it provided a barrier while he reached out and patted one of the horses on the neck. "What a sweetheart, Nash. What's this one's name?"

"Daisy. She's always been a little afraid of kids." Nash winked at Parker.

He went with it. "That's a shame. How about that, PJ? She's afraid of you. Maybe you could show her that she doesn't need to be."

If those gentle brown eyes of Daisy's didn't convince PJ that she wasn't going to hurt him, nothing would. Parker swiveled enough that PJ was within reaching distance.

PJ stuck his hand out for a quick pet before withdrawing.

"You just made Daisy's day. I can tell by the way she blinked," Nash said.

Parker wasn't sure whether Nash was making that up or whether it was a real thing. But he'd learned over the last several days to never pretend to understand anything.

"How does that work?" Parker asked.

"Horses blink less and their lids are more twitchy when they're stressed. When we first walked up, Daisy barely blinked. But as soon as PJ petted her, she blinked up a storm. And look at her now. No twitching either."

Parker couldn't have asked for a better gift from the universe.

"Did you hear that? You helped Daisy be less afraid. I'm so proud of you," he said.

PJ reached out again as if wanting to pet her, which Parker was more than happy to accommodate by stepping even closer.

Nash gripped his back and grimaced as if having some sort of muscle spasm. The whole thing sent a sympathy jolt down Parker's own spine.

"You okay?" he asked.

"Yep. It'll pass in a minute."

"Anything I can do to help?"

Nash half laughed through the pain. "You've already been a bigger help than you can imagine. If you ever want a job as a ranch hand, let me know. I'll hire you in a heartbeat."

He wasn't sure whether Nash was that desperate or simply delusional from the pain. Lately, Parker had wanted his hands to ache from physical labor. The most his hands had done lately was push a pen or tap on a keyboard.

With no other viable ideas to develop for his other clients at the moment, he could use some of his newfound cowboy skills to help here.

After all, Nash and the girls were family now. The cowboy said it himself. And family came first.

Always had, always would.

"A ZILLION YEARS AGO, the horses talked and decided to run away. And they never came back," Max began explaining, barely into the ride. Once again, his story cut a different path, although the timeline was always the same.

He was sandwiched between the couple, thus violating Hailey's single-file protocol. But that was okay. These weren't just any clients. Vern had booked the ride with Hailey and Max. And Sylvie was his date.

Instead of taking the lead, Hailey trailed behind the trio. Bad Boy was taking his demotion to follow in stride, which was a testament to all the training she and Cody had put the horses through.

While Max and Sylvie became further steeped in discussion about his latest theory, Hailey and Bad Boy trotted up to Vern's side.

"I thought group rides weren't your thing," she said, adding a knowing smile.

"They're not. But I was yearnin' to see Sylvie, and this was the earliest option. Thought it would also be an opportunity to wow Ms. Moss with my riding skills."

"Sounds like someone's in love," she said.

"I reckon you're right," Vern said. "But can you blame the woman? I'm quite the catch."

Hailey had to laugh. "That you are. Hey, what's that sound?" She craned her neck to look around.

Vern tilted his head and focused. "I don't hear anything. Then again, I need to change the batteries in my hearing aids. Probably one of those superheroes Max always talks about."

Hailey attempted to keep a straight face. "No. Sounds more like wedding bells."

Vern raised a single brow. "Is that so, missy? Would you be talking about mine? Or yours?"

"Definitely not mine."

Vern seemed to weigh the seriousness of her comment, which gave her chills.

"Do you know what Parker proposed?" she asked.

Specifically, barn weddings for Sunrise Stables? A revival of yet another Destiny Springs tradition? Not on her watch. She'd rather tear it down. In fact, knowing its history, she was tempted to do exactly that. But she'd pretended to love the story, just like she'd pretended to be okay with leading four children on the trail ride, so how was Parker to know. Putting up so many fronts was exhausting.

"Only thing I know is that my grandson has it bad for a certain cowgirl. But you didn't hear it from me."

"Hear what?" she teased. Yet, seriously, she wished she hadn't heard it at all.

"Let's stop up here and eat this bounty I've prepared," she said. It wasn't like any of them were interested in the scenery anyway. Sylvie and Max had already seen it, and the only scenery Vern was interested in had long, braided silver hair.

They all took care of their respective horses first, with Hailey helping Max, then settled in on the lunch blanket. Vern unwrapped and stared at his sandwich. Max pointed to the sliver of a burned edge and giggled. She'd almost caught it in time. Her skills in the kitchen were improving.

"That's cars again," Max said, although Hailey knew exactly what he meant. That confirmed her suspicion that the kiddo must have superhero hearing, because Parker had whispered the word so softly that evening, no one should have been able to overhear.

"Carcinogen," Hailey whispered to Vern.

"But the waiver you signed relieves me of all liability."

"Nonsense." Vern took a huge bite and practically swallowed it whole. "The cholesterol will do ya in long before that. But carcinogen isn't technically correct. I believe the term would be…" Vern looked to the heavens for the answer. And his personal angel answered.

"Acrylamide," Sylvie said.

Vern pointed at her. "That's the one. Quite the scandal that something so tasty can be bad for us."

Sylvie nodded in agreement.

"Brains *and* beauty," he whispered to Hailey. Except his whispers were almost at normal volume. Judging by Sylvie's reserved smile, her hearing was just fine.

"You two are beginning to sound like Parks with your million-dollar words," Hailey said.

"I know a zillion-dollar word," Max said while peeling his sandwich apart, then attempting to lick the cheese off one side like an Oreo.

"Do tell," Hailey said.

"Nincompoop." Max giggled uncontrollably.

Hailey raised her hands as if she were about to tickle him, which made him twist and dodge.

"Oh! A word you just used, Vern, sparked

my memory about the rides. There was some kind of scandal," Sylvie said.

"I was thinking that perhaps someone got injured," Hailey said.

Sylvie shook her head. "No. I would remember something like that. This was more subtle. A family secret, I'm certain."

"Whose family?" Hailey asked.

"Why, yours, dear. But I can't remember what the scandal was about."

Hailey gulped. Scandal? Her family?

"Someone's gotta remember something," Vern interjected.

"I've asked everyone I know. Unfortunately, my grandparents didn't leave any clues. At least, none that are obvious." Except, she was still coming across surprises in that old house. Perhaps she'd unearth something eventually.

As they rode back, Sylvie and Max were inseparable, while Vern continued to play an enthusiastic third wheel. Once again, Hailey trailed behind. Alone. Until Vern held back and waited for her to catch up.

"You're awfully quiet," he said.

"I'm thinking about PJ and hoping he's okay. Oh, and how my sweet grandparents were involved in some sort of scandal that caused the downfall of a Destiny Springs tradition. No biggie."

"I can't speak to the latter, but PJ is doing better than ever, now that his mommy's home."

Vanessa's back? That meant that Parker was no longer on babysitting duty. That, and his work with her was done, which meant...

"Is Parker planning to leave early?" They hadn't said goodbye, and she hoped they'd get that closure. But after her rejection of his latest proposal, she wasn't sure where they stood. In retrospect, she might have sounded a little...mean. But the whole proposal not only reopened a wound, it doused rubbing alcohol all over it.

Vern shook his head. "I doubt it. Nash is in a world of hurt since his ranch hands haven't been around. Parker's helping with the girls and around the property."

"That's awfully nice of him," Hailey said.

"He's never shied away from helping people he cares about. That's how Parker is wired. Of course, he has selfish reasons. He's as crazy about Nash's girls as they are about him."

"He's helping with the ranch, as well?" Had she heard that correctly?

"That's what he says. I'd pitch in too, if I

didn't have my own ranch hand woes. I'm down to only Trent for the next week."

She tried to imagine Parker juggling two little girls for Nash while helping around the ranch. Ordinarily, she couldn't imagine anyone handling that much responsibility. Nash had done it for far too long, and it was clearly taking a toll.

Then again, not everyone was Superman, like Parker. Or Superwoman, whom Hailey should attempt to become and insist on taking care of the twins. She'd have to sacrifice her quiet home for a few hours, and she wouldn't be able to pursue any of the trail-ride business-development ideas that kept popping into her head. But she'd survive.

Next stop, Buck Stops.

CHAPTER FIFTEEN

ONE LOOK AT Parker helping Nash with a damaged fence while keeping the two little girls occupied convinced Hailey that this was the right decision, even though facing him felt awkward.

Parker wiped the sweat from his brow and walked over. Nash looked up and nodded but otherwise continued working.

Meanwhile, the girls had barely acknowledged her. They kept calling out for their uncle Parker to watch them swing from a tire that Nash had tied to a tree limb. *Uncle?* Which, of course, Parker couldn't do. He didn't have an eye in the back of his head. And he wasn't Superman after all. But he was something, all right.

Something she wasn't destined to have.

"Hey there," Parker said.

"Hey. I led a trail ride with Vern. He tells me Vanessa is back and that you were over here, helping Nash," she said.

Parker put his hands on his hips. "She came

back sooner than expected. Couldn't wait to get back to her son. Can't fault her for that." He glanced down at his boots, then back up. His eyes looked a certain way when he was disappointed. She could safely guess why. He'd had a lot of fun playing *Daddy* for a few days.

At least, that's what she hoped the sad eyes were about.

"Let me guess. You're here because you reconsidered PJ's proposal." Parker punctuated the statement with a deep-dimpled grin.

At that, Hailey breathed a shallow sigh of relief. Her meanness hadn't caused irreparable damage after all.

"He did make a compelling case. If I would have accepted, I would have gone with the blue paint that he recommended," she said.

"My preference, as well."

"The real reason I'm here is because I want to help. I can take the girls off yours and Nash's hands for a few hours. After all, Nash is practically a brother," she said, although she wasn't sure why she added that last part. Was she trying to convince Parker that she wasn't some awful, antifamily person after all?

"That's a kind offer. Let's ask their daddy." Parker took the lead as they approached Nash. "Hailey wants to talk to you about something."

Nash stopped tightening a wire and looked up. "Is that so? I assumed you were here to talk to my ranch hand."

That earned an appreciative smile from Parker and a nudge from her conscience that, yes, these two men had indeed formed a bond. Despite their differences.

Or perhaps because of them.

"Now that the formalities are out of the way, how do you feel about me kidnapping the girls for a while?" Hailey asked.

Parker nodded, but Nash seemed to have to think about it. And think...

Finally, he put one hand on his hip and rubbed his chin with the other. "Well, let's see. Alone, it would take me about twenty hours to finish up everything with the girls underfoot. But without 'em, and with Parker helping, I imagine it could take a good forty hours instead."

"Wise guy," Parker said. "We're only talking about a few doodads and thingamabobs and whatchamacallits that need fixing over yonder. With my help, I have zero doubt we could knock this out by Christmas."

Parker's self-deprecating humor was charming, she had to admit.

"If that's the case, maybe I should put in my order to Santa to bring a lock and chain so that

I can secure that gate. Over yonder. It refuses to hold a half hitch. Either that, or someone keeps messin' with it, which is my suspicion because it happened with other knots too. I'd rather not carry around a bunch of keys, but I may not have a choice," Nash said.

Hailey laughed, but Parker turned so serious.

"What other knots have you tried?" Parker asked.

"What haven't I tried, that would be the shorter list," Nash said.

"Which way is yonder? I'll take a look," Parker said.

Hailey and Nash exchanged a skeptical glance. Parker could be quite the tease, but not about this.

They walked several yards to where a rope hung loosely between the gate's frame and a post. Parker untied what was left of the existing knot, then played with it for a while, tugging it tight once it was complete.

Nash leaned in. "I'm not sure what you've done, but I know every kind of knot there is, and that isn't one of 'em."

Hailey didn't know as much about them as Nash did, but she tended to agree.

"Oh, it's a real knot," Parker said. "My yacht-manufacturing client invented it. Taught me how to tie it on one of those outings that everyone likes to tease me about. He's calling it the Annabella, after his only child. It's almost as tricky to untie as it is to tie, as you can probably see. But I'll show you how to do both before I leave. He's applied for a patent, so I'd appreciate it if we keep this between the three of us for now."

Nash shook the gate and moved it every which way, but the knot didn't loosen. Nor did it constrict. "Well, I'll be…"

Hailey inspected it, as well. She couldn't help but smile, and he caught her doing it.

Nash exhaled and looked out over the property. "I spotted a couple other areas of fence that need mending. We could get 'er done by tomorrow morning if we work till dusk and get up at first light. Providing the girls don't get underfoot."

"You'd like for me to keep them overnight?" She hadn't anticipated that.

Parker looked at her and seemed to be mulling it over. "Or, they could spend the night at Grandpa's. He'd love it. Maybe Hailey could take them for a few hours, and I can pick them up from her when we're done here. Then take them back in the morning."

She studied this man who stood in front of

her, getting his hands dirty and putting his own career on the back burner to help a friend in need. He could be on his way to Chicago by now. She should rise to the occasion, as well. Help out these two hardworkin' cowboys.

Hailey called out to Lizzy and Kat. "Girls! Come here, please." They dropped what they were doing and ran over. "How would you like to have a slumber party at my house, and I'll bring you back in the morning?"

They didn't seem too excited. In fact, they moved closer to Parker, as if that's where they'd rather spend their time. Even Nash didn't come first anymore.

"We'll dress up. Y'all can take turns being Cinderella. And I have some new jewelry for you to play with too." Hailey covered the horse-hair bracelet. *Except for this.* Georgina had left plenty of other pieces behind specifically for the twins.

The lure of baubles captured their interest.

"Go pack your overnight cases," Nash said. And that was all the additional nudging it took.

Parker leaned in. "Thank you for doing this."

Hailey nodded, then went inside and helped the twins. Once done, they rejoined Nash and Parker outside, colorful cases in hand.

"Will you come visit?" Kat asked Parker.

It struck Hailey as so very precious that they didn't want to spend so much as a night away from him. Did they realize he'd be leaving soon?

"If your dad and I make good progress here, I will," Parker said.

"Can we make cupcakes tonight, Miss Hailey?" Kat asked.

"Absolutely. From scratch," she said without hesitating, even though she should have. Box mixes were her go-to. Making cupcakes from scratch was unheard-of in her house.

Hailey left Nash's ranch with more than she bargained for. Now she had another big decision. Whether to call Georgina for a lifeline on making cupcakes.

Then again... *Naw. You've got this, Hailey.*

However, she'd welcome a lifeline for a much bigger issue. Those pesky feelings she still had for Parks.

PARKER BLINKED. HARD. It was dark, but that sure looked like Vern carrying Sylvie over the threshold of the man's home. He knew his grandpa had fallen in love at first sight, but Sylvie seemed more sensible than to take things that fast. Had they gone to the justice of the peace after the trail ride without telling anyone?

He wasn't sure how to feel, except perhaps a bit envious at the romantic impulsiveness.

After a few moments, he decided to go inside and hopefully not interrupt Vern and Sylvie sharing a tender moment. Thankfully, Sylvie was sitting on the couch. More like lying back. Vern could be heard rummaging around the kitchen.

"I guess congratulations are in order," Parker said. As he got closer, it occurred to him that she wasn't dressed for even an informal ceremony. And her ring finger was bare. Then again, knowing Vern, she'd soon be sporting a nice one.

Sylvie shot him a glance that would have knocked a lesser guy flat on his back.

Vern shuffled into the living area with a glass of ice water and a heating pad, which he promptly plugged in.

"Can you run upstairs and get some of those extra-soft feather pillows from the guest bed?" Vern asked.

That's when the whole thing became clear. Took a little too long. His hands-on cowboy duties had made him a little rusty on adding two plus two.

"Sure thing." He raced up the stairs and passed PJ's room on the way, but it was empty.

He grabbed the softest pillows he could find, hurried back downstairs and helped Vern reposition Sylvie.

"Thanks, gentlemen," she said. "You don't have to dote on me anymore. I'll be fine."

Vern shook his head when she wasn't looking, thus disputing her claim.

"What happened?" Parker asked.

"I threw out my back," she said.

"On the trail ride?" Parker asked, although surely Hailey would have said something.

"No. She wanted to ride Sally after we got back from the trails," Vern said.

"Is that one of your horses?" Parker asked, a little ashamed that he hadn't bothered learning their names.

"She's my mechanical bull. The one Cody Sayers practiced on not that long ago for the national championship. Sylvie raised a bull rider and was a little curious. She charmed me into letting her go for a spin on the lowest setting."

"I have a newfound respect for the sport," Sylvie said. "I keep forgetting I'm seventy-four, and perhaps my reflexes aren't what they used to be. Speaking of which, I better get on the website and reschedule any bookings for the next few days unless Cody can take over."

Hailey. This could turn out to be a lengthy setback.

"I'll take care of the bookings," Parker said. "Your only job is to recover."

"Doctor at the clinic told her not to drive under any circumstances. Gave her some strong stuff to knock out the pain and likely knock her out, as well. Should be kicking in any second. Vanessa went to pick up PJ from his playdate with Max. They'll be back soon."

"If you think Vern is spoiling you, wait until you get into Vanessa's grip," Parker said.

Vern plumped another pillow and placed it behind her head. "I'm insisting Sylvie stay here tonight in case she needs any help."

"I don't want to be any bother to anyone. Besides, Vanessa doesn't even know me."

"Now, don't you worry. My granddaughter is a professional caretaker. I spoke with her while you were on the slab in the clinic, and she insists on helping."

Vern retrieved his favorite throw blanket from his recliner and draped it over Sylvie's legs. She was now having trouble keeping her eyes open. He threw some more wood on the fire and stoked it.

"When I first saw you carrying Sylvie over

the threshold, I thought you two had gotten hitched," Parker said.

"Trust me, if that would have happened, I would have taken her someplace a lot nicer than this for a honeymoon. But I have to confess, on the trail ride it did cross my mind to suggest that we keep riding until we found a chapel. But I'd want her to have whatever kind of ceremony she wants."

That reminded Parker of Hailey's comment about getting married at a Las Vegas drive-through chapel, with Elvis presiding. He never thought he'd admit it—even privately to himself as he was doing now—but that sounded much more fun than a royal wedding.

"That's…that's…" Sylvie mumbled as she struggled to open her eyelids. "Call…what's her name?"

"That's what?" Parker asked anyway. *And who's what's-her-name?*

"Got marrrrr'd," Sylvie added.

"No, pretty lady. We didn't get married and you're in no condition to call anyone. Try to get some rest." Vern turned to Parker and lowered his voice. "They said that painkiller was heavy-duty. They weren't kidding. I'll need to keep an eye on her—she's strong and stubborn. Might try to do something she's not supposed to do. Like your Hailey."

"Except, unlike me and *my* Hailey, you and *your* Sylvie have a lot in common. Cut from the same cloth. Isn't that the saying?"

"People can be cut from the same cloth but still come out different in the wash that life puts us all through. You, for instance," Vern said.

"How do you mean?"

"You've changed since coming here. Especially in the last week or so. If I didn't know better, I'd think you were a real cowboy."

Sylvie interjected with a slight snore that sounded kind of like a snort.

Vern nodded and led them down the hall, past the shelves stuffed with old albums and the dusty old turntable. Yet another reminder of *his* Hailey.

"So what's all this about you two kids not having anything in common?" Vern asked. "I see the way you two gaze at each other when you think the other isn't looking."

"That's not enough to make a relationship last. We're not on the same page about pretty much everything."

"Such as?"

"Financial stability. It's well documented that

money differences cause major problems in a marriage. Including divorce."

"Only if one or both parties value money *more* than the relationship. Next excuse."

That was an oversimplification, but it did make him think. Still, it wasn't an excuse. If anything, he was looking for a solid excuse as to why it *could* work with her.

"It is important if you want to have children. I'm not sure she even wants those either. And that's a huge issue for me, as you know," Parker said. Let Vern try to oversimplify *that* one.

"I see your point. Maybe she's been too busy with Sunrise Stables to give it serious thought. But that would be a gamble for you."

"Exactly," Parker said. He, for one, had given it plenty of thought. Couldn't imagine growing old without experiencing fatherhood. And grandfatherhood. Great-grandfatherhood, if he's lucky. But these feelings he'd been having for Hailey? Couldn't imagine growing old without her either.

"However, young man, the part about financial stability being important if you want kids is nonsense," Vern said.

"Felt pretty important when Mom and I didn't have it."

"There's a big difference between important and *most* important. A wise man chooses wisely."

Hailey's words came to mind. *Which one would you choose?*

Since everything else failed to produce any clarity, there was one other thing he might as well point out. "She likes bluegrass. I like opera. I rest my case."

Vern gave him a long look, then held up one finger. "This might take a while, but you stay right here. I'll be back."

"Good idea. Check on *your* Sylvie."

"Eventually. But first, I'm gonna prove you wrong."

"I'm betting you can't."

"You're on. If I win, I have your permission to play that goat movie for Sylvie when she comes to. That'll cheer her up."

"And if *I* win, you're gonna delete the video and never mention it again," Parker said. Did he really say *gonna*?

"You're on," Vern said.

"I'll take care of the bookings while you're wasting your time."

He didn't know how Vern intended to prove anything. He and Hailey had already exhausted the possibilities.

Parker retrieved his laptop from his room.

Sure enough, Sylvie had a large party booked for tomorrow afternoon. A family: two adults, four children. Yikes. But two other adults would be on the ride. Hadn't the child-to-adult ratio been the issue? Hailey was perfectly fine with Max riding again. It seemed as though she'd crossed back over that threshold that PJ's accident pushed her over. Besides, the trail rides were about to officially launch. All eyes were on her business. A cancellation wouldn't look good.

Speaking of thresholds, he kept envisioning carrying Hailey over a whole other kind of threshold someday. Seeing Vern carrying Sylvie had put that romantic notion in his head.

Cody was an option. Parker texted him to ask if he was available to fill in. But the cowboy's response was as swift and blunt as Hailey's rejection. Not available to lead tomorrow, but can help get horses ready.

Parker left the reservation as it was but changed the lead to Hailey. In the notes section, he explained that Sylvie was down until her back healed and that he and Hailey would discuss it further. He also warned her that he had one more proposal. One that couldn't wait another day. He was running out of time, but not on winning the promotion. Rather, on winning her.

As he was texting Hailey to give her a heads-up that he'd be stopping by tonight and to check the website, Vern came back in and handed him an old album. "Give this to Hailey, even though it's a gift for both of you."

Parker stared at the cover and smiled. He'd lost the bet with Vern, that was for sure. His terrified mug would soon be splashed across the big screen for Sylvie's viewing pleasure. And it was totally worth it.

Or, at least he hoped it would be.

CHAPTER SIXTEEN

HAILEY SCOOPED A very sleepy Kat Buchanan off the sofa and balanced her on her hip, then took Lizzy's hand and together they walked to the bathroom. Hailey put toothpaste on their respective toothbrushes.

"Y'all know what to do. Brush them fangs," she said.

From there, she made sure they changed into their nightgowns, then tucked them into the guest bed and gave each a kiss on the forehead. She imagined Nash putting them to bed that way at night. That's what her own father did when she was their age.

She flipped the switch on Max's animated-stars night-light, leaned against the doorframe and stayed put until the girls fell asleep.

Parker had texted that he'd be stopping by and to check the Sunrise Stables booking site, which was strange. Maybe he booked himself for a trial ride tomorrow, but that didn't sound right. He'd committed to helping Nash.

She hated that he was going to see her like this. Bone-tired. Kitchen in disarray from making and decorating cupcakes with the girls. Still, no regrets. She'd be returning the twins to their daddy in the morning. After that, she'd finally be able to breathe.

Lately, it seemed she couldn't take a breath without thinking of Parker and what the future could possibly hold. Even though they'd grown close, there was so much space between them. And that space was about to grow miles longer. Then there was Sunrise Stables. It was part of her family's legacy and was in her blood. She had to suffer some proverbial cuts to be able to see it. Furthermore, she was the only living Goodwin who cared enough to save it. Now, she not only cared, she felt overprotective of it—a trait she must have inherited.

By contrast, everything Parker had worked so hard to achieve was in Chicago. Funny, but the only common ground they seemed to share wasn't even on the ground—it was in the stars.

Hailey eyed Parker's first barn-razing proposal on a side table. He'd likely put a lot of effort into it, knowing him the way she did now. She collected the envelope, sat on the sofa and pulled out the paperwork. Clipped on top, his business card. *Mason, Shumway and Pinkerton Consulting. Parker Donnelly, Junior Consultant.* Plus his cell phone, direct line and company email, printed on clean white stock, with small black type and plenty of open space. Impressive.

She'd never been in a job that required a business card but always thought how cool it would be to have one. It would read, *Sunrise Stables. Hailey Goodwin, Owner.* The thought alone filled her with pride. Yes, she'd have some made for launch week.

The papers themselves were heavy with detail. Terms like footing options, insulation and ventilation, and structure costs based on different scenarios and materials. He'd included market research. Who offered what types of horseback riding and training within a specified radius, amount they charged, and how she could be competitive.

She sat up straighter as she dove deep into the numbers, trying to make sense of them and succeeding at times. Not agreeing with the destination but now having a full respect for the journey.

What time was it anyway?

She logged on to the site, and that's when she

realized why he'd asked her to check it. Sylvie hurt her back. When had that happened, and how? And Parker had transferred tomorrow's ride to Hailey as lead. He knew she didn't want to be put in that position.

Then there was the obvious thing: he no longer worked for Sunrise Stables. On top of that, he had another proposal to talk to her about. All with the added note that they would discuss everything when he arrived.

There was nothing to discuss. It was like every other situation in her life. Well-intentioned people thinking they knew what was best for her instead of listening to what she wanted and respecting that. It was as if she were a child all over again.

But she wasn't a child. Not anymore. This was her business, her rules.

To think she was entertaining the thought, mere moments ago, that somehow this could work out with Parker. He seemed to have changed so much over the past week and a half. Even becoming the cowboy she thought would be right for her. But with Parker, it always came down to the numbers. Not that she faulted him for it. He was a good man.

Just not a good man for her.

PARKER'S HANDS WERE TREMBLING. That was a first.

Even though it was awkward, he held the oversize envelope behind his back. Inside were two gifts, both wrapped in some lovely paper his grandpa had on hand. But this was a proposal, and he wanted it to look like one. Not a *will you marry me* proposal, but a big step in that direction. He, for one, did *not* want this to end with him getting on a plane.

He wasn't sure how this could ever work out, but he knew deep in the marrow of his bones that it somehow could. Asking her to come to Chicago was reaching for those stars they both admired. Yet, wonderful things happened to those who dared to try. She didn't want to further develop her property. She still seemed content on simply getting by. Which kept him wondering: Was she even happy here?

But as soon as she opened the door and he saw the sadness in her eyes, he knew he'd made at least one miscalculation. His gut had warned him about changing her to the lead, but he stubbornly ignored it.

He followed her inside and set the envelope on the dining table. The timing was already off for that.

Sergeant was immediately at Parker's feet.

He stood on his hind legs, jonesing to be held. Reminding Parker that he'd forgotten to take a pill before he came over. That wasn't going to stop him from getting at least one hug. He picked up the feline, who put his paws around Parker's neck and commenced purring.

"I'm guessing you checked the site. I wanted to discuss it with you," he said.

"Asking me first would have been the better decision."

"I know. I'm sorry. I was wrong to do that. My first instinct was to protect your business. It's too close to your launch date to get a bad review or negative publicity because of a cancellation. That's all."

She looked at him for an extended moment, then nodded. "Apology accepted. And I understand your reasoning. It's your first instinct I'm struggling with."

He started to approach her, but she crossed her arms.

"Cody couldn't take the lead. I checked with him first. If you don't want to do this, then cancel. Or I can go back in and cancel it."

"I'm considering that option."

"Just please don't cancel us," he said, because it sure felt like that's what was happening.

Silence.

"Hailey—"

"Parks. You're right. This *is* about us. We don't want the same things. If anything, we've been on different paths our whole lives."

"We can choose one path and see where it leads. I want to see us take that risk, so I'm just going to say what's been on my mind. I want you to come to Chicago."

"Chicago?"

"Yes. Check it out. If you want to stay, we can take the next step."

"As in, marriage?"

"Yes," he confirmed. Although this wasn't the way he'd wanted to introduce the topic. Far from it. But he'd started this. He had to follow through.

"A royal wedding," she said.

"You sold me on Vegas," he answered.

"Six children. Someday."

"Whatever number and timing you and I agree on."

"I can't have children, Parks. It's physically impossible."

What? It took a moment to process what she was saying. The pain in her eyes confirmed his interpretation without him needing any specifics. But this wasn't anything to cry about. The solution was easy. In fact, he'd always thought it was a beautiful option.

"We'll adopt," he said.

"That wouldn't be fair to you, just as it wasn't fair to my former fiancé. And I know this because that's why he left me standing alone at the altar. Let's spare us both a lot of grief and not take it that far. Please."

"I'll decide what's fair to me. I don't care where our children come from, just that I get to be their dad."

She bit her lip as her eyes dampened. He struggled not to do the same. What else could he offer her, except...*everything*?

"I have a lucrative job in Chicago, Hailey. I'll take care of the finances. The bills. Anything you need. All I ask is that you do the cooking. What do you say?"

She looked at the floor for several seconds, then looked back up.

"Here's the truth. I don't need someone to take care of me. Not in the way you described. I've built something here that's mine, and that I can be proud of. And I have you to thank for it. I've started looking at my business in a different way. I'm excited about helping it thrive."

"And I couldn't be happier for you. You did it," he managed to say.

She bit her bottom lip, looked away and wiped at a tear that had rolled down her cheek. "I love you, Parker Donnelly. As a business partner. As a friend. As someone who changed my life. But…"

He closed his eyes and braced his heart for the three words he didn't want to hear.

"I say Wyoming."

The long silence that followed felt like a weighted blanket, so heavy he had no idea how he could ever crawl out from under it. This was what he wanted in the first place, wasn't it? He simply hadn't foreseen that it was going to cost him…*her*.

He unhooked Sergeant from his shirt and set him on the floor. He never would've thought he'd get so attached to a silly cat in such a short time, but he had. He'd gotten attached to too many things and too many people here.

"There is one thing we agree on," she finally said, adding a bittersweet laugh that did little to soothe his broken heart. "Opera and bluegrass will never mix."

He was about to say he disagreed, but this was never about their differences in music.

Instead, he closed the distance between them and gave her a tender kiss on the cheek like she'd done for him twenty years ago. Her sharp inhale suggested there still might be some hope, although there was a chance he was misreading it. He'd misread so many things.

As he left and closed the door behind him, he was consoled by one thing: neither had said goodbye.

CHAPTER SEVENTEEN

THERE WASN'T ENOUGH concealer in the world to cover up the pain, Hailey concluded. But she did the best she could to patch herself up after a long, restless night of wondering whether she'd made the right decision. Especially after all of the beautiful things he said.

That kiss on the cheek? It might as well have been a dagger to the heart. His impulsive suggestion to adopt, the final twist. In the moment, he probably believed what he said. Her ex-fiancé had too. Until it was time to commit to a lifetime with her.

She returned to the kitchen where the twins were busy eating Pop-Tarts in their un-twin-like ways. The proposal that Parker had brought remained on the table. Looked as though he'd gone to great lengths, once again, considering the size. She could either throw it away or ask Parker to come over and pick it up if he wanted it back. But seeing him again would only make this whole thing more difficult.

Chicago? Did he really think that was a possibility?

Then it occurred to her. His mom lived there, and she was still recovering from cancer. He didn't remind her of that fact, but he shouldn't have needed to. At least now it made a little more sense. It also made her feel more than a little awful.

She went to the guest room and packed the girls' overnight cases and brought them to the den. They had already positioned the footstool and were washing their hands. When had they become so self-sufficient?

"Ready to go see your daddy?" she asked once they were finished with their task.

"Yes!" they cried in twin-like unison. It both warmed her heart and strangely hurt that they were so eager to get away from her.

She shook off the feeling and instead tried to imagine that lovely bubble bath she'd soon be enjoying in her quiet house.

"Let's go," she said, handing each case to its respective owner and getting everyone and everything loaded in her truck and on the road.

Lizzy and Kat practically jumped out of their car seats as she rolled to a stop. Nash was standing on the porch as if he'd been waiting there for hours. The girls nearly knocked him down in the process of collecting a hug. But he didn't seem to mind. In fact, she rarely saw Nash smile that big. Looked like the poor guy finally got some sleep.

She walked toward the three of them, feeling like a fifth wheel when there clearly wasn't even a fourth on this particular wagon.

"Thanks a million, Hailey. I hope they weren't too much trouble."

In thinking about it, they'd been no trouble at all. Making cupcakes with the girls had been a blast. Furthermore, the treats had turned out perfect the first time.

"They were a joy," she said.

He rolled his eyes, obviously mimicking her signature move. Not that she blamed him for being skeptical. But this time, she wasn't kidding. Maybe the moments simply seemed happy and effortless when juxtaposed against what happened after she'd tucked the girls into bed and Parker came over. When her entire world came untied.

"Go inside and unpack your things," he instructed while staying behind.

Hailey leaned against a column and tucked her hands in her front pockets.

"You and Parker have a few things to work out," he said.

"Is that what he told you?"

Nash shook his head. "He didn't say anything. But those puffy red eyes of yours sure do tell a story."

She hadn't imagined it. The concealer did nothing to hide it. "We've reached an understanding. No further working out is required."

"He stopped by late last night to say his goodbyes. Was gonna try to catch an early flight out. Looked like the life had been drained from him."

"It wasn't my best night either, but breakups are never easy. Not that we were ever a couple."

"Glad to hear it," Nash said.

"Excuse me? You're glad I had a lousy night, or that we were never a couple?"

"That you still have feelings for him."

"Thanks, *brother*. Good to know you take pleasure in my pain. If you enjoyed that, I can share some other stories that will both amuse and delight you."

"I take no pleasure. But you're not the only one hurting."

"We made the only decision we could make, Nash."

He crossed his arms and shook his head, as if he was now taking sides. And not hers. She almost turned to leave, but she'd already lost one important person in her life. She didn't want to alienate another.

Instead, she matched his gesture. "You want to say something, I can tell."

"I do, but I'd be violating a confidence if I told you Parker was terrified of riding horses, as of several days ago. Afraid of hurting his back after having spent his whole childhood getting it straightened out. He asked me to give him horseback riding lessons to impress you. But you didn't hear it from me."

She remembered that first ride. How nervous he was, but also how he did a commendable job.

"I figured someone gave him some pointers."

"And it probably wouldn't impress you to know that the man took allergy medicine so he could be around Sergeant without puffing up like a blowfish. Isn't even worth mentioning that he adores that cat, even though he's a dog person."

"Sergeant adores him too." That was an understatement.

He took pills?

"Anything else you aren't gonna tell me?" she asked.

"Can't think of a thing, except he did mention he was up for a partnership at his firm. The only thing missing was some proposal or such and such they were asking for. But he wasn't gonna give 'em one that the client wasn't one hundred percent happy with. The man can be his own worst enemy sometimes. But what integrity and heart. I'm still in awe of that knot. He's sure full of surprises, isn't he?"

He sure was. Couldn't argue with any of it. She thought about the envelope he'd left behind. It had been one of the surprises he'd wanted to talk about when he came over, but they didn't get that far.

Nor would she have let it. She'd specifically said no more proposals. Maybe if he'd been upfront about needing it and why, rather than saying that he only wanted what was best for her, things could have turned out differently.

Then again, they couldn't have. If she'd known, she would have agreed to one of his proposals, in theory, and he could have gotten the partnership, which would have put them in the same place they were now. The place they were destined to be.

Apart.

HAILEY COULD SWEAR the goats were bleating "Ave Maria."

That's what she got for playing her grandparents' albums. Was that a wedding song or a funeral dirge? She couldn't remember. Today, the two types of events felt interchangeable.

This barn and these goats had always been the surefire way to de-stress, but it wasn't working today. The family would be there in a few hours for their afternoon trail ride, and she'd yet to make a decision about whether to cancel.

"Do you kids mind singing something else?" Hailey called out to the goats. "Anything except 'My Heart Will Go On.'"

She transitioned from the cobra to the downward dog position, imagining the tension draining from her body as she visualized getting through the trail ride without some sort of disaster, then retreating to her house, locking the doors and drawing the most luxurious bubble bath ever. It wasn't working yet, but she still had a few hours of alone time.

At least, she thought she had the time. The familiar sound of the sliding barn door filled her with dread.

Fortunately, or perhaps unfortunately, it was Georgina. Holding a large paper sack.

"How did you find me?" Hailey asked without bothering to stand.

"When you didn't answer the door, I figured

you were out here. It always was your favorite hiding place."

Hailey broke position and stood. Her safe place didn't feel so safe anymore. "You knew I used to come out here?"

"Of course! We all knew. We also knew you needed to be alone, so we never bothered you."

"News flash. It's still my favorite hiding place. Maybe we can go back to pretending that you don't know." Although that wasn't exactly true. Ever since learning of the barn's history, every time she walked into it, she was surrounded by the ghosts of happy couples and weddings and celebrations.

"What have you got there?" Hailey asked. Might as well move this conversation along.

"Sandwiches and snacks for your afternoon trail ride. Becca helped. The family is staying at the Hideaway. This ride is all they can talk about."

Hailey had a sudden rush of nostalgia for her job at the B and B. Georgina was temporarily living Hailey's old life, complete with built-in best friend. In fact, she and Becca had barely spoken the last few days, which was unusual.

"That's nice of you to make these," Hailey said, stopping short of pointing out that she was perfectly capable of making sandwiches herself. She didn't need to argue the point or prove anything to anyone. She'd proven it to herself.

Georgina set the paper bag on a bench. "Mind if I join you?"

"Not at all." *Maybe a little.* Hailey got up and retrieved another mat.

Georgina took a seat. The goats began jumping around and brushing against her. She started laughing her trademark choppy laugh. Hailey hadn't heard it in years. And she just realized how much she missed it.

"Do you want the full experience?" Hailey asked.

"I'm not sure. I saw what happened to Parker in that video. Oh my goodness, that expression! *Ahhhh!*" Georgina tried to mimic the look of sheer terror on Parker's face and did a decent job of capturing it.

Giggles bubbled up in Hailey's throat.

"It's my Parker face. *Ahhhh!*" Georgina screamed out again, this time with eyes opened so wide it looked painful.

That did it. Hailey couldn't have stopped laughing if she'd wanted to. *They* couldn't stop. So intense that the tears flowed again, only these were the good kind. She didn't even care that all the concealer she'd piled back on to cover the redness was now washed away.

She finally stopped laughing and caught her breath, but the moment she looked at Georgina, it started all over again.

When had they lost *this*? The ability to have fun together?

Both exhausted, they laid on the mats. Thankfully, the goats had since become bored with the Goodwin sisters' private joke and were playing among themselves in a corner of the pen. Hailey wiped away the residual tears with the back of her hand.

"You have what's called an infectious laugh, Georgy Girl," Hailey admitted.

Her sister looked stunned. "What did you call me?"

Hailey had to think about it. *Georgy Girl.*

Georgina looked up to the ceiling. "You haven't called me that since you were little. I've wanted that nickname back for so long. You only hand them out to people who are on your good side."

"So I've been told," Hailey said.

"Does that mean I'm back there?"

"You were never on my bad side. You're just much more of a sophisticated Georgina than a quirky Georgy Girl."

Her sister looked at her. "Nice try, but I'll take it. You can't say my laugh isn't quirky. I inherited it from Dad. Remember his?"

She'd never forget it, although his laugh sounded much less like a jackhammer than hers.

"You were his favorite, you know," Georgina said.

"That's because he wanted a son, and I was the closest thing he was ever going to get."

"Oh, he wanted a son, all right. Wanted to name him George. Then I had to go ruin it for him. But he exacted his revenge. Named me Georgina."

"It's a beautiful name for a beautiful person. Inside and out," Hailey said.

Georgina and Hailey looked at each other. Really looked. Ordinarily, one or the other would turn away.

"Don't forget, he picked out my middle name. Alexandra. Alex, for short," Hailey said. "Maybe they should have adopted a son instead of having me."

"I'm quite sure they're glad they got Hailey Alexandra instead. Dad always bragged about you. How competent and brave you were to ride horses at such a young age. Honestly, I was a bit jealous. He always insisted you were the inspiration for that saying about falling off a horse and getting right back on."

"I remember." That feeling of hitting the

ground and, at times, breaking a bone. And the pure healing power of getting right back up again.

"You were probably too young to remember, but I wanted to be a professional barrel racer when I grew up," Georgina said. "Took a few lessons, but Mom freaked out, so I quit."

She looked to her sister. "That's awful. I never knew that." Although, after caring for children and with what PJ went through, she could finally relate to what her mom must have felt. Still feels, if her overprotectiveness was any indication.

"I admire you for exploring a new trail. Pun intended," Georgina said. "Forget barrel racing. I want to be like you when I grow up."

Hailey's breath caught in her throat. Georgina sure didn't look like she was joking.

"Thanks. I needed to hear that." *More than you'll ever know.*

"Hey, what's under that tarp?" Georgina pointed to the far corner of the barn.

"Who knows? I'm behind on going through Grandma and Grandpa's things."

Georgina walked over and lifted the edge. Looked like some sort of huge, antique candelabra. "That is gorgeous! You should hang it," she said, leaving it uncovered but returning to the yoga mat.

"Our great-grandparents hosted weddings in this barn. That's probably what it was used for."

"Mom and Dad brought me here to watch Grandma and Grandpa renew their vows. Her folks had already passed, though. I was too young to remember much. And I don't recall this piece. But Mom took pictures."

Funny, but Hailey remembered those pictures. Mostly close-ups. She never realized it had taken place in this barn.

Georgina cleared her throat. "Speaking of weddings… I've worried nonstop about what happened between you and me."

"I know," Hailey said.

"I'm sorry—"

"You did what you thought was best. You're a wedding planner, for goodness' sake. And it would have been the event of the century."

"But it wasn't what you wanted."

Hailey couldn't deny it. But it was what everyone else wanted. The hand-sewn dress from the top designer in Vienna. The guest list that stretched for miles. Then there was the woman who would've been her mother-in-law, footing the bill. She never did approve of Hailey, so she was probably thrilled when her son was a no-show at the altar.

She looked at her sister, who was wiping away a fresh tear.

"Ancient history, Georgy Girl."

There was a new unwanted thing Hailey had to face. She needed to start preparing to lead the ride, or to cancel it. Parker had chosen the direction he thought would be best for Hailey's business over what was best for Hailey, personally. He also made an excellent point. One, as a business owner, she'd be wise to consider.

Canceling the family's ride could impact the business with any negative publicity if it got around. Going through with it would be detrimental to the launch, should something bad occur.

But the final decision was hers. There was awesome power in that, but also tremendous responsibility. She still wasn't sure what the best decision should be.

Not only for the trail ride, but for the rest of her life.

CHAPTER EIGHTEEN

"WHAT DO YOU think you're doing?" Cody asked as Hailey eased the saddle from his hands.

"I'm putting this back. The trail ride is canceled."

"Says who?"

"Says Pumpkin. Trust her on this."

He tried to reclaim the tack, but she held tight. The whole thing turned into a tug of war.

Max ran over and chimed in. "I wanna play!"

Hailey relinquished her grip. "You win. For the moment. But only because I'm still undecided."

She turned to Max. "How about playing with the goats today?"

"But we're riding horses," Max said.

"Sorry, kiddo. I don't have enough for you to come along." She looked at Cody. "I should have told you that earlier. You could have left Max at home with Becca."

Max dropped his chin.

Being the bearer of bad news was no fun.

Cody knelt to his son's level. "This is great news, because PJ and Sylvie could both use some cheering up and would love to hear your latest theory about the trail rides." Cody looked up to her. "I think this is Max's best one yet."

"I want to hear it too. Can you give me a hint?" Hailey hoped to win some points back with her favorite kiddo. Plus his stories were usually summed up in a sentence, with the remainder of the time dedicated to Q and A.

"Okey dokey. Romeo and Jullet rode the horses last."

"Tell her what happened after that," Cody said.

"They got married," Max said with the biggest grin.

That was an interesting twist on a Shakespearean classic. He must have remembered Romeo and Juliet from the dinner conversation the other night. She didn't want to be the one to tell Max the truth about those two lovebirds. Let him enjoy his innocence while he could.

"Go say hi to the goats, cowboy," Cody said. "I'll join you in a few, and then we'll head over to Vern's."

"Don't go inside the pen until your daddy gets there," she added.

Max turned and ran toward his second-favorite activity at Hailey's place.

"So, are you riding or not?" Cody asked as a minivan pulled into the drive. Two young girls and two younger boys jumped out of the vehicle, followed by their parents.

"Ask me in a few minutes." Hailey walked toward the group. All were Western appropriate, except for one little boy who was wearing a bow tie. His mom was holding his hand.

"You must be Hailey," she said. "This is Tommy. He's so excited that he insisted on getting all dressed up."

Cody joined them, most likely to play devil's advocate in case Hailey wavered.

"And this is Cody Sayers," Hailey said. "Bull rider extraordinaire, legendary Rodeo Rascal and now copartner for Sunrise Stables."

"Yes, of course! Will you be going on the ride, as well?" the lady asked.

"No, ma'am. But you're in excellent hands. The best," he said.

"My husband will be disappointed. He's a big fan of yours and quite the equestrian himself. We've seen you around the Hideaway but didn't want to bother you."

"Please, bother me anytime. Hailey does," he said with a wink.

"I can vouch for that," she added, even though it took everything she had to muster the energy to be remotely playful.

"I'll say hello to your husband, and then we'll get the rest of your family paired up with the horses." He turned to Hailey. "Before I forget, Becca's stopping by after you get back from the ride. She wants to talk to you about something important but doesn't want to do it over the phone." He tipped his hat and turned on his heel.

Hailey would have given him grief about leaving her hanging if others weren't around.

"Nice man," the woman said as Cody walked away.

"I couldn't manage Sunrise Stables without him." Although she pretty much had.

Hailey looked over to the doting father and imagined that was how Parker would be—*will be*. As she envisioned how that would look, a mix of envy and regret washed over her.

Cody rounded up everyone while Hailey went back inside the house to retrieve the lunch items that Georgina brought. By the time she returned, Cody had managed to get all the riders matched and mounted.

She and Bad Boy took the lead, while the father rode in the back. The steady gait of the horses gave Hailey a sense of peace. She didn't do any talking as they ventured through the open trails and through grassy meadows, but she didn't need to. The parents and children largely talked among themselves. Joking around. Laughing. For the first time since the reboot, she felt like an outsider.

For the entirety of the ride, Hailey remained hypervigilant about keeping the entire family safe. And she did. No falls, no broken bones. Nothing had happened except a lovely family enjoying a beautiful day. She'd made the right decision—for her business, and herself.

When her house came back into view, something else did, as well. Vern, Sylvie and Max were waiting.

Sylvie was sitting in a folding chair, while Vern had one hand resting on her shoulder. Max was jumping up and down and waving his arms. The whole thing was odd.

Cody was there too. He jogged over to greet the group. "I'll take care of the clients and horses. Go," he said, nodding toward her surprise guests.

Sylvie was obviously uncomfortable, which meant Hailey should keep leading the rides for a while. And that was surprisingly okay.

More than okay. During the ride, while she

soaked in the beautiful Wyoming scenery, she thought about how there were only three trail-ride openings left for launch week. Then she thought about how she'd given Parker grief, at the beginning, about booking family members to fill empty openings. If he were here, would he give her grief for doing the same thing?

Her mom and sisters would enjoy these views. Furthermore, she wanted to be the one to lead them. If the B and B had any rooms, she'd reserve those, as well. Her mom and Faye had been angling to come to Destiny Springs to check on her. Maybe it's time they did. Even if this didn't end up being enough to convince them that she's all grown up and doing just fine, that would be okay too. She was convinced, and that was all that mattered.

Once she reached Sylvie, she had to state the obvious. "You should be at home, resting your back."

"Some things are more important than rest. Like what I'm about to tell you. I remember something about why the trail rides ended," Sylvie said. "In fact, thanks to Max, I remember everything."

CHAPTER NINETEEN

THE DOOR TO the modest one-story house swung open before Parker had a chance to knock, even though he had a key. He didn't want to startle his mom since he'd withheld the specifics regarding his arrival day and time.

Not that she was even around enough to get the message. Still, he wanted a raw, honest look at her. If Julianne knew when he'd be there, she would try to camouflage any physical clues of illness.

But this version of her, he barely recognized.

She apparently had trouble recognizing him, as well, because it took her a few seconds. The moment it sank in that the man in cowboy boots and a Stetson was her son, she couldn't pull him in close enough.

They took a couple of steps back to look at each other. Gone were her comfy warm-up suits and practical shoes. In front of him, a refreshed-looking woman in a lovely casual dress and heels. "What have you done with my mom?"

"I was wondering the same about you. Don't just stand there, come inside. It's probably a good thing you didn't let yourself in. I would've thought you were an intruder!"

"I would've thought the same of you. I don't want to keep you from wherever you were headed. I should have let you know, but—"

"You wanted to check on me."

"Guilty."

"I was about to run to the drugstore for some lipstick, but that can wait." She hurried toward the kitchen where she rummaged around the refrigerator and pulled out all sorts of food items. That was what she always did. Made sure he was fed. There had been such scarcity during his youth that she now went overboard.

"Does any of this look good? I can warm up some pot roast for you, or I can heat up this baked potato and pile on the butter and cheese and bacon bits. Oh, and I have half a Porterhouse leftover from last night. It's from your favorite steakhouse."

Which would you choose?

Parker walked to the pantry, pulled out a can of Campbell's Chicken Noodle soup instead and handed it to her. Not that he couldn't have warmed it up himself, but the little boy in him yearned for her to fix it. After all, he was in a lot of pain.

"Are you sure?" she asked.

"More than anything. Soothes the common cold. And the broken heart."

That elicited a look of concern he'd never seen. Not even when he was confined to that body brace. Or when the doctor told her that she had breast cancer.

"Does it have anything to do with that precious yoga gal?"

"What yoga gal?"

"The one with the goats. Vern sent me the video. You looked very handsome, by the way." She opened the can, poured the contents into a saucepan and added water.

"Only a mom would think that. I felt like Edvard Munch's *The Scream*. But, yes, you are correct. And the yoga gal is Hailey Goodwin. Not sure whether you remember her."

His mom stopped stirring. "The adorable little cowgirl you had a crush on for so long?"

"I never said I had a crush."

"No. You just never acted the same after she kissed you on the cheek. It was like she reached into your chest and ran off with your heart."

And has never given it back. "That would certainly explain the emptiness," he admitted.

"What are you doing back in Chicago?"

Parker tapped his index finger against his lips. "Let's see. My career, for one. And my mom, who has been avoiding my calls."

Julianne took the saucepan off the burner and poured some into a mug, then fished out a spoon from the utensil drawer and handed him the soup. "Here's dinner. Now I'm about to give you one less thing to worry about."

He followed his mom into the den, where she sat in her favorite chair next to a basket with needlepoint items. *New hobby?* He claimed his usual spot on the sofa.

"I'll come right out and say it. I've been seeing a nice man, and it's serious."

That's when he noticed the pattern on top. *Life Begins at Retirement.* His head spun in a good way.

"Mr. Mason, by chance?" he asked, to be sure his ability to add two plus two had returned.

Julianne nodded. "After you went to Wyoming, Teddy started coming by every afternoon and checking on me. We got to know each other better. Now that he's retiring, we're going to see where this leads. He made an offer on the Millers' house. Remember that one? I used to take you along when I cleaned."

He had to laugh. Yeah, he remembered. It was the same home he'd put an offer on. The one that was going to be a surprise. So his boss was the other interested party? They'd been in a bidding war for the past week, jacking up the price.

Teddy? "So he's retiring but purchasing a six-bedroom home with a separate master suite," Parker said.

"You *do* remember. He has several grand-children and wants to have them over as much as possible. Isn't that the sweetest?"

Parker looked down at his cup. That was about as sweet as it got. No way he could purchase the house now. Not that he was planning to. He simply had to be sure his mom was okay before he made any decisions.

"What's the matter?" she asked.

"I worry about you."

"Well, stop it. Teddy will take good care of me," she said as she played with her ring finger. How had he not noticed?

"You're engaged?"

"I wanted to tell you, but in person. I've been given a second chance in life. A do-over, and I plan to get it right. Even though I expect to make it to the five-year mark, I don't want to take any chances and miss out on the love of my life. He feels the same way."

"You deserve this, Mom. More than anyone else I know."

"So do you. Judging by your outfit, you're halfway there."

She was right. "You do realize I'm thinking of giving up a six-figure salary in favor of an hourly wage with no guarantee of enough hours to pay the bills." Not that he hadn't accumulated a nest egg, but it wouldn't go far enough.

Julianne joined him on the sofa and took his hand in hers. "I know this is going to sound wrong to you, but except for what you had to miss out on as a child, I wouldn't change the fact that we struggled all those years. It kept us close, and it shaped who we both became."

Parker was too choked up to speak. It didn't sound wrong at all. In fact, she summed it up perfectly. He'd found a better kind of security and stability: marry the woman you love, and commit the rest of your life to creating a wonderful life with her, and making her happy.

Of course, he had to make the marrying part happen first.

He stood, took his cup to the sink and rinsed it out.

"Are you leaving already?" she asked.

"Yes, ma'am. I want you to start your do-over as soon as possible. And I need to have a chat with my future stepfather first thing in the morning. Make sure this partnership he's considering me for is legit. I wouldn't want it simply because he's in love with my mom."

Not that he was even still in the running. Likely the opposite. But he did want closure.

"That's an interesting way to look at it. Teddy's saying the exact opposite. He said you're the clear front-runner, but he asked you to present one more portfolio piece for diversity so that the board decision would be unanimous. That way, he wouldn't be accused of nepotism once word got out about him and me."

A tingle raced up Parker's spine, reminding him of everything he'd worked so hard to achieve. It sounded like the partnership was his after all. Only, he wanted an entirely different kind of partnership altogether.

He was ready to say goodbye to the life he worked so hard to build and the stability and security it afforded. And hello to something even better.

Make that two things. Nash needed a ranch hand.

And Parker needed Hailey.

"Max, you do the honors the way we talked about," Sylvie said.

Hailey's hands were trembling, but she'd managed to make them all a cup of hot chocolate after they decided to take such an important discussion inside.

Max was the only one who didn't sit. Instead, he stood in front of Hailey, took a deep breath and started talking. "A zillion years ago, your grammy and grandy went on a trail ride. And they came back married."

Hailey looked to Sylvie, who simply nodded for Max to continue.

"Grammy's family didn't like him cuz he was poor. So he gave her a bracelet cuz her fingers were too fat for a ring. And that's what happened." At that, Max plopped into his recliner and grabbed the hot chocolate with both hands.

Oddly enough, Hailey was beginning to get the picture. What picture, she wasn't entirely sure.

Vern nodded and sipped his hot chocolate, as well. Except his eyes had barely veered from Sylvie.

"To embellish on Max's wonderful story," Sylvie said, "your great-grandparents didn't approve of their only daughter Estella's choice of a boyfriend. He came from the wrong side of the tracks, you might say. Because the Goodwins coveted their standing in the community, with all the local weddings and receptions they hosted in that barn, they forbade her to see the young man."

"So they loped," Max interjected.

"Eloped," Sylvie corrected. "Estella took him on a trail ride, just the two of them, and they kept riding until they reached a place to marry. Jackson, I'm guessing. Perhaps we can find their marriage records to confirm it. Shortly after that, your great-grandparents shut down the rides and stopped hosting the weddings. It was almost as though they went into hiding. Couldn't tolerate the speculation and gossip, I suppose."

"Tell 'em about the ring," Vern said. "That's my favorite part."

"Mine too," Sylvie said. "Before they eloped, Estella and her true love hid their engagement in plain sight. Your grandpa gave her a bracelet instead of a ring. My thoughts are that because he didn't have a lot of money, he made it himself. Out of the hair from both their horses' tails."

Hailey gulped hard and touched her wrist.

Sylvie continued. "That story circulated around town but was eventually dismissed as a rumor. I remember her wearing a horsehair bracelet and thinking how beautiful it was. But I was a child and didn't have a clue that the rumor might be true. Max mentioned that you came across such a piece the other day."

A chill ran through the entirety of Hailey's body as she pulled up her sleeve.

The color drained from Sylvie's lovely face as she placed both hands over her mouth. She leaned in, twisted it around and examined the suede ties.

"Yes. That's the one."

"We found it among her belongings in an envelope marked 'engagement ring.' We all thought it was a mistake," Hailey said.

"Max's version of Romeo and Juliet is what unlocked my memory, when he insisted they'd taken the horses and come back married. But the bracelet was the key that opened the floodgates," Sylvie explained.

"My grandmother kept her maiden name and passed it along to their children. I always figured it had to do with keeping Sunrise Stables under the Goodwin name. Maybe at least that much appeased my great-grandparents, because they clearly never disowned her."

"That would be my guess too," Vern said. "We love our children, even when we don't agree with their choices. I also bet they ended up lovin' your sweet grandpa as much as Estella did."

Sylvie nodded and sat up straighter. "I bet you're right, Vern. I remember seeing the whole lot of 'em in town one day, a few years later. And if memory serves, Estella's dad was pushing a stroller. Might have been his grandchild, Hailey's own momma, tucked away inside."

Hailey rested her head on the back of the chair and looked up at the ceiling.

Sylvie stood and picked up Vern's empty mug along with hers, rinsed them out in the kitchen sink and placed her hands on her lower back.

Vern noticed the gesture. "We should probably get you home and on the heating pad."

Sylvie nodded. "I want to talk to you more about this later, Hailey. I have an idea which route they would have taken, if I'm right about Jackson. Probably passed through Hoback Junction and Snake River Canyon. Max is excited about getting to tell the real story, although you and I might want to figure out the timeline first. I'm old, but I'm not *that* old."

"We'll need a name for the trail ride, once it's in place," Hailey said. "Any ideas?"

The room turned quiet for a good minute or two, until Vern broke the silence.

"Max will be tellin' the story, right? How about Tails of Two Horses," he said.

Max giggled. "I like it!"

"Why, Vern, I think that's a wonderful idea. What do you think, Hailey?"

"It couldn't be more perfect," Hailey said.

She had to smile. What once felt like a zillion years ago seemed like it was happening now. As she escorted Vern and Sylvie out the door, she noticed Becca turning up the drive. At least one mystery was solved. She was about to face another one. Hailey went back inside but left the door wide open.

Becca walked in and closed the door behind her. As soon as Max realized his mommy was there, he jumped out of the recliner and ran over to hug her.

"The kiddo and I were having hot chocolate. Want some?" Hailey asked.

"No, thank you. I'm fine. Cody might want some when he's done." Becca turned to Max. "Hey, cowboy. Why don't you go outside and help your daddy finish up?"

The fact that she was sending Max away warned Hailey that the news was going to be bad. There was only one topic she knew of that Becca wouldn't want to discuss in front of her son.

"Let me guess. You're gonna tempt Georgina

with a job offer, and you want my permission," Hailey said, once Max was gone.

Becca cocked her head. "Seasonal or part time, if she could manage some duties along with her other career. How did you know I was going to talk to her about that? And why would I need permission?"

Ouch! On multiple levels. Of course, Becca didn't need her permission.

"Sorry. I didn't mean for it to come out that way." Hailey crossed her arms. "To be honest, I'm a little jealous. You and I have barely spoken since your honeymoon, yet my sister gets to enjoy your company every day."

Becca shook her head and stepped forward. "I know I've been an absentee friend, but there's a good reason. I haven't been feeling well. I didn't want to say anything until I knew what was going on."

Hailey's heart sank. She closed the distance between them and embraced her friend. "What's wrong? And why has Cody been keeping this from me?" She pulled away and studied Becca's face for any clue.

"Nothing's wrong. In fact, everything is perfect." Becca placed a hand on her own belly.

Hailey covered her mouth.

"I wanted you to be the first to know," Becca

continued. "The third, actually. Cody was first and Mom was second. We haven't decided how to break the news to Max, but he'll be next."

"As it should be. They're family."

"So are you. But you're also my best friend." Now Hailey felt super silly and more than a little emotional. "Okay. Since you put it that way, I give you permission to hire Georgina," she teased.

Becca softly laughed and bit her lip. "Actually, I will need the extra help down the road. I'd hire you back in a heartbeat, except what you and Cody have going here is so much more important."

"I wouldn't say that. The Hideaway is your family's forever home. Doesn't get more important than that."

"I do need your permission on one thing," Becca said.

"You need for me to look after your kiddo until your upset stomach is all better?"

Becca shook her head. "We want to borrow your middle name. If it's a girl, we want to name her Alexandra Rose Sayers. Alexander Lee Sayers if it's a boy."

Hailey stepped back in and gave her an even bigger hug than before. This had to be the best day ever. She went to her kitchen cabinet and retrieved her last can of chicken noodle soup and held it up. "I hear this does wonders for an upset tummy. I insist you take it. Better yet, if you want to have a seat and get comfy, I'll make some for you now."

"I better take a rain check and get my boys back home." Becca walked to the door and paused, then pivoted back around. "On second thought, I'd love that, Mom."

"Don't tease me. I'd adopt you in a heartbeat," Hailey said.

Becca placed both hands over her heart. "And I'd be the luckiest girl in the world."

CHAPTER TWENTY

HAILEY WATCHED THE bubbles expand and multiply beneath the running stream of warm water in the claw-foot tub. Aside from that sound, the house was perfectly quiet.

Her mind, however, was anything but. The smiles and giggles of the children on today's ride tickled her thoughts. The unbridled happiness of their father, who was horsing around a bit too much for his wife's taste, reminded her of her own dad.

While that was happening, the lady had asked her, "Do you have any little ones?"

"Not yet," Hailey had said, although that wouldn't have been her usual answer. It caught her so much off guard that she'd changed the subject. But her own words still haunted her.

Even after easing into the tub and closing her eyes, those giggles played in the background of Hailey's conscience. And when they finally stopped, the silence was almost spooky.

Music. That's what she needed.

She got out of the tub, patted herself semidry and wrapped the towel around her as she tracked damp footprints on the hardwoods to the guest room. She pulled out a random album from the stack then went to the den. There to greet her once again was the envelope Parker had left behind.

She'd promised herself she'd throw it away, but when she lifted it, the contents shifted. There was something other than paper inside. She undid the clasp and pulled out the contents: two wrapped packages.

Odd.

One was clearly an album, based on the shape. The other box was more of a question mark. She mustered the nerve to unwrap the latter one first. Those bossy horse-head earrings that she'd given him stared back at her. Inside the box, a note: *I found one.*

Found what? Then she remembered. She squeezed her eyes shut. So he was going to propose that she be his girlfriend? That was what the whole proposal thing was all about?

The sweetness and innocence of it went down bitter as she thought of how it ended. More so when she thought about how it all began, twenty years ago. She set the earrings down and tore through the wrapping paper of the other gift.

The note taped loosely to the album said it was from Vern, which should have made it easier.

It didn't.

The feelings that rushed through her could only be described as a tsunami that crashed into her with full force. Parker had neither agreed nor disagreed when she reminded him that opera and bluegrass don't mix. Turned out, she was wrong. She read the cover again.

Nashville Bluegrass Opera. The Cumberland Mountain Boys.

She tried to swallow but couldn't. Her hands trembled as she set the record down and looked around the place. All of a sudden it felt so empty. On the kitchen counter was the cupcake pan for when she and the twins had made them together.

It was so quiet now. Too quiet. She thought of Lizzy and Kat, with their silly arguments. Kat wanting to come live with Hailey because her sister was being mean. And their ability to forgive and forget and go back to being best friends twenty seconds later. And little PJ wearing Parker's tie and wanting to grow up to be like him.

Then there was Max, when he'd wake up in the morning and come padding into her kitchen in his flannel pajamas, sleepy-eyed and clutching his stuffed horse, acting like whatever she fixed for breakfast was the best thing ever.

Most of all, she thought of Parker. In fact, she'd never stopped.

Hailey took a deep breath and picked up the envelope containing the original proposal, complete with his business email address. The seriousness of what she wanted to say would be best articulated in his language and on paper, because this had to be perfect. After all, two partnerships were at stake.

She could picture the perfect outcome now. It gave her that same warm, safe feeling she had as a little girl. True, neither of Parker's proposals were what she wanted for her property. However, he was everything she wanted in a man. With a lot of imagination, a little luck and a full pot of coffee to fuel an all-nighter, that barn just might bring them back together.

Looked like this cowgirl from Destiny Springs had some proposing of her own to do.

WITH THE LEVEL of clarity and energy that only a solid night's sleep could provide, Parker straightened the horse tie and walked through the door of CEO Theodore "Teddy" Mason's office for the last time.

He sat in the chair across from the man who

would soon be his stepfather. But for the time being, the man was still his boss. He displayed the framed needlepoint Parker's mom had given him as proudly as Parker wore his tie.

There they were. Unexpected family. Both in love with the same six-bedroom house. And both in love with the respective woman of their dreams. Only difference was, his boss had "gotten the girl." Parker still had some work to do to convince his. And the only place to do that was Destiny Springs.

"Timing is everything, isn't it?" Mason picked up a printout and put on his reading glasses.

Parker blinked. "I don't follow." At the same time, he agreed wholeheartedly.

"A proposal landed in your inbox this morning. From one Hailey Alexandra Goodwin of Destiny Springs, Wyoming. Says she's one hundred percent satisfied with it. I have to admit, I had no idea you could be quite this creative, although the numbers are a little off."

Parker's first thought was that his numbers were *never* off.

His boss let out a hearty belly laugh. "What exactly is goat yoga, anyway?"

He should have known Mason had seen one

of the most embarrassing moments of his life. Everyone had. "So my mom showed it to you."

Mason looked up and over his reading glasses. "Showed me what?"

"The video."

"What video? Are we speaking the same language here?"

"You mentioned goats."

Mason nudged the printout toward him. "You mentioned them first."

Parker studied the proposal. It was for her property, all right. But the whole thing had changed. He couldn't help but smile. And he thought he'd been the only one to learn a whole new language. Kind of scary how brilliant it was, even if the numbers were off. Scary *and* thrilling. Just like her.

Summary: Owner is considering painting the barn blue, per the advice of the consultant and his assistant. Price estimate included. All other changes to the barn will be facilitated using movable parts so as to not compromise the structure's integrity. The barn's money-making activities will include goat yoga for adults, and goat feeding, a petting zoo and pony rides for children.

Parker's breath hitched at the last item, but he continued.

Sunrise Stables could either bring in a comfortable revenue, or fetch a nice asking price, if there's any reason the owner would consider selling it. Owner's note (delete before presenting to management): There are only two reasons the owner would consider selling it: if she decided to move; or when she and her husband need a home with more bedrooms for their adopted little ones. If Mr. Parks Donnelly concurs, they can seal the deal with a kiss on the cheek.

Mason was right. Timing was everything. And Hailey's timing and proposal couldn't have been more perfect.

Parker looked up at his boss as he swallowed back the emotion.

A huge smile spread across the man's face. "Obviously, you didn't put this together, and I wasn't meant to see this version of it. The 'Confidential' subject line made me pause, but we agreed I'd open everything in your absence. And since I have... A kiss on the cheek? Does this have anything to do with that tie you're wearing?"

"It has everything to do with it." Of course, she wouldn't have known about his blind cc agreement with Mason, and he never imagined needing any reason to alert her.

Parker thought about all of Mason's years with this firm, as well as his own. Soon, that man's chair was going to be filled by someone else. And that someone could be Parker if he wanted it.

Mason stood and walked around the side of his desk. "I'm not trying to tempt you, but would you like to give it a test spin? Just to be sure. Of course, you could pick out one of your own if you prefer. But something tells me the only chair you're interested in isn't a chair at all. It's a saddle."

Parker stood, but not because he was even remotely tempted.

"I'm already sure, but thank you for the offer. Besides, that chair will fit beautifully in your new six-bedroom house. With all that space, you could have an amazing home office for any hobbies. That's what I was planning to use it for."

Mason paused, then chuckled. "You mean, you're the one I'm bidding against?"

Parker shook his head. "*Were* bidding against. I've found a house I like even better. In fact, it's not actually a house. It's a whole state." *And a new state of mind.*

Cowboy boots, flannel shirts and Stetsons? That was only the beginning. He was getting a do-over. Furthermore, there was no one else he'd rather *get by* with in life than Hailey.

Looked like this wannabe cowboy was getting the girl.

CHAPTER TWENTY-ONE

"NICE TIE," Cody said as Parker strolled past him through the opened sliding barn door where the restoration was already in full swing. Even though he'd been gone only a week, it had felt like a lifetime.

Parker straightened the knot and smiled. "Special occasion."

Cody offered up his trademark grin and resumed his task of replacing some damage on the upper track of the frame.

Georgina was off to the side, unpacking and unrolling banners that announced the official launch of a Destiny Springs tradition, with additional activities for wranglers of all ages. Pony rides and a goat petting zoo for children. Goat yoga for adults (by appointment only).

Up ahead, Nash and the twins were busy assembling a pony-go-round. Make that, Nash was assembling while the twins asked a million questions. As Nash's new ranch hand slash babysitter, Parker couldn't wait to take over the answering duties.

"It's about time," Nash said as Parker walked by. The cowboy stopped what he was doing long enough to give him grief. If that was a preview to how their working relationship was going to be, he was onboard. One hundred percent.

Max came running over and tugged on Parker's arm. "Guess what?"

"I give up. What?"

"Hailey's gonna get some ponies, and I get to be pony master!"

"Oh, yeah? What's their story?" Parker asked as he continued to his ultimate destination: the beautiful tomboy cowgirl at the far end of the barn who had yet to look up and still had no idea he was back in Destiny Springs. He'd had to tie up some loose ends in Chicago first but otherwise took the earliest possible flight. Not only did he want to be here for the official launch in less than a week, but because he had a proposal to accept. With one important revision of his own.

Max tagged along, saying something about how the ponies were the original trail-ride horses' babies. Or something to that effect. It wasn't that Parker wasn't interested or listening. But the closer he got to Hailey, the more his nerves kicked in. What if she'd changed her mind? What if she said *no*?

Vern and Sylvie were standing there, chatting. Looking suspiciously in love. Vern did a double take when Parker was about to walk by but didn't say anything. He simply winked. His grandpa was the only person he'd alerted as to his arrival.

Sylvie did one better. She pulled him in close and gave him a huge hug. Had to love those strong, determined women who weren't afraid to take the lead.

Arm still in a cast, PJ was busy playing with the goats under Vanessa's supervision. Mirrors and several mats for goat yoga were arranged in a designated corner outside the pen.

Parker spied the little critter who had ruined his tie and nearly made him somewhat of a viral video sensation among family and friends and miscellaneous acquaintances. If he didn't have something more important to do, he'd pick up the little four-legged kid and give him a huge hug.

Maybe later. After he changed clothes. That silly horse tie was his now-and-forever favorite, and he wasn't going to take any chances with it. He brought a few ties to give to PJ and donated the others along with his suits and wingtips to a charity for men in Chicago. Ones who were down on their luck and trying to get a job.

Hailey was sitting cross-legged, polishing an antique candelabra and sipping on a Coke. With peanuts, he assumed. What a beautiful puzzle piece she'd come across. Looked like something used during one of those weddings. With a little luck, it would grace at least one more.

Maybe even two more, if he could talk his mom and Teddy into reciting their nuptials here, and if Vern and Sylvie decided to take the leap.

Hailey looked up as Parker approached. Her breath visibly hitched. She dropped the polishing cloth and scrambled to her feet.

"I wasn't expecting you. When—"

"Just now. What we need to discuss has to be done in person and as soon as possible. It's about your proposal for the barn." He tried to maintain his most serious, professional expression.

She straightened her back and her smile faded. "Okay."

He pulled the printout from his pocket and unfolded it. "I have a major issue with your changes, and I'm afraid I can't sign off until this is resolved."

She raised a brow and crossed her arms. "Oh? Really? You need to sign off? I thought this was about maintaining your perfect client satisfaction score and securing a partnership. So much for doing you a favor."

"Oh, believe me, you did me a huge favor. But I'd be remiss as a consultant—but most important, as a man who is in love with his client—to not insist upon adding a line item. That said, there's something we have to agree on first. Since you've already said you love me, albeit as a business partner and friend and someone who changed your life, I expect those negotiations to go smoothly."

She bit her lip, then smiled. Those beautiful, high cheekbones of hers turned the prettiest shade of pink. "I love what I'm hearing so far. But exactly what would that something be?"

Parker dropped to one knee.

EVEN THOUGH HAILEY didn't have an actual recipe for such a situation, she could see the label perfectly.

Directions: Say "yes" to the man of your dreams.

"Yes, yes, yes! And I love you too," she said.

Okay, so her directions to herself specified one *yes*, but one simply wasn't strong enough for how she felt in the moment.

"I haven't even asked the question," he said.

She dropped to her knees and closed the distance between them. "Then perhaps you should."

Parker seemed to struggle with the words. In the meantime, everyone in the barn had formed a cautious semicircle. Hailey looked around, having all but forgotten anyone else was there but the two of them.

"Hailey Alexandra Goodwin, I love you with all my heart. Ever since that day you kissed me on the cheek, so I've had plenty of time to think about this. I say you and me, and Wyoming. That is, if you don't mind being married to one of Nash's ranch hands."

"I say I've waited twenty years for you to ask."

They leaned in, sealing it with a kiss. He wrapped his arms around her waist, and she put hers around his shoulders, fitting together like pieces to a puzzle. She didn't want this moment to end, yet she couldn't wait for their future together to begin.

Once they stood, Vern didn't waste any time

moving in to claim a hug. Sylvie, meanwhile, kidnapped Hailey's new fiancé, leaving her alone with Vern.

"Do you have any advice for me?" Hailey asked.

Vern wrapped her hands in his and couldn't seem to speak. Was he about to cry?

"Hey, remember, you're not losing a grandson. You're gaining a granddaughter," she offered, which only made him more emotional. First time she'd ever seen the man cry, although he always wore his heart on his sleeve, and it was therefore susceptible to injury.

Vern nodded, then confessed, "I was actually wondering if I could ask *you* for advice. All this proposing has me itching to do some myself. If I had a ring on me, I'd probably get down on one knee. Except, unlike my grandson, I wouldn't be able to get back up without assistance."

She looked to Sylvie. Hailey could totally picture her as a grandmother-in-law. At the same time, she knew Vern had been moving at breakneck speed.

"It never hurts to ask. The worst that can happen is she'll say *no*." Although Hailey couldn't imagine anyone turning Vern down.

"*No* is a scary word," he said.

"But missing the opportunity to hear *yes* is even scarier, isn't it?" Hailey asked.

Vern nodded and inhaled a sharp breath.

"There is a way we could stack the odds in your favor." Hailey untied the horsehair bracelet, placed it in Vern's palm and closed his fingers around it.

"Hailey, no. I can't—"

"Yes, you can. Now that you've confided in me, you have to. But it doesn't have to happen today. Sleep on it, and see what your heart tells you in the morning."

At that, he seemed to breathe a little easier.

"I don't know what my heart will tell me, but it wants to tell *you* something. Welcome to the family," he said, giving her one more superlong hug before shuffling back over to one of the luckiest women in the world, in her opinion.

Speaking of weddings... Georgina stepped forward and gave Hailey a hug. Just the person she needed to talk to.

"I've got a job for you, Georgy Girl," Hailey said.

Georgina shook her head. "Oh, no. I can't. This time, it has to be all you. Right down to the flowers. If you even want any."

"Sorry, but you don't get to say *no* to the bride-to-be. Ask Vern. He just learned the same lesson. My barn, my rules. You're a part of me, and I want your input. All I require is that it be held in here."

"I suggest outside. Beneath our stars. Have the reception inside," Parker said.

How long had he been standing there? Hailey looked at him sideways, then called in the reinforcements. "Max! Can you come here for a minute, kiddo?"

The adorable little boy came running over.

"Guess what? Mr. Parks and I are getting married. Just like you always said we would."

Max giggled. Parker looked perplexed. She'd explain later.

"Are y'all gonna lope, like Romeo and Jullet?" Max asked.

"Not a chance," Hailey said. "We're having it at Sunrise Stables, but there's something we can't agree on. I think you can help. Parker wants to have the wedding outside, under the stars. I want to have it inside this barn."

"Cool!" Max said.

"Except, we can't have both. Unless you can solve the mystery of how to get the stars inside," Hailey said, adding a private wink for Max only to see.

Max's mouth formed a huge O. "I can do that!"

The night-light of Max's that was still in her guest room? The one with the animated stars that she'd kept forgetting to return to him? It was about to be given a very important job.

Max ran over to his mommy and daddy, most likely to fill them in on his and Hailey's plan. Parker still looked a bit confused. She moved in close again.

"You're not scared, are you? Truth," she insisted, because she was more than a little scared and didn't want to be the only one.

"Can I choose dare instead?" he asked.

Hailey shook her head.

"Okay then. I'm terrified. But in a good way," he said.

She totally got what he was saying. His life was about to change even more than hers. For now. Hailey looked over at Becca and Cody, who couldn't have looked happier. Without inviting the thought, Hailey envisioned her and Parker's children, growing up alongside her best friend's. Inevitably breaking bones and hearts along the way. And forming lifetime bonds.

The only directions she intended to follow were in her heart. Everyone deserved a second chance. Like Georgina. Sunrise Stables. And this old barn.

So did this cowgirl. And her kind of cowboy.

EPILOGUE

One month later

PARKER'S MOM ADJUSTED the lapel of his black blazer like she always used to do when he was a little boy, then admired the boutonniere Hailey had picked out for him. A single white rosebud. Elegant and understated. Strong enough to stand on its own without unnecessary embellishment. Like Hailey herself.

"Your beautiful bride has good taste in flowers. And in men. I'm so proud of you," she said.

"For trading a corner office for horse stalls that, by the way, I'll be in charge of mucking?"

"That too, but no. For following your heart. Cowboy."

Now, that was a nickname he could get used to. He shifted from one foot to the other. He'd always envisioned wearing a tux and wingtips to get married, but cowboy boots and jeans, paired with a white button-down and blazer, with no tie, felt so right for this new beginning.

Even though he did allow his mom to press a crease into his jeans. After all, it was a special occasion, to put it mildly.

Never in a million years would he have imagined he'd be getting married in a barn, of all places. Much less, to the little tomboy cowgirl who stole his heart twenty years ago.

Then again, it all made perfect sense. Like opera and bluegrass.

"Julianne and I have already talked about it. You and Hailey will always be welcomed at our house," Teddy said. "There will be a room for you, anytime you want to come visit."

To have his mom so close to being considered cured, and to see her in love with a good man—one that he'd privately thought of as a father figure all along? Warmed his heart nearly as much as his bride-to-be.

He'd yet to talk to Vern, who remained focused on the entrance, waiting for his signal to start the processional—which apparently had come, since Vern set the needle down on the record. Parker swallowed hard when he realized it was opera instead of the bluegrass song they'd agreed upon. That's what he got for leaving Hailey in charge of the details.

His mom took her seat, but his soon-to-be stepfather remained by his side as *best* best man. That wasn't an easy choice, since every man in Parker's life was the best. His other best men were about to walk down the make-shift aisle with Hailey's maids of honor on their arms.

Lizzy and Kat paved the way with rose petals. Max, the keeper of the ring, walked a little too fast and nearly tripped.

Cody and Becca appeared next, with huge smiles pasted on both their faces. Followed by Nash and Georgina, who looked almost as nervous as Parker felt. Last but not least, PJ, wearing one of Parker's nicest ties and escorting Hailey's other sister, Faye.

Vern scurried out the door and returned with Sylvie on his arm. That's when Parker noticed the bracelet that Hailey had been wearing was around Sylvie's wrist.

Parker had never seen a collection of men with such huge smiles, and the beautiful women who had put them there. It was like someone spiked the punch with a love potion. There wasn't a finer collection of people than in this barn, with the wedding party almost outnumbering the other guests.

It seemed like forever before Hailey walked through the door, escorted by her mother. She looked like an angel. They both did.

Trent closed the barn door behind them. The candelabra provided the only lighting until Max temporarily abandoned his post and turned on another light. Stars danced across the walls and ceiling, splashing across the lovely bride's beautiful full-length white sheath dress. Her long, usually straight hair was shiny and wavy, adorned with strands of rhinestones braided into its length in lieu of a veil. They sparkled and swayed with her gait.

He had to stifle a huge grin, thinking about how Max and Hailey had solved the mystery of how to bring the stars inside. That further confirmed what he knew all along: Hailey was capable of accomplishing anything she set her mind to.

The officiant had taken her place at some point. When Hailey's mother handed her off to Parker, he felt as though the last piece of this puzzle-of-a-life had finally fallen into place.

He tried to focus on what the officiant was saying, about how they'd all come together to witness the union of this couple and thanking the guests for being there. But he kept looking at Hailey instead. And she kept looking back, until the officiant finally picked up on it and instructed them to go ahead and face each other instead.

When it came down to the question of whether anyone objected, the barn was silent except for one lone goat bleat, which made the small crowd laugh.

The officiant asked him first if he took this woman to be his lawfully wedded wife. He enclosed Hailey's strong, beautiful hands in his and gave them a gentle squeeze. Even though there was only one answer—and he was dying to say it—he paused instead to savor this moment.

He paused perhaps a bit too long, so her reaction shouldn't have surprised him. As a matter of fact, it both thrilled and terrified him in the most wonderful way.

She squinted.

He smiled.

This marriage is gonna be fun.

* * * * *

Get 4 FREE REWARDS!

We'll send you 2 FREE Books plus 2 FREE Mystery Gifts.

FREE
Value Over
$20

Both the **Love Inspired®** and **Love Inspired® Suspense** series feature compelling novels filled with inspirational romance, faith, forgiveness and hope.

YES! Please send me 2 FREE novels from the Love Inspired or Love Inspired Suspense series and my 2 FREE gifts (gifts are worth about $10 retail). After receiving them, if I don't wish to receive any more books, I can return the shipping statement marked "cancel." If I don't cancel, I will receive 6 brand-new Love Inspired Larger-Print books or Love Inspired Suspense Larger-Print books every month and be billed just $6.49 each in the U.S. or $6.74 each in Canada. That is a savings of at least 16% off the cover price. It's quite a bargain! Shipping and handling is just 50¢ per book in the U.S. and $1.25 per book in Canada.* I understand that accepting the 2 free books and gifts places me under no obligation to buy anything. I can always return a shipment and cancel at any time by calling the number below. The free books and gifts are mine to keep no matter what I decide.

Choose one: ☐ **Love Inspired**
Larger-Print
(122/322 IDN GRHK)

☐ **Love Inspired Suspense**
Larger-Print
(107/307 IDN GRHK)

Name (please print)

Address   Apt. #

City   State/Province   Zip/Postal Code

Email: Please check this box ☐ if you would like to receive newsletters and promotional emails from Harlequin Enterprises ULC and its affiliates. You can unsubscribe anytime.

Mail to the Harlequin Reader Service:
IN U.S.A.: P.O. Box 1341, Buffalo, NY 14240-8531
IN CANADA: P.O. Box 603, Fort Erie, Ontario L2A 5X3

Want to try 2 free books from another series? Call 1-800-873-8635 or visit www.ReaderService.com.

Get 4 FREE REWARDS!

We'll send you 2 FREE Books plus 2 FREE Mystery Gifts.

FREE Value Over **$20**

Both the **Harlequin® Special Edition** and **Harlequin® Heartwarming™** series feature compelling novels filled with stories of love and strength where the bonds of friendship, family and community unite.

YES! Please send me 2 FREE novels from the Harlequin Special Edition or Harlequin Heartwarming series and my 2 FREE gifts (gifts are worth about $10 retail). After receiving them, if I don't wish to receive any more books, I can return the shipping statement marked "cancel." If I don't cancel, I will receive 6 brand-new Harlequin Special Edition books every month and be billed just $5.49 each in the U.S. or $6.24 each in Canada, a savings of at least 12% off the cover price, or 4 brand-new Harlequin Heartwarming Larger-Print books every month and be billed just $6.24 each in the U.S. or $6.74 each in Canada, a savings of at least 19% off the cover price. It's quite a bargain! Shipping and handling is just 50¢ per book in the U.S. and $1.25 per book in Canada.* I understand that accepting the 2 free books and gifts places me under no obligation to buy anything. I can always return a shipment and cancel at any time by calling the number below. The free books and gifts are mine to keep no matter what I decide.

Choose one: ☐ **Harlequin Special Edition**
(235/335 HDN GRJV)
☐ **Harlequin Heartwarming Larger-Print**
(161/361 HDN GRJV)

Name (please print)

Address _____ Apt. #

City _____ State/Province _____ Zip/Postal Code

Email: Please check this box ☐ if you would like to receive newsletters and promotional emails from Harlequin Enterprises ULC and its affiliates. You can unsubscribe anytime.

Mail to the **Harlequin Reader Service:**
IN U.S.A.: P.O. Box 1341, Buffalo, NY 14240-8531
IN CANADA: P.O. Box 603, Fort Erie, Ontario L2A 5X3

Want to try 2 free books from another series? Call **1-800-873-8635** or visit www.ReaderService.com.

---

*Terms and prices subject to change without notice. Prices do not include sales taxes, which will be charged (if applicable) based on your state or country of residence. Canadian residents will be charged applicable taxes. Offer not valid in Quebec. This offer is limited to one order per household. Books received may not be as shown. Not valid for current subscribers to the Harlequin Special Edition or Harlequin Heartwarming series. All orders subject to approval. Credit or debit balances in a customer's account(s) may be offset by any outstanding balance owed by or to the customer. Please allow 4 to 6 weeks for delivery. Offer available while quantities last.

HSEHW22R3

THE NORA ROBERTS COLLECTION

Get to the heart of happily-ever-after in these Nora Roberts classics! Immerse yourself in the beauty of love by picking up this incredible collection written by, legendary author, Nora Roberts!

Get 4 FREE REWARDS!

We'll send you 2 FREE Books plus 2 FREE Mystery Gifts.

FREE
Value Over
$20

Both the **Romance** and **Suspense** collections feature compelling novels written by many of today's bestselling authors.

YES! Please send me 2 FREE novels from the Essential Romance or Essential Suspense Collection and my 2 FREE gifts (gifts are worth about $10 retail). After receiving them, if I don't wish to receive any more books, I can return the shipping statement marked "cancel." If I don't cancel, I will receive 4 brand-new novels every month and be billed just $7.49 each in the U.S. or $7.74 each in Canada. That's a savings of at least 17% off the cover price. It's quite a bargain! Shipping and handling is just 50¢ per book in the U.S. and $1.25 per book in Canada.* I understand that accepting the 2 free books and gifts places me under no obligation to buy anything. I can always return a shipment and cancel at any time by calling the number below. The free books and gifts are mine to keep no matter what I decide.

Choose one: ☐ **Essential Romance**   ☐ **Essential Suspense**
        (194/394 MDN GRHV)   (191/391 MDN GRHV)

Name (please print)

Address   Apt. #

City   State/Province   Zip/Postal Code

Email: Please check this box ☐ if you would like to receive newsletters and promotional emails from Harlequin Enterprises ULC and its affiliates. You can unsubscribe anytime.

Mail to the Harlequin Reader Service:
IN U.S.A.: P.O. Box 1341, Buffalo, NY 14240-8531
IN CANADA: P.O. Box 603, Fort Erie, Ontario L2A 5X3

Want to try 2 free books from another series! Call 1-800-873-8635 or visit www.ReaderService.com.

HARLEQUIN
PLUS

Try the best multimedia subscription service for romance readers like you!

Read, Watch and Play.

Experience the easiest way to get the romance content you crave.

Start your **FREE TRIAL** at
<u>www.harlequinplus.com/freetrial</u>.

P9-CCJ-414

By Keith Douglass

THE CARRIER SERIES:

CARRIER
VIPER STRIKE
ARMAGEDDON MODE
FLAME-OUT
MAELSTROM
COUNTDOWN
AFTERBURN
ALPHA STRIKE
ARCTIC FIRE
ARSENAL

THE SEAL TEAM SEVEN SERIES:

SEAL TEAM SEVEN
SPECTER
NUCFLASH
DIRECT ACTION
FIRESTORM
BATTLEGROUND
DEATHRACE

SEAL TEAM SEVEN
DEATHRACE

KEITH DOUGLASS

BERKLEY BOOKS, NEW YORK

Special thanks and acknowledgment to Chet Cunningham
for his contribution to this book.

SEAL TEAM SEVEN: DEATHRACE

A Berkley Book / published by arrangement with
the author

PRINTING HISTORY
Berkley edition / February 1999

To my longtime friend and
editor, Tom Colgan, who keeps
the wheels turning and the
books rolling.
To the writers bunch—Cyndy, Mark,
Ken, Lee, Peggy, and Rosie—who have
given beneficial criticism, comments,
and aid in researching.
It would have been a lot harder
to write this book without
the help of all of you.

Foreword

SEAL stands for SEa-Air-Land. This specialized group of fighting men was created by President John Fitzgerald Kennedy in 1962 to meet special quick-strike needs of the U.S. Navy. Today the Navy SEALs are among the leaders of the elite special-operation forces in the world.

SEALs undergo a six-month training course that is enough to break the back and the will of all but the most dedicated, and the strongest. On average, 60 percent of those who start the SEAL training course drop out.

During the Vietnam War there were only two SEAL teams, One and Two. Each was composed of a number of fourteen-man platoons. Today SEALs function with sixteen-man platoons.

As modern warfare changed, in the eighties, the Navy realized that it had to meet the challenge. Through the Ronald Reagan administration, the Navy lobbied for more SEAL teams, pointing out the greater emphasis on "small wars" and covert operations.

By 1990 there were seven SEAL teams. Teams One, Three, and Five were headquartered in Coronado, California, under the direction of the Naval Special Warfare Group

One. The plan was to use these units for emergency actions in the Pacific and Far East.

Teams Two, Four, and Six were assigned to Little Creek, Virginia, under the command of NAVSPECWARGRU-TWO. They would be deployed in the Caribbean, the Mediterranean, and the Middle East.

The Navy's special warfare groups are highly security conscious. They give out no press releases on SEAL actions. Most of the SEAL work is never known to the U.S. public, let alone other nations. They work quietly, often deadly, to achieve the purpose of intense national security that has been handed them.

At my latest report, there is no SEAL Team Seven in real life. That makes this series of books more interesting and exciting, since all manner of actions, problems, crises, coups, takeovers, terrorists, and "small wars" can be dealt with by a realistic prototype of an actual SEAL unit.

After the book *Seal Team Seven: Specter*, Team Seven's Third Platoon was assigned for full-time use by the Central Intelligence Agency. They selected the best, highest rated team, and the team with the best in-action record for this task. Now SEAL Team Seven, Platoon Three, is at the top secret whispered call of Don Stroh, its CIA control.

If you have any questions about the SEALs or comments on the books, please drop me a line at: Keith Douglass, 8431 Beaver Lake Drive, San Diego, CA 92119. Hope to hear from you.

Keith Douglass
December 1998

SEAL TEAM SEVEN

THIRD PLATOON*
CORONADO, CALIFORNIA

Lieutenant Blake Murdock. Platoon Leader.
WEAPON: H&K MP-5SD submachine gun.

FIRST SQUAD

David "Jaybird" Sterling. Platoon Chief. Machinist Mate Second
   Class.
WEAPON: H&K MP-5SD submachine gun.

Ron Holt. Radioman First Class. Platoon radio operator.
WEAPON: H&K MP-5SD submachine gun.

Martin "Magic" Brown. Quartermaster's Mate First Class. Squad sniper.
WEAPON: H&K PSG1 7.62 NATO sniper rifle or McMillan M-87R .50-
   caliber sniper rifle.

Joe "Ricochet" Lampedusa. Operations Specialist Third Class. Platoon scout.
WEAPON: Colt M-4A1 with grenade launcher.

Kenneth Ching. Quartermaster's Mate First Class. Platoon translator.
   Speaks Chinese, Japanese, Russian, Spanish.
WEAPON: Colt M-4A1 with grenade launcher.

Harry "Horse" Ronson. Electrician's Mate Second Class.
WEAPON: H&K 21A1 7.62 NATO-round machine gun.

James "Doc" Ellsworth. Hospital Corpsman Second Class. Platoon
   corpsman.
WEAPON: H&K MP-5SD or no-stock, 5-round Mossburg pump shotgun.

*Third Platoon assigned exclusively to the Central Intelligence Agency to perform any needed
tasks on a covert basis anywhere in the world. A top secret classified assignment.

SECOND SQUAD

Lieutenant (j.g.) Ed DeWitt. Leader Second Squad. Second in Command of the platoon.
WEAPON: H&K G-11 automatic rifle.

Al Adams. Gunner's Mate Third Class.
WEAPON: Colt M-4A1 with grenade launcher.

Miguel Fernandez. Gunner's Mate First Class. Speaks Spanish and Portuguese. Squad sniper.
WEAPON: H&K PSG1 7.62 NATO sniper rifle.

Colt "Guns" Franklin. Yeoman Second Class. Speaks Farsi and Arabic.
WEAPON: Colt M-4A1 with grenade launcher.

Les Quinley. Torpedoman's Mate Third Class. Explosive specialist.
WEAPON: H&K G-11 caseless rounds, 4.7mm automatic rifle.

Rodolfo "RG" Gonzalez. Damage Controlman First Class. Speaks Spanish, Italian, and Russian.
WEAPON: Colt M-4A1 with grenade launcher.

Joe Douglas. Quartermaster First Class. Machine gunner. Second radio operator.
WEAPON: H&K 21A1 7.62 NATO-round machine gun.

Fred Washington. Aviation Technician Second Class.
WEAPON: H&K MP-5SD submachine gun.

1

Friday, October 21

1040 hours
Chocolate Mountain Gunnery Range
Niland, California

Lieutenant Blake Murdock rubbed the stinging sand out of his eyes, and watched the target ahead. Nothing moved. Good. He glanced to his right and saw the first two men in his Third Platoon flat on their bellies in the hot rocks and dirt.

Their weapons were up and ready.

They both wore full combat gear.

Their faces were daubed with black and brown paint.

Their desert cammies showed the grime of a long crawl two hundred yards up to this vantage point.

Murdock nodded sharply at the first two men.

David "Jaybird" Sterling, Machinist Mate Second Class, and platoon chief, surged off the ground into a crouching run and charged the squat building directly in front, twenty yards away. He held his H&K MP-5SD submachine gun ready, his finger on the trigger set for three round bursts.

Right behind him, Ron Holt, Radioman First Class and the platoon's communications man, jolted to his feet and charged the low building. He carried a Remington 870 shotgun with no stock, a pistol grip, and virtually no barrel. The pump-action weapon carried five 12-gauge rounds.

Sterling hit the door first, kicked it open, and darted inside. Ron Holt went in right behind him.

From long practice, Sterling took the right-hand side of the room. Two terrorists stood over a woman tied to a chair. Sterling put three-round bursts into each of the terrs, and looked for more.

As he did, Holt dove through the door covering the left-hand side of the room. One terr held a knife, and was about to move toward a captive tied to a table.

One round from the shotgun cut the terr in half.

The sound of the shots in the small room were like 155 howitzers going off in a cave. Both men wore earplugs, but still the sound rattled around in their heads.

"Clear right," Sterling said into his Motorola MX-300 personal communication radio. To his left, Holt heard the words through a small speaker in his left ear.

"Clear left," Holt said. They looked at each other through the dimness of the room, then charged through the door eight feet away, into the second room.

This time Holt went first. He scanned the inside of the room but found no terrorists.

Sterling came right behind him, his submachine gun searching for any terrs in his zone. Suddenly one popped up from behind a table. Sterling riddled him with three rounds, and kept scanning.

Holt checked his section again, and saw a form with a weapon leap up from behind a couch. Holt had pumped a new round into his shotgun as soon as he shot the first time. Now he jerked the Remington around and triggered off a round. The terr was blasted against the back of the room and dropped to the floor.

"Clear left," Holt said.

"Clear right," Sterling said. They nodded, and ran hard through the last door in the room, and out into the sunshine.

They trotted fifty yards to the left and bellied down in a shallow irrigation ditch near the rest of the platoon.

Back in front of the low building, Lieutenant Murdock looked to his left. He pointed to the first two men in line there, and they both scrambled to their feet and charged the structure.

Martin "Magic" Brown, a black man carrying one of the new H&K G11 automatic rifles, hit the door first. He had put aside his usual sniper rifle to try out the new weapon, which had rounds without casings. He kicked open the door and charged inside, taking the right-hand section. Two terrs showed themselves and he fired, pouring twelve rounds into the two of them before he got his finger off the trigger.

"Holy shit," Magic growled. "Clear right."

Behind him Joe "Ricochet" Lampedusa, the platoon lead scout, had hosed down one terr with a three-round burst from his Colt M-4A1 carbine.

"Clear left," Joe said. "Sure you got him?"

Magic grinned in the room's dimness, and waved them forward.

They charged into the next room where the G-11 blasted again, this time set on three-round bursts.

Out in front of the Kill House, Lieutenant Murdock made a double check. He pointed at Kenneth Ching and Harry "Horse" Ronson, sending them into the small building, where they practiced room clearing with surprise dummy targets—some stationary, some jolting upward from behind furniture.

Murdock watched the two burst into the Kill House, then turned, hearing a new sound in the desert land not far from the small town of Niland, California, in the near edge of the Navy's Chocolate Mountain Gunnery Range.

The foreign sound turned out to be a new Buick easing up to the twenty-four-man bus with Navy markings. The rig had been home, and chow hall, for the Third Platoon of the U.S. Navy SEALs from SEAL Team Seven, now in the third and last day of a training session to sharpen their weapons skills.

Murdock had three new men in the platoon since the last walk in the park down in Kenya, and he wanted all the live firing time he could wring out to be sure the new men blended in, meshed, with the thirteen other men in his command.

He watched the car come to a stop. A familiar figure stepped out and waved.

Big news coming, Murdock knew. He wasn't sure if it would be good news, or bad, or something in between. Whenever the platoon's contact with the CIA showed up, there was a damn good reason.

Murdock waited until the last two men had stormed through the Kill House. He didn't do a critique. The men knew what they had done right and what wrong, and how to correct the mistakes. They would learn from them.

He stood, but didn't bother brushing the desert dirt off his cammies. He cradled the H&K G11, and waited for Don Stroh to come to him. The CIA man had flown over three thousand miles to get there; another hundred yards wouldn't hurt him.

Stroh was their boss, the next step up in a new chain of command, their pipeline to the CIA. A year ago the Third Platoon of SEAL Team Seven had been placed under the direct control, and command, of the Central Intelligence Agency, with Stroh as their contact. Since then Third Platoon had undertaken some ultra-secret, clandestine operations, usually on the direct orders of the President.

Anytime Stroh showed up, something was afoot.

Two months ago, in a phone call to Murdock in Washington, D.C., Stroh had indicated something big was brewing, but it wasn't quite time to move on it. Now must be the time.

Murdock held out his hand as Stroh walked up. He'd left

his suit coat in the car, stripped off his tie, and was unbuttoning his shirt.

In October the California desert could still throw up a heat wave. Some said September and October were the hottest months in Southern California. The desert went along with the plan.

Stroh grinned. "Nice little frying pan you have here."

"Not bad today. You shoulda been here yesterday."

"Come back to my office. We need to talk."

Murdock looked over to where Lieutenant (j.g.) Ed DeWitt stood in front of the platoon. He gave two curt hand signals. DeWitt signaled back and got the men up to take the planned five-mile hike at double time.

"Your office?" Murdock said.

"The car. It's got air-conditioning."

Five minutes later, they sipped ice-cold Cokes from Stroh's cooler. He never forgot the Navy's strict code about no alcohol on base.

"It's about ready to go down. Two months ago I told you something was brewing. We've got word from some of our people that the pace has quickened and it's time for us to move."

"Stroh, you sound like you're running for office. How about some specifics, some facts."

"In the near east, one of our not-so-friendly nations is about ready to build one or more nuclear devices. We don't want them to do that. You and your platoon are going to stop them."

"You make it sound simple. When and where?"

"Murdock, you're hard to figure. I thought you'd yell or groan. You've never been up against anything like this before."

"What about the North Atlantic and that oil drilling platform? We had a nuke there. The Arabs were bound to get a nuke put together sooner or later. We've been talking about it. Hell, what else in the world can go south? Now some specifics."

"First breakfast. We're going back to the huge town of Niland. They have one air-conditioned cafe I saw, and I haven't had breakfast. I'm ugly before I get my coffee and flapjacks."

"I've got more training operations this morning."

"I saw you tell Ed to continue the program. They'll be just fine. You can wash your hands and comb your hair in town."

Twenty minutes later, they were served breakfast. Murdock had a cup of coffee.

Stroh started talking as soon as he finished eating.

They were in a corner booth with no one else around them. The cafe was deserted except for one woman in the end booth.

"So, it's a nuclear problem in an Arab country, Iran to be exact. We have a simple job. To insert your platoon into the country, find the nuclear device assembly complex, destroy it and all of the nuclear components. Then you have to deal with the plutonium without causing a five-hundred-mile death zone across Iran."

"Did you say 'find the assembly complex'? You don't know where it is?"

"We've got two good men on it right now in Tehran. As soon as they tie it down, we move you and your men."

"Good to know where we're going. But you realize my platoon hasn't been cleared for combat duty yet. I had five men shot up in that Kenya picnic, and I have three new men I'm integrating into the team."

"You've had two months. I thought your guys were fast learners."

"They are, Stroh. But when you're staking your life on the guy behind you, you want to be fucking certain he knows the ropes, and the routines, and what to do and when to do it."

"Granted. The President says he wants you ready to fly out of North Island in a week."

"We can't do it. Some of my men are still hurting. We still need the platoon exercises to get everyone integrated. We're probably two weeks away from being ready for duty."

"Not a chance, Cowboy. When the President says a week . . ."

Murdock grunted. "You've got something else to spring on me. I can see it in those little blue eyes of yours. What is it?"

"How are you at dismantling nuclear warheads and stand-alone nuclear bombs?"

"Piss-poor, to coin a phrase. My best idea is to drop them down a mile-deep oil well and let them rot away for the thirty-five thousand years of plutonium's half-life."

"So you know something about plutonium."

"Enough to stay as far away from it as possible."

"So how are you going to dismantle those half-made nukes and dispose of the plutonium?"

"Have to study up on that. I still like the drop-the-plutonium-down-a-well idea."

"Fact is, Murdock, not even you and your crew can handle those nukes. We'd like to take in a NEST team. That's Nuclear Emergency Security Team. Let them handle the hot stuff. But we can't do that. DOD has no one who has a military background who can go in and do the disman-tling. So, we're calling on a civilian expert who will go in with you, and do the dirty work once you get on site. You'll be protection, guard dogs, and exfiltration experts."

Murdock slammed his palm down on the table. "A civilian? Not a chance. We can't accept a civilian on a mission. We'd be slowed down, compromised, lose some people right off. What civilian?"

"An expert on dismantling nuclear weapons. Be handy to have somebody like that around, wouldn't it?"

"Yes. But your expert first has to make it into the target.

We'd have to guarantee that, right? I could lose four or five men protecting a damned civilian. What if we have a five-mile underwater swim or a HALO jump? How can a civilian keep up with SEALs? It just won't work."

"The President says it will work, Murdock. So it's up to you to make it work instead of bitching. You think about that for a minute. I'll be right back."

Murdock watched Stroh walk away, then stared at his coffee. A mission, fine. Any mission. But taking a civilian along into Iran? He'd been in Arab countries before. No damn fun. He looked up as Stroh came back.

"Murdock. I saw an old friend down the way. Lieutenant Blake Murdock, this is Katherine 'Kat' Garnet. Kat, Murdock."

She reached out her hand. Murdock fumbled his way out of the booth to stand, and took her hand. She had a surprisingly firm grip.

"Pleased to meet you, Miss Garnet. Stroh usually doesn't have such attractive friends."

"Murdock, Kat is the civilian we're sending along with you to take care of those small toys we talked about."

Murdock's eyes went wide; his frown came at once. He shook his head. "Stroh, you've got to be joking."

"No joke, Lieutenant. The President has cleared it. It's a done deal. Kat goes with you. Last time I looked, the President was still the Commander in Chief. That would mean he outranks you, and is your boss. Right?"

Murdock sat down quickly. "Yeah, Stroh, right."

Kat Garnet grinned, and slid into the booth beside Stroh.

2

Friday, October 21

0800 hours
104 Tabas Street
Tehran, Iran
Jomhuri-ye Islami-ye, Iran

It was called the street of thieves in Farsi, and George Imhoff still couldn't pronounce it correctly. He'd slipped into the country two months ago and had been working with Shahpur Shamil, an undercover Iranian national who drew his pay from the CIA.

Together they had been trying to find out the exact location of the secret Iranian nuclear development project.

So far they had come up with little.

"It is somewhere far south and in the center of the area where there are few residents," Shamil said. "That we know for sure. I have coffee with one of the scientists working in the area in an hour in the back room of a small shop a kilometer from here. He said you couldn't come. He's taking enough risk just talking with me. He's home to attend to some family business. He returns tomorrow."

"Maybe you can get a look at his airline ticket," George said.

"Oh, no. Not fly. No airport anywhere near there, he said. He'll go by car and truck all of the way."

"You mean this area is so isolated there isn't even a railroad in there? Good, now we're making progress. Can you get for me a complete map of the train system in Iran?"

"Of course, but it will cost us."

"How much?"

"Two hundred American dollars."

"Do it. Make a phone call, whatever it takes."

George washed his hands over his face. He was thirty-five, still single his mother kept telling him, and somewhere near the top of the bracket for CIA field agents. So why did he feel like his life was going down the toilet? His Farsi was weak. He couldn't speak a word of Turkic, and his Kurdish was minimal. You needed all three languages to function well in this part of the world.

So, he would maintain. The Far Eastern Desk said they absolutely had to have the intel on this one by next Friday. He had a fucking week to find out what he hadn't been able to get in two months. Great. What was he supposed to do . . ."

Shamil had said something.

"Sorry, I was far afield thinking."

Shamil nodded. "It is good for one to think from time to time. I do not do enough thinking. Now I must go and make that phone call from the booth, then go see our friend from southern Iran. He's given me no clue where the facility is situated." He hesitated. "It will cost us."

"How much?"

"My guess is a thousand dollars, American, will loosen his tongue."

George pulled a money belt from around his waist and opened it. He counted out fifteen used one-hundred-dollar bills and gave them to the Iranian. He had no way of knowing how much of the money Shahpur would keep and how much he would give to the informant. It didn't matter. Both men were putting their lives in peril for having anything to do with George and the Organization.

"So, good hunting. There is a British student I need to see this afternoon. Remember, I'm a tourist with all the proper stamped papers, passport, visas, the works. So far nobody has asked to see my papers, which is a good sign. I must be blending in with the life and times of Iran well enough to get by."

"I pray to Allah twice a day that I, too, can escape detection. The secret police are everywhere. The fundamentalists . . ." He stopped and shook his head. "Not even here can I criticize them. I must be going."

As soon as George saw his new friend get to the street and walk away, he lowered the front window blind on the second-story apartment, and waited. Before he could fully enjoy the anticipation, a knock sounded on the two-room apartment's front door. He unlocked it and pulled it open.

Yasmeen stood there looking back over her shoulder. As soon as the door opened, she rushed inside and closed it behind her. She was breathing hard and the fire in her eyes made her pretty face glow with excitement.

"I thought they were following me, but it was only two young boys out to trap a girl." She put her arms around his neck and pulled his face down. She kissed him, long and deep. Her body pressed hard against him and he felt her shiver. He wasn't sure if it was because she was thrilled to be here, or because of the danger and the mystery of it all.

Yasmeen let him go and smiled up. She was five-one, a slender figure dressed in dark brown with her head covered with a thin shawl that was used to cover her face as well when she was in public.

She kissed him again and led him to the bed in the far room, where they sat.

"You know what they would do if they caught me here?"

He kissed her and rubbed one breast.

"First they would publicly humiliate me, then they would cut off one breast. Then they would take away all my identification cards so I could not get a job or buy food. I will not be caught here."

He kissed her again, and lay her on the bed, on her back. He started to say something, but she shook her head. "First make love to me the way you do American women. You are so thoughtful, so tender, so gentle.

"Iranian women have no rights. We can't vote, we can't be outside without our faces covered, we can't drive a car, we can't own property, we can't get a good job anywhere. We are little more than baby-making machines. I hate it all."

She pulled at his belt and tried to get his zipper down.

"Quickly now, before someone comes. One of them might have followed me after all. They are extremely good tailing people."

A half hour later she lay in the sheets, her heart still beating wildly. He sat beside her, kissed her lips once more, and nodded.

"Now, Yasmeen, tell me your news. Help me strike back at the dictators who run your country."

She sat up, and her breasts bounced. George noticed and enjoyed the moment, then watched her face. With this woman he knew for sure he could tell if she were lying.

"My father's trucking company was hired to haul goods from a port far down to the south. I know they went as far as Chah Bahar, which is almost in Pakistan. They picked up the loads at Bushehr well up on the Persian Gulf."

"Why truck material all the way down the coast when it could have been off-loaded from the ships at Chah Bahar?"

"Oh, everything was supposed to go to Shiraz, the biggest town in the southern half of the country. But then they changed the orders and it all went south."

"Any idea what these goods were?" he asked.

They began to dress then, and she put on her clothes without embarrassment.

"Oh, yes, Father talked about it. They were huge machine tools, heavy as the gods, as Father said. Then there were high-precision optical instruments. Tons and tons of cement to make concrete from, and three huge electrical generators and fuel to run them. Hundreds of other things, including construction materials. They all were loaded on Father's trucks and taken south. Even he didn't know the exact destination. This was all two years ago."

"Where could the trucks go once they got to Chah Bahar? It seems to me there is little down that far. A few mountains along the coast, then the desert plateau inland for hundreds of miles."

She nodded. "Not much in there. Why would somebody want to put up some kind of a plant in the middle of a desert?"

They were dressed then. George checked out the window. She should leave soon. He wondered if anyone would be waiting for her. Out the window, he saw movement. A man with a military-type rifle hurried from one doorway to the next. He scanned the street both ways.

Yes, there were more of them. Civilian clothes, but definitely military-type movements. Where were they going? Then he figured it out. They were closing in from both directions on this building where he lived.

He caught up a small bag that he always had ready, with everything incriminating about him inside it. He took out a .45 pistol with an extended 15-round magazine in the handle.

Yasmeen's eyes went wide. "What?"

"Troops in the street. I have an idea they're coming here. Quick, we'll go out the back window and across the roofs. Maybe they haven't got that covered yet. Now."

They hurried into the back room, and he opened the window. Before they could leave, they heard the front door smashed down. It sounded like two men in the front room. George stepped to the door and looked around it. Two shots slammed into the doorjamb just over his head.

He leaned out again, firing with the automatic. Both Iranians went down with chest shots.

He surged to the window, helped Yasmeen out, and they rushed down a narrow ledge to the first-floor roof of the building behind them.

Before they got there, two shots snarled from the window they had just left. Chips of plaster rained on them as they dropped to the roof. George fired twice at the open window, driving the men there back.

Then they came to the roof edge. They hung by their hands, and dropped six feet to the alley.

"Run," he said, and they rushed down the alley hidden from their former room by the houses. Half a block down they slowed. "We need to get away from here. Any ideas?"

Her face was pinched and frightened, but she nodded. She had pulled her head covering up to mask her face now and they hurried along the street.

"We walk, not run. Make it as casual as possible. You stay ten meters behind me. I know a place you can hide. Why are they shooting at you?" She didn't wait for an answer as they hurried down the first alley.

They walked for what he figured was a half hour, going from one alley to the next, working away from the downtown area. He heard sirens and some trucks grinding along, but saw no soldiers or the civilian-garbed enforcers.

George noticed that they had entered a poorer section of the city of 7.2 million people. The buildings were of stucco, but in poor shape. They left the alley, and went halfway down a long block before Yasmeen turned in at a walkway. They went to the back of a two-story house a little better than some of the others.

"A friend from our small freedom group lives here. Don't be surprised, he's a little different."

She knocked on the door, and when it opened, the largest man George had ever seen stared at them. He wore nothing but a pair of shorts that barely covered his crotch. George figured the man weighed at least four hundred pounds. His face had been grim, but when he saw Yasmeen, he smiled and screeched in delight.

"Little flower," he said in Farsi. He picked her up like she was a feather and whirled her around. He planted a kiss on her forehead and set her down.

"Who the fuck is this?" the man asked in Brooklyn-accented English.

About an hour before George's mad dash from the apartment, Shahpur Shamil had arrived at the coffee shop early, passed eighteen thousand rials, about six dollars U.S., to the shop owner, and hurried into the back room reserved for special customers.

His contact was already there sipping one of the thick native coffees.

"You are early," the tall, thin man said in Farsi.

"We have much to talk about."

The owner brought in a coffee for Shamil, and he tasted it, then looked at the other man.

"We don't need names, as I told you before. I just want to know where you work. How close to what town."

The man smiled. "We spoke of some compensation."

"I have five hundred American dollars."

The man held out his hand.

Shamil had carefully counted out five hundred from the fifteen hundred before he arrived, and now he drew it from his pocket.

The man pulled his hand back and shook his head. "I'm taking a great risk. It must be a thousand."

"You said . . ." Shamil shrugged. He would still have five hundred dollars left. He reached in the other pocket and pulled out the second five hundred. The man took it and smiled.

"My new friend, you have just won yourself a place in the hearts of your countrymen."

As he said it, two doors burst open and four men with machine pistols stormed into the room. Two grabbed Shamil and threw him against the wall and held him there. A third searched him, took out the other five hundred dollars, and put it in his pocket. He backhanded Shamil with a gloved hand.

Then the same man went to the table where the tall engineer still sat, and held out his hand. The engineer gave all but one of the bills to the secret service police. They both nodded. The tall, thin man stood and, without looking at Shamil, left the room by the back door.

The secret policeman turned to face Shamil. "We didn't even suspect you at first. You were so clumsy. Surely the American CIA wouldn't rely on one as stupid as you are. The money proves we were wrong.

"Where is your American CIA agent? No one in Iran has this kind of American money without getting it from an American agent."

Shamil turned his head and looked at the wall. He remained silent. He didn't even see the policeman draw his gun. He fired the pistol once. The small round blasted through Shamil's right knee and jolted him to the floor.

"Now, Shahpur Shamil, you have two minutes to live unless you tell us exactly where we can find the bastard American CIA agent."

Shamil shook his head. They would kill him anyway. His knee hurt so bad he couldn't think straight.

Then a second shot hit him in the shoulder, shattering two bones there and bringing a great wail of pain. He almost blacked out, but fought to stay conscious.

When he recovered enough to have a coherent thought, he told the secret service officer the address.

The officer wrote it down, then nodded to the traitor.

"Thank you for your fine service to Iran and the greater Islamic Republic." He scowled, then shot Shamil twice in the head, and hurried out the back door on his way to find the American spy.

3

Friday, October 21

Murdock sat in the booth and stared at the pretty woman across from him. She was slim, looked fit, had short brown hair, maybe five-eight, tanned and with penetrating brown eyes that watched him with barely concealed amusement.

"Stroh, you aren't kidding, are you? I'm surprised."

"Blown out of the water seems a better Navy phrase, Lieutenant Murdock," Kat said. "I've had that reaction before at other good old boy's clubs."

"Can you swim, Miss Garnet?"

"Yes, and I'm a SCUBA instructor." Her mouth formed half a smile.

"Good. What about parachuting?"

"I've had twenty jumps so far, concentrating on free fall." The half smile grew.

Stroh gave a short laugh. "Let's forget the twenty questions, Lieutenant. Here's her short biography: Kat is twenty-eight, has a Ph.D. in nuclear physics from M.I.T. Has been working on dismantling our overstock on nuke warheads.

19

She's a C-12 on the civil service scale. Is she in good shape? She won the second Hawaiian triathlon ever held for women. Now she keeps in shape running marathons. I'm wondering if your SEALs will be able to keep up with her."

Murdock closed his eyes and lifted his brows. He took a deep breath. Then he nodded and looked up at Kat.

"Well, it looks like I have my orders, Miss Garnet. Welcome to the Third Platoon of SEAL Team Seven."

She smiled, and it erased the harsh lines of a frown.

"Thank you, Lieutenant Murdock. Please call me Kat. I'm looking forward to working with you."

"Kat, our first job is to survive. Our next job is to get to the target. Then we, or in this case, you, do the dismantling and destruction. Then we have our biggest task—trying to exfiltrate out of some hellhole without getting ourselves killed."

She unclenched her hands where they had been gripped in her lap, and smiled. "First things first, Lieutenant Murdock. I especially like that part about surviving. I did hesitate before I took on this job. Then the President called me. One advantage you have over me: Nobody has ever shot at me trying to put big holes in my body."

"Our job is to protect you, Kat, and call me Murdock. No sense our getting to the target if you're riding along dead in a body bag."

"I don't like body bags." She looked up and a small frown creased her pretty face. "Oh, one more thing. I've never fired a gun in my life. I figure I need to learn how."

"No problem. We've got sixteen experts who will be falling all over themselves to teach you." Murdock looked over at Stroh, who couldn't stop grinning.

"This shoots your timing schedule all to hell, Stroh. No nonsense about a week for our DOD. I can rely on the current sharpness of my men, but I'll need at least a month to get Kat integrated and up to speed. How big a pack can she carry? What weapon for her? Check her out underwater with the rebreather. Can she jump with forty pounds of gear? Has she ever parachuted into water? Hell, we've got a year's worth of training for her to jam into a month."

"I'll talk to my people and they will talk to the President. State is all out of joint on this one. They say if any one Arab state gets a workable bomb, they can blackmail half the rest of the Arab states and form the biggest Muslim nation in the world. That will upset the balance of power over there, and jeopardize the whole Middle Eastern oil flow. The oil, of course, is the biggest worry."

"Have your people talk to my people," Murdock said, and Kat laughed.

Murdock looked at the woman again, only then noticing what she wore: a skirt, mid-calf, and a brown blouse with short sleeves.

"What kind of shoes are you wearing?" Murdock asked Kat.

"Shoes? Oh, one-inch heels. Sturdy enough?"

"Good, we might as well get started. We won't be back to the Kill House for a while. Let's get out there and I'll run you through it for a cold-shower approach to what you're letting yourself in for."

"Right. I want to do some shooting today, too."

Murdock stood, and Kat was up with him.

"You have any gear?" he asked.

"Just one bag in the booth."

"Bring it," Murdock said, and headed for the door. Kat looked confused for a moment, then hurried to the booth, picked up her black travel bag, and ran out the front door. When she got to the Buick, Stroh held open the rear door for her.

On the drive out to the range, Stroh said he'd arranged for Kat to have quarters at the Amphibious Base Officers Quarters.

"On the books, Kat, you'll have the temporary rank of Lieutenant," Stroh said. "That's not a field rank, but in the

SEALs rank doesn't count anyway. As the President told you, your main job is to stay alive going in so you can do the job on the nukes."

"So it doesn't matter a hell of a lot if I make it out of the country alive or not?" Kat asked.

"Getting those nukes destroyed and the rest of their nuclear capacity blasted into rubble is our only job," Murdock said. "If we do that, it isn't important if any of us come out." He hesitated and watched her shiver. "Of course to each one of us it's damn important to get out of there in one chunk."

Kat lifted her brows and smiled. "I like that last part the best."

They pulled up at the Navy bus on the range, and Kat and Murdock got out. Kat carried her bag.

Murdock talked to Stroh through the open front window. "Remember, I need a month to get this crew put together, and to safeguard Kat. Won't do any good to get to the target in there if we lose her going in. Make your boss and the President understand that. A month. No less."

The platoon was still out on one of the training exercises. Murdock motioned to Kat. "Over this way, sailor. Leave your bag in the bus, and we'll take a look at the Kill House."

He went with her to the bus, picked up a Colt .45 pistol and three extra magazines and the new H&K G11 they had been testing. Kat looked at the weapons. He pushed the safety on, on the .45, and pulled out the magazine, racking back the slide and catching the forty-five round that spun out. He handed the weapon to her.

"Get the feel of it. This could be one of the weapons that you'll carry."

She took the gun and frowned. "Heavy, isn't it?"

"Heavier with a loaded magazine in it."

They stopped twenty yards from the Kill House. It was especially built of bullet-absorbing material so the rounds wouldn't go all the way through and outside where they could hurt anyone. It had a roof and four rooms all rigged with the "terrorist" dummies.

Murdock took the weapon from her and pushed in the magazine. Then he gave the forty-five back to her.

"Grab the slide on top and pull it backward."

She tried. It didn't move. He put her hand forward and showed her how to grip it.

"This weapon is no good unless you can rack the slide back. That pushes one round from the spring-loaded magazine into the firing chamber. Then it's ready to fire."

She tried again, and this time pulled the slide back, and let it snap forward.

"Locked and loaded," Murdock said. "That means you're ready to fire." He reached over and pushed off the safety. "This is the safety. You can't pull the trigger when this is on. Now it's off. Always keep the muzzle of a loaded weapon pointed down-range."

She lifted the forty-five and pointed it at the building. She held it in her right hand. It wavered a little, but she was strong.

"Fire it," he said.

She looked at him and lifted her brows. "Remember you've got a virgin here. My very first time."

"So we go slow and gentle."

She grinned, and pulled the trigger. The weapon went off, and the recoil swung her hand well above her head.

"Wow. I did it, I shot a firearm. What a kick. I didn't expect that much."

"With an automatic you have a new round every time you pull the trigger. Try another shot, and try to hold the muzzle down a little this time."

They worked for fifteen minutes on the forty-five. Toward the end she used two hands to hold the heavy weapon. He showed her the overlapping grip.

As they finished the last magazine in the forty-five, Lieutenant (j.g.) Ed DeWitt brought the platoon up to the side of the Kill House. DeWitt's cammies were sweat-soaked on the chest and under each arm. He carried a Colt M-4A1 with the 40mm grenade launcher over his right shoulder, and stared at Murdock and Kat.

"DeWitt, get over here and stop gawking."

DeWitt walked up and kept staring at Kat.

"Kat Garnet, I'd like you to meet Lieutenant (j.g.) Ed DeWitt, second in command of the Third Platoon. Ed, this is Katherine Garnet, Lieutenant Garnet to you."

Ed saluted sharply and stepped forward. "Pardon me for staring, Lieutenant, but it isn't often that we have a pretty lady on our little training site out here in the desert."

"I'll be around from now on, Lieutenant. Call me Kat. I'd expect that Murdock has some interesting news for you and the rest of the platoon." That half little smile edged her face again, and Murdock wasn't sure if she were really smiling or laughing at him.

"Oh, yeah, there's that. Kat, maybe you'd like to tell the troops?"

"Not a chance, Murdock. I'll be interested to see how you handle the news."

"Me, too," Murdock said and they both laughed. DeWitt didn't understand what was going on.

"Murdock, past chow time," DeWitt said.

Murdock chuckled. "Oh, yeah, great idea. Put this off, and let me think on it a minute."

DeWitt called, and the platoon broke out of its position on a run and converged on the bus.

"While we're here, let me show you the new H&K G11. It's an automatic rifle. Works this way. Two positions on the fire selector. Fully automatic and three-round bursts."

Murdock moved the selector to three-round and charged a round into the chamber, then leveled the boxlike weapon at the Kill House and blasted out three rounds.

"Fully auto it works this way."

He pushed the selector lever to auto, and chattered out a dozen rounds into the Kill House.

She tried it. He fit the butt to her shoulder and she fired. The three rounds stuttered out, and the barrel hardly moved. When he shifted the selector to automatic she looked at him.

"I just pull the trigger and hold it back?"

"Right. It fires up to fifty rounds as long as you hold back the trigger."

She looked at him, then set her mouth. Her finger closed around the trigger, and she aimed at the Kill House. The first three rounds hit it, then the rounds climbed into the sky. Murdock caught the weapon and brought it back down. She eased off the trigger.

"Forgot to tell you that you have to really hold this one steady or it climbs on you."

"Now you tell me."

"Enough for today. You'll need daily training on weapons. Now how about a delicious meal at the mess hall?"

Her dark brown eyes evaluated him. "Murdock, how can I figure out when you're teasing me and when to believe you?"

"Tough question, Kat. So far few people have figured that out."

The mess hall was the bus. The delicious meal was the famous MRE, Meal Ready to Eat. This particular one was Menu No. 6. The MREs are stable, long-lasting field rations and not the favorite of most of the GI's who use them now and then. For the SEALs they were a lot easier than hauling a kitchen out to the firing/training range at Niland.

"Thought we were getting McDonald's takeout this time," Harry "Horse" Ronson called. The SEALs shouted him down.

Murdock gave Kat one of the dark brown MREs and sat in the dust on the shady side of the bus with one of his own.

"Have a seat, anywhere," he said.

Murdock cut open the heavy brown plastic envelope on

Kat's MRE, which was a foot long and seven inches wide. "Enjoy."

Kat poured out the contents. The largest olive drab plastic envelope was the main course: "Chicken à la King, #2117."

"Heat it up or eat it cold," Murdock said.

She investigated the rest: one plastic package of cocoa beverage powder, a plastic spoon, a paper package of beverage base powder, a plastic package of peanut butter, crackers, and an accessory brown envelope. Inside it was a small bottle of one-eighth of an ounce of Tabasco sauce, paper matches, a moist towelette, instant coffee, salt, toilet paper, sugar, nondairy creamer, and chewing gum.

"All this for lunch?" Kat asked.

"If we ever had time to heat it up and eat it," Murdock said. "No fire, no coffee. Cocoa maybe. Peanut butter on crackers for sure. The chicken à la king isn't bad with a little of the Tabasco sauce on it."

The men kept looking at Kat. Ed had told them only her name and rank. That made them even more curious. Murdock finished his quick meal and stood.

"You may have been wondering about our guest. Her name is Katherine, call me Kat, Garnet. She's a G-12 in government service, and for this assignment holds the temporary rank of full Lieutenant. You will at all times treat her with proper respect.

"Kat is going to be training with us for the next three or four weeks. No, this isn't for a movie. As you saw, Don Stroh, our old buddy from the CIA, was here this morning. He brings us some news. Part of it is that we have an upcoming mission. We'll be going into Arab lands somewhere to deactivate, dismember, and generally destroy that nation's nuclear bomb building program.

"How many of you know how to deactivate a nuclear bomb and destroy the plutonium inside it?" He looked around, but no hands went up.

"Yeah, me, too. Kat is a Ph.D. in nuclear physics from

M.I.T. Not a bad school but their football team stinks." He waited for the laugh that came.

"What this all means is that Kat will be training with us for what we hope will be the next four weeks, then she will be going with us, infiltrating into this Arab nation, where we will find, and Kat will destroy, the nuclear capability, and take care of the plutonium."

He heard some groans from the troops.

"Yeah, I know how you feel. By the way, Kat won the second Hawaiian triathlon for women. She keeps in shape running marathons for fun. That's over twenty-six miles, girls. Our job will be to try to keep up with her.

"She's with us. That's on special Presidential orders. Not exactly a rank we can buck. She'll train with us, go in with us, do her job while we play guard dogs, and then we'll come out with her and all the rest of you. Now, any comments?"

"Lieutenant, ma'am. Did you check first with Demi Moore?" Magic Brown asked.

A smattering of laughter.

"No, but I did see her movie."

"Will you hold us back, ma'am? Meaning no disrespect?" Jaybird Sterling asked it.

"Not if I can help it. I'm tougher than I look. I could have said no to this offer. The President didn't order me in here. I have no problem with swimming. I'm a SCUBA instructor. Jumping, I've made twenty jumps, want to do more. Damnit, SEALs, I'll be trying as fucking hard as I can."

The SEALs gave a shout of approval.

Murdock took over. "That's a wrap, folks. Let's get on the bus and head back. We need to outfit Kat and set up a new training sched. Things will change, but they will be the same, only tougher. You may think the next four weeks are going to be worse than hell week from the Grinder days. Let's get to it."

Three hours later, they were back in Coronado at the

SEALs training base. Lieutenant (j.g.) DeWitt took Kat to base operations, where he found arrangements had already been made for Lieutenant Garnet. A complete set of SEAL uniforms and gear had been put in her quarters.

She stared at the pile of uniforms and equipment.

"So, you're set, Lieutenant. Uniform of the day tomorrow will be cammies like I have on, and boots. Report to the quarterdeck promptly at oh-eight-hundred and you'll be brought to our area."

DeWitt hesitated. "Oh, Kat. Out here in Navy world, your temp rank will carry weight. Inside SEAL country rank doesn't mean squat. Some of the guys might get on you. Take it in good spirit. These men depend on each other for their very lives when we're out there on a mission. Somebody fucks up, somebody dies. We don't want that to happen. That's why we've got four weeks to make you into the best SEAL there ever was."

Kat bit her lip and squinted her brown eyes. "Lieutenant DeWitt, I like to think I'm a fast learner. I'll do my damnedest to learn what I must, to do what I have to, and to make sure that I don't cause any glitches in the traditional SEAL procedures. Thanks for the escort, and I'll see you bright and early at oh-eight-hundred tomorrow."

4

Friday, October 21

George Imhoff didn't believe his eyes or his ears. The four-hundred-pound man had demanded to know who he was. This Brooklyn blubber ball was an American.

Yasmeen moved into the void quickly. "Please let us in, and I'll explain everything. Come on, Tauksaun, it's an emergency."

The huge man waddled back from the door and made a narrow passage for them to enter. It was a single room, with a small kitchen on one side, a bed on the other, and two chairs in between. The bed was a mattress on the floor. George figured no bedsprings or frame could support all that weight.

The man she had called Tauksaun settled down on the bed and stared at George.

"He's a fucking American government man, FBI or the damned CIA or something. I don't want him in my place."

"Tauksaun, he just shot two, and maybe more, Secret Police. They have a dragnet out to find him. I figure he must be on our side."

"So he is CIA. I can spot you guys a mile away. What the fuck you looking for?"

29

"Where are you from, Tauksaun?" George asked. "Where in Brooklyn?"

"What do you mean, Brooklyn. I'm from Hempstead out on the Island."

"Sure you are. My guess would be Flatbush Avenue, down toward the Marine Park. Maybe Nostrand Avenue."

"Hey, man, you're way off. No fucking Flatbush Avenue. We had more class than that. Hey, you are CIA, right?"

"Why else would I be in this hellhole? What are you doing here?"

"Hiding from the damn IRS. Claim I owe them over a hundred thousand, with all of their penalties and interest. CIA, damn. What the hell you looking for?"

"Important shit. I don't know if Yasmeen thought you could help me, or just hide me for a couple of days."

"Hey, anything I can do to put a hot poker up the ass of the Secret Police, I'll do in a second."

Yasmeen looked at George. "Tauksaun knows a great many people in Tehran. He's lived here for five years. Most of the protest groups seek his advice."

"Is there a protest group against nuclear weapons?" George asked.

Tauksaun laughed and slapped his bare thigh. "Now we're getting down to where the rubber meets the road. Nuclear weapons, of course. What else would the CIA be interested in? I have contacts, but they are not easy to locate. I'm not good at running through the rat warren this town has become. They should starve half the people here, and start over."

"You know about the work the Iranian government is doing to make nuclear weapons?"

"Yes, we hear talk. We go to meetings. We have some sources of information, but sometimes they turn out to be spies for the Secret Police. Then that whole cell is wiped out. As in gravestones."

"We need a little information," George said. "Yasmeen

said her father had done some heavy hauling deep into the southern section of Iran. We think it was building materials and supplies, and tools for work on a nuclear bomb."

"You want to pinpoint the location of the facility," Tauksaun said. "Yes, we, too have been working toward that end. We have little. Somewhere in the mountains of lower Iran. We also know that it is carefully camouflaged and can't be detected from the air by plane or satellite."

"That makes it tougher," George said. "It must have a road that leads into it."

"We've heard of a road, but it ends abruptly at the side of a mountain. There's a sheepherder's cabin there. The problem is there are thousands of sheepherders' cabins in those southern mountains and the high plateau. Finding the right one would be a wonder."

A door opened a few inches at the back of the room. Yasmeen watched it, then lifted from her chair and, without a word to the two men, went through the door and closed it.

"Tiny," Tauksaun said. "My woman and Yasmeen are good friends. Haven't seen each other in a month or two. We've been busy."

"Do the Iranian authorities know you're here?" George asked.

"Hell no. If they did they'd deport my ass in a minisecond."

"How do you survive?"

"Tiny works at a store. Slave wages, but it's enough for us. I'm not what you'd call easily employable."

"I've had a deadline kicked in my face," George said. "I have six more days to find the exact location of that nuke facility. I've been working on it two months, and thought we had it knocked. Then my rep here goes to meet this engineer we know works at the plant. Next thing I know I'm up to my asshole in Secret Police shooting at me."

"Your rep?"

"Either in jail or in the morgue."

"They don't have morgues here. If they killed him, he's probably on a trash heap somewhere. If the family finds him, they can bury him. Did he have any U.S. dollars with him?"

"Fifteen hundred."

"He's dead."

"I figured."

They sat there for five minutes without a word. Then George broke the silence.

"Tauksaun, can you help me?"

"You have a radio in that kit?"

"Yes."

"You have plenty of U.S. dollars?"

"Yes."

"Either one of those could get all of us in the place killed in a heartbeat. First we hide the radio, and all but twenty bucks of the cash. They won't burn us for a twenty. The fucking Secret Police keep all the dollars they find. Always have, always will."

"Hide them?"

"Yes. I'll know where they are. So will Tiny. A way to keep you alive. You have papers?"

George nodded and handed over his tourist visa and other papers, including a U.S. passport and a letter ascertaining that he was a professor of Middle Eastern history at New York University on leave to study some ancient manuscripts.

"Ever had to show them to anyone?"

"Just some hick cop to the north."

"Parachute in?"

"No, came across the border from Russia."

They were silent again.

The door opened, and Yasmeen came in followed by an extremely small woman. She was only a little over four feet tall, delicately proportioned, with long black hair to her waist, and flashing black eyes. Her skin was the color of toasted almonds.

Yasmeen took her to George, who hurriedly stood. Tiny stepped back. Yasmeen told her in Farsi that in America a man standing when a woman entered a room was a mark of politeness and respect. Tiny frowned but nodded.

"George, I want you to meet Tiny. She takes care of Tauksaun. Tiny, this is George." Tiny bowed briefly, her eyes downcast. At last she glanced up at him, smiled, and hurried back through the door they came in.

Tauksaun smiled. "Usually Tiny doesn't meet my friends. She's shy."

Yasmeen went back to her seat.

"Can you help us?" she asked, looking at the huge man.

He waved, moved a pillow on the couch, and took out a cordless phone with an antenna. He dialed a number, and waited. He spoke rapidly in Farsi. The conversation lasted no more than thirty seconds. He smiled and hung up.

Tauksaun's bloated face was serious for a moment, then he smiled thinly. "There is a chance. We may have someone who knows something. He grinds lenses for glasses. A year ago he was pulled off his job, and sent to Chah Bahar. He went into the hills, and did much the same work, only not on glass, on some kind of metal that he had never seen before. He's still not sure what he did or where he was. Still he might help us."

"Lens grinding?" Yasmeen asked.

"Some of the metal in a nuclear bomb is similar to stainless steel," George said. "It takes careful machining, but any skilled craftsman, like a lens grinder, can do the job."

"Exactly," Tauksaun said. "This little man can be contacted tonight. He's extremely cautious. He'll talk only to Tiny. If he's convinced he'll be safe, she'll bring him here. Then he'll talk only to me."

"Sounds promising. Your phone. I thought they were few and far between in this town."

"True, but I can't get out, so I call out. Easier that way. Fact is I have two lines, three extensions."

George smiled. "Good plan. Hey, I need to check in with the office. Is there a balcony or a roof where I can use my little SATCOM without being seen?"

"Let's see it," Tauksaun said.

George took out the latest development in the satellite communications field. The dish traveled folded like a fan that extended into a circle six inches in diameter. It had a small tripod three inches high. The send/receive set was minimal, with only voice/data capability. It had sensors to angle the antenna at the orbiting Milstar satellite at 23,300 miles over the equator in a geosynchroness orbit.

The small keyboard had a built-in crypto unit that automatically scrambled the message. He would type it out, approve it, then hit a button to scramble the message. A few seconds later it was shot out of the small antenna in a data burst of no longer than a tenth of a second. It was almost impossible to triangulate the signal, even if one listening post picked it up.

"That one's a lot more advanced than the old ones I used to use," Tauksaun said. "Don't be surprised, these are off the shelf now. Not calibrated to the mil frequency, but good for the satellite."

"The roof?" George asked.

Tauksaun nodded, and Yasmeen led the way through the closed door into a second bedroom, and up a steep flight of open stairs to a pull-back door on the roof. There were no taller houses close by. He found a good spot behind the structure that topped the stairs, and settled down.

Yasmeen sat beside him. He set up the small antenna aiming it generally southward. He turned on two switches and checked the glowing lights. He plugged the lead from the four-inch-square transceiver unit into the antenna, turned on the set, and began to type in his message.

"George. One contact might be productive. Name: Tauk-saun. American. Suspect location still southernmost area. Shahpur KIA. Any intel for me?"

He read over the message on the small screen, nodded, and punched the crypto button. A moment later an indicator light glowed, telling him the transmission had been completed.

"That's all there is to it?" Yasmeen asked.

"That's it. Shoots it directly to a satellite which relays it to a receiver in the States."

"Can they talk to you?"

"On a schedule. Midnight and noon local time. I set up the antenna, turn the set on to receive, and wait for ten minutes. If nothing comes through, they aren't sending." He folded up the antenna and put the unit back in the heavy plastic carrying case. He stuffed it in the shoulder bag that held everything he owned in Iran. His clothes and some other items were by now in the Iranian Secret Police hands.

"What now?" she asked.

"We wait and see if Tiny can talk this lens grinder into coming to see Tauksaun. We don't have enough. We could wander around those desert roads down there east of Chah Bahar for months, and never find the right sheepherder's shack."

"For my father's trucks, the road would have to be wide, and well made, not the narrow little trails that the shepherds use. The road should stand out from a light plane flying over."

George agreed. Also it would show up well on a satellite photo. He'd send that on his next transmission. Have them move the satellite enough to cover the Iranian southern area on an every hour basis. The road had to be there. You couldn't camouflage a heavy truck road through the mountains and across some desert plateau. They had to find it.

They went downstairs, and into the front room, where
Tauksaun now lay on the bed snoring softly.

Tiny looked up and put her finger over her lips. She
motioned them back into the other room and showed them
to chairs.

"Coffee?" she asked in English. They said fine, and
watched her work on a small hot plate to boil water.

"I practice English," she said.

"You're doing very well," George said.

"You wait here. Tauksaun say. Maybe tonight the lens
grinder comes. Now, we wait. You want sugar?"

5

Friday, October 21

Lieutenant (j.g.) Ed DeWitt watched Katherine Garnet walk away and through her door in the officers quarters. It hadn't really hit him yet, a woman on a SEAL mission. Unthinkable. Impossible. Outrageous. Dangerous as hell.

But they were going to do it.

Had to. The President said so.

He turned and walked out the gate, and across the highway to the SEAL headquarters. A few minutes later he entered the small offices where the Third Platoon hung out when they were on base.

Platoon Chief Jaybird Sterling worked over some papers on his desk, and only looked up and nodded. They were informal where they could be.

DeWitt walked into Murdock's office and dropped into a chair beside the battered desk.

"We have to go through with this?"

Murdock looked up and laughed. "Just how in hell are we going to get out of it? Not a chance." He threw a wadded-up sheet of paper at the wastebasket across the room. He missed. DeWitt saw that there were a lot of misses around the target.

37

"Makes sense, in a way. Having her go in with us. But why couldn't they have found a man just as good at taking apart nukes? Now, that I could have lived with a lot easier."

"Living with it, the key phrase," DeWitt said. "How much is she going to compromise us? Are we going to take any extra KIAs because she's along? Can we get in there, and out, without getting her killed?"

"Wish I knew. If I did, I'd ask for another two months to make her the best shot in the outfit."

The two career naval officers looked at each other. The silence stretched out.

"So, what we have to do is turn Kat into a damn good SEAL in a month," DeWitt said.

"About the size of it." Murdock kept staring at DeWitt.

"You wouldn't."

"I would. Lieutenant, your new task for the Third Platoon is to be personal training officer for Kat Garnet. You will be with her twelve to fourteen hours a day. You will train her until her little buns fall off. You will make her an expert shot with pistol, and the MP-5 sub-gun."

"How in hell . . ."

"You will do it. Start with the most important first—shooting. Work her with the five and a pistol, probably a nine-millimeter with fourteen rounds. Work out a training sched to show me in the morning. Hot rounds first. Might take two weeks. Then we'll work her into the first squad as our ninth man and try to get her integrated into the platoon conscience. She has to know what we do and how we do it, so she'll know instinctively what to do and when to do it."

"It's a three-month job, Murdock."

"True. So we'll be lucky to get four weeks out of the brass back on the fucking Middle Eastern desk and from State."

"Oh, damn."

Murdock grinned. "Hey, what's Mildred going to say you

ass-to-elbows all day and half the night with a pretty, sexy woman like Kat?"

"Oh, damn. I won't tell her. No, I have to. No secrets. Damn, already I'm going to be sleeping on the couch."

"Milly might surprise you."

"Yeah, you're right. I'll be sleeping in the garage and eating on the patio. We don't have a dog house."

DeWitt yelped and looked at a small notebook he took out of his pocket. "Oh, damn. Murdock, I need a favor. Tonight you were due at our place for a fried chicken dinner. Call Milly and cancel out. I've got at least five hours of work to get a training sched to map out for my CO tomorrow."

"Done."

"Don't say anything about Kat. I'll have to break that news to Milly a little at a time."

"But don't tell her why Kat has to go with us."

"Naturally," DeWitt said. But both he and Murdock knew that he'd have to tell Milly. There was no way around that kind of a challenge.

Ed arrived at his Coronado apartment off base at 1815. Milly was pacing the kitchen. She scowled at him, and her fists went onto her hips. Ed wished he was a religious man so he could say a prayer.

"I know, I know, he had to cancel out. That leaves more chicken for me." He swept forward and kissed her, then kissed her again until her akimbo arms dropped and she grinned.

"Hey, maybe this isn't such a bad deal, after all."

Milly looked at his sandy, dirty cammies. "Shower," she said and pointed.

A half hour later, they were eating the fine meal, when Ed began.

"We had a double whammy, Navy style, today. We got a new assignment, almost, but Murdock told them we needed another month for training."

"Will you get the extra time?"

"I hope so. Think we will. Murdock can be damn convincing when he's talking about the platoon."

"What was the other whammy?"

"Oh, that. We have a new person to work into the platoon for this assignment, a damned civilian."

Milly stopped the fork halfway to her mouth. "You're joking. The SEALs have never taken along a civilian on a shooting mission. What is Washington thinking of?"

"Whatever it is, they don't tell me. Now, how did your day go?"

Milly looked at him and smiled. "Hey, did I tell you that I'm just delighted that you're back from your little three-day camping trip. I missed you. I don't want you ever to go away again."

They both laughed. It was a standing joke. She knew he had to go away, and he did, too. But in more than a year now, the two of them had weathered the separations. Twice he'd asked her to marry him. Twice she had said no.

"Ed, this is a dangerous game that you're playing," she'd said the last time. "I know it. You know it. I've read all the books about the SEALs. I know now that you do some covert work that nobody can be told about. I can accept that for now, this way. But I just can't marry you, and start a family, knowing that you might come home the next time in a damn body bag." Tears had welled up in her eyes and spilled over. She slashed them away with her hand.

For now they both accepted that, and made the best of what they had. Long, quiet walks along the crashing Pacific Ocean. Dinners out at curious and different eateries around the San Diego area. Bicycling up and down the streets of Coronado and then playing racketball. Going to plays and concerts. Walking through the zoo and Balboa Park. For now it was enough. Ed wasn't sure how much longer it would be. She had never asked him to quit the SEALs, but he was sure that was what she was hoping for.

He helped her with the dishes, and cleanup, then they sat on the sofa, their thighs touching.

"So, tall Navy officer, what's on the agenda for tonight?" Before he answered, she leaned over and kissed him, and eased him down on the sofa, so she lay on top of him.

The kiss lasted a long time. When she came up for air, he chuckled. "Mrs. Robinson, are you trying to seduce me?"

She hit him on the shoulder. "That's from an old, old movie. And yes, I am. After three good sessions, what do you have to do?"

"About three hours of planning out a training schedule for this civilian so nobody in the platoon gets killed. First weapons, then conditioning, parachute jumping, under-water—the works. Never know what we'll need to do once we get in the field."

"But you're not going to tell me why it's so important that this civilian go along with you on the mission."

"Absolutely not. Top secret. Anyway, I don't want to tell you anything to upset you while you're looking and sounding this sexy."

"Like the way you think, sailor. So, roll me over in the clover, big guy. As the English song used to go. Do they still sing that anymore?"

He didn't know. He didn't care. He had more important things to do right then.

Milly agreed with him, passionately.

6

Saturday, October 22

0700 hours
SEAL training base
Coronado, California

Kat Garnet had been up since 5 A.M. She frowned. No, that would be 0500 Navy time. She had to immerse herself totally, unrelentingly, in Navy now, specifically Navy SEALs. She could do that. She had a fast breakfast, then tried on her clothes. They almost fit, probably the smallest that the Navy issued. Not exactly from some fancy downtown store. She grinned when she looked at the beige boxer shorts. So they were a long way from Jockey ladies' briefs. She pulled them on. They nearly fit.

She rolled up the cammies legs two narrow turns, then put on the Navy bra and the cammie shirt. It didn't nearly fit. She stuffed it in the pants and tightened the belt, then looked in the mirror and saw silver bars on her collar. She took them off and put them in her shirt pocket. The black jungle boots came next, with the socks rolled down over the tops to keep them from snagging. Like the boxers, the boots almost fit. Somebody must have checked. She realized she'd be spending a lot of time walking and running in those boots, so they better fit right. She'd know after the first day.

She put on the cammie-splotched floppy hat and took another look. It would have to do. She picked up the plastic-enclosed pass she had been given, and an ID card, also sealed, and put both in the big front-flap shirt pocket.

Kat paced the floor of her small quarters a minute, saw that her waterproof wide-plastic-banded watch set for military time showed that it was 0730. Time to move.

She pushed open the door and headed for the main gate, to go across the highway to the SEAL headquarters on the other side of the road.

When she stepped into the SEAL "quarterdeck," she found it to be only a lobby for the headquarters. She showed her ID card to a sailor behind a counter and he snapped a salute.

"Good morning, Lieutenant. I'll have a man take you down to SEAL Team Seven, Platoon Three."

At once a sailor in blue dungarees appeared at a locked door to her left and motioned to her.

"This way, ma'am."

For a moment, Kat felt almost pampered, but she knew that wouldn't last. She had to become "one of the guys" to make this mission work. She had made up her mind about one thing: She was going to be so damn tough nobody would question her, and she wasn't going to get herself or anyone else killed on this mission.

A short walk later and she was shown into a building and to an open door. She stepped inside an office.

"Lieutenant Garnet, we were just talking about you," Murdock said from behind his desk in the eight-by-eight-foot room. He didn't get up. Two others were in the room. She knew one was the other officer in the platoon, DeWitt. The third was an enlisted man she remembered seeing. They all wore desert cammies.

"Good morning, Lieutenant Garnet," Murdock said.

"Good morning," she said, trying to keep her voice even, neutral.

"One suggestion, Kat. While we're at the base and in training, we all wear our rank. For you it will mean a certain amount of on-base respect, and some protection. The regular Navy likes to know who is who. Do you have the bars?"

"Yes." She took them out, and DeWitt pinned them on for her.

"As I said, we've been talking about you, Kat. You must have figured that out. Lieutenant DeWitt has been assigned as your personal trainer. He'll turn you into a SEAL so fast you'll wonder why you run those marathons."

He handed her an H&K MP-5SD. It was almost two feet long and weighed a ton. She reconsidered—maybe five or six pounds.

"This is called an MP-5. It's a Heckler & Koch submachine gun. It can be set for single-round, three-round fire, or fully automatic. Don't be afraid of it. This weapon is going to be your constant companion. You'll work with it, shoot it, swim with it, hike with it, sleep with it if you want to.

"The first priority for you is to learn to fire this weapon, to get good with it so you can hit what you aim at. This is a form of insurance for you, and for the rest of the SEALs who will be with you. That's first up for you this morning— lots of weapons training, and live-round firing. DeWitt."

"Right this way, Kat. We've got packs waiting." They left the office and picked up backpacks.

"Usually we don't use these on a mission, they're for training. Oh, carry that weapon in both hands with the muzzle facing left at a forty-five-degree angle across your chest. Easiest way to carry it, and it's ready to use in a half a second."

She lifted the pack.

"Only ten pounds, Kat. Mostly ammo. Want to get you started off easy."

She slipped into the pack, adjusted the straps, and held the submachine gun the way she had been told.

They walked away from the buildings, through a gate and onto the sand. A sand dune had been dozered up to replace the sand ripped out by winter storms. They went down to the hard sand along the water and turned south.

"We've got about three miles down to a spot we use for live firing. Since time is important, we'll run. How about a six-minutes-a-mile pace."

"That I know about," Kat said. She had resolved to talk as little as possible, to record everything, and to remember everything. She started off at the six-minutes-a-mile pace, and was soon glad it wasn't a five-minute mile he wanted. The pack bounced and jolted on her back until she worked out a slightly different stride to move with its sliding motion.

DeWitt looked at her and smiled. "Yes, you know what a six-minutes-a-mile pace is. Can you do that for twenty-six miles?"

"Not with this pack on, for damn sure."

DeWitt grinned. "Good, you're human, after all."

Twenty minutes later they stopped at a twenty-foot-high sand dune with grass and shrubs growing on the top. The face of it had been bulldozed out almost vertical to set up a safe twenty-yard shooting range. DeWitt got down to business.

"At this point we don't care if you can field strip the MP-5 or not. All we want you to be able to do is shoot it, and hit what you're aiming at. That's our job this morning. This weapon has a folding stock so you can hold it close or, if you have time, pull out the stock for a better aim. It has a thirty-round magazine, and will fire single-shot, three-round bursts, or fully automatic. However, we like to think that SEALs are better shots than to have to hose down a spot with thirty rounds to hit one man."

He watched her. She had a slight frown, and seemed to be memorizing everything he said.

"Understand yesterday you fired a weapon for the first

time. First a forty-five pistol, and then the G-eleven. This isn't quite so hot as the G-eleven. But it will do the job. Now, let's do some dry firing for position."

Back in the office of Third Platoon, Murdock had tried again to lay out a training schedule. He and DeWitt had worked over it since seven that morning, and it still didn't look right.

"This whole thing might be useless if Stroh says we have only ten days to get on that plane," Jaybird Sterling said.

"Not a chance. Stroh saw how serious I was. I'll call the President direct if I have to. No sense slaughtering a whole platoon and still not get the mission accomplished. We'd just show our hand, and the Arabs could throw a division of troops around wherever the factory is and make it impossible for any outfit to get in there."

"So, we keep the same sequence for Kat: weapons, fitness, water training and rebreather, then jumping?"

"Still looks the best. We can modify it as we go along. After her individual training, we still need two weeks to work her in with the rest of the troops."

"At least. In our combat formation, where does she walk?" Sterling asked.

"With our squad. Lampedusa out front, then me, then Holt with the radio. You're behind Holt and right in back of you is Kat. You'll baby-sit her."

"Figures. By the time Mr. DeWitt gets her trained, I hope to hell she'll be able to work right along with the rest of us."

"To be prayed for. Now for the rest of the troops. Get them up and ready—we're hitting the obstacle course. No tadpoles over there this morning. Every man gets timed. Anybody who doesn't do it in ten minutes, drops, and does a hundred pushups. Ten minutes later he does the course again—until he's under ten. I'm the first one out of the chute."

Two hours later, all but two of the men of Third Platoon

had done the beast of an obstacle course in under ten minutes. Those two ran it again. This isn't any ordinary course. It includes the usual barriers, plus a twenty-foot vertical wall climb, a go up and down a sixty-foot-high cargo net, a rope climb, a shinny up a sixty-foot tower, a slide down from it on a rope, the stump jump, parallel bars, a rope climb up a wall, a thirty-foot barbed-wire crawl, the weaver, a rope bridge, the log stack, the five vaults, and the swing rope combo. When the men finish, they are told their time, then drop, and do twenty push-ups.

Murdock gave the last two men through the obstacles a five-minute break, then he stood.

"Gentlemen, let's go for a little run."

They hit the hard sand and ran south for a mile at a seven-minute pace, then moved into the soft sand and did another mile. When they were two miles from the gate, Murdock turned them around.

"Too damn hot out here today," he said. He led the twin line of SEALs into the surf, running, splashing along at the seven-minutes-per-mile pace in sometimes wet sand, sometimes a foot of swirling ocean water, depending on when the waves broke.

Within two minutes the SEALs were soaked to the skin from head to toe.

Murdock watched the men as he ran backwards. Yes, they were doing it, holding up. The three new men had settled into their places now that they knew an assignment was coming up. His wounded troops were responding as well. In two weeks they would all be hard and fit, and ready to try something new: like working with a civilian woman on a mission where the smallest misstep could mean death to yourself, and some of your fellow SEALs.

It was entirely new territory. No woman had ever participated in a SEAL covert operation before.

• • •

By 0900, Kat's right shoulder was sore from firing the submachine gun. She had lost count how many 30-round magazines she had burned up. She liked the three-round burst. Only twice had she fired it on full auto. In two bursts she emptied a full magazine.

"All right, Kat. You have a full mag. We're hiking along this trail. I'll be behind you. Without warning we start taking enemy fire from the left. I'll say 'Fire from the left!' When I shout that, you drop to your stomach, have the MP-5 up, and return fire into the dune. Use up the magazine with three-round bursts. Got it?"

Kat nodded.

They moved back to the start of the range and began walking across the face of the big dune. DeWitt waited until they were almost across the mouth of the range before he called out.

Kat dropped to her stomach, broke her fall with her elbows, aimed, and fired at the carved-out sand dune within three seconds. She fired all thirty rounds, ejected the empty magazine, slammed in a new one, and worked the slide to push a round into the firing chamber the way DeWitt had showed her.

"Cease fire," DeWitt said. He squatted beside her. "Yes, Kat. Good. I didn't even tell you to change magazines, but that's a basic. In any firefight you keep a loaded magazine in your weapon at all times. If you can change from a partly used one to a full one, do that. Never get caught with an empty magazine, or you and half the platoon could be dead."

"Got it," Kat said.

They did the firing on command six more times, three from each side so she learned how to twist her body to return fire to the right. Each time she did it quickly and the right way.

DeWitt sat down across from her and stretched out his legs. He watched her. She looked at him.

"What?"

"Nothing. It's break time. In your pack is a canteen. I filled it with Coke and ice cubes before we left the Grinder. Strongest thing we have on base."

A grin flashed across her face as she grabbed the canteen and drank. She smiled. "Oh, yes, I needed this. Like Navy grog of old."

"Kat, I know you have a Ph.D. in physics. Any minors like law?"

"How did you know? I went into prelaw for two years, then switched."

"How did I know? You have a sharp analytical mind, I'd guess. What I've seen this morning is that I don't have to tell you or explain anything to you twice. You listen, you see, you learn, you memorize I'd bet, and then you do. Traits of a good trial lawyer. I had prelaw and then a year of law school before I went to the Academy."

"Still happy with your choice?"

"Remarkably. I'm so Navy that it hurts sometimes."

She nodded. "I can see that, DeWitt."

They worked on the canteens of Coke.

"What's next?" Kat asked.

"Easy, we have all day. You seem determined."

"I didn't really want this job. They told me I was the best person to do it. Now that I'm into it, I'm determined not to get anybody killed, and to get in and out, and stay alive myself."

"That's exactly our plan. So, you ready to work with a pistol?"

"I'll be carrying one besides the MP-5?"

"Right, we all have at least two weapons. Some of the guys also have a hideout, a little twenty-two or a thirty-two."

He reached in his pack, and took out a pistol. DeWitt gave it to her. "This is an H&K P7. It fires a nine-millimeter round and holds eight of them in the magazine in the handle.

It doesn't have the hitting power that the forty-five you shot yesterday does. But neither does it have the weight or the recoil."

She held it, careful to keep the muzzle pointing down-range.

"One interesting feature on this weapon is that it has no safety. Most pistols have a safety. You can't just draw and fire like in the old westerns. You have to push off the safety, then fire.

"This pistol has a unique grip catch in the front edge of the butt. When your hand grips this, it engages the trigger with the cocking and firing mechanism. That all means that to fire the weapon you simply grip the handle and pull the trigger. If you drop it, the weapon's grip catch isn't engaged, so it can't go off accidentally."

DeWitt stood. "Give it a try. It's loaded."

She stood, aimed at the sand dune, and pulled the trigger. Nothing happened.

"That's an automatic," DeWitt said. "First you need to pull the slide back like you probably did on the forty-five. You need to do this on any automatic just after loading an empty weapon with a fresh magazine."

"Right," she said. She pulled back the slide and let it snap forward, then lifted the weapon, gripped the handle, and squeezed the trigger. It fired. She nodded. Aimed again, and fired. Soon the 8-round magazine was empty and the slide stayed open.

DeWitt handed her a full magazine. "How do I get the empty one out?" she asked.

"The magazine catch is at the left side of the butt, behind the trigger. Push it and the magazine drops out. Slide in the new one."

"Then I pull the slide back to chamber a round. Got it."

"Now hold your fire while I set up some man-sized targets." He went to the face of the sand dune, pulled six targets from a closed wooden box, and leaned them against the back of the carved-out sand.

Back beside her, he motioned at the targets twenty yards away.

"This is a common target distance, twenty yards. That's sixty feet, three times as far as the Old West gunmen liked to be for a gunfight. Twenty feet was plenty for those old six-guns.

"We'll move up to ten yards and give you a try. No weapon is any good if you can't hit what you're aiming at. Anyone we start shooting at won't be afraid of the sound. It'll take hot lead to discourage him. We use the point-and-shoot technique with pistols and handguns. It works.

"Just push out your finger and point at something. You'll do the same thing with the H&K in your hand. When you are pointing at your target, pull the trigger. Give it a try on the first target. Hold the pistol at your side. Then lift your hand almost shoulder high and point at the target. When you're on target, squeeze the trigger."

Kat did. The first two shots hit the first target. Then she missed three, and the last three she hit.

"Yes," DeWitt said.

They fired forty rounds through the P-7 then tested two other handguns, both with 14-round magazines. Kit liked the H&K P-7, without a safety to worry about.

They packed up, finished the canteens of rapidly warming Coke, and cleaned up the brass from the rounds they had fired. Then they headed back down the beach.

"Packs are a lot lighter this time," Kat said.

They ran back the three miles to the Grinder and dropped into chairs in Murdock's office.

"Boots," DeWitt said. "How do they feel?"

"Blisters," Kat said. "They're half a size too big. I need eight-and-a-halfs instead of nines."

"I'm on it," Jaybird Sterling said. "I'll pick up a pair this afternoon."

"How's the shooting eye?" Murdock asked.

Kat shrugged and pointed to DeWitt.

"Good. Point and shoot with the pistol was right on. Kat likes the H&K P-7. We'll keep at it. The MP-5 is coming along. Didn't do much on accuracy. Down the road. What about longer guns? We still have that friendly rancher up by Boulevard?"

"Last time I knew," Murdock said.

"Think Kat and I'll slip up there in the morning for some work on the long guns. Kat, we want you to be able to fire any weapon we carry in an emergency. Not that you have to qualify, but you should be familiar enough to pick up one and use it if you lose yours or you run out of rounds."

"Sounds reasonable. What's next?"

DeWitt looked at Murdock.

"A run?"

"We did six miles already," DeWitt said.

"What about the obstacle course? I'd like to try it."

"Not on your agenda," DeWitt said.

"You don't think I can do it," Kat said.

Murdock grinned. "Might be a good welcome to the SEALs," he said. "Yes, Kat, I'll lead you on a tour of the obstacle course. Any one of the stops you don't want to try will be fine."

"I'll do the whole course. Let's go."

7

Friday, October 21

2242 hours
Tehran, Iran

George Imhoff sat in the second room of the small apartment and tried to make sense out of what went on between the huge fat American and the Iranian lens grinder. George belched and his stomach growled at him. He hadn't had anything to eat since that morning. The four warm French beers hadn't helped any. He had no idea where Tauksaun, the huge one, found French beer in Tehran.

George looked at Yasmeen for the hundredth time and lifted his brows. They sat near the door that had been opened three inches so they could see, and Yasmeen could hear. Most of the conversation was in Farsi.

"They still talk about the soccer match. Each time Tauksaun brings up the lens grinding, the man changes the topic."

George swore softly, and watched Yasmeen's eyes light up. She seemed to be excited by the dirty words, but he didn't have time for that now. He slipped the forty-five from his pocket and checked the magazine. Full. He held it in his right hand and reached for the door.

"No," Yasmeen said softly.

"Yes, I don't have time for this shit. Past time for some action." He stepped through the door and cleared his throat. Both men near the bed looked at him. Tauksaun shook his head when he saw the weapon.

George didn't hesitate. He pulled the forty-five's slide back and let it snap forward, slamming a round into the firing chamber. He carried the pistol low as he walked up to the Iranian.

"Tell him the bullshit is over. Do it, Tauksaun."

The huge man tried to roll to one side a little to ease the pressure on his hips. He sighed, then stuttered out some Farsi.

George brought the forty-five up to aim at the lens grinder's chest.

"Now, tell him I want to know exactly where he was taken to do the grinding work on the polished steel. Exactly. None of this blindfolded crap."

George waited as the translation came. Then he put the pistol's muzzle against the lens grinder's chest, directly over his heart.

The Iranian was thin, small, with a full dark beard and bushy brows. He slumped back toward the bed and George moved with him, increasing the pressure of the forty-five. The Iranian looked up with black eyes that showed stark fear.

He chattered once, and paused, then came out with a flood of Farsi.

George waited.

Tauksaun nodded. "He says he knows they went to the southern port city of Chah Bahar. From there they drove north by truck into the mountains on a good gravel road. He says they never got all the way through the mountains into the great plain. So the spot must be in the mountains."

"Could he find the place again?" George asked.

When the Iranian heard the translation, he looked at George and shook his head.

The translation came that they had been kept in covered trucks all the way from the port. He only knew they went north. They did not go into Pakistan.

The questioning went on.

The man had no idea what kind of project he had worked on. He was grinding some kind of metal. He never saw a finished product. He and ten others had worked around the clock on twelve-hour shifts.

Yes, they had completed the project and then were sent home. Yes, they each received wages, and a bonus of 210,000 rials. That would be about seventy dollars, not a lot of money for a lens grinder.

"That's all he knows, CIA agent," Tauksaun said. "I don't appreciate your use of the weapon in my house. It wasn't needed."

"It worked, nobody got hurt."

"So far," Tauksaun said. He spoke with the lens grinder for a few moments, then Tiny came. They put a blindfold around the small man's eyes, and Tiny led him out the front door.

It would take Tiny a half hour to get the man out of the area and safely away. Tauksaun didn't talk to George. He tried to find some American music on his short-band radio. He got mostly static, then located an American station on one of the Air Force bases in Germany. The music came through loud and clear.

The Andrews sisters had just finished a golden oldie, when Tiny came in. She closed the door, then tried to turn, but staggered a step before she fell to the floor. George went down beside her and held her head.

Her eyes rolled for a moment, then steadied in place.

Blood seeped from her mouth.

"Police," she whispered in English, then passed out. George carried her to a pallet beside the floor bed and stretched her out. He had tears in his eyes. Yasmeen knelt beside Tiny on the pallet, making a quick examination.

"She's been shot in the chest," Yasmeen said. "Probably hit one lung, and for sure lots of internal bleeding. If she doesn't get to a hospital, she'll die."

"No hospital," Tauksaun said. "The police would recognize her and let her die there. Tiny isn't exactly unknown to the authorities. This is all on your head, CIA man."

He stared at Tiny for a moment and blinked rapidly. He nodded to himself, and then used the telephone. He spoke quickly in English and Farsi, then hung up.

"A friend, a nurse, will be here quickly. Before she comes, you two must go. Now."

"Can I help?" Yasmeen asked.

Tauksaun watched her; his eyes seemed to narrow as a frown tainted his round face. "Perhaps. Your father is wealthy. We always need money. Yes, you can help. Twenty million rials would be good. That's only a little over sixty-six hundred dollars, George, don't look so surprised." He rolled, and sat up straighter with a great effort.

"Now both of you out of here with your radio and your American dollars that could get us all shot on sight. The Secret Police will be here shortly. Somebody will always rat on me for a few thousand rials. Out."

"Thanks for the help," George said. He picked up the radio and put it away in his shoulder bag, then pocketed the forty-five after making sure the safety was on.

"No thanks needed. I just hope you haven't got me killed."

Yasmeen and George went out the front door and hurried down the street. George could almost smell the Secret Police coming. He frowned as they rushed along. He had a little more information, but not nearly what the Company demanded. How the hell was he going to find out anything else without going into the region? The idea of a small plane was good, but he'd have no chance at all renting such a plane down in that area. There might not even be an airfield down there. He didn't know that much about Iran.

They saw a military vehicle moving down the street toward them. It was still two blocks away. Yasmeen pulled at his arm, and they drifted into an alley, then ran full speed to the next street. Yasmeen looked both ways, then they darted across the street into the alley, and ran through it until they both were panting so hard they had to stop. They leaned against a wall.

"I think we got away from them," George said.

Yasmeen scowled at him, her eyes almost closed. "I hope nothing happens to Tauksaun. He's a friend. He helps with the protest movement."

George shook his head. "Tauksaun will come out smelling like a bunch of violets. He's a survivor. Not even the Secret Police will be able to hurt him."

"What are you going to do now?" she asked.

"Not the faintest."

"Come to our house. It's big and I'll tell Papa that you're teaching me better English. He wants me to be good in English. But we can't even touch at my home. You understand. Iranian women aren't that free. We have tremendously strict rules."

"You mean, we can't make love in your father's house?"

"He'd chop off your head if he caught us."

George chuckled. "I think I can keep my hands off you. Which way do we go?"

Before they could move, a man jolted around the corner twenty yards from them and shouted in Farsi for them to put up their hands.

"Run," Yasmeen barked. She went right, he went left. The Secret Policeman with the submachine gun tracked his best target and fired a 6-round burst. Four of the slugs caught Yasmeen in the back and she stumbled, tried to call out, and pitched into the dirt. Yasmeen died before she hit the ground, where her face dug a foot-long furrow in the dust and garbage of the Tehran back alley.

Before the Secret Policeman could turn his weapon on the

second person, George had sprinted around the corner to safety. He ran hard down the block to the next alley and surged into it. He paused. No one chased him. George panted. He had to get more exercise and stay in shape.

He'd seen Yasmeen fall. Damn them. She was dead or as good as dead by now. Which left him absolutely at the end of his string of contacts. He was running in fucking hostile Tehran. The Secret Police were hunting him. He had lost his luggage, all of his clothes, and personal gear. He had only his "vitals" in the shoulder bag. He had a deadline of six days to find out for sure where the Iranian nuclear manufacturing site was situated. How in the hell was he going to do that?

8

Saturday, October 22

By the time Murdock and Kat returned from the obstacle course, it was nearly 1700. Murdock dropped in his chair, and looked at DeWitt and Jaybird.

"So, how did Kat do?" Jaybird asked.

Kat came in the door standing as tall as she could, and grinned. "I did it all except the ten-foot wall."

"That takes good upper body strength," DeWitt said.

"Hey, I'm a long-distance swimmer, remember."

"Any word from Don Stroh on our request for more time?" Murdock asked.

DeWitt shook his head. "Not a word, which might be good news. He should be fighting for those four more weeks."

Murdock looked at the chart in front of him. He passed it to Kat.

"Your schedule. First things first in case we get short sheeted. Weapons training the next two days. Then two days of parachute jumping. Can't see any other way we can get into Iran fast and quietly. Then comes rebreather work in the

61

ocean, and some underwater techniques. Last we'll get you working in the first squad, so you'll know who does what and when."

The phone rang.

Murdock picked it up.

"Third Platoon, SEAL Team Seven. Murdock."

"Stroh here. Murdock, you've got friends in high places. You get your four weeks. State is unhappy, but my boss said we don't have the target tied down for you yet. That has to come first."

"We'll make good use of the time."

"We're having another small problem. Lost our local in Tehran. We might need some fast muscle in that area and I'm touting the idea of sending in two of your men to help protect and cover our sales representative there. If he can't pinpoint the target, the whole operation is off."

"Two men? To serve as backup and some firepower? Remember, we're action guys, not your average Company spook."

"Our man's still there—he'll lead the way and do the digging, but he's lost his cover and been chased twice now. He needs some backup with some firepower. Nothing definite that we can drop two men in. We'll know by Monday. Pick out two men who can use a radio and who can take care of themselves. Anybody speaking Arabic or Farsi would be helpful."

"Oh hell yes, half our guys speak Farsi. Anything else?"

"No. You've got four weeks, and hang loose. How is Kat doing?"

"She just came back from the range and the obstacle course. She's looking good, for a Ph.D."

"Remember, she has a round-trip ticket to Iran. You'll be hearing."

They hung up.

"So, we got our four weeks?" DeWitt asked.

"We have. They still haven't located the target. Might

need some help in Tehran. Soon you guys will be taking a pleasure cruise into Iran."

"Iran?" Jaybird said. "Already they don't like us there."

"True. Jaybird, find out if any of our guys speak Arabic or Farsi."

"Should be in the personnel files." He left the office.

Murdock looked at Kat and DeWitt. "We've got a job to do, so let's revise that training schedule. Kat, we'll want you to check it out and see how fast we can push you." He watched as she flexed her shoulders.

"Your arms and shoulders getting sore?"

"Yeah. I haven't been swimming enough last few weeks."

"We'll take care of that. Of course, you'll be swimming in your cammies most of the time and with your boots on. It's harder."

"I'll start tomorrow. Now, where's that training schedule?"

Jaybird came back in. "Found a guy who speaks Farsi— Colt Franklin, one of the new guys."

"Who else can run a SATCOM besides Holt?" Murdock asked.

"Joe Douglas, second squad."

"Get Franklin and Douglas in here now. We've got something coming up."

Kat looked up from the training schedule on Murdock's desk. "I want to do a mile swim and a three-mile run every day besides the other training. Unless it doesn't fit in."

Murdock grinned. "Young lady, we'll try to arrange it. No solo swimming. You'll have to have a buddy. We don't want to lose you to a Great White."

"I'd like to take that swim now, Lieutenant Murdock. Who wants to go with me?"

"Now?" Murdock asked.

"Unless it interferes with your schedule, Lieutenant."

Murdock lifted his brows, and pointed at his platoon

chief. "Jaybird, take Kat on the one-mile course on the bay side. Then see that she gets to her quarters."

"Now, sir?" Jaybird said, surprised.

"Now, sailor. A SEAL is always ready for the unexpected."

Jaybird snapped a salute at his commanding officer. Murdock was so surprised to see it, that he only half returned it.

"Get out of here, Jaybird."

When they left, DeWitt concentrated on the schedule a moment. "Murdock, I think Kat is going to fit in nicely. She's tough as old leather, has lots of heart, and is a worker. No wonder the brass wanted her along. She'll do a lot better than most of the men the AEC could have sent us."

"Agreed. But she's still a civilian. We can't get her SEAL trained in four weeks, so there will be a lot of chances to fuck up. Our job is to make damn sure we get her into the target with all of her bodily parts working."

DeWitt checked his watch and moved toward the door. "Thanks for sending Jaybird on that swim. I didn't want to be late getting home tonight. Time I tell Milly about Kat. Last night I just told her the person was a civilian. Sure you don't want to come over for dinner?"

Murdock waved. "Count me out. I hate bloodshed among the civilian population. Let's hope Milly is tremendously understanding. Starting tomorrow, you'll be with Kat twelve to fourteen hours a day. Be sure Milly understands that."

"Oh, yeah, easy. Maybe I'll just sleep on base tonight."

"Sure you will."

"Right, I better get home and face the firing squad."

"Won't be that bad. We'll have Doc Ellsworth ready with his medical kit for you first thing in the morning."

At the end of the Navy Amphibious Base pier extending into San Diego Bay, Jaybird looked at Kat.

"Lieutenant, you have anything in your pockets you don't want to get wet?"

"Just have my I.D., which is sealed. I'm ready when you are."

"Let's do it."

They dove into the bay and both gasped at the coolness of the October water. Jaybird did his famous side stroke until he saw Kat surface from her shallow dive and strike out with a strong crawl. He kicked into one himself, and caught up and stayed with her. She went out much faster than the usual SEAL crawl, but he didn't say anything.

"We'll go east to that first point of land," he called. She nodded, and angled to the right.

Five minutes later, Jaybird saw that he was falling behind. Kat's strong crawl stroke had picked up in tempo, and she pulled away from him.

When she came to the turnaround down from the point, she stopped and treaded water waiting for him to catch up.

"This the turnaround?" she asked.

Jaybird said it was, and she kicked out for the pier.

By the time Kat went up the ladder to the pier they had left, she was three minutes ahead of Jaybird. He came up the ladder puffing. He squeezed water out of his cammies, and nodded.

"Lady, you won't have any trouble keeping up if we have to take a swim getting in or out of country over there."

"Good, Jaybird. Next time maybe we can try the ocean side."

Ed DeWitt made it home ten minutes before Milly came from her job as a computer network analyst at Deltron Electronics. She was an expert in her field, and was making a salary twice what Ed made even counting his housing, food, and uniform allowance.

He checked the menu written out on a pad on the refrigerator door. They tried to specialize in healthy yet quick-to-fix meals. Tonight it was Spanish rice, a green salad, French cut green beans, and rolls. Whoever got home first always started dinner cooking. Sometimes it was murder for Milly to get across the Coronado Bay Bridge from San Diego. Tonight, DeWitt thought, must be one of those times.

He had the Spanish rice simmering when Milly came in the door.

"Don't ask," she said, tossing her purse on the kitchen table and dropping into a chair. "Everything went wrong. I've never seen such a foul-up. I never get the little problems, just the ones nobody else knows how to fix."

He kissed her and put his arms around her, chair and all. "Bet you solved the problem in a rush. Hey, you have to earn the big bucks they pay you."

She sighed, and kissed him back. "I guess. Sometimes I just wish that I could stay home and raise babies. There, I said it. My nesting instincts are high right now." She gently moved his arms and went to the stove.

"Smells good. Spanish rice always is great the first day, but a bummer for warming up. I wonder why."

She turned. "Hey, I'm sorry. Me, me, me. So how was your day? How is that new civilian working out?"

"Need to talk to you about that." He led her back to a chair and pulled one up facing her. He sat down.

"Hey, you look serious. You proposing or something?"

"Something, yes. I never tell you much about what I'm doing, or where we go. I can't. This time I've got to. Top secret—not even your best friend can find out about this. Our civilian is from the AEC or some such group. This person is an expert at dismantling nuclear warheads and bombs. This person is a woman."

He stopped, and watched her. Milly frowned. "You mean the CIA is sending a woman with you on your next mission to dismantle some atomic warheads or bombs?"

"Exactly right."

"No woman can take all the physical punishment you guys go through. I've seen you black and blue with bruises from head to foot. I've watched your bones knit back together and changed bandages on your bullet wounds. They must be crazy sending a woman in with you."

"That's what we thought. The problem is the President said that this woman is going. We can't really get around an order from our Commander in Chief."

Milly eyed him seriously, then her face melded into a small frown. "Have you met this woman?"

"Yes, she's on base, began training this morning."

"I'm curious. What's she like?"

He gave a quick description of Kat.

"Yes, yes, but is she pretty? You said she was about thirty. Is she pretty?"

"Pretty? A vague term. She's attractive, fit, seems to have a good attitude. Did I tell you she's a Ph.D. in nuclear physics?"

"No. How can she hold up on your long marches, your swims? Can she parachute?"

"She won the second Hawaiian Iron-Man woman's triathlon—the swim, bike riding, and marathon. Yes, she's fit and strong."

"I just don't understand why they would pick a woman for this job."

"Evidently she was the best person to get the work done."

"So you got the job of training her in SEAL techniques."

"Afraid so. We were on the small arms range this morning. We ran both ways, six miles round trip. She never faltered."

Tears welled in Milly's eyes. They spilled over. "You want me to move out?"

"Milly, of course not. Why on earth would I want that? She's not personal. It's my job to train her well enough so we can get her to the target. After her work is done, she has to be able to get out of there with us, and not be such a liability that half the platoon gets killed."

Milly began sobbing, and reached out and clung to him.

"Oh, God, not that. I pray every time you leave me. I know you're doing something important for our country—but it's so dangerous. I don't sleep much while you're gone. Did I ever tell you that? I'm not sure if I eat anything. I always lose about ten pounds when you're gone. Oh, damn, I wasn't ever going to tell you that."

"I didn't know." He took her in his arms and held her.

After a while, she stopped crying.

"I'll be putting in some extra time. It's my job to teach her how to shoot our weapons, show her what we do, and how we do it. If I do my job right, then she won't cause any of us to get wounded or worse. Yes, we'll be baby-sitting her, but unexpected things always happen. If she can defend herself, so much the better."

"She, she. Does this woman have a name?"

"Katherine Garnet. She has the temporary rank of full lieutenant and she said to call her Kat."

"How nice." Milly sniffed. "I'm sorry, Ed, I didn't mean to sound so snide. She's probably a fine person. I want you to invite her over to dinner tomorrow night. If you aren't having any kind of night drills."

"I'll arrange it. Yes, good idea. I think you'll like Kat. Now, I think your marvelous dinner is ready. May I seat you at the table and serve you?"

As they ate, they talked about her work, and the new theater season coming up. All the while DeWitt remembered what she had said about losing ten pounds while he was gone. She shouldn't do that. But who could they trust? Then he remembered one of the men in his squad, Fernandez, who lived with a woman in Coronado. He'd talked to him. Maybe the two women could get together when the platoon was on a mission. He'd never met the woman. They would have one huge thing in common. It might just work. He'd talk to Fernandez in the morning.

That night, Milly clung to him. She had slipped into bed beside him without wearing her usual nightgown. She kissed him, and put his hands on her, and whispered in his ear.

"We're going to make love every night from now until you leave."

Ed laughed softly. "We're not shipping out for a month yet."

Milly nodded. "Good, I'll keep you so worn out you won't even know that Kat is a woman. She'll just be another one of the guys you have to train. Now, roll over. I want to be on top the first time tonight."

9

Saturday, October 22

0214 hours
Tehran, Iran

George Imhoff had struggled with his decision for three hours, as he went from one small cafe to another, nibbling at rolls and drinking the bitter tea. There was no other way. He had used up his best prospects. The British student he was supposed to see that afternoon might be hard to find now.

He worked his way slowly to the right street and paused in the shadows for five minutes watching it and the surrounding half-block area. Nothing moved. No one walked or rode by. Only one light showed in the whole area. He moved cautiously to the front of the small building and found the gate where it was supposed to be.

It was unlatched. He pushed it inward.

Nothing happened.

He darted quickly through the opening and closed the wooden gate. A walkway led to the rear of the structure. It had two stories. The front of it was some kind of a retail store with windows covered by wooden panels locked in place.

Trust your fellow man and he will trust you.

Right.

George found the rear door and knocked on it three times. He expected no reaction. Picking the lock would do no good. Everyone in this part of the world used locks with steel bars on the inside as well.

To his surprise the door opened a crack, and a small voice asked him a question. He caught only one word and that didn't make sense. He used the code word with hesitation.

"Armageddon," he said.

There was a pause, then a sucked-in breath.

"Just a moment," the voice said in English.

He heard movement inside, then the door opened more. "Not if we can prevent it," the countersign came.

"Thank God," George said. The door opened to a dimly lit interior.

"Come in, my friend. Come in. We have been expecting you. Things are not going well for us on this adventure."

The tall Iranian man, dressed in work clothes, held out his hand and George shook it.

"I'm George," he said.

"Call me Peter." The door closed and the two men went into a small room with cushions on the floor and a single light bulb burning in the corner.

"We know about Shahpur. His family claimed his body. Have you eaten? You need sleep? What can we do for you?"

George leaned against the wall. Suddenly he was tremendously tired. "Some sleep would be good, but first, do you know my mission here?"

The man called Peter shook his head. "None of us know."

"Yes, usually it's better that way. But now you must know. I need help in locating a facility. I have only two more contacts, and I'm afraid one of them has been picked up by the Secret Police already."

George told Peter about needing the exact location of the nuclear bomb fabrication plant in southern Iran.

The tall man sat on one of the cushions on the floor and

rubbed his beard. "From time to time we hear stories. Nothing solid, no two alike. It's some marvelous weapon that will make Iran king of the whole Arab world."

"With one or more nuclear bombs, Iran could threaten all of the Arab states, and ensnare them into one giant confederation that could rule all of the near east," George said. "It would disrupt the balance of power and pit the Muslim world against the West."

"Yes, yes, it would be even worse than that," Peter said.

"Do you know anyone who might help us locate this facility? We know it's in the mountains somewhere north of the port city of Chah Bahar."

"That is many hundreds of miles away."

"Do you know anyone who has traveled down there, or used to live there? Anything we can learn will help."

"I know of no one who could aid us. Let me talk tomorrow to several friends who will not betray me. Now it's time for you to sleep."

"First I need to get to your roof. I must send another radio message. Don't worry, not the best radio receivers in Tehran could intercept the message and pinpoint it here."

Peter led him to the roof, where George set up the small dish antenna, aligned it, and sent off his message in a half-second burst.

The message said: "George. Out of contacts. Site is in mountains north of Chah Bahar. Check satellite photos. Good road to it a must. Am at sight A. So far not compromised. Any ideas? George out."

Downstairs, George fell on a floor mattress, and went to sleep in minutes. Peter carefully checked the contents of the shoulder bag. There was no money in it—a few personal items, the radio, and a blank notebook and pens.

Peter watched the American for a time, then went to his own pallet. He would do some talking at the market tomorrow. If he could tie down the exact location, he could charge the Americans a year's wages. Peter smiled at the prospect. If everything worked out right tomorrow, he could be well on his way to achieving his retirement.

Across town in the Minister of Defense's office, four-star General Reza Ruhollah sat back at his desk, and frowned. His Secret Police had uncovered something sinister that made him nervous. They had caught a suspected agent for the United States with more than fifteen hundred U.S. dollars on his person.

He had tried to talk to, and probably bribe, an engineer who worked in the south on Project Equalizer. The engineer had told them of the traitor, and they had grabbed him and the money. When they went to the place where the spy's control was known to be, they were shot at, and whoever had been there escaped.

Could that person have been a U.S. CIA agent? General Ruhollah pondered it. There was a good chance. He stood, paced to the window, and stared out over his beloved Tehran. Well over seven million people lived here now. His nation held almost seventy million. Iran should be leading the Arab world in a once-and-for-all battle to drive the Western powers out of the Middle East.

When Project Equalizer was finished, they would have the power to do just that. It had been difficult. Iran had no history of such scientific wonders. Neither did it have the agencies, and the mechanics, to keep such a huge project secret. Somehow traces of news had leaked out. He knew the U.S. and Israel had agents in his country trying to gain the critical information they would need to halt or destroy the project.

He would not permit anything to happen to his facility the way it had near Baghdad, Iraq, in 1981. There Israeli jet fighters destroyed a nuclear reactor. Israel claimed the reactor would produce plutonium which could then be used for Iraq's nuclear weapons program already in development. They had been wrong. Iraq had no such program, and the

Iraqis were too stupid to even try for something so compli-
cated.

The problem was that Israel got away with the act of war
against the traditional power in the Middle East without any
world censure. It would not happen again. One Israeli agent
had been caught and killed in a gun battle late last month.
Now one U.S. agent—true, an Iranian—had been caught
and eliminated. But where was his control, his master from
the U.S.?

An aide came in after knocking. He was a trusted friend.
He stopped three feet in front of the desk and waited to be
recognized. The Defense Minister turned and nodded at
him.

"General Ruhollah, we have good news. The huge
American we have so long sought has been found. We
haven't brought him here, because he's so big he won't go
through the door to his quarters. But we have questioned
him."

"This is the American we have been watching for, the one
who supports every wild-eyed student protest, and several
small groups agitating for rights for women?"

"The same, my General."

"Is he a spy for the United States?"

"We don't believe so, my General. He had no radio, no
spy equipment, no code books, that sort of thing."

"What about U.S. currency?"

"Only ten dollars U.S. He said his mother sent it to him
in a letter. Not enough to bother with, and U.S. dollars are
not illegal in this country."

"On the other hand, Colonel, the U.S. dollar is much
sought after by our oilmen, and merchants looking for hard
currency. So, does this huge one have any tie-in with the
U.S. spy your men did catch today?"

"Not that we know of, my General."

"Very well. Release the man. Put a camera in a hidden

place and take pictures of everyone who enters or leaves his rooms."

"It shall be done."

General Ruhollah waved the colonel away. At least they knew where this huge American was now. He'd heard the man weighed more than six-hundred pounds. How much must he eat every day to keep up that much weight? Amazing.

General Ruhollah took a file out of a locked drawer in his desk and looked over the engineer's last report.

The machining of the metal similar to stainless steel was well under way. They still needed blanks for the manufacturing process.

He looked at some sketches the head engineer had done. One showed a folded cylinder of plutonium. Situated around this was a cylinder of beryllium. This is a very light, stiff metal, which would form an X-ray window, and become a neutron reflector.

"Beryllium is difficult to machine," the engineer wrote. "We must use cubic boron-nitrate tools. Anything else, such as carbon or steel tools, will not give satisfactory results. We still need the powder form of tungsten-rhenium. We will sinter this into cylindrical segments."

The General stopped. Sintering, sinter. What did that mean? He checked a dictionary. Sinter: heating matter just hot enough so it will form.

"The tungsten-rhenium will be used to form a cylinder around the beryllium for density. Around this cylinder goes our explosive-lens assembly."

General Ruhollah put down the report and rubbed his eyes. He had never taken science classes at the military academy. It was enough to learn to read and write, and then study the history of their country, the *military* history, and then to learn the ways of warfare. He had been trying to catch up ever since. Most of the reports by the engineers made no sense to him whatsoever. He did have two trusted scientists at the university who checked the reports weekly and gave him advice.

"Why does the project move so slowly?" he asked out loud. He knew that the science, the physics, of a nuclear bomb was no longer a secret. There were schematics of bombs on the Internet, and papers and manuals telling how to build a crude one.

They wanted one step up from crude, so it was taking longer. He dreamed of the day he would have the first operational bomb ready. He would tell the world about it, then threaten one neighbor with the total destruction of their capital city, if they did not surrender and become a part of the Greater Iranian Islamic Republic. What a day that would be!

There would be outrage around the world, but no nation would challenge him with its own nuclear weapons. He would use his if he had to, and the whole world knew it. Who would be the first Arab nation to capitulate and join forces with him? Iraq with its 25 million people? Maybe Syria with ports on the Mediterranean would be good. Then Jordan and Saudi Arabia. Yes!

He would put together a united nation of over 135 million people! That would be enough strength so the other world powers would have to recognize him.

Israel, with only 5 million people, would be a terrible problem. They never would capitulate. He might have to waste a bomb on them, or simply ignore them, and in time, bit by bit, drive them all into the sea.

He stared out the window, and dreamed his dream of great power and wealth. No one could stop him once he had the might of the nuclear bombs under his control. No one.

He looked back at his desk and saw the report on the dead Iranian who had been working for the U.S. Who had his control been? Where was the American CIA spy who pulled the man's strings? He had to find that infidel American spy quickly.

10

Sunday, October 23

0730 hours
SEAL training base
Coronado, California

Murdock looked up as Jaybird Sterling came through the door.

"You called, L-T?"

"Right, we've got traveling orders for two men, Douglas and Franklin. They're flying out of North Island at thirteen hundred riding shotgun in a pair of Tomcats."

"This is a workday. The platoon knows. Everyone to report at oh eight hundred."

"Cut some orders for those two going to Saudi Arabia."

"What uniform, what gear?"

"Send them in cammies. To take small arms. Give them both MP-5's and thirteen-round H&K P7 automatics. They'll be going in by air, HALO, and will be outfitted with Iranian clothes, and I.D. in Saudi. They'll get rials there as well for cash, and changes of clothes. They can get ammo in Saudi, so don't bother with that. Get both of them in here as soon as they show up."

"Aye, aye, L-T. This have any bearing on our month of training?"

"Probably not, Jaybird. Unless they can help root out some vital intel that the bombs are farther along than the brass thinks they are. We'll keep to our sched for now at least."

Murdock paused and gulped at his coffee. "Seen DeWitt yet?"

"No, sir. Shall I get Doc Ellsworth up here just for laughs?"

"Better not. This could be a damn touchy situation. Depends on Milly."

"Right, sir. I'll bring in the guys when they come."

When Murdock looked up from his desk a minute later, a pretty face surrounded by short brown hair poked around the door frame.

"Any room at the inn?"

"Kat, come in. How many sets of cammies do you have?"

"Two."

"I'll order you six more. You'll need them. You on for long-gun shooting today, right?"

"That's what Lieutenant DeWitt said."

"He should be here shortly. Jaybird has ordered a car, and has laid out enough weapons, and ammo to sink a battleship. How was the swim?"

"Fine, but I'm a little out of shape."

Murdock grinned. "Really? That's not what Jaybird said. You left him in your wake."

"He's not used to competitive swimming. When I get in the water, I hate to have anybody ahead of me."

"Even the men triathlon swimmers?"

"Especially them."

"Swimming shouldn't be a problem for you here. We'll go in by air, almost for sure, but I'd guess our only way out will be to fight our way to the coast of southern Iran and take a long swim."

Jaybird came in towing his two SEALS. "Captured a pair for you, L-T."

"Good. Kat, I want you to listen to this." Murdock went over what he knew about the mission.

"So, that's about it. You don't have to play spy, although you will be going in with civilian clothes and gear, international brand weapons, and lots of rial to spend judiciously so you don't attract attention. You'll be meeting a man named George at site B, wherever that is."

"So we back up this guy, as he tries to tie down the exact location of the nuke plant?" Douglas asked.

"Right. Iran is tough with its Secret Police. We lost our native contact there, and George is feeling lonely. CIA would rather risk some of us than send in two more of their own. So we get the assignment."

"We HALO in," Franklin said. "How the hell do we get out?"

Murdock waved them over to look at an eight-by-ten fax of a map of Iran.

"Advice on the wire this morning is that once your mission is over, you radio out the pinpointed location, and then exfiltrate out of the area. They say the least sensitive route is to the north of Tehran, to the Caspian Sea. It borders Iran and Russia. The water is about sixty miles from Tehran. Then you should be able to find a boat, or work your way along the coast north to the border with Russia, and get across.

"At Baku, in Russia, there will be a CIA man. Baku is about two hundred miles north of the border with Iran."

"Sounds like a walk in the park," Douglas said.

"Yeah or a long hike," Franklin said. "We volunteered for this duty, right?"

"Right, Franklin, and brush up on your Farsi—you'll be the mouthpiece for your twosome," Murdock said.

Franklin laughed. "Grandma said I'd be glad someday that she taught me to speak the old country language."

"You fly out of here at thirteen hundred, so get moving it," Jaybird said. The three walked out of the office.

At the stroke of 0800, Ed DeWitt came in the door. His uniform was crisp and fresh, his face cleanly shaven but showing traces of strain and fatigue.

"Well, shipmates, look what my pit bull dragged in off the beach," Murdock said. He grinned. "Or is it roadkill?"

"Roadkill is closer to it," DeWitt growled. He sat in the chair across the desk and glanced up at Kat.

"Good morning, Lieutenant Garnet. I believe we're going to be doing some long-gun shooting today."

"Looking forward to it, Mr. DeWitt."

Jaybird came in and motioned to Kat. "Ma'am, we didn't set you up with a locker for your gear and personal things. We even have locks to show you how much we are a family here. Let me get you set up before you go on your picnic."

Kat nodded, and followed Jaybird into the squad room.

"So, what did Milly say?" Murdock asked when they had left.

"About what I expected. She cried. She asked if I wanted her to move out. All the damn female emotional things. Then she seduced me three times last night. But the real surprise was this morning at five A.M. The alarm went off and she was all over me again. She said she'd totally satisfy my male libido so I'd think of Kat as nothing but another one of the guys. Oh, damn, she's right. It's really working."

Murdock chuckled. "One of Hollywood's leading men in the fifties had the same problem. His wife did him every morning before he went on the shoot. They were married for twenty-seven years."

"Sorry to hear it." DeWitt took a long breath, then grabbed the cup of coffee Jaybird handed him. "If I pass out on one of our training runs, don't call just any doctor, get me straight to my urologist for a hormone transplant."

Jaybird came back in grinning and tossed DeWitt a small plastic bottle. He read the label. "Might help," he said holding it up. "One-a-day vitamins." They all laughed.

Kat stowed the gear that Jaybird had issued her in her locker. It included all sorts of items she wasn't familiar with, including some kind of a SCUBA device she figured must be a rebreather for underwater swimming. She had everything in shape when Jaybird came back.

He had a black tow bag beside an assortment of weapons.

"Long guns, today, Lieutenant. I'll drive the car around and load this for you. Also I've included some MREs and two six-packs of Coke. I think the L-T will take along a cooler with some ice. Might as well make it a real picnic. Not many fast-food places where you'll be going."

Kat went back to Murdock's office.

"The atmosphere in here has changed since yesterday," she said. "Now there's an excitement, an electrical charge. Reminds me of the last few minutes before a race."

"True," Murdock said. "We've got those two men heading for Saudi Arabia. It's like this is the real start of our mission. Now all we have to do is get the rest of the troops ready and get into Iran. Let's hope they do a good job."

Jaybird ordered the additional cammies for Kat, got the travel chits cut for the two SEALs, and grinned at the open-ended orders. The two men were to report to an Air Force base near Ridyah, Saudi Arabia, for an indeterminate time period, and would SEE to the base commander for further instructions. He'd never seen orders quite so vague before.

Kat and DeWitt got off on their drive to the east country, where the Navy had an unofficial firing range.

Murdock and Jaybird drove Franklin and Douglas to North Island with five minutes to spare before flight time. They put on flight suits and stowed their MP-5's beside their feet. Five minutes later, the two Navy F-14 Tomcats raced down the runway and lifted off. They would do midair refueling three times and set down in Saudi Arabia, nonstop.

The Tomcat can do about two-thousand miles to a tankful on a hop in ferry mode.

The Toms carried minimum arms—two Sparrow missiles and two Sidewinders. They would be flying over no disputed territory. At a top speed of 1,500 mph they would be doing nearly Mach 2.34 and searching for favorable tailwinds.

Yeoman Second Class Colt "Guns" Franklin sat in the rear seat of the F-14 and marveled at the wonder of it all. It was his first ride in a supersonic fighter of any kind. He'd almost lost his lunch when they took off from North Island. He listened to the chatter between the pilots. He could see the other F-14 to his right, just far enough away so the two planes wouldn't interfere with "clean" air ahead of them.

He knew they would do air-to-air refueling. That would be something to see. He'd watch the other plane get the fuel, since he couldn't see much out the front.

Guns wasn't even sure where they were flying. He figured they'd have to cross the U.S., pick up some fuel partway there, and then head for where—Greenland? They weren't going over the pole; he knew that from their talk.

Fifteen hundred miles an hour. In two hours they would be all the way across the U.S. Damn! That was moving. He didn't even want to figure how fast that was in feet per second. He looked at the radar and intercept instruments in front of him but didn't touch anything. They fascinated him but scared him, too. He didn't want to push a button and fire a missile. Could he do that? He didn't know.

A little over six hours later, the two fighters contacted the control tower at a U.S. Air base outside of Riyadh, Saudi Arabia. Both pilots had landed there before. Guns couldn't figure out why.

Once out of the planes, Franklin and Douglas were taken to the field's commanding officer. He sent them down the hall to a small room where a civilian sat waiting for them. He shook hands with them and began chattering in Farsi.

Douglas shrugged.

Franklin cocked his head to one side, then replied in the same language: "Sir, your accent is rather weird, or maybe it's mine, but I can understand you with no trouble. Is you accent the correct one for modern-day Tehran?"

The CIA man smiled. "Mine is out of date, I'm sure, in a growing, changing language, but the important thing is that you understand, and can communicate. Your friend isn't so lucky."

"He knows no Farsi, but he's a whiz with a SATCOM."

"Good. We'll need you both."

They went back to English.

"Welcome to Saudi Arabia, men. I understand you're both SEALs from San Diego. Yes, we know that you're not spies, not trained to gather intelligence on foreign soil. What we'll want you to do is to back up and protect our man who is in country doing that job.

"You'll get civilian clothes, and two changes. You have H&K M-5's, I understand. Good German make. There will be nothing except your English to tie you to the U.S. Now, we'll get you fed, and then you can catch some sleep. You passed several time zones, so you'll take a day or so to adapt.

"You'll have identity papers if you need them, but try to stay away from anyone who might ask for them. You were told you might go in HALO. A change here, gentlemen. We have too far to fly to penetrate the Iranian airspace at that altitude, which would show up on their radar.

"Instead we'll go in low and mean, hope to stay under their radar. You'll be riding in a big mother, a specially equipped MC-130 Combat Talon. It's also called a Hercules and can carry seventy-four troops fully combat-ready. You'll have the space all to yourselves.

"This plane is especially equipped for exactly this type of deep-penetrating covert missions. She's painted all black and with no U.S. Air Force markings or insignia. The crew will be carrying no U.S. identity and their uniforms are strictly non-U.S."

"So if we get shot down, nobody can say we're Americans," Franklin said.

"Quite right and for good reason we won't claim you are. You'll get on board, and jump off, a rear loading ramp on the plane. Plenty of room. We'll be dropping you off at no more than a thousand feet, depending on the terrain. Your chutes will be on static lines for instant deployment. You should have fifteen seconds before you reach the ground, so be ready. Have you ever jumped this low before?"

"Ten times or so," Franklin said. "No problem."

"We'll go in at night, right?" Douglas asked.

"Yes. You'll get a ride up to Kuwait, and from there the MC-130 will take off for Tehran. We plan on dropping you about fifty miles this side of the city. Tehran has seven million people now and growing. We'll try to hit near a main highway where you can catch a bus to get to the city, and find the meet. It will all be spelled out on a paper for each of you. Don't let anyone see that paper."

The civilian looked at them for a moment. "That's about it. Any questions?"

"Does the Company put any restrictions on us? We're basically a shoot-and-scoot-type operation. This won't quite be that, I'd guess."

"No restrictions. However, if there's a body count, it will bring out the Secret Police by the hundreds. They don't like anybody but themselves killing people in Iran."

"Foul-ups," Douglas said. "Say we get to the meet, and this George isn't there? Say George got himself killed. What do we do then?"

"You have a SATCOM. I'd hole up somewhere and ask for instructions. We'll be listening for you twenty-four hours a day. You should listen for us at midnight and six A.M."

"We know what George is trying to find out," Franklin

said. "We're not spooks, but we'll do what we can to help him, as well as protecting his ass."

"Good. You'll be shown to quarters now for some food, and then sleep. Tomorrow you'll get a ride up to Kuwait." The man pointed at the door, and two Air Force men came in.

"Right this way to your quarters, men," a corporal said.

"Where's the food?" Franklin asked.

The corporal grinned. "Hey, you get to order what you want, and we'll bring it to you. How about that for service?"

The tension, the long flight, and the change in time all hit Douglas at the same instant. "Hey, if I drop facedown into my steak and go to sleep, just roll me over and let me snore. I've never been so damn tired in my life."

11

Monday, October 24

1004 hours
Kuwait City, Kuwait

Franklin and Douglas had been outfitted with Iranian clothing an hour before. Now they looked over their I.D. and other papers that made them out to be Iranians.

"We don't even look Arabic," Douglas said.

"Make that Persian, Kurd, or Azerbaijani," Franklin said.

"Whatever. We going to be able to pass?"

"We damn well better, or we'll be dead meat."

Douglas groaned. "We go in tonight as soon as it gets dark?"

"Yeah. What a kick. That great big bird for just the two of us. Think they would have used something smaller, faster."

"Could, but we wouldn't have any way to bail out. Hell, they say this plane has been prepped especially for runs like this. Covert as all hell."

"Just so it gets us in without getting shot down. We'll worry about how to get out."

Douglas scowled. "You still have that map? Let's take another look. Tehran is a humongous place, seven million bodies. We've got to find one certain apartment?"

"Yeah, if we're gonna do any good."

They both were surprised when Don Stroh, their CIA guardian, walked in the room two hours before flight time.

"Any problems?" he asked.

"Yeah, Stroh. I'd like to get some of your frequent flyer miles." Franklin said. "You must have built up a few million by now."

"No such luck, mostly military aircraft. Problems?"

"Yeah, the handguns they gave us. A piece of shit," Franklin said.

"We got the Polish copy of the Makarov, the P-64. A nice light little nine-millimeter with six rounds. Best part is it can't be traced to the U.S. Everything you have is sterile of any U.S. tie. We planned it that way."

"Rather have fourteen rounds in my magazine," Douglas said.

"Sure, and you'd rather take the MP-5 you brought, but no chance. Anything else?"

"We get out via Russia, right?" Franklin asked. "Baku?"

"Correct. First we need to know exactly where that nuke plant is. If our man in there can't find it, you two will have to. I know you aren't trained for this. Mostly it's just common sense. Find the people who know what you need to know, and persuade them to tell you."

"We'll get the damn intel some way," Douglas said. "Otherwise there can't be a mission."

"That's the rub." Stroh brightened. "But our man said he had a new lead, so maybe all you'll need to do is be backup for him. Oh, he'll have some more weapons for you when you get inside."

"When do we leave?" Franklin asked.

"A half hour," Stroh said. "Let's get out to the plane. You'll take off a half hour before dark. The plane will move north up through Kuwait, and then through the no-fly zone in Iraq. After that it turns to the right into Iran. This means we'll have only about two hundred and fifty miles to penetrate into Iran before you drop."

"How low?" Franklin asked.

"You're set for eight hundred feet. Takes about three hundred feet for a round chute to open, then twenty seconds or so to the ground."

"Damn, I feel naked going in like this. No weapons, no gear, almost nothing." Douglas shook his head.

"This is the way that it should work best. Let's get out to the flight line."

Ten minutes later, they were in the big plane. The Hercules C-130 is a monster, especially for two passengers. It has four Allison T56-A-15 turboprop engines, good for 4,591 horsepower each. It has a high wing and has flown off aircraft carriers. It has a 132-foot wingspan, is 98 feet long, and the tail extends up 38 feet.

The C-130 has a crew of five, cruises at 375 mph, and with a maximum fuel load can cover 4,894 miles without gulping more juice.

Douglas looked at the cave-like interior of the big ship, and then at the Air Force sergeant who was the load master.

"How in hell do we get out of this thing?" Douglas asked.

"Easy. We lift the rear cargo door and you run down the wide ramp, and one step later you're outa here. We've got you attached to static lines so you'll have instant opening of the chutes. Nothing to get in the way except our prop wash."

"How long we got, Sarge?"

"Our flight time to the DZ is an hour and twenty-three minutes. I'll alert you fifteen minutes before drop time."

They nodded, and the crew chief went back to the cabin. Douglas looked out the small round windows. It had grown dark quickly after they took off, and now he could see nothing but pure blackness.

The two men slumped in the bucket seats, and worked their own thoughts. Douglas had been restoring a 1931 Model A Roadster in a garage near his apartment in Coronado. It had yellow wire wheels, a rumble seat, and a cloth top. He wanted to keep it all original but soon found that parts for a sixty-seven-year-old car were almost impossible to find. So he had been replacing some with remanufactured parts from specialty houses. He'd keep it as pure as he could, especially the outside. He loved the gas tank that sat over the engine next to the inside of the fire wall. No fuel pump. Gravity flow.

He looked at the SATCOM radio he carried. It was much smaller than the multiple-use one that Ron Holt had for the platoon. This was a simple transceiver for the satellite only. He would turn it on to receive at midnight, and at noon. He could send at any time.

That was the one item that could tie the team to the U.S. If they faced capture, that was the first destroy job he had. He had been with the Third Platoon for almost two years now, had been through three big operations before. He'd get through this one if he had to walk every damn step to Baku.

First they had to find where the Iranian nukes were being made. South, somewhere south. At least this was something different from the shoot-and-scoot he'd been involved with so far.

He knew Iran was a mountainous place. One hill went over eighteen hundred feet, which was higher even than Mammoth Lake, where he came from in California. Mammoth was around eight thousand feet, in the middle of the Sierra Nevadas. He yawned—no time for a nap.

Colt Franklin took out the pistol again from deep inside his three layers of strange clothes. It wasn't even in a holster, just nestled into some folds of cloth. Safer that way, they told him.

Skydiving and parachuting were not new to him, but this low jump would be a first. Sport jumping usually makes you go out at least twenty-five hundred feet. He thought of writing a letter, but didn't have any gear. He'd write when he got back. He'd heard about the mountain near Tehran. They said it was 18,934 feet. Damn. He'd love to get a shot at climbing it. But not this tour.

Rock climbing was his passion, but he'd never seen a mountain almost nineteen thousand feet high. Maybe later he'd have a shot at it. If he didn't get shot on this run. He looked out the window again, but there was nothing out there. Just blackness. Good. He'd hate to see the slash of a jet fighter slamming past them. Much prefer to be alone in the dark, and get to the damned DZ in one fucking piece.

Ten minutes later the load master came back and yelled.

"Time: We're about fifteen away from the Drop Zone. I hate this low-level stuff. You probably felt us rolling around a little. So far we've not had any radar tracking us, which is great. About five minutes until drop, I'll open the rear hatch and get you hooked up on the static line."

He vanished. They tried the windows again. Nothing.

When the load master came back into the cabin, the two SEALs stood. He hit a switch somewhere and there was a grinding, whirling sound and the rear ramp section of the big transport swung down revealing a square of pure black space. For a moment Franklin thought he saw lights below, but he wasn't sure.

The Air Force sergeant hooked up the SEALs to the static line, one on each side of the wide hatch. The static line would automatically pull the rip cord, and their round chutes would deploy as soon as they jumped out the door. Douglas had heard that it took a chute three hundred feet to fully deploy and start slowing a man's decent. Then within a few seconds they would drop through the other five hundred feet to the ground.

They couldn't use the rectangular steerable chutes this close to the ground. The round chutes would spill air on one side or the other for some control. But not much. Soon now. They were both hooked up to the static line and ready.

"Stand by," the load master shouted against the roar of the wind behind the plane. They watched the red light on the bulkhead over the door. In a heartbeat it turned to green.

"Go, go go," Douglas shouted.

The two SEALs ran the ten feet to the gaping hole in the back of the big transport and raced into space.

The slipstream of the big transport battered Douglas for a moment, then he felt the chute open behind him. The big round chute caught the wind with a shrilling crack. At the same time the parachute harness jerked at his legs, thighs, and shoulders. He'd been halfway upside down in the slipstream, the chute yanked him savagely upright. It was harder than Douglas had ever felt on a chute opening, even with sixty pounds of gear.

He shook his head, and looked above him. The glorious jet-black canopy billowed there, fully open, and cutting his rate of descent to a modest speed. He looked around, but couldn't find the other chute.

The ground. He looked down, and in the faint moonlight he could see it. What appeared to be some kind of a road showed to the left maybe half a klick. That might be the highway they were to use to get to Tehran.

Suddenly there were trees ahead of him. He pulled the cord on the right side of the chute, spilling some air on that side and drifting him to the right of the trees.

Then the ground rushed at him. He took it the way he had dozens of times, with his knees slightly bent and his hands on the chute release. He hit the ground and ran, dumped the chute, and began pulling it into a big wad. For a moment he didn't make a sound, and listened. He heard a grunt from his right.

"You okay?" he said, half aloud.

"Hell yes," the short reply came.

The found each other a minute later. Franklin used the entrenching tool he carried to dig a hole for his chute and harness. He covered the spot with some branches and dead leaves. Douglas did the same with his chute and gear, then pushed the digging tool under the pile and looked around.

"Thought I saw a road when we came in," Douglas said.

"To the left, half a klick," Franklin said. "We better move."

They found the road twenty minutes later. There was little traffic. It was paved and two lanes, looked like a main highway for this country. Half a dozen trucks sped by. The two SEALs moved down closer. The route ran generally northeast by southwest. From there they had to go northeast.

After a half hour's wait near the road, they heard an older rig coming that had to be smaller than the others. Franklin watched it come through the darkness, then walked out near the side of the road and waved both arms in the glare of the headlights. The old, much used farm truck, with a stake body, slowed, then stopped.

Franklin chattered for a moment in Farsi with the man in the small truck, then waved at Douglas. They both crawled into the cab, They saw the rig had crates of live chickens in the back.

Franklin took some bills from his pocket and gave the farmer two 10,000 rial notes. The old man grinned, showing snaggle teeth, and then he nodded. He said something to Franklin. They both laughed.

"Told him we missed our bus to Tehran," Franklin whispered.

They got to the big city before daylight. Franklin told the farmer where they wanted to go, and he explained how to get there. The farmer stopped at an open-air market that was almost filled already with merchant booths.

The sun had been up for two hours when Franklin knocked on a door in a falling-apart neighborhood. A small man answered, and stared at Franklin in surprise. Before he could say anything, the small man was pushed aside, and a tall man who looked remarkably American stepped into his place. He carried a huge-looking .45 automatic in his right hand and waved it at Franklin.

"George?" Franklin asked.

"Oh, God, yes," the man said, and motioned them inside.

Douglas checked out the place. It was sparsely furnished—no modern appliances, a cot, a small cooking area, and a mattress on the floor.

They introduced themselves and George sighed.

"Am I glad to see you guys. The Secret Police have been hounding me the past two days, and I haven't made any progress. I was afraid you'd get lost."

"Okay, George, we're here," Franklin said. "Now what the fuck happens?"

12

Tuesday, October 25

1032 hours
Safe house "B"
Tehran, Iran

"What are we going to do?" George asked. "We're going to
find out exactly where that damned Iranian nuke plant is.
I've been on the phone this morning. The damned Secret
Police can't keep tabs on every one of the seven million
people in town."

"So?" Douglas asked.

"Peter, my last contact was a total bust. Now I have a
noon meet with a guy who says he worked at the nuke plant.
He may have; he may just be looking for some cash."

"Or he may be ready to turn you in to the cops if you
don't pay him," Franklin said.

"True. That's why I'm glad for some backup. I've got this
one laid out just right."

"Stroh said you'd have some better firepower for us,"
Douglas said.

"What are you packing?" George asked.

They showed him.

"Yeah, good for a hideout, not much on stopping power.
I like a forty-five."

"We saw it. Where's ours?" Franklin asked.

George chuckled. "They told me you might be a little gung ho. Look, one thing I don't need is a bunch of bodies around here. The cops here are tough as shit about that. I need security, not a couple of hit men. Understood?"

"Roger, that," Douglas said. "So what do we do?"

"This is my last safe house. I want to keep it safe. The Secret Police don't know a thing about it. My other two were raided. Two of my friends were killed. I don't know about the third one, Tauksun."

"Tauksaun?" Franklin asked. "Sounds like the Japanese word for big, large, a lot."

"That he is, maybe six hundred pounds. The point is he's compromised now and I can't use him even if he is alive."

"So, how close are you to getting the exact spot down south?"

"Not far enough. We know it's inland somewhere from that port city down there. The satellite is supposed to get some better pictures of the area. We're trying to follow roads. There has to be a big hairy road leading into the site. Unless they bulldozed it out after they got the place built, and all the structures in place."

"Camouflaged?" Rogers asked.

"The main plant, yes. It's either that or underground in a big natural cave, or a dug-out one."

"So who is this guy you meet this noon?" Franklin asked.

"I know him only as Lefty. He's another lens grinder. They used a lot of locals to grind some of the finely tuned parts of the bombs. Not sure what parts, but it's our best local tie-in.

"I'm talking with him in the middle of a soccer field. I'll tell him the location fifteen minutes before the meeting time. He won't have time to set up anything with anybody if he's crooked. I'll want you two on the sides of the place to give me some support. Anybody who tries to get on the field, you stop. Gently, not with bullets."

"What can this guy tell us, if he's for real?" Franklin asked.

"What we need to know is what highway they took out of the port city, how far they went, how long they drove. We know the trucks were closed so the riders couldn't see out except occasionally. Time will be a big factor. If we know they traveled north for over an hour up into the mountains, we're starting to get a general idea on the location, but that's about all."

Both the SEALs nodded.

"Now, how about something to eat? My man, Coman, has been working on it. Figured you haven't eaten since yesterday sometime. Not your usual American meal, but we have some goodies."

As if on command, the small Iranian, who had vanished through a curtained door, appeared with a tray. It was filled with food: two kinds of meat, thick slabs of bread, a jar of American peanut butter, and steaming cups of coffee. On another platter were four kinds of fruit.

A half hour later most of the food was gone.

George watched them eat, had some himself, and then asked the question of the day: "The meat sandwiches, how did you like them?"

Both said they were good. Different, but good.

George grinned. "Probably the first time you've ever had a dog meat sandwich." He held it for a moment then laughed at the wild expression on the two men's faces. "Just kidding. I don't think they eat dog meat over here. It was most likely goat or lamb. I try never to ask what I'm eating."

Twenty minutes later they had walked to the soccer field. It was bare brown earth with no chalk lines but with goalposts on either end. No one was there practicing. George left the SEALs on the side where small buildings evidently housed equipment. Franklin went around the end of the field to the shacks on the far side, where he vanished. Both had their 9mm pistols.

Douglas saw the Iranian come from the other side of the field. He came partway, looked around, saw only George and then slowly walked up, and evidently began to talk with George. Douglas watched around him—the street, half a block away—and checked out anyone walking nearby. One man came directly toward the field, then when he saw the two men there, he turned and walked away quickly.

Douglas kept one hand on the gun under his outer garment, but relaxed when the stranger left.

He looked back at the conference in the middle of the field. All seemed to be going well. They did not shake hands, but he saw a curt nod from each man. The contact went back the way he had come, and George waved at Franklin, who followed him back to where Douglas watched.

George smiled. "All right. So far, so good. This lens grinder said he was sure that they traveled fifty miles almost due north on a new road. There were no seasonal gullies washed through it, so it was new or finely maintained. From the fifty miles, he isn't sure where they went next.

"This does nothing more than corroborate information we already had. But it's good to know we have at least two witnesses who put the work north and into the mountains. He thinks he fell asleep after the fifty miles. He does know a woman here in town who he thinks may be able to help us. She's at one of the city's good restaurants. He will meet us there tonight and introduce us."

"How did he come up with fifty miles?" Franklin asked.

"Time and speed. He said the truck had a governor on it so it couldn't go over forty miles an hour. The roads would support that speed, but not much more. He says he had a stopwatch feature on his wristwatch, and timed it at an hour and fifteen minutes. That would be fifty miles at forty miles per hour. But where did they go after that? This woman might be able to help us."

"I thought women were like slaves in this country," Douglas said.

"Oh, they are, believe me. Can't vote, can't drive a car, can't hold a job worth anything. They are baby makers and child raisers. That's about it."

"But this woman you want to meet?"

"She's remarkable. I've heard of her. Something of a star performer in this country. She's married with two boys, and is one of the best belly dancers in the country. Persia, remember, the heart of the belly dancing trade. Because of that, she has been given certain allowances and privileges."

They went to the cafe that night. George's man, Coman, led the way and eased them into the place. He knew someone there. It was more like a nightclub than a restaurant, but there was no alcohol. Not in a Muslim country. The surroundings seemed typically Persian to Douglas: curtains, drapes, incense, low lighting, strange music on even stranger stringed instruments, and far off some woman's singsong voice echoing through the eatery.

They met the man George had talked to in the soccer field. He kept looking around as if someone were after him. At last he relaxed. He had them seated in a corner away from most of the other diners. A few minutes later he brought a beautiful woman to their table and introduced her to them. He didn't used their names. She said her name was Murrah, the Arabic equivalent of Mary.

Murrah smiled at them, and spoke in heavily accented English. "My friends. I will see you later and dance for you. Enjoy yourselves. Perhaps we can do something good for Iran and the rest of the world. It could start tonight."

She left then, and their food came. Again the Americans weren't sure what they had for their dinner. It was good. Soon, Coman stood and motioned the five of them to a private room, where they sat down at a low table. The room had heavy drapes, more incense, and soft lilting music. On the table were five tall glasses of some kind of special drink. They sampled it and talked quietly. A few moments later the music changed, and then took on a throbbing, intense beat.

From the drapes, a belly dancer came out and did her dance to the accompaniment of the faster and faster sensual music. It was Murrah.

Douglas tried to figure out how old she was. He'd heard that belly dancing was an art that took years to learn. This woman had to be in her forties, he decided. Yet she was still slender, with well-rounded hips, which are the featured part of the body for the dance. She had changed from the dress she had worn in the cafe. Now it was the traditional belly dancer's skimpy and revealing costume.

Before it was over, the four men were tapping the low table in front of them to the beat of the music.

She came to the end of the dance, but the music continued, and she sat down close to George. She whispered to them in English.

"I can help you," she said. "But not here. Too many know me and watch me. They pay to watch me." She laughed. "I know what they are doing in the south. I don't like it. The devil bombs are too many already. Iran does not need them. I will help you. Come to my house later tonight." She gave Franklin a piece of paper.

"Be there at midnight, and we can talk in private."

Then she was gone.

The five men stood. Franklin looked at the note. "It's an address." He showed it to George, who smiled.

"Yes, a good address in the better part of town. The three of us will go; Coman will keep the home fires burning." They said good-bye to the man from the soccer field, after giving him a sheaf of rial notes.

They took a taxi most of the way back to the safe house, then walked in twos the last eight blocks. They paused, backtracked, and circled around. No one followed them.

Douglas sat in the safe house and field-stripped, cleaned, and oiled his pistol. It didn't need cleaning. He looked up at George, who was reading a newspaper, trying to understand the Farsi.

"George, how far are we from Chah Bahar?" Douglas asked.

"What? How far? To hell and gone way down there in the south almost in Pakistan. Must be fifteen hundred miles." He frowned. "Won't do. We have to find the location here. Somebody here knows exactly where that facility is. All I have to do is make the right contact. Maybe Murrah is the one. She seems to know that they are working with nukes down there and doesn't like it."

"So there are a few people here who know the spot. How do you find them, George, out of seven million foreigners?"

"With a whole lot of luck."

"We don't believe in luck, George," Franklin chimed in. "I'm with Douglas. Be one hell of a lot easier to pinpoint the spot if we were in the neighborhood. So how can we get down there to that southern town?"

"Practically impossible. You don't just waltz up to a ticket counter and get an airline ride down there. I don't even think it has an airport. It's a port, but it would take a month to sail down there the way these coast boats run. That leaves a car. You know how much trouble it would be to drive from here to Chah Bahar?"

"No, George, tell us," Douglas said.

George stood and walked to the window, then came back. "You're serious, aren't you? I'm about tapped out up here, true. I've gone through four leads, and nothing but those damn fifty miles. What happens tonight, I don't know, but I'm not overly enthused. What could this dancer know?"

"Could we drive down there?" Franklin asked.

"Possible. If we had some good reason for going, and a car and the permits we would need."

"What about flying partway?" Douglas said. "Didn't I see a big town about halfway down the country, Shiraz, something like that."

"Yeah, it's down there, about halfway. But they check papers on all commercial flights. Travel in this country isn't automatic. Our papers wouldn't stand up to a detailed inspection."

"I still think we need to go down there," Douglas said.

"Maybe Murrah will have some ideas," George said. "At least I hope she will. If she knows there are nukes down there, she may know more about it than we do. She's evidently in some group that is fighting the nuke development. Lots of luck to her."

The played poker for matches for two hours, then took off to find the address Murrah told them about. They walked away from the safe house almost a mile, then caught a taxi, and arrived on the right street.

Again they left the cab several blocks from the address and walked in a roundabout way. When they were sure no one was following, they went to the side door of the address and knocked.

This was in the more modern section of Tehran, which had business buildings right beside ancient bazaars and markets, with winding mazes of narrow streets and lanes that came up against circle highways around the city. Now broad avenues cut through most large towns in Iran, such as Tehran, in contrast to the traditional labyrinth of crooked streets and cul-de-sacs lined with narrow arcades of individual shops, grouped according to the products or services sold.

This building looked like a single house, but was large by most Iranian standards. It was two stories, and made of some kind of stone.

They were early, but soon a woman with a long white robe came to the door and let them in. She had led them to a living room that looked much like one in the States.

"Pleased to sit," the woman said. "She will be with you in a minute."

George looked around with a slow grin. "This could be in Portland or Denver, or Washington, D.C. It's so damn American."

George bobbed his head. "It is well known that Murrah is a fan of the Western world, and would like to go there someday when travel restrictions are lifted."

They looked up as a woman came into the room from the shadows beyond. The three men stood quickly. She wore a body-hugging blue dress with sequins, and that draped off one shoulder. It looked like something off a Paris runway at a big fashion designer's show. Her dark hair was formed high on her head, in a frothy buildup.

She smiled. "Gentlemen, welcome to my home. Please sit down. Yes, I'm a mere woman in Iran, but still I have the clout to demand a few things, and those who love my dancing can't deny me them."

She came on into the room and sat in the ornamental chair the others had avoided. It was her chair and she settled into it, and waved her hand.

The same woman they had seen before, in the long white robe, came in with a tray of drinks.

"Sorry, no bourbon on the rocks or old-fashioneds or even gin and tonic. This is Iran." She watched them for a moment, sipped from her drink, and then a small frown touched her face.

"I hope I was not wrong in my assumption. I have the impression that the United States government knows more than I do about the nuclear facility Iran has built far to the south. It is my hope that we can work together to help damage or destroy that plant without unleashing a rain of deadly radiation clouds that would sweep across the Middle East."

George took the lead.

"Murrah, your intel is right on target. We have hopes of doing some work at that plant that will indeed leave it in such a state that the Iranian government will need to start over in its drive to build a nuclear-powered weapon."

"Good. Then we are in agreement. How can I help you?"

She sipped the drink, and watched them over the rim of the delicate stemware.

"We need to know the exact location of the nuclear plant," George said.

"When do you need this information?" she asked.

"As soon as possible. We understand the construction phase is nearing completion. We have at the most three weeks."

The woman shook her head, then stood gracefully and paced the room, more like a ballet dancer than a stalking tiger. She shook her head a second time, then looked at the Americans.

"Impossible. I've been trying to find out that same fact now for almost two years. I have seen two of my friends killed by the Secret Police. Another man I talked to was severely beaten and is still recovering.

"Yet the Secret Police do not suspect me. They can't see past my dancing. Since I am not suspect, I can learn more. But I am tremendously careful. Did you know that I had someone follow you here tonight?"

"Follow us?" Douglas asked. "We were careful, we saw no one following."

"That's what I pay my people for. You were followed by my man to be sure that you were not followed by the Secret Police. I know, of course, where your last safe house is, George."

George chuckled to relieve some of his anger and frustration. He had no idea how she did it. He moved ahead smoothly.

"We're grateful for your help, Murrah. Now, what can we do here in Tehran to find out the location of that nuclear site?"

She frowned, and held up her hands. "George, I have no idea."

13

Tuesday, October 25

Lieutenant Murdock put down the phone and looked at Ed DeWitt and Jaybird Sterling, who had been listening to this end of the conversation with their CIA contact, Don Stroh.

"Our boys are in Tehran. Franklin and Douglas checked in by SATCOM this morning. The CIA guy there isn't making much progress. They're not sure what they will do. A chance they make a move fifteen hundred miles to the south, and try to find the nuke plant in person."

"Sounds dangerous moving over that much enemy territory," DeWitt said.

"Like walking through hell with an ice cream cone," Jaybird said.

They all looked up when Kat Garnet walked in wearing her spanking new cammies.

"Morning," she said.

"Good morning to you, Kat. How's the shooting eye?"

"Better after yesterday. Two days with the long guns is about all I get, Ed tells me. I might want some more in a week or so."

107

"Good swim last night?"

Kat grinned. "I'm not used to an open-ocean swim at night. Different, especially on the surface. Soon I get to use the rebreather, I hope."

"Before you know it, Kat," DeWitt said. "Today you get to blow up things. Ever throw firecrackers as a kid?"

"Not many. They were outlawed early on in Virginia. Hand grenades?"

"Right," Jaybird said. "And then there's plastique C-4, and the new stuff TNAZ."

"A long ride?" she asked.

"Just down the beach to the pit," DeWitt said.

"First the run? It gets me loosened up."

"We can set up each day with the run first, if you want," Murdock said. "You're getting up to speed, how about ten miles today?"

"In the sand?"

"Soft or hard, your pick. You lead."

"Good. Who do I run with today?"

"Ron Holt is your patsy. He's our communications man, and works right behind me in the squad formation. You'll be right behind him, so I want you to know his moves inside out. Jaybird, give Holt the word. Holt will know the five-mile point to the south."

"Thanks, Murdock," she said, and snapped him a proper salute.

He returned it. "Hey, you even learned how to salute the right way."

She laughed. "Got caught on the amphib base a couple of times, and had to return salutes to some men. Figured if I was going to play the part, I better get it all down right. See you in about an hour." She went out the door.

Jaybird came back. "She's doing the ten miles in an hour? Ron Holt is gonna be sweating by the time they get back. That's a six-minute mile."

"Yeah, be good for him," Murdock said. "Wait until you see what I've worked up for the rest of the platoon."

"Skipper, that must be the planning session I missed," Jaybird said.

Murdock tossed him the clipboard. "Check it out."

Jaybird looked down the six lines on the paper, and collapsed on the platoon leader's desk. He revived, and staggered to a chair.

"If that was a dive from the ten-meter board, I'd give you no more than a six," DeWitt said.

"All of this, today?" Jaybird finally stammered out.

"That's just the morning drill," Murdock said, and laughed at the expression on Jaybird's face.

"Of course, we could always add a few problems and marches to get the new men totally integrated."

Jaybird dropped the clipboard on the desk. "L-T, it looks just dandy to me."

"Waves are kicking up out there this morning from a storm. Be a good time to get in some refresher work on the IBS. We'll start with that just after oh-eight-hundred, Jaybird. Have the men on the beach ready to get wet at oh-eight-ten."

"Boats, sir?"

"Two reserved for us in the yard. Take your pick."

Jaybird went into the squad room and let the men know the first order of business. It would be with full combat gear, vests, full ammo load and issue weapon, including the heavy H&K Mark 23 .45 pistol with silencer on the belt of each SEAL.

"Hey, Jaybird, you don't make it easy, do you?" Magic Brown called.

"Sure I do. The only easy day around here was yesterday, remember? We've got ten minutes to pick up those two boats. Let's move."

Back in the platoon commander's office, Murdock looked at DeWitt. "How is Milly taking your official duties?"

"She's still pissed. Says there isn't any excuse to have the expert be a woman, and no reason you gave her to me to train except that you're trying to split up me and Milly."

Murdock chuckled. "Milly knows that's a bunch of crap. She's just playing female for a while. She doesn't have a worry. You look so wrung out every morning no other woman would stand a chance. Thought you and Milly had Kat over for dinner."

"Kat said she didn't think that would be such a good idea the first couple of days. Put her off for a week. I think Milly thinks that by then she'll crash and burn, and get out of the operation, and go home."

"You really think so, Ed?"

"Hell no. She's tougher than half our guys. The only thing I'm worried about is how she'll stand up under actual enemy fire. We've seen some good SEALs come apart at the seams when the bastards start shooting at us."

"True, 2IC. But that's one test you can't give a SEAL. You have to wait and have that trial under fire to be sure. My guess is that she'll be twice as good in action as she is in training. Let's go jump some waves and surf in on some of those five footers out there."

14

Wednesday, October 26

Joe Douglas watched the dancer for a moment, then snapped his finger against the expensive stemware. It rang like a silver bell. Everyone at the table looked at him.

"If we can't find out from here where the damn plant is, then it's logical that we have to get down there to the south and dig out the location on the spot."

"But it's fifteen hundred miles or more all the way to the southern border of the country," George said. "How can we get down there?"

"Hitchhike, steal a car—I don't know, but we've got to be on-site down there to find the damn place," Douglas said.

"I might be able to help," the dancer said. "Tomorrow I have to go far south to the town of Bandar-e 'Abbas. It's on the Straight of Hormuz. That's only about four hundred miles north of Chah Bahar."

"Going down there," Franklin said. "Could I ask how?"

"Yes. I rent a plane at the airport here and fly down. I understand there's a small airport at Chah Bahar, but the four of us arriving for no obvious reason would stir up a lot of Secret Police and military questions."

"You mean we could ride in your plane down to Bandar-e without the authorities asking about us?"

"I do have a little bit of influence in this country. You'll be going as my bodyguards. I always travel with one or two. Three is not unheard of."

George frowned. "So we get that far, how do we get on to Chah Bahar?"

"Rent a car," Murrah said. "I can do so without a question. I'll tell them it's for a vacation, and I've never been that far south before. You'd be surprised how many people, and officials, will let me break a lot of the rules."

"If we're voting, I'd say it's a go," Franklin said.

"Sounds good to me," Douglas chimed in. "Once we get to that town, we can start working our way out those roads and feel our way along until we find the sucker."

George still had his frown. "I don't know. I'm not comfortable exposed that way. In Tehran, I can melt into the community. I'm going to have to check with the Office on this."

"Don't bother," Douglas said. "You stay here and we'll go with Murrah down south and find the damned location."

George sighed, and at last nodded. "Yes, you're right. I haven't done the job up here. I'd say it can't be done here. So we go south. If it's still all right with Murrah."

"I'd be delighted. You'll stay here tonight. I'll outfit you in some different clothes, and we'll take two or three suitcases. I have jackets that are just alike that should fit the three of you. Yes, let's do it. I have some phone calls to make. Lotus will show each of you to your room. We'll be up early. I like to fly out before seven A.M. It's an hour to the airport in my car."

Lotus, the maid, arrived on cue, and motioned the three men to follow her. Murrah took a cordless phone from its set in a drawer in the arm of one of the large sofas, and made her calls.

A half hour later, Joe Douglas had turned off the light in

the room he had been shown to. He had stripped to his shorts and slid between white sheets. Murrah lived like a queen in this poverty-drenched country.

He had just closed his eyes, when he heard his door open. Damn. His pistol was halfway across the room.

"Don't be alarmed, Joe Douglas," Murrah said softly. She turned on one of the small lamps and sat down on the bed beside him. She wore a thin, wispy see-through gown.

"Joe Douglas, did you enjoy my dancing tonight?"

"Yes, fantastic. I still don't see how you can shake that way."

She laughed. "It is a gift and a craft. Tell me, was I sexy?"

"Oh, yes, absolutely."

"Did you fantasize about me just a little?"

"Yes."

"Good." She slipped off the light robe and stood naked in front of him. Then she slid into the bed beside him.

"Joe Douglas, tonight I want you to dance with me many times."

Douglas couldn't stop a big grin. "Hey, that's one dance I think I can do good enough to keep you happy."

"Enough talk, Joe Douglas. Enough talk."

The early morning at Murrah's house was a blur for Colt Franklin and Joe Douglas. They were awakened about four, fed, given new clothes with matching brown jackets, then ushered into a Mercedes Benz sedan and driven swiftly to the Tehran airport. They went through a side gate to a private hangar.

In ten minutes, they had loaded onboard a six-passenger aircraft, of some European make not even Joe Douglas could determine, and taken off. Douglas checked his watch. It was a little after 0653.

"We'll be flying at one hundred seventy-five miles an hour, and have to make one stop for fuel in Shiraz," Murrah told them.

"When will we get to our destination?" George asked.

"It's about seven hours with the stop," she said. "We should land in Bandar-e 'Abbas a little after two in the afternoon."

"Then what's the program?" Douglas asked. She had made sure to sit beside him in the rear two seats, and when no one was looking, her hand strayed over to his thigh.

"In Iran, speed is not important. If we try to move too quickly, we could stir up some suspicion. I have canceled my performance for tomorrow night, a case of the flu. We'll stay tonight at a small inn where I have friends. That will give them time to find a car for me that won't be noticed. We'll leave early in the morning. Will that be fast enough?"

"Sounds fine," Douglas said.

"Take us most of the day to drive on to Chah Bahar, I'd guess," George said.

"The farther we go south, the worse the roads become, but we should be able to maintain a forty miles per hour average." Murrah hurried on. "I know that's not fast by American standards, but it's the best we can do on our secondary roads."

"Only a ten-hour car ride," Franklin said. "We'll be getting on-site faster than I had hoped."

"Tonight I'll find a spot, and send our plans to Don Stroh and company, unless George wants to unlimber his SAT-COM," Douglas said.

The CIA agent waved. "Help yourself."

Conversation tapered off then. Murrah went to sleep with her head on Joe Douglas's shoulder, and her hand halfway up his thigh. He moved it away gently.

They made their fuel stop, and took off without incident. Later they landed at the small airport at Bandar-e 'Abbas. They taxied to a small private hangar where a car waited for them.

"Nothing like traveling first class," Guns Franklin said. The other two Americans agreed with him.

There was no military security at the airport, which surprised Douglas.

Two miles later, they drove into a courtyard and a big door closed behind them. A woman rushed out of the inn and hugged Murrah. They talked for a minute, then the men got out of the car. There were brief introductions, then they went inside.

Ten minutes later, on the roof of the three-story inn, Douglas set up the SATCOM and worked on his message.

"Flew three-quarters of the way to Chah Bahar. Going on there tomorrow by car. Have help of famous person who is sympathetic. George is with us. Will listen at regular times. Any suggestions?"

He read it over twice, let George look at it, then hit the send button, and the burst of energy shot out of the antenna in a millisecond, straight to the satellite.

The men stayed inside the compound. Douglas and Franklin were feeling antsy, so they had a push-up contest. Franklin, the former gymnast, won with a hundred and forty-seven. After a short rest they ran around the courtyard until they sweat through their clothes.

At midnight, Douglas had the SATCOM set put up, the antenna tuned in, and the radio turned to receive. The message came through promptly at midnight, local time. Douglas had no idea what time it was wherever Don Stroh had landed.

The encrypto mechanism in the set spilled out the message in plain English on the readout screen.

"Douglas. Approve move south. Keep body count low. Make any KIAs look like accidents. Security is high all over Chah Bahar area. Douglas is CO of operation. New satellite photos of area coming in. Will give you layout of major roads out of Chah soon. We need location of target to within a quarter mile. Be careful. Stroh."

George and Franklin read the message. George waved.

"Hey, down here I'm out of my element. I'm not a country kind of guy. I'll follow your lead."

"The fucking highways out of town are the key," Franklin said. "Wish we had a fax on this thing. We'll have to use compass directions. Can't be many roads to go nowhere."

"Yeah, but getting on them, following them without being stopped by those military guards, will be the trick," Douglas said.

About the same time in Tehran, General Ruhollah paced his office. They were too close now to permit anything to go wrong. Another three weeks and the men at the plant said the first device would be ready.

Only three weeks!

General Ruhollah could hardly believe it. He had pushed hard for the development of their own nuclear capability. He had had trouble at times, but had bulled through every roadblock. He had pinched money from many sources to fund the program. Now only three weeks away!

But there was something going on that he didn't like. The U.S. CIA had been too active lately. One Iranian agent had been killed, the top CIA man was on the run. They had quashed three small Iranian groups who had fought the very idea of a nuclear facility. The large man, Tauksaun, was contained in his apartment. Anyone who came to see him was picked up for questioning. They would soon have a phone tap on his three phone lines.

Still there was something else. It was more a feeling than any hard facts he had. The dancer, Murrah, was one he had not been able to touch. He knew she was involved with one of the small anti-nuclear groups. He wasn't sure which one or what they could do. His last report today was that she was not at her usual performance restaurant.

He checked and found that she had a series of dance engagements in Bandar-e 'Abbas. Yes, his men reported that she had rented the usual plane she often used and flown out that morning with the southern city her destination on the flight plan.

Her plane had landed there earlier today.

Still he wondered. It was only four hundred miles on to Chah Bahar. There were no indications that she was going to go there. Still it worried him.

More and more people knew that "something" had been built in the mountains above the southern city. A project this big could not be done in secret. The construction people alone numbered over a thousand. But they didn't know what they were building.

The lens grinders had been the biggest security leak. They didn't know what they worked on, but educated guesses could be made. Secrecy plus the intricate grinding process must have led many to speculate.

Only three more weeks.

He made up his mind in a flash, the way he always did. Tomorrow he would fly to Chah Bahar. The small airstrip was large enough for his personal plane to land. In the morning he would order two more companies of infantry troops to report to the main security building in Chah Bahar. That would make four companies, about eight hundred men. He wished he could station some of their jet fighters there, but the runway wasn't long enough. Perhaps at the Bandar-e 'Abbas airport. He would have to check it. He could send six attack helicopters to Chah Bahar. The French ones they bought last month would do fine.

If anyone tried to disrupt the work at the nuclear plant, they would be in for a huge surprise. He had no idea what to expect. He guessed that the CIA knew of the program by now. Such a huge undertaking was hard to keep totally under wraps.

General Ruhollah went to his telephone and made three calls. The plane would be ready in the morning at six o'clock. It was the smaller one that could land at Chah. At 200 mph top speed, it would take most of the day to get there. Then he would look over the security, and welcome the new troops that would arrive in three days.

If anyone tried to get within ten miles of the plant, they would be met with deadly force.

General Ruhollah poured a small glass of bourbon from a secret bottle in his desk. No good Muslim drank liquor. He sighed and tipped the glass. He had spent too much time in England as an attaché. Maybe he wasn't a good Muslim. It didn't matter one way or the other. He had little patience with the old-timers, the hard-liners who wanted Iran's 70 million people to turn back the clock and live the way their grandfathers had.

It was a new world.

Iran must be ready to compete.

Iran must be ready to defend herself with nuclear weapons.

Iran must be ready to conquer the five big Arab states on the peninsula. Then they would speak with one voice to the West. They would dictate the terms of world commerce and the price of their oil.

Iran must be ready!

With six nuclear bombs, they would be ready.

15

Thursday, October 27

1826 hours
A safe house
Bandar-e 'Abbas, Iran
They heard the news just after dinner. A young man on a scruffy-looking motorcycle pulled in through the inn's main doors and was met with food and a long drink of cold water. He talked quietly with the owner of the inn and Murrah. Douglas watched the conversation from his second-floor window looking into the courtyard, and he could tell it was bad news.

Douglas took the steps three at a time and ran down into the courtyard. The talk continued. It was in Farsi or something else he didn't understand. After two exchanges, Murrah turned to Douglas.

"We have problem. There is an army unit at Jask turning everyone around who tries to go toward Chah Bahar. Even those who live there must stop and give details about their lives, and their identification papers. The roadblock is tight."

"How far is Jask?"

"Halfway, about two hundred miles," Murrah said.

"I move we get there as fast as we can. Leave in a half hour. Then we'll be there in the dark."

Murrah shook her head. "How will that help us?"

"We'll share riding the pony. We travel down that way, and as soon as we spot the roadblock ahead, the three of us will get off while you and your driver continue on. You're a star in this country. Tell them that you're going to Chah Bahar to entertain the soldiers stationed there. It's a sudden impulse you had to cheer up the troop on such rigorous duty."

Murrah began to smile as he outlined the plan, then she smiled broadly, and kissed his cheek.

"Yes, it will work. I've gotten into war areas more than once in the past. Yes, they will let me through."

"While you chat with the guards, the three of us will circle around the roadblock well into the darkness of the countryside. When we see you get through, we'll head for the road well down and out of sight of the block. We'll get back in the car and hope that's the last roadblock we meet."

Murrah nodded. "Yes, yes, it could work. I'll have a good story worked up, but we have two hundred miles for me to figure it out. Yes. I'll get talking to some people and get things ready. They have the car for us. Good enough to make the run on one tank full of petrol, but not flashy enough to get us in trouble.

"You round up your two friends, and get them down here in fifteen minutes. I'll need that long to get some basic supplies and some of my performance gear packed in the suitcase. I'm never without at least two outfits. Hurry now."

Murrah questioned the cycle rider again. He told her that the roadblock was just past the far side of Jask, so it didn't interfere with local traffic. When he was stopped, there were three soldiers and an officer in a closed car. Two full-sized trucks stretched across the two-lane road from ditch to ditch. One older car had tried to run the blockade going around the side. It had been shot full of holes, and rolled into the ditch, where the driver and two passengers died.

The soldiers left it there as an object lesson.

The soldiers all had submachine guns. He didn't know what type, but they scared hell out of him. He turned around the first time he was ordered to do so, without a word of protest.

"Love to have those sub-guns," Franklin said. "How can we make it look like an accident if we take out that block?"

"No way. Besides the officer in the closed car must have a radio and the word would be out on us before we could go to cover come daylight."

"Afraid so," Franklin said. "Maybe the next roadblock will be smaller, and we can do some good. Hate to be here in enemy territory with only this little peashooter."

"That's a Roger. We'll see what develops. You can't make an oyster stew without killing a few oysters."

"Huh?"

"Nothing. Let's get in this car, and try to look like natives."

The road south was worse than they had imagined. By the time they got to Jask, it was after midnight. Their Iranian driver found the right road south but mostly west along the shoreline of the Gulf of Oman. Five miles out of the main port of town, they spotted the roadblock ahead.

Just as the cyclist had said, it was a good one. The death car had been pulled away, but the two large trucks with trailers still blocked the road. A jeep sat in front of it with a mounted .30-caliber machine gun. A staff car showed to one side. Two armed soldiers stood at the barricade.

The three Americans bailed out of the sedan while it kept moving. They vanished into the inland side, and moved cautiously through the sparse vegetation. It wasn't a desert land, but almost.

Douglas watched the sedan roll on down the road, and soon stop at the checkpoint. They jogged then, moving as fast as they could over the uneven ground.

George lagged behind. They waited for him twice. Douglas. cut the speed down so the big CIA man could stay with them. They were a hundred yards into the landscape when they came even with the barricade. There were no wires or warning devices they could see or feel.

They saw the two soldiers talking with Murrah, then an officer came from the staff car. There was some laughter. Then as they hurried on past, the Americans heard one of the big trucks' engines start, and the truck pulled out of the way for the star dancer's car to slip through.

"Could have taken the three of them easy," Franklin said.

"Easy, but how would it have looked like an accident? Remember, we can't leave a bunch of bodies around, at least not until we get some backup—like the rest of Third Platoon."

They went faster then, and slanted toward the road. They were two hundred yards down the blacktopped highway when they got back to the road. The car had moved away from the barricade slowly. Now they ran to match its ten-mile-an-hour speed, and get on board.

"Made it," Murrah said when the three were safely in the backseat. "There's one more roadblock ahead, but the Captain said I should have no trouble. All I had to do was mention that I was coming at the specific invitation of General Reza Ruhollah. He's one of the big movers in the new Iranian Army."

"How far to the next block?" Douglas asked.

"Halfway, about a hundred miles. That's about three hours the way we're moving. At least we won't have to worry about any other traffic on the road."

It was a little after 0300 when they spotted the next roadblock.

"This one we're taking out," Douglas said. "We need some weapons. We'll make it look like an accident somehow. Pull up the same way, go a little slower as you get close. If there's an officer, get him out to talk. We'll come in from the darkness at each side. Try not to get too close to any of them, and don't get between them."

Franklin watched the dancer. "He's saying there's going to be some shooting. The closer we can get with these little parabellums the better."

They left the car the same way, hit the ditches on each side of the road, and ran, keeping pace with the car. It slowed more as it came up to the headlights that now shown from the two vehicles. There were no big trucks at this spot.

The car stopped fifteen feet from the Army vehicle, and the driver got out quickly. He jabbered something, and the soldiers came forward.

When Murrah left the car, it was a grand entrance. The soldiers let their submachine guns swing down and gawked. An officer came out at once. He showed no weapon, and was all smiles.

Franklin and Douglas had agreed to shoot over the heads of the Iranians. They didn't want bullet holes showing up in the bodies later.

The SEALs shot almost at the same time. Franklin barked out in Farsi, telling the men to lay down their weapons at once or they would be riddled with bullets. The soldiers did as they were told. The officer made a lunge for his car, where he must have left his weapon. Murrah's driver tackled him, and by then Franklin and Douglas were on the scene. They had noticed a cliff of sorts that dropped off here almost into the Gulf of Oman. It would be a hundred-foot fall.

Douglas took one of the soldiers, put him in the jeep, and backed it out. He drove toward the cliffs and parked. He kept the man under his own submachine gun.

Douglas found the right spot, then pushed the Iranian into the jeep's driver's seat and slashed him with the butt of the submachine gun. It took two blows to put him out. Then Douglas started the jeep, put it in gear, and steered it straight for the drop-off. It went over with a scraping of the undercarriage. He heard the crash far below, and glass breaking, then silence.

He went back to help Franklin. He had tied the officer's

hands, and had both men in the officer's car. Franklin drove the rig to the cliff and got out.

They put the soldier in the driver's seat and the officer in the back, then slugged them with their weapons. They took the ties off the hands of the officer, then angled the small sedan off the same cliff. It crashed far below in the rocks and incoming tide. It should take the Iranian police, and the military, at least a week to figure out what happened at this poorly manned roadblock.

Back at Murrah's sedan, they said nothing, just motioned the rig forward. George started to say something, then thought better of it. They had the two submachine guns and found six 30-round magazines for each one. They were simple to use. George also found a 14-round pistol in the officer's gear.

Murrah broke the silence. "I'm glad that's over. At least now we'll have a clear run into Chah Bahar. I know a few people there. We should be able to find a safe house before morning. Then I and my driver will see what we can find out about the highways to the north. Somebody must know something. How can such a huge project be kept so secret?"

"There's a chance that most of the people living here are paid by the Secret Police and the army not to say a word about it," George said. "I've heard such talk."

Murrah nodded. "I've heard that talk as well, but there is no chance to keep this many people quiet about something like this. We had a small group of protesters here for a while, but three of them were killed when they were said to be trying to escape from jail. They were simply murdered. I've got a lot of scores to settle."

The car crept into Chah Bahar with lights off. They sat in shadows watching the main street. They saw no police cars, no roving military patrols. They turned off the main street into some sparsely settled areas, and soon came to a house better than the rest. Murrah sent her driver in to knock on the door.

Five minutes later, they all were inside the house, and the car had been hidden behind it. A man and woman came into the room, and there was much hugging and crying by the two and Murrah. Then she wiped her tears, and introduced them to the three Americans.

"These people are my dear friends who used to live in Tehran. They have kept out of trouble here with the authorities, but have been our listening post, and sent us mail reports.

"Now it seems that security has been stepped up. They know the main road into the hills, but have no idea where the trucks vanish to after that."

Douglas rubbed his face and nodded. "Is there any way that Guns and me can get back in there? Fifty miles and then a turn. Do they agree with the distance?"

Franklin asked the question in Farsi, and the man, who was tall with thinning gray hair, smiled. He replied in the same tongue.

"I'm pleased you speak our language so well. You can't drive in there. The road is constantly patrolled and no one is allowed in that area. The only solution may be to disguise you as prospectors. There are still crazy men who risk being shot hunting for copper and chromium back here in our hills to the north. There's a huge chromium mine up by Bandar-e, and nuts think they can find another one in the mountains down here."

Franklin briefed Douglas on what the host had said.

"You mean a prospector with a donkey, a pick, and a sack full of food?"

The Iranian chuckled. "More likely a beat-up old jeep or a falling-apart sedan, and a backseat full of food and water. That would give you cover, and let you move longer distances. Most of the wildcat prospectors use this kind of a rig these days."

"They get shot at?" Franklin said.

"Routinely. When they get too close to a closed area or

one patrolled. The guards, and the helicopters, do it mostly for sport, and target practice. They don't really chase them unless they really move in too close."

"Which way do you guess the big plant is, to the left or right of the end of that highway?"

"I simply don't know. It could be either way."

Douglas figured their host was in his fifties. Murrah said he was a teacher in the local school system, teacher and principal. He was a highly respected man in Chah Bahar, and had the full respect of the local authorities, and the military units posted to the town.

"How much army is there here?" Douglas asked. Murrah interpreted for him.

"Roughly two hundred men," the host said. "They rotate in units of fifty up to guard duty around the facility. They are gone for a week, then another fifty go up to replace them and the first group returns in trucks."

"Do you have military law here?" Franklin asked.

"Yes and no."

The woman of the house left, and soon returned with rolls and coffee. It was almost daylight outside.

"We have civil law. Judges, courts, but this is strongly slanted toward the religious leaders. If there is any problem, the military have the final say, or so it would seem down here. We are a long way from Tehran."

When the rolls and coffee were gone, Murrah said now was the time for some sleep. She would need to put in an appearance at the town's main meeting hall the following night. The guards at the first roadblock would be sure to radio their men down here that the famous dancer was coming.

"Between now and then I'll help arrange for a prospector's car for the two of you. It'll be all outfitted with food and water and supplies and ready to roll."

Douglas brought out a stack of ten-thousand-rial notes and gave them to Murrah. "I know this sort of thing costs money. Uncle Sam will pay his way. If that's not enough, we have more."

Murrah leafed through the bills and smiled. "Do you know how much money this is? It's a fortune to the average Iranian. I'll put it to good use, without tipping our hand. Now, off to bed, all of you. I need to make some early morning arrangements before I get to sleep."

Douglas went to the flat roof on the house and set up his radio antenna. He adjusted it to the satellite, then sent off a quick message to Stroh: "Stroh: At Chah Bahar. Contacts here good. Will be moving out in old car into hills as prospectors. Many do this in these hills. Try to penetrate to the road and see which way it turns. Any satellite photos to help us? Read them and send us directions. Be a big help. All else cool. Three Iranians had an accident at a roadblock, but all is taken care of. Douglas."

Douglas folded up the fanlike antenna and stowed it, then hit his bed. It was going to be a long day even after he woke up.

16

Friday, October 28

0814 hours
SEAL training base
Coronado, California

Sixteen SEALs and Kat Garnet swam fifteen feet underwater in the blue Pacific Ocean a half mile off the Silver Strand that linked Coronado to Imperial Beach. They moved forward with a steady stroke using their Drager LAR-V rebreathers. They use pure oxygen that is recycled through the device to eliminate any of the telltale bubbles that follow ordinary SCUBA divers.

This new model Drager was worn on the chest, and the SEAL's personal weapon was strapped on his back. They had on their usual black wet suits, hoods and boots.

Lieutenant Blake Murdock looked around through the clear greenish water. Visibility good, at least twenty feet. Slightly ahead, and tied to him by a buddy cord, swam Joe "Ricochet" Lampedusa, his new lead scout. The rest of them were also paired with six-foot-long cords so they could stay together.

Tied with Ron Holt was Kat Garnet. Holt was the platoon radio operator who carried the fifteen-pound SATCOM set.

Next in line were Magic Brown and Kenneth Ching.

Murdock watched Kat. She had taken the first two days of training with the Drager in stride. But then she had been an instructor with SCUBA back in Washington, D.C., so the Drager was no stretch.

She carried the full load of combat gear the other SEALs had, including the combat vest with ammo for her MP-5, K-bar knife, canteen, and the belt Mark 23 MOD O .45 pistol.

So far so good.

They had entered the water a half hour before, swam out a half mile, and now were on the way back. This was another exercise to get Kat integrated into the platoon operation as smoothly as possible.

They all had live rounds in their weapons. Kat was getting used to her MP-5 and firing it. She had daily firing practice now. During the past two days she had taken six parachute jumps at Brown Field, a civilian airport near the border with Mexico. A jump school over there contracted with the SEALs for refresher jumps and in this case shepherded Kat through her jumps with full gear. Murdock had limited her load to forty pounds, which still make a big difference in the way her rectangular chute opened and drifted.

"A lot different than the round chutes I used before, with no load other than me," she told him.

They had completed her rush training course in the elements that SEALs must know. Now they were in a crash operation to get her used to working within the group. Most was land training, since they would most likely drop into the mountains of Iran, and go by ground to the suspect facility. By now, Kat was more than trained on the Drager to make an exit from Iran by water if they needed to.

As they neared the beach, Murdock held up his hand and stopped the first pair of swimmers. They passed the sign along until the platoon was assembled, then they went to the surface.

It was to be a normal assault landing on a beach. They treaded water with their mouths barely out and the Dragers unhooked.

Murdock waved his right hand, and Lampedusa ducked underwater and swam hard for the beach. He came out of the last wave and lay in the sand without moving. Slowly, a half-inch at a time, he turned his head to scan the beach. When he was sure it was secure, he lifted his right arm and brought it down toward the sand.

Six more SEALs from the first squad powered toward the beach, surfed in on the last wave, and lay motionless on the wet sand, where an occasional wave washed over them.

Half a minute later the rest of the platoon surfed in on the four-foot waves and lay on the beach. Kat knew exactly what to do. She had rehearsed this with Jaybird a dozen times on dry land. When she saw the hand raised, she moved with the others. They had cut their buddy cords. She swam furiously, surfed down the last breaker, and was the second man in the platoon to go to ground on the wet sand.

On another signal from Murdock, the SEALs crawled forward, pulled their weapons off their backs, emptied out the water, and charged a round into the chambers. Kat was in sync with the rest of the platoon.

The two snipers leaped up, charged across the dry sand to a small dune, and went prone behind it, simulating fire to the front. On signal the first squad charged the dune and spread out around it, facing the shore. Kat bellied down in the sand, her MP-5 up and ready to fire. She lay six feet from Ron Holt, where she had been assigned.

Second squad raced out of the wet sand, came near the dry dune, and spread out facing the water as a rear guard. Murdock gave another hand signal and Miguel Fernandez leaped up, raced up beside the snipers, set up his machine gun, and chambered the first round. He held up his hand to show that he was ready.

Murdock gave him a signal and he simulated firing.

The next move came as Murdock leaped up. The rest of first squad lifted as a unit with him, and charged past the machine gunner, through the sand toward the highway fifty yard inland. At the edge of the highway, Murdock went prone, and the squad followed.

A moment later the machine gunner Fernandez and second squad charged up beside them.

Murdock stood. "Gather around," he barked, and the SEALs pulled up nearby and sat.

"Not bad. A little ragged getting the second squad to shore. Get your buddy lines cut quicker so you're ready. Kat, any problems?"

"No. That Drager is a sweetheart. I want to take one home with me."

"You can. They price out a little over three thousand dollars."

"On the other hand . . . ," Kat said, and the SEALs laughed.

"Kat, you kept up with us, you stayed in your position, you took to the sand in good form, and you charged across it like a veteran. How does it feel to swim and run with forty pounds of gear?"

"Better than if had sixty."

The SEALs hooted and jeered at Murdock.

Murdock grinned. In a week this small lady had won the hearts of every man in the platoon. Now all he had to be sure of was that she could carry her load, keep herself alive, and didn't cause any of his men to get wasted. Oh, yeah, and he had to be careful that none of his SEALs put himself in danger trying to help out Kat.

"Let's get back to the OP shack. I want you to change into dry cammies. We're going for a ride in forty-five, so hustle."

"Where we riding to, L-T?" Jaybird asked.

· "Didn't tell you chief? We're headed for Niland and a

little bit of live firing practice, in formation. Kat, you can change in my office. Let's move it. Jaybird, a column of ducks and double time."

The squads formed in a column of twos automatically, and Murdock and Jaybird led them the two miles down the wet sand to the SEAL Grinder. Kat ran beside Holt. She had no trouble keeping up. Holt looked over at her and gave her a thumbs-up.

Kat Garnet, physics professor, nuclear weapons break-down expert, and temporary SEAL, grinned.

Four hours later, the Third Platoon had saddled up with full combat gear, personal weapons, and regular ammo load, and headed across country from their Navy bus at the edge of the Navy's Chocolate Mountain Gunnery Range in the California desert.

Murdock had given them the orders before they started out from the bus. "Our mission today is to take Hill 284. It's about five miles out to the left. First we find it, then we assault it, and we hope we don't kill any of our own men—or women. This is a live-fire drill."

He turned to Kat.

"Lieutenant Garnet, do you read me?"

"Yes. We have live rounds. We follow standard proce-dures, and fire in our designated areas, and do not endanger any friendlies."

"Right, remember that."

They hiked out in combat style. Lampedusa led off as scout, working a hundred yards ahead of the rest. They had two diamond formations side by side. Murdock led the point on first squad, followed closely by Ron Holt with the radio, and then Kat. She carried her MP-5, and six extra maga-zines.

From time to time, Kat stared down at the safety on the weapon. It was on. She didn't want to stumble and fire off a half dozen rounds. When the order to fire came, she would check to be sure her field of fire was clear of any friendly force, then fire in the indicated direction on single-shot or three-round burst. Yes. Now all she had to do was do it right. This was her first live-fire training exercise with the rest of the platoon.

They were halfway out to the mountain in the hot afternoon sunshine of October, when Holt touched his mike button once, creating a one-shot *tsk* on the radio. Sixteen SEALs hit the dirt, and lay without moving. Kat tried to look ahead. All she could see was Ron Holt's boots. She looked over at Magic Brown. She'd watch him.

Magic stood. Kat stood and saw the rest of the platoon on its feet and moving forward slowly toward where the scout remained on his stomach looking forward to the right.

The radio receiver in her ear came on. It was Murdock. "We have some activity to the right front. First squad on the double, and form a line of skirmishers in the dirt on the scout. Move!"

Kat held her MP-5 in front of her and charged forward. The men raced ahead of her, but she caught them by the time they came to the scout, and all flopped on the ground with weapons pointing outward in a menacing line.

Kat knew there would be no open-fire command. In the SEALs, when the platoon leader began firing, that was the signal for the rest of them to fire.

She heard the stutter of Murdock's MP-5 and leveled in her own weapon, pushed off the safety to three-round burst, and fired six rounds. The weapon sounded strange. She fixed six more rounds. The earpiece gave three *tsks* and the squad ceased fire.

"Second squad form on our left flank," the radio speaker ordered. "Open fire when in place."

Kat watched to her left and saw the second squad run into position, and the weapons chattered. She'd never heard so many guns firing at the same time in her life.

"Cease fire, reform in diamonds," the radio whispered.

As Kat moved back into formation behind Holt, Murdock fell into step behind her.

"Good work back there, Kat. You moved well, stayed in position. Always remember before you fire to check for friendly forces in front of you. Somebody might get out of line, or get held up, even wounded. Check that field of fire first. It has to be an automatic every time you're in combat."

Kat nodded, and he slapped her on the shoulder, and went back to lead the squad on toward the hill.

Twice more in the next mile they had fire missions. On the last one the first squad went into line and second squad formed up on their left flank at a 45-degree angle. Murdock fired, and the whole platoon fired, then stopped at the cease-fire three *tsks* on the earpieces.

"Kat," the earpiece spoke. "Take a look at the squad on the left, then lay down covering fire twenty yards in front of them. Now."

Kat lifted her MP-5, pushed it to three-round bursts, and scattered a dozen shots in front of the Second Squad.

"Cease fire, cease fire," the excited voice came over the radio. "Man down, we've got a man down, Second Squad. Get Doc over here fast."

Kat's eyes went wide. She pushed the safety on her submachine gun. She had been the only one firing. Had she shot one of the platoon?

Murdock appeared at her elbow. "Kat, on me. Follow me." The two ran over the desert rocks, and past straggling sage and some dwarf plants to where the second squad had gathered around a man on the ground.

They moved up, and the men gave way. Les Quinley, Torpedoman's Mate Third Class, lay on the rocky ground on his back. His eyes were closed, his chest a mass of red blood. Doc Ellsworth worked on him quickly, taking his vitals, trying to stop the blood flow from his chest.

Doc turned, and looked at Murdock. "Gonna need some

help. Better have Holt ring up a chopper to get out here from North Island or Pendleton."

"How bad is he, Doc?" Murdock asked.

"Can't tell. Must have taken two right in the chest."

Kat dropped to her knees and stared at Quinley. She picked up the SEAL's hand and then let it down. It was limp.

"Murdock, I didn't mean to—"

He cut her off. "Holt, get over here on the double and warm up the SATCOM."

"Ed, was Quinley too far off line down there on the end?"

"No. He was within ten yards of the next man. Should have been safe."

"Kat, didn't I tell you to give support fire, *in front* of Second Squad?"

"Yes, sir, you did. I thought—"

"No excuse!" Murdock thundered. "The only answer to a fuckup like this is to say, no excuse."

Kat lowered her head to her hands and blinked. She would not cry. There might not be any "crying in baseball" as the movie said. There sure as hell wasn't any crying in the SEALs.

Somebody snickered.

Kat looked up.

A belly laugh launched from somewhere in the Second Squad.

Kat stared around, wiping just-formed tears from her eyes.

She looked down at Quinley, who now had one eye open.

Murdock's face was still grim. "Lieutenant, are you absolutely sure that you fired in front of Second Squad?"

She stared back at him. "Absolutely certain, Lieutenant. Fucking absolutely certain."

"Atta girl," somebody shouted from the Second Squad.

"Would you hurry this up?" Quinley brayed from his

apparent deathbed. "I've got a shithouse-sized fucking rock in the middle of my back."

Kat punched Quinley in the belly and he rolled over and sat up. The blood pack fell off his cammies and the whole platoon roared with laughter.

"You fuckers, you set me up," Kat screeched.

Murdock squatted beside her. "We had you, though, didn't we? Kat, I want you to check your magazine."

She frowned, swung her MP-5 up, and pushed the mag release. She caught the magazine in her hand, and looked at the rounds still in it.

"You really set me up. They're blanks. I've been firing blanks all afternoon." She turned toward Murdock, the weapon dropped to her knees. She balled her fists and bellowed in rage.

"You whore-mongering, sonsabitching, mother-fucking, gonad-eating, umbuquatious assholes. You won't get me again. As I remember, Murdock, sir, you volunteered to load my magazines for me." Then she grinned. "I'm nominating the rest of you fifteen shit-kickers for a fucking Academy Award for best actors."

"Welcome to the SEALs, Lieutenant Garnet," Jaybird said. "It's good to have you aboard."

Everyone cheered. Quinley cleaned up the blood pouch Doc had begged from the base infirmary, and they got ready to march.

"Two more miles," Murdock said. "Let's get back in our diamond formation and haul ass."

Going up the last two hundred yards to the top of the small rise, they laid down assault fire, then secured the peak and spread out in a protective formation on the reverse slope. Twice they fired down the slope. Kat had stowed magazines of blanks, borrowed hot rounds from some of the other MP-5 shooters, and joined in the exercise, glad to have live rounds again.

DeWitt remembered that Kat hadn't fired any of the

40mm grenades from the Colt M-4A1. Murdock approved, and she fired six HE rounds and then two WP. The white phosphorous started a small fire that Jaybird and four men attacked with entrenching tools, and had out before it had burned ten feet. The desert land offered little fuel, but at times annual grass could be a problem.

Murdock checked his watch: 1725. He called the troops together. "Anybody want to camp out tonight, and have a twenty-mile hike tomorrow morning?"

He heard a few boos.

"Good. It's now 1725. We're five klicks from the bus. If we get back there by 1800, we turn turtle, and drive back to Coronado. That's six minutes to the mile. Kat will lead out; she knows this pace. Let's do it."

They headed downhill. A six-minutes-to-the-mile pace is just a little slower than the professional marathoners go. With full combat gear it was a struggle and a strain. Kat held it for two miles, then checked the troops. They were strung out for a quarter of a mile.

Murdock called a halt while the stragglers caught up. When all were assembled, he relented.

"Sorry some of you ladies couldn't keep up with our newest recruit SEAL. I see more hikes coming up. Okay, you've had a good drill, we'll walk the rest of the way, and still have that bus ride. Now, are we happy?"

"We're happy, sir!" the SEALs bellowed in unison.

"I asked if we're happy?"

This time the bellow came twice as loud followed by raucous cheers and shouts.

Murdock gave them the old Infantry signal of forward with his hand high over his head and then brought down to the front.

The Navy bus pulled up in front of the SEAL quarterdeck just after 2100.

Murdock motioned to Kat as she stepped off the bus. "Lieutenant, there are some matters we need to discuss.

Dinner tonight at the officers club at the Amphib Base. I'll meet you there in thirty minutes."

"Cammies? That's all I have."

"I think I can get you past the cop at the door."

An hour later they sat at a back table next to the wall and worked on medium-rare steaks. Murdock took the lead before dessert came.

"Kat, I owe you an explanation." He held up his hand when she started to protest. She relaxed.

"Our little stunt today is standard for most of the new men we get in our platoon. A kind of wringing out and checking out. There's one thing we can't know when we train a man. How is he going to react in actual combat when the bad guys are shooting back trying to kill his ass dead.

"It's the one intangible that every combat commander worries over until all of his men are blooded. This problem was magnified about tenfold when you were assigned here. You're a civilian, you had never fired a gun before, and you were a woman."

"So?" She watched him with a faint smile.

"So far you've stood up to our training and physical regimen better than I expected. Far better, in fact. You didn't panic when you thought you might have killed one of your platoon. You took the guff and came up smiling. All A-plus in my book."

"So far, so good, Lieutenant. You didn't buy me dinner—you did say you were buying; I don't have any money with me."

He nodded.

"Good. We're not here to take a look at my report card. What else is in your craw?"

"Don Stroh, but he's another problem. I don't know if you researched us before you arrived?"

"I did. The U.S. Navy SEALs were established by presidential order in 1962 by John Kennedy. SEAL stands for SEa, Air, and Land. Most say that the SEAL teams are the foremost elite special operations forces in the world today. SEAL teams One and Two served in Vietnam. At that time they were fourteen-man platoons.

"By 1990 there were seven SEAL teams to meet the expanding use of special operations and for covert work. They put teams One, Three, Five, and Seven here in Coronado at the Naval Special Warfare Group One. The rest of them, Teams Two, Four, and Eight, were headquartered at Little Creek, Virginia, in the command of the NAVSPECWARGRU-Two. The teams here were to be used in the Pacific area; the east coast teams would handle jobs in the Atlantic and Mediterranean areas."

Murdock grinned as she clicked off the history of his outfit. "You have done some homework."

"SEALs have the toughest, roughest, baddest training of any elite forces in the world, including the British SAS. It lasts six months and officers go through the same training as the other Bud guys, with one added duty. Officers must score at least ten percent higher on all tests than the enlisted men do.

"This creates a strange and magnificent bonding between SEAL officers and men. SEALs know their officers have done the BUDs course—lifted the log, manned the IBS, run the obstacle course—and done it in the ocean on a ten-mile swim combat ready.

"It's a spirit and motivation that few units have. These men depend on each other on every mission for their very lives. I've seen more dedication and devotion and dependent-bonding here in the past week than ever before in my life."

She stopped and took a bite of the desert. She wasn't sure what it was, or how it tasted. She watched his eyes. They seemed to light up for a minute, then a grin spread over his handsome face and she smiled. "Coach, how did I do?"

"Glad we could have this little talk."

They both burst out laughing. Neither of them said a word for a while. They concentrated on the desert. When it was gone and the final sips of wine vanished from their glasses, he picked up her hand and held it on the table.

"Katherine, you did fine, to answer your question. One thing I noticed about you the first day you reported. We told you something once and you learned it and remembered it. We never had to repeat anything to you. It's an exceptional ability. Now for the big question of the day: Has DeWitt's lady invited you over for dinner yet?"

"No. Ed mentioned it once, but said the time wasn't quite right yet."

"I'll see if I can get that worked out tomorrow. We got word today from Don Stroh that our men, Guns Franklin and Joe Douglas, are now somewhere near the nuclear facility north of the town of Chah Bahar in Iran. If they find that place in a rush, we won't have our month of training. I'm telling Don that as of tomorrow, we're combat ready. We can fly out anytime our boys find the target."

"We'll probably drop in by parachute?"

"Fifty miles inland is a long walk. We'll probably go in my air for a low-level drop. Static line on the chute from a thousand to twelve hundred feet off the deck. Quick down and ready to fight."

"Can we practice it once or twice here?"

He looked at her for several beats, then slowly shook his head. "Negative. There's a certain risk factor such as a broken arm or leg, maybe a bad landing and a broken back. We can take the risk on the actual hot drop. No way I'm risking you on a low-level training jump."

She gave a quick sigh, and nodded. "Good. I wasn't looking forward to it. I've got bruises over half my body now from those other parachute jumps. Those straps really jerk you around when the chute opens."

"True. Lieutenant, I think I better get you to your quarters. We have an oh-seven-thirty call in the morning."

At her door, she turned to face him. She wasn't sure what he would do. He was single, she knew that. Of all the men in the platoon, she had guessed he might be the only one who would try to come on to her.

He touched her shoulder. "Hey, Kat, have good dreams. See you in the morning." He turned, and walked away. Kat smiled faintly, and felt just a little rejected.

"What the hell, Kat," she whispered to herself. "You're a grown-up girl, you could have reached out and kissed him first." Then she shook her head. He was right. They had a mission. No entanglements, no baggage. She was just one of the guys. She had to be, at least until this mission was over, and they were back in the U.S.A. Then, who knows? She grinned as she unlocked her door and went inside.

17

Friday, October 28

1040 hours
Safe house
Chah Bahar, Iran

Joe Douglas dug the sleep out of his eyes with a pair of HE fraggers and stared at the new day.

Iran.

Hot already.

Wheels. He jumped off the bed and pulled on the loose-fitting Iranian clothing they had provided, stepped into his black Iranian shoes, and hurried down the stairs to the ground floor. He heard a motor kicking over in the interior of the quadrangle.

A minute later he saw it, a French-built Citroen sedan, at least ten years old. It had been repainted brown, but the driver's side front door was from another car, and still held the blue paint job. The motor sounded good.

Franklin pulled his head out from under the hood, and waved.

"Damn thing looks like it's been taken good care of. Should run a ton of miles unless somebody opens up on it with an Uzi or an MP-5. Look what we have in back already."

143

Franklin opened the rear door on the four-door model. There were heavy plastic bottles, each holding five gallons of water. There were a dozen boxes filled with food, most of it freeze-dried or dry, two loaves of bread, baskets of fruit, four rough brown blankets, an assortment of picks and shovels, and other prospecting gear to make them look legitimate.

They spent another hour going over the car and its contents. Murrah and her helpers brought more items they might need, such as a small butane bottle for cooking and a large piece of brown camouflage-painted canvas they could use to hide the car. The tank was filled with gasoline, and there were two 10-gallon tanks built into the back that were also filled.

"When's the best time to leave?" Douglas asked Murrah.

"As soon as it gets dark. Seven hours from now, maybe more." She frowned. "We need to have a private talk before then."

Douglas smiled. "Just how private?"

"The most private—in your room."

She left then, and the two SEALs looked at the captured weapons. Both were short, compact, with an extension stock. With the stock folded, they were less than a foot long.

"It's an MGP-15, what it says on the side," Franklin said.

Douglas grunted. "Yeah, heard about it. Made in Peru. Rate of fire only seven hundred rounds a minute, but you can shoot the sucker with one hand with the stock folded. Kicks out a lot of firepower with one hand."

"Magazines look like they should hold thirty rounds, nine mike, mike," Franklin said.

"No three-round bursts, but can go fully auto or single."

Franklin nodded. "Yeah, I think I'll keep this one until I can rob, plunder, or steal something better."

At high noon, Douglas set up the SATCOM in the courtyard and aimed the round antenna at the satellite.

When it was aligned, a light popped on, and he switched the set to receive.

A minute later a voice came loud and clear from the small speaker after the set processed the encrypted message through the code breaker.

"Douglas. Uncle Don here. We've found some interesting tracks in your wilderness. Widest highway goes forty-five miles almost due north, then splits. Best road heads east toward Pakistan. Estimate fifteen miles, then comes south another five, and vanishes into what looks like a fairly tall mountain.

"Gives you a place to start. Third Platoon reports ready to go when you are. Careful on that prospecting run. Stroh out."

Murrah brought out a local map, and they traced the roads. The one going north wasn't on the map. She plotted it in with a ballpoint pen, then at the forty-five-mile point, she turned it hard to the right for fifteen, then back south for five miles.

"How the hell do we get in there?" Douglas asked. "Are there any small trails or little-used roads, maybe old mines up in there?"

Murrah shrugged. "I don't know this area. Let me get Tabib, he can tell you."

She came back a moment later with the teacher, who was Iranian despite his Turkish name. He had a map of the area that did show some dirt roads and trails.

"Most of these are little more than trails, and often they run into a mountain and stop. One or two go through. I'll mark those. But those will be the ones that the military guards will be watching."

They bent over the map. He sketched in where the satellite photos had shown where the end of one wide roadway could be.

Tabib nodded. "Yes, there could be something there.

That's an exceedingly tall peak for this range. Some of them are at the ten-thousand-foot level."

"So we should bear to the left as we head north," Douglas said. "If we can get within ten miles of that place on the map, we can hike in and take a look."

"If you leave the car, camouflage it carefully," Tabib said. "They do have several helicopters in this area. We never know where they stay, but it isn't at our small dirt-strip airport."

"Choppers," Franklin said. "That would make it hard to hide the Citroen in a wadi somewhere, but we'll try."

"Enough," Murrah said. "Time for you both to get some sleep if you're going to be driving most of the night. There will be a full moon tonight, so that will help. Get some rest, now, both of you."

The two SEALs laughed, and went up the stairs to their rooms.

"This going to work?" Franklin asked.

"Damn well better. George didn't get the job done, so it's up to us. No location, no drop-in by the platoon."

Douglas smacked his fist into his palm. "Damn, wish we had a small chopper. We could tie down that location in a few hours, and have the platoon on their way loaded for nukes."

"Yeah, now you think of it," Douglas said. He turned into his room and closed the door.

He figured five minutes. It was no more than three minutes before his door opened gently, and someone slipped in.

"What took you so long?" Douglas asked.

"You Americans always make the jokes," Murrah said as she lay down on the bed beside him.

They left the house a little after 1930. Darkness was gathering quickly, and Tabib rode with them to the far edge of town. He headed them out a track of a road he said would parallel the main truck road for twenty miles or more. Then they would need to move carefully, working through a maze of roads, to try to get another dirt road that might or might not lead closer to their suspected target.

At the edge of town Tabib shook hands with them.

"We hope you destroy the bombs, my friends. The world does not need a wild-eyed Iranian General calling the shots in this section of the world with nuclear blackmail." He stepped back from the car, and waved as they moved into the countryside with their lights off, and only the pale moon to help them see the way.

Douglas drove. Every few miles, Franklin turned on a small flashlight and checked the creaking odometer.

"That's fifteen miles, we're getting there."

Douglas hoped he was right. Now and then they had seen a series of headlights moving along the road to their left. It seemed like most of the traffic was heading into the mountains. Why would that be? Maybe vital supplies were still needed to finish the fabrication of the weapons.

Two hours into the drive, the engine sputtered, stopped, came to life again, then died.

Franklin crawled out of the rig and lifted the hood.

"Try the starter."

Douglas ground it over.

"Oh, damn!" Franklin yelped. "Okay, we've got lots of hot spark on the plugs. Now we check for fuel. Did this old rig have a fuel filter on it?"

Douglas had no idea, and didn't answer. Franklin hummed a little tune as he checked the engine with the small light held in his mouth.

"Yeah, here it is. Let me get it apart." It was a twist-and-pull type cylinder half an inch in diameter and two inches long. He pulled it off and checked it with the light.

"Sucker is plugged up solid. Must be great gasoline they sell in this shit hole."

He poured a cup of water into one of the small cooking

pots they had in their gear and began shaking and washing the filter and thumping it on his hand.

At last he had it clean, then blew on it until it dried out. He wiped it off with a cloth and put it back in place.

"Give it a whirl."

The engine ground twice, then the third time until enough fuel had worked through the inlet pipes and through the filter to get to the engine. It fired, caught, and purred contentedly.

In the half-light, they had to drive slowly, carefully. They traded off driving every half hour. Just before 2300, they came to what looked like the end of the road.

They had moved deeply into the barren hills that now rose higher and higher around them. The small valley they had been in came to an end suddenly against a mountain. To the left they saw a scratched-out road that seemed to climb the side of the hill and vanish.

Douglas did a scouting run on the road, and was back in twenty minutes.

"Looks like it keeps going to the right. We need about five or six miles that direction. Let's give it a try."

They had trouble on the first incline. Douglas rolled rocks out of the way, and they scraped through. Then the slant down was so great that Franklin used the brakes all the way. At the bottom of the grade, the mountains seemed to close in around them. In the shadows they could see no road or even a trail.

"Better wait for some daylight," Douglas decided. They took out the camouflaged brown canvas and staked it down over the car, stretching it out ten feet on each side. From a couple of thousand feet the little car should be invisible.

They rolled out their blankets on the ground, put their small submachine guns at their sides, and tried to get some sleep.

•   •   •

It was daylight when Douglas awoke at 0510. He lay perfectly still. Something had disturbed his sleep. What? He looked around without moving his head. At once he saw a man at the side of the car. He had just pulled out one of the five-gallon cans of water.

In one swift move, Douglas whipped back the blanket, jumped to his feet, and leveled the sub-gun at the thief.

Franklin came up a second later, his gun trained on the man as well.

"No, no, don't shoot!" the man pleaded in Farsi.

Franklin moved forward quickly, pushed the man away from the car, and told him in Farsi to sit down on the ground.

He sat and began talking so fast, and with such emotion, that Franklin had a hard time keeping up with him.

Douglas stared at him, then waved to Franklin. He came back and whispered.

"Says he's just a prospector like us, but not as well set up. He's a poor man who owes everyone in town, and he can get no supplies. He has to steal what he needs."

"Ask him where his car is, and how far this road goes."

Franklin sat down across from the man, who had lost some of his fear since he hadn't been shot. Franklin talked to him gently in Farsi, and gradually learned the rest of his story.

Franklin relayed the story, now speaking in English openly. "Says his car broke down, engine blew up. He ran out of oil. He was going to steal what he could from us and hide it, and come back for it later."

"Ask him how well he knows these hills."

Franklin nodded at the answer. "Says like his own backyard. He's been prospecting for chromium up here for ten years."

Franklin nodded to himself, and asked the man if he knew where the big construction site was where the big trucks went.

His eyes grew wide, and he nodded. "Yes, but it is a bad place to go. The soldiers shoot at anything that moves. The helicopters fly out and shoot at anyone they see. Very bad place to go."

"How far from here?"

"Oh, twenty kilometers, maybe thirty. Long ways."

They all heard the sound of a plane about the same time. It was a propeller aircraft, moving slowly. All three ran under the tent part of the camouflage canvas. Franklin had forgotten his blanket. He dashed out and pulled it under the tarp just as the small plane came in sight over one of the mountains. It was a high-wing spotter-type aircraft.

"Looks like a Piper Cub," Franklin said. "He's at least four thousand feet over us. If we don't move, he'll never see a thing out of the ordinary down here. One nice thing about these hills. They keep the spotters up high."

"Unless they decide to scoot and shoot down through the valleys," Douglas said.

They held their places as the plane vanished to the north, and the sound slowly faded.

"Can you take us where we can see this huge plant that the soldiers guard?" Franklin asked the man in Farsi.

"Why would I do that?"

Franklin showed him six 10,000-rial notes. The man leaned forward and had to hold himself back from reaching out.

"We have money," Franklin told him. "Could you lead us to where we could see the place?"

"I might. You have food, could we eat while I think about it?"

"He's hooked," Franklin said. "With some persuasion, and some cash, he'll take us through this maze of roads, trails, and hills to the damn nuke site."

"Good, let's eat. We feed him, we watch him, we tie him up every night so he doesn't steal our car, and all our gear. Then maybe he'll do what he says he can."

They ate fruit and bread for breakfast.

"How far is the plant?" Franklin asked.

"Far, maybe thirty kilometers, maybe twenty. Roads go up to about, maybe . . . oh eight kilometers. Walk from there."

"Six miles from the end of the road," Franklin told Douglas.

"Can we trust him?" Douglas asked.

"Hell yes, as far as I can spit. We watch him every minute. We make him take us to his stash, and see what he has. Then maybe we let him lead us toward the place. Shouldn't take more than two days. We could even promise to give him our prospector's rig if he gets us there without any problems."

Douglas grinned. "Now, there is a payoff this guy would love to get. Talk with him."

The two talked for an hour in the shade of the tent. They drank water, and ate figs, and at last shook hands.

An hour later, the man, whose name they learned was Nard, a Persian name meaning the game of chess, led them toward his supplies. They were only half a mile away, in the start of a tunnel someone had dug six feet into a mountain before giving up.

From his gear, and his lack of food, they decided he must be who he said he was. A bargain was struck. They would pay him well to take them as close to the big plant as was possible.

The rest of the daylight hours they slept. One of the SEALs was always awake to watch Nard. He made no move to leave. He had his sights set on the car, and all of the supplies. Douglas was sure the man would kill both of them to get it.

When dusk came, they took down the canvas, stowed it, and moved forward to pick up Nard's gear, then he angled them down another track deeper into the mounts, north and east.

All three of them rode in the front seat of the car as it edged along slowly in the dim light. Twice they stopped to move rocks from the trail, and once they almost slid off the track into a ditch.

The hills loomed over them.

They drove until midnight, then stopped and let Nard look over the land. The full moon was still out, and he nodded.

"More to the east," he told Franklin, and they swung down another small gully between the brown, dead hills.

"He could be leading us into a trap," Franklin said.

Douglas didn't agree. "Why would he? He's got nothing to gain by killing us now. He can take us where we want to go, and then bargain with us for the rig. He gets paid either way. It isn't like he's going to run into a dozen buddies at the next gully who will mow us down with shotguns."

They came to a fork in the road about 0400 and decided to call it a night. Before they sacked out, they covered the Citroen with the camouflage canvas, stretching it out on both sides.

Then Franklin explained to Nard why they had to tie him up. He agreed, and let them tie his hands and feet.

Douglas awoke the next morning when the sun blasted into his eyes. He rolled over, then came up in a rush. It was 1006. Franklin snored softly. He looked where they had left Nard. The Iranian prospector was gone. The ropes they tied him with were in a neat stack.

Douglas came to his feet in a rush.

"Franklin, our friend has escaped."

Franklin came awake at once and brought up his submachine gun.

A shrill laugh caught them both by surprise. Nard stepped from behind the vehicle eating a large piece of bread and some fruit.

"You see, I did not run away. You can trust me. Neither did I slit your throats. I am poor, but honorable. We made an agreement; I will honor that pact. We eat more, then sleep again. It will be a hot day."

The spot they had stopped was where two small valleys came together. They had pulled the car into the lee of the tallest hill, and now the morning shadows covered it. By noon it would be in the direct rays of the sun.

The sun scorched everything in sight. The three men stayed under the shade of the canvas, and hoped for a slight breeze up the canyon. They cooked the last of the fresh meat they had been sent, and made instant coffee over the butane burner. Douglas had listened on the SATCOM at noon, but there were no messages from Don Stroh.

Before two that afternoon, Douglas lay down on his blanket, and tried to think cool. The throbbing sound of a helicopter brought him out of his dreams of a swimming pool.

"The choppers often fly over," Nard said in Farsi. "They try to find something. Usually they don't. It is part of a routine they do to insure their security."

The chopper moved away from them, then circled back. This time the helicopter was just one ridge over and they could see it from time to time.

A loudspeaker blared. Franklin translated it as the words came.

"You on the ground. We have followed your car tracks. We know you are there. If you do not show yourself and reverse your direction, we will send down a squad of soldiers to hunt you down like dogs, and kill you all. Give up, and return to the Chah Bahar area. There are no minerals in this area worth prospecting for. Show yourselves now."

Douglas groaned. "Damn. We did leave tracks. Most of this area hasn't had a rig through it since the last cloudburst stormed in off the Gulf of Oman. Tracks lead straight to us."

"I have heard this talk before," Nard said. "Many times they say so when they see nothing, to try to bring out prospectors. We have learned to doubt them."

Franklin translated and nodded. "But they sure as hell got tracks from our car. Sounds like a little chopper. He won't have a squad of troops on board. Maybe two or three. He lands, and sends them along to find us, or goes back for a bigger bird with more men?"

"He's got to send in who he has, otherwise we might vanish down here," Douglas said. "What we need to do is set up a grand reception for the two or three shooters."

Franklin grinned. "That's a Roger. Which side do you want?"

They put Nard up a side canyon, then studied the layout. The chopper could land easier to the left, where the canyon was broader. Yes, they would come that way.

With a little additional work they transformed some large rocks along the side of the fifty-foot-wide gully into good shooting spots. They heard the chopper voice come twice more, then it seemed to pull back a ways. They heard it again later, and the sound came gushing up the gully.

"They're down," Douglas said. "Give them twenty minutes to work up the gully. I've got the left side."

Douglas wondered if they could waste the two or three men who came after them, then charge down the little valley, and capture the chopper. He shook his head. Not a chance. The pilot would be jumpy as hell. The first sign of firing, he probably would lift off, and wait at a safe altitude for his troops to return.

Three of them. There would be three shooters. It was a four-man chopper, so three guards with rifles or sub-guns. Either way, the element of surprise would win the day.

Douglas wiped a line of sweat off his forehead, and waited.

Ten minutes later they heard the men coming up the slight incline of the canyon. Three of them, Douglas decided before he saw them. The Iranians talked back and forth. Then forty yards away, the canyon bent a little and the three men came around it. All three had rifles with small sub-guns

slung around their necks. They walked slowly, the rifles at
port arms, up and ready. One man kept to each side of the
canyon, here about fifty feet wide. The third one moved
along the tire tracks the Citroen had left in the Iranian dust
and rocks.

Douglas pulled out the metal stock on the Peruvian
MGP-15. He braced it against his shoulder and turned the
lever to full auto. Then he zeroed in on the man on his
side of the canyon and tracked him. If he kept coming on the
same line, the soldier would be less than twenty feet from
where Douglas crouched behind the rocks.

He waited. They were at forty feet.

Then the men moved forward again. One of them
shouted. Evidently he had seen the car. The others rushed
forward.

Douglas waited a moment longer, then tracked the man,
and pulled the trigger. Ten rounds slammed out of the short
barrel. They sprayed in shotgun fashion, but four of them
caught the soldier in the chest, and smashed him backwards
into the dirt, dying as he screamed.

An instant later, Douglas heard the other sub-gun roar,
and the far Iranian soldier crumpled. Douglas angled his
weapon at the lone survivor in the middle, and jolted out six
rounds. Franklin fired again as well, and the third soldier
screamed in rage as he died before he hit the ground.

Both SEALs waited, but no more troops arrived. They ran
to the bodies and dragged them up against the side of the
gully. Quickly Douglas pushed rocks down from the side of
the slope until they covered the dead soldier. He had set
aside the rifle and the sub-gun and all the magazines he
could find.

Franklin had buried the man on his side, and they both
dragged the third dead man to the far side, where the slope
crumbled more easily. They kicked at it until they had rolled
enough dirt and rocks down to cover the dead soldier.

They picked up the three rifles, three sub-guns, and the ammunition, and ran back to the car under its tarp.

Nard came up grinning. "You are not prospectors at all," he said. "You are soldiers, commandos, you are killers."

Franklin told Douglas what Nard had said.

"But we have not harmed you," Franklin said. "We wish nothing but the best for you, and we are paying you well. It may even be that we won't need our vehicle, and all of our supplies, once we know exactly where the big plant is. Would you like to have all of this material for your own?"

Nard smiled broadly. "Indeed Allah is all knowing, and all kindness, and wonder. I am your loyal servant until you no longer need me."

Just then they heard the chopper's engines rev up, and the bird took off. The gully was too narrow for the helicopter to make a close inspection, but it hovered overhead and moved slowly up the passage, then swung away. Douglas had no way of knowing if the pilot had seen the car under the camouflage or not.

"We've got to pack up and move," Douglas said. "They won't take kindly to losing three of their hotshot guards. They'll be sending out all the troops they can carry in their choppers. We've got to be several miles away by that time."

18

Sunday, October 30

1523 hours
Hill country north of
Chah Bahar, Iran

Franklin gunned the engine as soon as everything was loaded in the Citroen, but Douglas waved him off.

"We need a drag, something to pull behind the rig to brush out our tire tracks so they can't follow us. A bunch of brush usually works, but there ain't none here."

"Tie one blanket on the bumper behind each rear tire," Franklin said. "Should do in a pinch."

They tried it.

Douglas walked behind the car for a hundred yards, and couldn't make out the tire tracks. Nobody could see them from the air.

They drove.

Franklin rattled the old car along as fast as he dared in the rock-strewn dirt track. Sometimes he hit fifteen miles an hour. It should be enough.

Twice Nard had them stop and back up to take a different branch of the dirt trails. They climbed a slope that Douglas was sure would tip over the rig, but it was built heavy, and low to the ground, and made it up and over, then down the far side. They came to a spring that had spawned a palm tree and fifty square feet of green grass. They paused only a moment. The choppers would search this area carefully.

Douglas checked the drags again. Yes, they blotted out the tire tracks well. Now if they could just get enough miles between them and the dead bodies, all would be well. Maybe.

"Getting low on gas," Franklin said.

"Those two 10-gallon tanks. Were they piped into the fuel line?" Douglas asked.

Franklin pulled into the shade of a towering peak and took a look. He crawled into the backseat, moved a ton of stuff, and come out smiling. "Both have valves on them. I switched on one, which should take us for another day at this pace. Which way there, our dependable scout and guide?" He had asked the question in Farsi.

Nard was catching on to some of Franklin's jokes. He pointed to the left again, and they rolled.

Every ten minutes they stopped to listen. They could hear no aircraft, fixed-wing or rotary.

"So far we is staying alive," Franklin said. He repeated it in Farsi and Nard grinned.

"Twelve miles," Douglas said. "We've come twelve fucking miles today. Are we getting too far to the east?"

Franklin repeated the question to Nard in his language. He looked out the window, then, when they came to a break in the hills to the north, asked Franklin to stop the car. He got out and stared at the hills for some time, then nodded and went to Franklin.

"See that second mountain up there, the one with the twin peaks and saddle in the middle. Saddle Mountain, we call it. The place you look for is just beyond that mountain two, three kilometers."

"You're sure?"

"Oh, yes. Almost got killed near Saddle Mountain.

Soldiers came, searched all day. I lay in a small canyon with sand and gravel covering me except for a breathing straw made from a desert plant with a hollow stem. One soldier stepped on my leg, but he didn't notice. Oh, yes, I know that spot. Almost died there."

"Where do we turn north?"

"Another short ways, half a kilometer. Then only drive another two kilometers or so before road runs out. No more trail. Only mountain goat climb from there on."

Franklin told Douglas what Nard had said.

"We might just be getting somewhere."

Before they could get moving again, they heard the chopper.

Quickly they pushed the car into the shadows of the mountain, then spread the camouflage tarp over it. This time they didn't tie it down, just draped it, and crawled underneath.

All three men under the canvas had rifles ready. The long guns were nothing that either SEAL had ever seen before. But they had 30-round magazines. Douglas snapped off the safety and turned the selector switch to fully automatic fire. Then he waited.

Franklin found a small hole in the canvas he could look through.

"Damn chopper is still a ridge over. He's looking for anything he can find."

"If he spots us and hovers, we all get clear of the canvas, and fire at him on full auto. If he's only four or five hundred feet, we should be able to hurt him a lot."

"Shoot the fucker down," Franklin said.

Nard pointed the other way. "Helicopter," he said in Farsi and Franklin grunted.

"Another chopper south of us. Wonder how many they put out to try to nail our hides?"

"All they've got, my guess," Douglas said.

They listened then.

"Nearest bird is moving away," Franklin said.

"Hope we're outside their containment area. They must think we're still inside their web."

"So, we wait, or we move?" Franklin said.

"I'm too tired to spit. When did we get any sleep? Let's conk off here until dark. I think we beat them for right now. The closer we get, the tougher their security should be."

"Yeah, but out maybe ten miles?"

"That's where I'd put my first line." They listened for a moment, and both grinned. "No more choppers up here. Good. Ask Nard how much farther we can drive."

Franklin had the answer a moment later. "He says maybe three more kilometers. We turn north again until we run out of the next canyon. Then it's almost due north to that saddle mountain. He says we will be able to see the nuke plant from the far side of the saddle."

"We better rig up something to use for packs. We'll need to carry food, ammo, and our weapons."

"Yeah, and don't forget water. We can't order shakes from Jack in the Box."

"Chogie straps," Douglas said.

"What?"

"Chogie straps. The Koreans used them during the Korean war to carry shit with. My dad told me about them, and I saw pictures. Take a box or a sack full of stuff, use this long loop strap made out of canvas or cloth and loop it around the box, and two loops to put your arms through. Works fine, or at least it did for the guys over there."

They began sorting through the gear to find something to make the straps out of. Franklin snorted and used his knife to cut two eight-foot-long strips two inches wide from the camouflage canvas.

He tied the ends together.

"Show me," Franklin said.

"Damned if I know. Let's figure it out."

Ten minutes later they figured it, and then concentrated on picking out the gear, food, and water they would need for the hike on to Saddle Mountain.

"How much we taking?" Franklin asked.

"Enough water for three days—no, four days. How long will it take our guys to get in here from Coronado?"

"Three or four days. We better leave a batch of supplies at the end of the road so we can come back and get them if we need to."

They continued to sort out food and water. There would be plenty for a cache, and to get Nard on to his next dig in his continual search for chromium.

Franklin took the first watch, and Douglas went to sleep. They decided not to trust Nard this late in the game. He could bug out with everything, and leave them dying of thirst in the high desert.

Two hours later, Franklin took his turn sleeping. As soon as the sun went down, and the shadows grew into dusk, they hung out the blanket drags and began driving into the night.

Four hours later, Franklin switched on the car's head-lights.

"Yep, like the man said, this is the end of the line. No way a car or a camel is going to go up that cliff."

He killed the lights, and they began checking the gear they had laid out.

Franklin explained to the Iranian what they were doing. He nodded.

"Good idea to have water and food here. You might have longer stay, and need to get back out. Should I wait for you for two days before I leave this spot?"

For a moment Franklin was sorry that they hadn't trusted their guide. He shook his head.

"We'll have enough supply here to last us even if we had to walk out to Chah Bahar. You take the rest, and get the rig moved away from here. Keep the drags on the rear to wipe out your tire tracks. Remember, the choppers will be looking for this vehicle. Hope you make a rich strike."

They left six of the five-gallon cans of water, and half of the freeze-dried food, behind under a small shelf of rock, and covered it all with slabs of stone to keep away any predators. There were various big cats in the mountains, but Douglas wasn't sure if that was down here or farther up north in the forested areas.

They waved at Nard, and sent him down the canyon and on his way. He said he would travel well out of the danger zone, so there would be no chance the soldiers would destroy his new transport. They also gave him half of the rials they had left, something like one hundred thousand. That figured out to three hundred dollars, but was probably more cash money than Nard had seen in years. The Citroen was probably worth twice that much. Nard was now a rich man by Chah Bahar standards.

They began hiking north. The chogie straps cut into their shoulders, but they simply bent over more and endured. You weren't really a SEAL if you weren't in pain somewhere. They had to detour around the shear cliff in front of them, but found a canyon leading up a quarter of a klick to the left.

Douglas took a bearing on a star, and kept it as his guidepost. By the time they had climbed up halfway on the hill in front of them, they could spot the dark blotch of the saddle mountain where it blotted out the stars in silhouette.

"Only five miles forward," Douglas said. "That doesn't count another six to ten straight up, and straight down."

They stopped after an hour for a breather. They had been up and down four smaller hills, and still the saddle mountain seemed as far away as when they started.

"A mountain always looks closer than it really is when you're sighting across a bunch of other hills and empty space," Franklin said. "That's what my Boy Scout scoutmaster always used to tell us."

"You believed him?"

"I was ten, what did I know? Yeah, I believed him. I still do. We might not get onto that saddle before daylight."

"Bet you a case of beer we do," Douglas said.

"You're on, sucker. I'd like some of that German beer."

"That'll be the day. Let's haul ass."

19

Sunday, October 30

1830 hours
Lieutenant (j.g.) DeWitt's apartment
Coronado, California

The dinner party had progressed well. Ed DeWitt had asked Kat to come to his house for dinner with him and his lady friend, Milly.

"Frankly, Kat, she wants to meet you. She's a little jealous, and wants to be sure you don't have real claws."

Kat had understood at once, but said she'd come only if they had Murdock along as a kind of buffer person. It had worked out.

Now they sat around the dinner table scraping up the last of a delicious cherry pie à la mode.

"Cherry pie has been my favorite since I was a tomboy climbing trees in our backyard in the wilds of Virginia," Kat said.

Milly had taken a liking to this nuclear physicist at once. They had chatted in the kitchen while getting the last of the dinner ready for the table. Milly had seemed to understand at once that this pleasant woman with short brown hair and impressive credentials was no threat to her love for Ed. From there on the friendship grew.

They pushed back from the table and went into the small living room.

"Don't worry about the dishes," Milly said. "Our maid will clear, and take care of everything."

"Oh, yeah, by that she means me," Ed said. They all laughed.

"Let's just talk," Milly said. "We got off to a good start in the kitchen. I understand you showed up a few of our vaunted SEALs on one of the open-ocean swims."

"The guys aren't used to competitive swimming," Kat said. "If it's just an exercise, I tend to go out a little faster then the rest of the platoon."

"Yeah," Murdock said. "Then she stretches her lead in the middle part, and churns home so fast we can't even see her wake."

"Only part true," Kat said, smiling. "When we're in a combat situation, I'll keep my stroke exactly on sched. Hey, you've drilled that into my brain."

"You better," DeWitt said. "Or we'll let you swim the twenty miles out to the carrier." They all laughed again.

Milly leaned back and relaxed. It was so clear to her now. Kat was indeed "one of the guys." She had an extremely difficult job to do once they got to the target, but she had to be able to endure a lot of tough physical activity before they got there. Ed had told her that Kat had to be able to fire her weapon to protect her own life, and the lives of the rest of the platoon. Now Milly totally understood.

"Are we ready to drop in on Iran?" DeWitt asked. He looked at Kat.

"I don't know about you, but I feel ready. I know the routines. True, I'm not sure how I'll function when the bad guys start shooting real bullets at me, but, I think I can pass muster. Am I ready to blend in and be an integral, functioning part of the platoon? You'll have to ask Murdock that."

They looked at him. He scowled for a moment, then did

the old Jack Benny motion with his arms folded and a
curious look on his face. "I'm thinking, I'm thinking." They
broke up.

When the laughter simmered down, he nodded. "Yes, I'd
like to have two more weeks for platoon-size drills, but if
we get the word to fly out tomorrow, I won't be the least bit
hesitant to ship Kat and her submachine gun right along
with us."

"Oh, thank god, no more sixty-mile hikes," Kat said.
They laughed again.

The phone rang. Milly picked it up. "This is the DeWitt
residence." She listened for a minute, then smiled. "Yes.
Yes, just a second."

She held the phone to Murdock. "Someone wants to talk
to you."

"Our orders from Don Stroh?" DeWitt asked.

Murdock lifted his brows, and then took the phone.
"Murdock here." He listened for a moment, then smiled.
"Yes, I think I can arrange that. The Del in ten minutes."

He handed the phone to Milly.

"Duty calls," he said, straight-faced. "Did I tell you about
my friend in Washington, D.C.?"

"Yes. Ardith, I think her name was," DeWitt said.

"Like I say, duty calls. I'll see you sailors in the
morning." He grabbed his hat and headed for the door.

It took Murdock only seven minutes to get to the Del
Coronado Hotel and park in the far lot. He wore his off-duty
favorites—blue jeans and a Western shirt. As soon as he
came into the big Hotel Del lobby, he saw her. For just a
moment he paused, watching her, remembering those fine
times in Washington, D.C.

She stood in a pose that had to come from years of ballet
training: straight and tall, feet placed just so; long, golden
hair swept down across her shoulders. She turned and saw
him. The best smile he'd ever seen brightened her already

pretty face. High cheekbones accented her face under the mischievous light blue eyes that could always keep him guessing.

She turned and hurried toward him, reminding him of a prima ballerina moving across to stage left for her solo number. Instead of a tutu she wore a frilly white blouse and a brown skirt showing off just enough of her svelte figure to be interesting.

"Did I surprise you?" she asked, as he caught her shoulders for a quick kiss on her ready lips. He pulled away, and smiled.

"You surprised me, and I can't think of a better one."

"I'm glad. I hear you might be going on a long trip. Wanted to get here before you left."

His face clouded for a moment as what she said registered fully. "Damnit, why doesn't somebody just put a story on the front page of the *Washington Post*?" He relented at once. "Sorry, not more than half a dozen people know about this. Who was your source?"

"Do I have to tell?"

"Absolutely. I might need to kick some tail. It wasn't my dad, was it?"

"No, nor my father."

"So, who?"

"Let me tell you later. The elevator is right over here."

"Elevator?"

"Why don't we stay here? If we go to your place, I'll have to prove what a lousy cook I am. Here I can fake it."

Murdock laughed and caught her arm. "Lead on, Mac-Duff."

She shook her head. "That should be, 'Lay on, MacDuff.'"

Murdock guffawed. "Hey, I thought that part came later." She punched his shoulder, and they walked into the elevator.

In her room, Murdock kicked the door closed, and she moved into his arms for a long kiss. It was a full-body-pressure kind, with them pressed together from hips to lips.

Their mouths opened, and they explored dark passages. At last they broke apart.

"Oh, yes, Blake. Now, that was worth waiting for."

"I might find some more of those." He held her at arm's length. "Really, I need to know who told you."

"Nobody told me anything, actually. I just happened to be talking with Don Stroh the other day—okay, yesterday—and I told him I was going to Los Angeles on business and wondered if this would be a good time to come down and see you."

"Stroh—I might have guessed."

"He only said that now, this week, would be an excellent time. Any later, and I might miss you. So he told me nothing secret, not even when or where you'll be going. If and when you go."

She kissed him seriously. "So, Mr. Secret Man, that was all I found out. I made reservations yesterday, and here I am, weary, flight-torn, but able to stand up . . . for a little while yet."

"Good, I'll take care of that problem, too. I'm glad that's all he told you. This one is really top of the shop. I bet not even dear old Dad finds out about it until we're done and back home."

"When?"

"We don't know. We need some more intel, then make out our flight sched. It won't be more than a few days, I've got a hunch."

She kissed him again, and they moved to the bed and sat down. The kiss came apart, and he reached for the buttons on her blouse.

"Did I tell you about . . ." He stopped. "Son of a bitch! I almost did what I accused Don of doing." He shook his head, and kissed both her cheeks and her nose, then a butterfly kiss on her mouth, barely touching her lips. Her eyes closed, and she sighed, and pulled him down with her on the bed.

"Ardith, you vixen. You should have been a spy during the Cold War. You could have charmed the pants off any diplomat on the other side. You could have seduced the secrets right out of Brezhnev himself."

She unbuttoned the fasteners on his shirt. "Thank you if that was a compliment. The only one I want to charm, and seduce, is you." She pulled his shirt out of his pants and reached for his belt. "How am I doing so far?"

An hour later they lay naked side by side on the king-sized bed. Her fingers toyed with the dark hair on his chest.

"Here you thought that three times was too many, and too fast. You sure fooled yourself."

"And happy to do so."

She turned on her side and propped up her head with her elbow. He enjoyed the way it made her full breasts move, bounce, and then sway.

"Oh, yes. A woman's breasts, her most perfect artistic delight."

"Sexist."

"Absolutely. I wouldn't have it any other way." He shut up then; from her expression he knew she was getting serious.

"Have you thought any more about . . . about some other kind of work for the Navy?"

"Haven't had time. We had to integrate three new men into our sixteen-man platoon. Not an easy or quick task. If they aren't right, or aren't trained right and blended in, the whole platoon could be in trouble on a live-fire mission."

She rolled over, and kissed him deeply, then eased back and lay half on top of him.

"You know how terrible I feel when you're off on a junket somewhere. Junket. Ha. I wish they all could be nice safe missions to countries where we at least have embassies."

"Maybe I'll pick up a million-dollar wound, and not be

able to get back in the outfit. Do you know that we lose fourteen men washed out of the SEALs for medical reasons for every man who gets killed? So the odds are . . ."

She smothered his mouth with her own, and didn't move until they both had to breathe.

"Now we talk about things more pleasant. I'd guess you'll be working tomorrow."

"Yes."

"Could you give me a guided tour of your office, your training area?"

"Oh, boy. We usually don't do that . . . I mean it's not secret or anything. I'd have to get a pass for you from the NAVSPECWAR headquarters. I have planned an all-day exercise for the platoon . . ."

"All right, I understand. Damnit, that's the trouble, I really do understand."

He kissed her.

"I'll be at your command after five tomorrow afternoon. We can have a picnic on the beach, take a hot air balloon ride, go play at Sea World, make crazy faces at the animals at the San Diego Zoo. Or we can cuddle up in my place while I fix dinner, and then we could have a long, relaxing evening before we have a long, sexy night."

She grinned, and tickled him under the chin. He pulled away from her.

"You remembered that."

"Lieutenant, I remember everything I know or read or discovered about you. Especially that little strange noise you make just before you explode when we're making love. It's delightful, and then I know what's coming, and . . ."

She stopped, and they watched each other.

"Hey, I'd like to vote we go to my place tomorrow. When do you head back to Nutsville?"

"Day after tomorrow on the eight-fifteen A.M. American."

"Oh, damn."

"True."

"What time is it?" he asked.

"It's oh-one-hundred-fifteen, as you Navy types say."

"How about a late-night sandwich, and some champagne? I understand the kitchen is open all night here."

"Yeah, let's give it a try. I want a crab salad sandwich on toasted dill rye, with a pair of kosher dills."

"Crazy lady, you're on."

The sandwiches were delicious.

The champagne bubbling.

The rest of the night a delight.

20

Monday, October 31

0330 hours
Hill country north of
Chah Bahar, Iran

Guns Franklin and Joe Douglas pushed up another ridge in the middle of an unending series of hills that all worked upward toward the saddle mountain.

"How many more of the fucking hills are we going to have to climb to get there?" Franklin brayed.

The chogie straps due deeply into their shoulders now as the strain of the sixty pounds of food, water, and ammunition bore down. Douglas went to his knees in the rocky soil a hundred yards from the top of the ridge, then sat down and lay back against the heavy pack.

"Oh, damn but that feels good," he shouted. "So fucking good I could shoot my wad right here."

"Strange what turns some guys on," Franklin said, doing the same drop, sit, and roll motion to get the weight of the pack off his shoulders.

"What day is this?" Franklin asked.

"How the hell should I know? What am I your fucking walking calendar?"

"You should be. I don't even remember when we dropped

173

into this garden of plenty. I still say we'll get to the saddle before daylight."

"Hell no. You'll owe me that case of German beer when we get back to civilization."

"We're on the last ridge. When we get to the top of this, the next slant up will be the saddle mountain."

"That's what you told me the last two ridges, hotshot."

"You'll see, Guns. Let's move it."

They rolled over, lifting the packs off the ground and getting to their knees, then pushed upright with a pair of groans.

"I still say three hundred pounds is too much to expect even a SEAL to carry on his back," Franklin said.

They hiked upward.

The last few yards they had to use their hands on the steep slope to get to the top. Franklin made it to the ridgeline first. He stopped, and stared.

"I'll be fucked on Friday. There the big bastard is."

Douglas got there a moment later and he grinned. Even in the darkness, they could tell that there were no more ridges between them and Saddle Mountain. They could see only one peak, but this had to be it. The other half of the mountain was behind the one they could see.

They had a fifty-yard slope down the ridge, before the longer slant upward to the saddle mountain began.

"An hour to the top," Douglas said. "It's now oh-four-twenty. The sun shouldn't be up until about oh-six-hundred. Plenty of time for you to owe me that case of good American beer."

"If we make it, it'll be worth it." Franklin shrugged, and began the slower move down the slope.

They struggled up the last rise to the side of the saddle mountain. They weren't going all the way to the top. They quartered around the mountain peak, and within another half hour saw the saddle opening spread out before them. Through the saddle to the north they saw the glow of what

could only be electric lights. In this starkly dark countryside, they stood out like beacons.

"Jackpot!" Douglas screeched. "Look at those shit-kicking
lights. We've found the nuke plant sure as little green apples
get riper in the summertime."

Franklin couldn't suppress a grin. "Hey, yeah. Looks like
it could be. We need to get to the far side of the saddle—
what, a half mile. Then we'll have a better look. Why in hell
didn't we bring a twenty-power scope with us?"

They hiked again.

The comparative flat bowel of the saddle was either part
of a huge volcanic eruption, or just neutral ground between
two volcanic peaks. Douglas didn't worry about it too much.
The nearness of their objective pushed him forward. The
straps cutting into their shoulders didn't hurt so much either.
As he moved, Douglas wondered if the saddle would be a
good drop spot for the rest of the platoon. Depended how far
it was on to the big factory. It could still be ten miles away.

Dawn crept up on them, and before they realized it, the
sun peaked over the far hills. They were in the open here,
and with daylight they thought of their own security.

"What happens if one of them spotter planes flies over?"
Franklin asked.

"We go prone and stay as still as an ant. Movement is
what the spotters watch for. If we stay quiet, they'd have to
be right over us at a thousand feet to pick us out."

Another twenty minutes, and they came to the edge of the
saddle bowl and stared across to where they had seen the
lights. They saw only a haze, with a bluish tinge that could
have been from ground fog, or smoke.

"Why would there be smoke up here in the hills?"
Franklin asked.

"We didn't see any power lines coming in anywhere.
They'd need lots of power up here. Maybe they have a huge
oil- or coal-burning electrical generating plant."

"Sounds reasonable."

They stood there a minute staring at the place where the Iranian nuclear plant could be. Gradually the mists or smoke began to lift.

"Yeah, clearing up," Douglas said. "Shouldn't take long. If it's what we think we can have the old SATCOM up and working in five minutes."

They waited.

The mixture ahead of them turned out to be half smoke, half some kind of ground fog. The smoke showed prominently when the fog was burned away by the bright sun. Smoke was to the right of the rest of what they could now see.

"Damn it to hell on Sunday, look at that," Franklin said. "Big bunch of buildings with camouflage all over them. No wonder the satellites couldn't find them. Got to be the fucking nuke plant."

"Yep, I think we've found the nuker. Let's get to some kind of protection or cover, and we'll get the SATCOM set up."

They found a spot near the edge of the half-mile-long saddle. It had almost no vegetation—some low grasses and a shrub here and there. The place they picked was near a boulder that screened them from the nuke plant and gave off some deep shade from the already burning sun. Douglas set up the SATCOM and aligned it with the satellite high overhead.

He took the cellular phone–sized instrument out of his pack and pulled open an eight-inch antenna. It was the MUGR, or the mugger, as the SEALs called it—the Miniature Underwater GPS Receiver. This was a modified version for land use, with a pull-out antenna instead of a floating one that went to the surface.

Douglas turned it on and the antenna began searching for the four closest Global Positioning Satellites. The MUGR picked up the satellite's positions, and with quadra-angulation, pinpointed the location of the MUGR to within ten feet.

After a few seconds the small device beeped and the screen showed a readout of longitude and latitude.

With that data in hand, Douglas composed his message on the SATCOM screen.

"Found it. About five klicks due north of this position." He then put in the longitude and latitude the mugger gave. "This position good for LZ. Outside of their major security area. No positive ID but nothing else up here but snakes, desert mountains, and scorpions. Will stay in on-mode for your response."

He read over the message, made a small change, then hit the send button that automatically encrypted the words, and blasted them out of the set toward the communications satellite in a burst that lasted only a fraction of a second. He left the set turned on and sat down on the sand, moving into a patch of shade near the rock.

"So now we watch and wait?" Franklin asked.

"Have a nap if you want to. We wait for a reply."

A helicopter lifted up from the side of the saddle and raced to within a hundred yards of their position before it paused, then climbed to more than a thousand feet off the saddle, and hovered.

"Don't move," Douglas said. "If we move he'll spot us for damn sure."

"Least we have on these damn brown-and-beige Iranian clothes, and we're in the shadows," Franklin said.

They watched the Iranian chopper. Douglas didn't know what make it was, but he did see a machine gun angled out the side door. He'd heard about door gunners from the Viet Nam vets and knew they could be deadly.

The chopper made a slow circle over the saddle. When it was at the farthest end, about a half mile away, the two SEALs draped themselves with spare beige shirts, so they covered their faces, weapons, and the twelve-inch-diameter SATCOM antenna.

They heard the helicopter swing back toward them. It was now higher, Douglas could tell by the sound.

"They must check this area routinely as part of their security," he said. "Might not be such a good LZ after all."

"Best in the whole damn place I've seen. Shit, we get the platoon in here on a night drop, and we can fade into the gullies on both sides before daylight. Even if they patrol this area every day, they wouldn't find a trace."

"Yeah, hope so."

They heard the chopper make one more circle search. Douglas checked out from the cover, and saw the bird much higher now. A minute later it flew off to the north working lower, and out of sight.

When he took the shirt off his face, Douglas saw the SATCOM light pulsing.

"Incoming message," he said.

He turned another switch, and a voice came on the small speaker.

"Douglas. Received. Now plotting out your position. Stay out of sight. Will get Murdock in gear immediately. Shooting for a drop there within thirty-eight hours. Second dark from now. Hole up. Stay out of sight. Good work. Stroh."

The message repeated three times. When it stopped, Douglas sent a two-word reply: "Douglas, Roger."

"So, we hole up. Exactly where?" Franklin scowled.

"Just off the side somewhere, and on the shade side," Douglas said.

They found their spot an hour later. It was a gully that evidently drained water from the flat top of the saddle whenever there was a downpour. The rocky ground wouldn't soak up much of a cloudburst.

The water had dug out a respectable gully, leaving some sharp edges. At one place a small waterfall must have formed and resulted in a fairly flat place below it. It was on the shady side. They unloaded their packs and found room enough for both of them to stretch out.

First came food. They couldn't risk a fire. While there might not be much smoke, the smell would slide downwind like a beacon for anyone on foot in the area. Instead they ate some of the freeze-dried foods, much like the familiar MRIs. They had plenty of water.

"That would make their drop in here not tonight, but tomorrow night," Douglas said. "Means we have two days and a night to get through. I wonder how much of that I can sleep."

Franklin snorted. "Hell, Douglas, knowing you, I'd say you can sack out for about ninety percent of the time. Go ahead. I'll take the first watch. Not much to see. We can spot anyone coming up the gully for half a mile. If they drop troops on the saddle up on top we'll hear them. So, we've got nothing to worry about. Sack out. I'm going to try one more of these freeze-dried pastrami cakes."

21

Monday, October 31

Lieutenant DeWitt awoke slowly.

Something was clanging, like a police car in England.

No, more like an ambulance in France.

Oh, damn, the phone. He sat up, fully awake now. He grabbed the instrument and glared at it.

"Yeah, what the hell do you want?"

"Well, good morning to you, too, Lieutenant DeWitt. I know it's about three-thirty in the morning out there in Lotus Land, but some of us have been working all night back here in D.C."

"Stroh? Don Stroh?"

"Damn, you still remember me. I can't get hold of your boss. He unplug his phone or something?"

"Why would he do that?" DeWitt asked.

"I don't know, why?"

"Oh, yeah. The good Lieutenant was, shall we say, busy tonight with his friend from D.C."

"So if he unplugged the phone, I'd still get a ring on that end?"

"Right, the phone rings, but the ring you hear comes from the switching station here in town."

"Thanks for the intel. Hey, we're in business. Just got word about six hours ago that we have the exact location of the picnic grounds we were looking for. We did some tail twisting, and got the final okay to move out. You have travel orders for as soon as possible. No later than sixteen hundred today. Your headquarters there has a fax on it now, and will get a phone call later. You better roust your crew out for an early call, and get cracking. You'll take all the goodies you expect to use."

"Including ammo?"

"That's right. Everything for land and sea. You'll be able to get some extra ammo when you land with the Air Force. This is not a secure line. You have a telephone tree of some sort?"

"That we do. I call four, they call the rest."

"Do it, now. Have your boss call me when you dig him out. I'll see you across the pond."

They said good-bye and hung up. DeWitt looked over at Milly, who was sitting up listening.

"You're going?"

"This afternoon."

"Once more, Ed. Just once more, then call the guys."

"I'll call first, then once more," he said and began dialing. Milly pulled off her nightgown and waited.

The phone rang, and Murdock shook his head trying to stop the ringing. Then he figured it out, and grabbed the phone.

"Good morning, this is your four A.M. wake-up call from the front desk of the Hotel Coronado. You have a nice day."

Murdock hung up the phone, and scowled. "I didn't leave a four A.M. wake-up call."

He heard a giggle beside him, and looked over at Ardith.

"I know, I'm wicked and evil and oversexed, but I just

wanted to be sure to love you one more time before you went to work."

"You are wicked . . . and wonderful. I don't have to leave here until oh-seven-forty-five. That leaves me five minutes to get to the office and five more to get into my cammies."

"Shut up," she said, "and slide over here."

Lieutenant Blake Murdock rolled into his office at oh-seven-fifty-five in his blue jeans and a blue Western shirt. He lifted his brows at the rush of activity from men in the platoon. Inside he saw Lieutenant DeWitt at his desk working over a form.

"What happened?" Murdock asked.

"Your phone must have been unplugged," Ed said. "Stroh called me at oh-three-thirty with our marching orders. Douglas and Franklin found the damn nuke place. We fly out of North Island at sixteen-hundred."

"Oh, yeah. All the guys here?"

"All except Magic Brown, who must have had his phone off the hook. If he isn't here in thirty, Jaybird will run him down."

DeWitt got up from the chair. "We're to take everything we'll need for the whole operation, land and sea. All our ammo, weapons, rebreathers, uniforms—the works. I'd figure no wet suits. Too heavy to pack out to the coast from our drop."

"Right. Is Kat here?"

"She's checking her gear."

"Ask her to come in here."

Kat walked in a minute later, looking trim in her cut-down cammies, but her face had flushed, and a line of perspiration beaded on her forehead.

"We're taking that much ammo?"

"You'll be glad you have it. Kat, sit down. One thing we

haven't covered." He explained to her that each of the SEALs had to have a last will and testament. Platoon policy.

"A will? God, I haven't thought about that in years. I have one, wrote it myself so I know it's good. It's on file with a lawyer back in D.C. You need a copy?"

"No, just your word that you have one, and where it can be found, and your next of kin. File those with Jaybird. Now, how's everything else coming?"

They talked for a few minutes, then she hurried back to her gear. She was surprised when some of the guys showed her all the things she had to take with her.

Murdock had his carry-on bag and special backpack ready in two hours. The backpacks would be used for ground movement, to let the men have full use of both hands. That was in addition to the nylon-mesh American Body Armor special operations vest. They had two- to six-magazine pouches across the front, depending on the type weapon the person carried. Their Motorola personal radio fit in back in a watertight bag. Grenade pouches showed on the web belt.

Murdock moved around the big squad room. There was a tension in the air that hadn't been there yesterday. A sense of purpose, of expectation.

The banter and the jokes flew hot and heavy, some of them landing on Murdock. He grinned, and shot back at them, and they all laughed.

By noon most of the men were ready. Magic Brown had come in about 1100 and dug into the task of getting his gear together. He asked Murdock if they could requisition a hundred rounds of .50-caliber HE armor piercing to be picked up at their land base in Saudi Arabia or whatever their Air Force plan would land. Murdock make a quick call to Don Stroh and asked for that plus several thousand rounds of other ammo they might need. It would be on hand.

Murdock sat at his desk. He had the paperwork signed and off to Seal Team Seven headquarters. He had checked with North Island and they would have an Air Force plane on the runway ready to take off on schedule. He didn't ask about the route. He didn't want to know. They might be en route for twenty-four hours; he wasn't sure.

What was he forgetting?

Ardith!

She was expecting him at sixteen hundred for an early supper. He closed his office door and called the Hotel Del. She came on the phone on the first ring.

"Bad news, Ardith. We're moving out today at four o'clock. I won't be able to see you before we go."

"Goddamnit!"

He let the silence stretch out. "I was afraid this might happen, but I hoped it wouldn't, not while you were here. I'll stop in Washington when we get back."

He could hear her crying. She tried to stop it.

"Darling Blake, I'm sorry I'm such a ninny. I so hoped that we could have two or three days. Oh, God!"

She cried again.

"Hey, let's talk. I even shut my door, and nobody wanting to keep his head on will come in. Let's talk about last night."

They did.

It was almost an hour later when he hung up the phone and opened his door. Nobody said a word.

DeWitt came in to report that his squad was all packed and ready to go.

"I inspected each man. We're ready. Chow at the regular time?"

"Yes, or go an hour early if you want to. I'll check my squad."

When he got to it, he found that Jaybird had done it for him. Everyone including Kat was packed up and checked out. They would wear their cammies on the trip, and on the mission. They each had a spare pair. They had rebreathers and flippers, and six sonoboys that would send out locator signals for the submarine.

First they had to get to the LZ, and then take down the nuke factory.

He checked with Kat. She sat on a bench by her locker staring straight ahead.

"Hey, Kat, sorry you volunteered for this trip?"

"Volunteered? Who the fuck volunteered?" She said it sharply, then grinned. "How did you know I volunteered?"

"Nobody does SEAL work with SEALS without agreeing to it. Besides, I checked with your boss in Washington. He gave you two thumbs-up."

"He better. He owes me." They both laughed.

"Ready?"

"As ready as I'll ever be. I feel comfortable here with these guys. It's like I've found a whole new family, with sixteen brothers."

"Good. Our job is to get you to that nuke plant alive, and ready to blow up the damn place. We've got more explosives with us than you want to know about. Lots of that new TNAZ that you and Ed shot off. Hot stuff."

"I've got my handy dandy nuke destruct tool kit," Kat said. "Everything I need, from pliers to a miniature cutting torch, and a radiation safe suit folded up you wouldn't believe how small."

"Good. You ready to travel?"

She grinned. "Almost. I may need to go to the bathroom again."

They both laughed. "That happens to all of us. The nerves are a marvelous diuretic. I was thinking more like a phone call. You get a long distance call on the Navy if you want one."

"There's just my mom. She's in Connecticut and doesn't know I'm here or anything about this. I do a lot of traveling. No, I don't think a call."

Three of the platoon used Murdock's office to make calls. Then it was time to saddle up and move out. Every man carried his own gear and ammo. Three had drag bags, including those for the big .50-caliber sniper rifles.

They boarded two trucks outside the quarterdeck and headed for the North Island Naval Air Station, about three miles away.

22

Tuesday, November 1

**2010 hours
Hill country north of
Chah Bahar, Iran**

Joe Douglas looked at Franklin where he lay in the shelter on the side of the gully.

"Hey, you awake?"

"Sure, asshole. I always snore when I'm awake."

"It's past twenty hundred, maybe we should go topside, and wait for the guys."

"When did the radio say they were coming in?"

"Last SATCOM message said between twenty and twenty-two hundred tonight."

"How can they see this saddle in the dark?" Franklin asked.

"Same way we did, where it blocks out the stars."

They worked their way up the slope to the top of the saddle, and walked into it a hundred yards. Then they stopped and waited.

"I still don't like the signal light idea. How will we know it's them?"

"Who else would be flying a big plane over this area, exactly at this time? We'll know. They make one pass, we flash the light three times. They key in on it and make their low-level jump, and all is right with the world."

"If it works. What's the odds of losing at least one man on a night low-level jump?"

"Ten percent, but both of us made it."

"Yeah, but what about Kat?"

"She's made more than two dozen jumps now."

"None at night at low level."

"Quiet, what's that?"

Douglas held up one hand, and they both listened. The sound came from the south. The small purr grew into a sizable one, and then a growl.

"Sounds like one of them turbo props, maybe the same C-130 that brought us in," Franklin said.

They listened and watched, then it was obvious that the plane was heading straight for them. The pilot would have the exact position. Douglas picked up the strobe light and flicked it on and off three times, aiming it south. The powerful, surging flashes jolted south toward the plane. There was no recognition signal from the plane.

Then the sound was almost on top of them. Douglas stabbed the light three times again just before the big bird thundered over them at less than a thousand feet. He was sure the big plane was below the tops of the mountains on both sides of the saddle.

The plane made a turn away from the nuke plant to the north, and came back, and this time it seemed to be throttled down. Again, Douglas hit the strobe. It was aimed away from the nuke plant so they couldn't possibly see it.

"There," Franklin said. "Hear the change in the sound? Like the big rear hatch came open." A moment later he nodded in the darkness. The engine speed had picked up, and sounded different. "The engine picked up when those fifteen fully loaded SEALs ran out the ass end of that C-130. Our buddies are coming down."

Douglas kept hitting the strobe now as they stood there

watching the sky, trying to find the black chutes blotting out the stars. For a moment Douglas thought he saw one, then he wasn't sure.

He hit the strobe light every five seconds now.

Somewhere ahead they heard a yell.

Closer by something hit the dirt and skidded.

"Ho, SEALs," Douglas called.

"Ho yourself," somebody said from close by. "Hit that light and aim it along the ground," a voice said.

"L-T, that you?" Douglas asked.

"Me and my buddies. On me, you landlocked SEALs." His last was a bellow. It brought a series of calls from around the area.

Murdock came up to them dragging his black chute. He unhooked the straps and stepped free, then put down his pack and the bag he carried.

"Morning, Franklin, Douglas. Good to find you guys. Black as the inside of an inkwell out here. Hooooooo. This way. Men, assemble on me."

They straggled in then in ones and twos. One came in who was shorter than the rest.

"Kat, that you?" Murdock asked.

"What's left of me. This low-level jumping shit has got to stop." Half a dozen of them laughed.

"Glad you made it, Kat. Any tears, rips, broken bones?"

"I'm all in one chunk, but a little bruised up. What else is new?"

"Is Jaybird here yet?" Murdock asked. "He was the last man out. Somebody get me a body count. Stand still, everyone." Four more SEALs came in. Magic Brown came up a minute later.

"I've got a count of thirteen chutes, L-T. We still need two more."

"Keep the light going, Douglas. Fernandez and Franklin, take a hike and see if you can find anybody. We might have lost one over the side. Douglas, where can we see the damn nuke plant?"

Douglas took them to the north two hundred yards and showed them the glow of the lights.

"Oh, yeah, that's more lights than we saw since we left Saudi Arabia. Got to be it. Five miles from here?"

"What we estimated in the daytime."

"The plan is to get situated here and make a move toward the plant tomorrow night. We'll send out a recon patrol tonight to figure out the best way to get there. We'll need some cover closer than this. How tight is the security?"

Douglas told Murdock and the rest of them about the daily chopper overflights of the flat area of the saddle, and about the chopper attack, and the three soldiers who chased their car.

"The car went back south so they probably are still hunting it," Douglas said.

They went back where they had dumped their chutes and packs. Magic Johnson was there with the missing Al Adams and Doc Ellsworth.

"Adams has a badly sprained right ankle where he hit some rocks on landing," Doc said. "I put a bandage on it but he won't walk too well for twenty-four."

"Got it," Murdock said. "Any other hurts, sprains, rips, or tears?"

Kenneth Ching had a slash on his left arm that Doc treated and tied up.

Murdock called them all around him in the dark.

"Yeah, we're on-site. Now we get down to business. Lampedusa and I will take a recon and be back before daylight. We've got to be invisible tomorrow. Douglas and Franklin will get you situated in the gullies around the sides of this place. Use your camo cloths and lots of sand when the chopper comes over. Remember, don't move when you can see the chopper. That means he can see you. No firing. Let him look and scoot.

"I want every man to take care of his own chute and harness. Bury them down the sides in the gullies where moved dirt won't be a clue. Lampedusa, we'll leave our gear and chutes here for Franklin and Douglas to take care of. All of you find a hide hole and get situated. You can get some sleep in before dawn. Lam, let's get the hell out of here."

They used their NVG, night vision goggles, and that helped out at once, showing a gentle slope down from the saddle to a small valley below and then a ridge beyond it. They climbed the second ridge without finding much in the way of an easy route to the nuke plant. It would be muscle versus the mountain.

Murdock checked his watch every half hour.

They took a break at the top of the third ridgeline. From there they could see the lights of the factory.

"Not sure if they have a night shift or if those are security lights," Murdock said.

"They must have barracks or houses, supply and stores, a whole damn city up here. Wonder how many workers they have inside that place."

"Too many, I'd guess," Murdock said. "I hope they are beyond the point where they need a night shift. We'll have to chase all the civilians out of there before we blow the place."

An hour later they lay just outside of a high wire fence around the nuclear bomb operation. The wire could be electrified; they'd find out about that later. Here earth-moving machines had widened a good-sized valley by shaving off the sides of hills until the space was big enough for the complex.

Murdock figured it was about a half mile long, with a series of large and smaller buildings. They'd have to find out which one held the final assembly.

"Up there, L-T. See where that cut is on the hill? The fence is not quite as high as the cut. We could jump over there easily if the damn fence is juiced."

"Noted," Murdock said. "Which building is the one we want?"

"We watch them for a while," Lam said. "My guess would be the smaller one in the middle with the extra lights around it."

As they watched, a jeeplike vehicle came around the corner of the structure, paused, and two men in the rig went up and checked on the doors. They got back in, and drove around the far corner of the place.

"So, probably no workers inside that one at night," Murdock said. "Does it get special protection, I'm wondering."

They ducked low into the smattering of weeds and boulders as a vehicle swung out from the nearest building and drove to the fence, then along it, as it made a circuit around the part of the fence they could see.

When it was gone, Murdock lifted up and checked his watch. "Better time this one. I figure the jeep is on a schedule, and makes the rounds of the fence every so often. Be good to know. We'll have to be through our hole, and have the fence rewired, and be out of sight forward before the driver comes back here."

"L-T, we gonna move up during the afternoon and get here just after dark?"

"Sounds good. That will give us ten hours of darkness to get the job done and haul ass out of here. They'll hound us all the way to the coast. Probably bring in a blocking force once they see where we're headed. That could be rough. First we have to get those bombs taken care of."

A half hour later the jeep did its run around the fence again.

"A half hour should be time enough," Lam said.

Murdock stared at the complex. Where would be the best place to breach the fence? There should be the least security at the far end, but then they'd have a longer run to whichever building they needed.

They heard a chopper. It lifted upward from the far side of the largest lighted building, and swept over the complex end-to-end, then it did a circuit of the fence with its brilliant spotlight tracing a twelve-foot-wide circle on the ground, as it moved along little faster than a walk.

"That could be real trouble," Lam said.

"We'll have to take it out early on. I hope they have only one. Wish there was some way we could know how many troops they have inside that wire."

"Looks like we'll need a diversion hit," Lam said. "We send three guys up to the far end, maybe one of the fifties, and an MG. We put some forty mike-mikes in there and blast a building with the fifty, and MG, and get them all shook up."

"At the same time we breach the fence and go through silent as a ghost," Murdock said. "Yeah, it might work. We've got our work cut out for us on this one."

Lam rolled over and stared at his commander. "Skipper, I've got an idea. Why don't I go in now, move around enough to find which building is the final assembly? I can work around there until almost daylight if I have to, and then get out, and wait for you guys to come tomorrow night. That's later on today, I guess."

Murdock shook his head. "Too dangerous. They could nail you, and know we were coming, and be ready."

"No chance they could grab me, L-T. I can hide in a damned tomato can. Been doing it all my life. How in hell we gonna shoot our way in, and then try to find the right building? Not a chance. If I go in, and find the right spot, and get out and tell you, we're well ahead of the game. If I get in, and don't find it, and get out, we're no worse off. I can find it. No shit, L-T. Think it over."

"Nothing to think over, Lam. Your idea is good. Should I risk you or not?"

"Not much of a fucking risk, L-T. The big risk is not knowing where to go once we get inside. As soon as they know we're here, they'll put all their guns inside that final assembly building we want, and hold us off until they fly in reinforcements. No other way. I got to get through the fence and see what I can find out."

"Jump over down there?"

"Yeah."

"How will you get out?"

"Dig under at one of the gullies the cloudbursts make. There's one over there, a foot deep under the fence already. Quicker to jump over now, and then dig out when I find the assembly area. Is it a go, L-T?"

Murdock scowled into the darkness. The kid was right. They needed more intel. He'd had no idea the place would be so big, so many buildings. Slowly he nodded. There was no other reasonable way.

"Okay, Lam. You take my MP-5 and four mags. The silenced rounds might help."

"Hey, I won't waste anybody unless I have to. The first body that shows up in the morning, they'll have security scouring all the hills around here. No bodies, I decided that. I might have to knock out one or two."

"Okay, Lam. One other thing. While you get over the fence, I'll move up with my K-bar and dig out that gully under the fence so you can slip right under it when you need to. I'll be in the light so it will have to be a low motion kind of operation."

"Done," Lam said. He handed Murdock his issue Colt M-4A1, took the MP-5, and extra mags. He dabbed more cammie makeup on his face, hands, nose, and ears. He tugged down his floppy hat. "I'll see you right here if I find the right building quickly. If not I'll have to move back a couple of ridges after I get under the fence. No sweat. I'll either find the right building or give it one hell of a try. What I won't do is tip their hand. See you around, Skipper."

Lam moved away in the darkness, toward the cut in the hill three-hundred yards away. Murdock watched him go,

sent along his best wishes, and then began working toward
the small wash under the fence so he could dig it deeper.

Lam lay near the splash of light along the fence, and
evaluated it. He could spot no lookout towers or sentries in
the area. If somebody watched the area with binoculars, it
would be on a casual and intermittent basis. He had a good
chance of going over the eight-foot fence, and not being
seen.

He was about to move when he heard the chopper
coming. He blended in behind a two-foot rock, well out of
the airborne spotlight, and waited for it to pass.

When it vanished down the way, he came up and moved
to the edge of the fence. The slope of the hill put it higher
than the fence here, and he held the MP-5 in one hand to his
chest, and jumped. He hit on the hard ground, and did a
shoulder roll to take up the force. The MP-5 stayed on his
chest. He rolled once, and then lay perfectly still.

Nothing happened.

Good. He crawled out of the lights on the fence slowly, so
anyone watching would not notice him by movement alone.
After what seemed like two hours, but was only about two
minutes, Lam was in the shadows between the lighted fence
and the buildings. He was about in the center of the
complex. He came to his knees, then his feet, and ran bent
over toward the nearest building.

Just then the jeeplike rig's headlights cut a path through
the darkness, as it drove around a building two down from
the one he aimed at.

He paused and watched the small truck move away, and
darkness return. There were two nightlights outside the
small warehouse-type structure. He had no idea what kind
of uniforms the Iranian soldiers wore. Be nice to get a set to
put on over his cammies. An idea.

He walked casually through a bloom of light to the
building and then along it to a door. He tried the handle. It

wasn't locked. Trusting souls. He pulled it open. No alarm. A moment later, he was inside with the door closed.

Lam took a penlight from his shirt pocket. He used it to check the building. It looked to be a machine shop of some kind. Definitely not a final assembly plant. Check one off the list. He headed for the same door he'd come in.

Just before he reached it, the knob turned, and the door opened outward. Someone spoke in normal tones. Then another voice answered, before a man came through the door, and closed it. In the dim light, Lam saw that the man was an Iranian soldier.

Lam was six feet from him. He lunged forward. Just as the soldier turned to see what was coming, Lam slammed the heavy butt of the MP-5 into his head. He went down with a grunt, and fell unconscious to the floor.

Yeah, he was big enough, Lam decided.

Five minutes later, Lam left the building dressed in the soldier's uniform and cap. The unconscious form had been tied hand and foot, gagged, and stuffed into a closet in the machine shop. Nobody would find him until morning at least.

Lam moved easier now. If he met anyone, he'd growl at them, and go on by. He checked six more unlocked buildings. None was the final assembly. Then he came to a one-story structure set apart somewhat from the rest. It had brighter lights around it. Lam walked up to it in the open and began checking doors, as if he were a security man. The first three were locked, the next opened, and he stepped inside.

All the lights were on. The interior was laid out in six individual areas. In each one was an elaborate worktable, a hoist, a battery of tool cabinets, and what could be shelves for parts. On each worktable was what looked to Lam like a partially assembled nuclear weapon. They were larger than he had figured. But these would be crude and unso-

phisticated compared to the U.S. atomic weapons. He'd
found it. This had to be the final assembly building.

Three men worked at each assembly area. He turned and,
as casually as he could, walked outside, shielding the MP-5
from view. He had no idea what weapons the Army men
here would carry. The one he met had been without any
firearm.

Just before he went out the door, he heard the chopper
coming overhead. He paused at the door, felt as much as
saw the brilliant beam of some kind of stream-light spot
from the chopper wash over the building, and then it was
gone.

He stepped outside, and headed back the way he had
come, angling toward the fence. One of the military-type
jeeps came around the corner, and caught him in its
headlights. He slowed to let the rig pass him, but instead it
rolled up beside him, and stopped. One man in the jeep said
something to him. He growled, and waved the man on past.
The question came again, and Lam screeched some words
he was sure weren't Farsi. The man behind the wheel
shrugged and drove on.

Lam let out a breath, and walked directly away from the
building into the shadows. He paused beside a pile of
wooden boxes. No one seemed to have noticed him, or to
question his presence. He waited a minute, then walked into
the darkness between the buildings and the lighted fence. He
angled to the left where he had left Lieutenant Murdock.

When he got closer, he saw slight movement at the
lighted fence area. He stopped and concentrated on it. Yes,
that was the small gully under the fence. Now it was
considerably deeper. He watched again, and saw a hand dig
a knife into the dirt and slowly drag it backward. The L-T
was still there working on the opening.

Lam ran then through the semidarkness between the
buildings and the lighted fence. He came close to the spot,
and called out softly.

"Lieutenant Murdock. Lam, coming out."

He heard a grunt, and the hand and knife moved backward.

Just then the chopper began its run along the fence. Lam saw the figure on the other side of the fence roll several times away from the wire. Lam dropped to the ground rolled into a ball, and lay perfectly still. He was outside the direct beam of the powerful light, but it splashed to the sides a dozen feet.

Lam held his breath, expecting at any instant to be shot by a door gunner working a machine gun. The chopper moved slowly but didn't pause at the escape spot. Then it was past.

Lam wanted to run, but he walked to the lighted area, dropped to the ground, and crawled as slowly as he could stand it toward the fence, and the enlarged escape hole. It looked big enough.

It took him three minutes to cover fifteen feet. Headfirst, he decided. He turned on his back and worked his head under the wire in the little gully. Good so far.

He pushed with his heels. The MP-5 caught on the bottom of the wire. He pulled it to his side, and pressed forward again with his legs. The wire snagged his ammo pouch, then came off. A moment later he was under the wire, and crawling slowly away from the light.

Twenty feet later, he was in the darkness.

"You do fast work," Murdock said just behind him.

"Oh, damn, sir, you scared the shit out of me. How do you like my new uniform?"

"Iranian military, I'd say. Keep it, we may need it later on tonight. You found the place?"

"Roger that, sir. It's the one-story building down from that intensively lighted one. Eighteen guys in there. Three of them working on each of six different bombs. I have no idea how close they are to finishing anything."

"Kat will know. Let's get the hell out of Dodge City."

They hiked back the way they had come. For a minute

Lam felt the tension draining out of him. He'd been higher than a comet while he was inside. What a fucking rush! He shook his head. Now it was back to work as usual. They had five miles to hike, then to get hidden for the daylight hours. He wondered when the Iranians would find the naked soldier in the closet. By then they would be wondering, but there should be no special alert. Somebody might just have been playing a joke on the soldier. At least that's what Lam hoped.

As they walked, he filled in his L-T on what happened.

"Good work, Lam. We may keep you in the squad."

Lam grinned, and kept hiking. In two hours they should be back on the saddle, and find a hide hole. Yeah, and then some sleep. He suddenly was more tired than he could remember.

23

Wednesday, November 2

1734 hours
Near nuclear bomb plant
Chah Bahar, Iran

The helicopter with the Iranian flag on the sides made three sweeps across the barren saddle between the two mountains, hesitated as if for a third look, then drifted to the north and swept down a valley, and out of sight of the seventeen SEALs.

The sixteen men and one woman had plenty of time to hide from the chopper. This was the second time it had been over the area that day. Some SEALs had found crevices to lie in, and simply covered their body and packs with the camouflage cloth made of desert cammies material. It blended in perfectly with the surrounding brown and sandy colors.

Some SEALs had dug out trenches in the shade of the mountain, in a gully on the downslope, leading from the top of the saddle. They dug in and covered up with the camouflage cloth when needed.

Both times the chopper came over, Magic Brown asked for permission to shoot it down with his .50-caliber sniping rifle.

"Come on, L-T. I've got him in my sights. Just one trigger squeeze and he's history."

"So are we, Magic, when they realize there are more than rattlesnakes and scorpions out here in the hills. We don't want to give ourselves away."

"Hell, I know that, Skipper. Just had to ask."

Murdock and Lampedusa had straggled into the position about 0200 and found half the SEALs up and eating.

"It's a two-hour hike into the target," Murdock told those awake. "We'll plan on leaving here about 1700 tomorrow and should get there at first dark."

That had been the plan. Now Murdock watched the chopper vanish over the hill. He had cautioned the men to keep under cover for another ten minutes after the bird left. He could pop up over the edge of the mesa without warning and surprise them.

This time he didn't.

Murdock checked his watch. "No chance we're going to leave here now before it gets dark," he told the troops. "Pass the word. We'll keep secure here until that time. Fucking chopper could check back this way anytime and catch us on the trail."

He looked over at Kat. She had functioned perfectly so far. She had her hole dug and camo ready before half the men did. Of course she had a smaller hole to prepare. She was about ten feet down the gully from him.

"Kat, you might as well have something to eat. Might be some time before we can take a break for food again. Try the chicken à la king."

Kat laughed. "Hey, we had that out at Niland, remember? I think I'll go for the beef stroganoff."

Murdock tore open an MRE and picked out the crackers and peanut butter. He made a cold drink from the powder. He looked over at Douglas, who was nearby. Douglas had a stack of water bottles and food behind him.

"Douglas. How in hell did you get all that stuff in here?"

"Chogie straps, remember them?"

"Never heard of the term."

"Korea. Some of the old Army guys told me about them."
He explained how they worked. "We didn't know how long
we'd be here or how much water we'd need."

"We might use some of it before we leave. Have all the
guys fill up their canteens. Then we're hoping for water at
the nuke factory."

They had talked half the morning about the strategy for
hitting the big plant. What it came down to was what Lam
had suggested the night before.

"So it's set," Murdock had said. "Three of you will work
to the west end of the complex. Up at least a quarter of a
mile from our attack point."

"Got it," Magic said. "We go on your signal on the
Motorola. We keep as many of them occupied up there as
long as we can, then we drift south, and give you guys
support fire when you're inside the fence."

Kat had talked for more than an hour with Lampedusa.
He had described to her as much as he could remember
about the worktables, and how far assembled the devices
were.

"None had an outside shell on it?" Kat had asked.

"No, none of them. I didn't even see anything that looked
like a bomb casing."

"Good. They may not be halfway along. The problem
will be finding the plutonium and disposing of it. Wish we
had a nice deep oil well we could pour it down."

"We'll figure it out," Lam said.

"If we don't, it stays there in a safe container. I'm not
going to scatter it over the hills and kill a few thousand
people."

"That's a Roger, Kat. I understand."

At 1930, Murdock had them packed up and ready to go.
They all had filled their double canteens. Some of them
carried an extra two-quart plastic jug of water that Douglas

and Franklin had packed in. Two quarts of water weigh
another four pounds.

"Let's use our NVGs," Murdock said. "It helps in this
uneven terrain. We'll use regular squad order. Let's move
it."

Kat had broken down her tool kit at Murdock's insistence.
He had half of it, Kat had a quarter, and Ron Holt, who
hiked right behind her, had the other quarter. Kat still had
almost forty pounds of gear and ammo.

The first hour went easily. They were more than halfway
to the objective, when Murdock called a halt. He went from
man to man, checking on assignments, making sure the
battle plan was clear to everyone.

An hour later, when they topped the last ridge, and could
look directly at the facility, there were soft whistles.

"Big sucker," Magic said.

"Glad we don't have to level the whole thing," Gonzalez
said.

They quieted then as Murdock led them down the last
slope, and up the next small rise to where the ground had
been leveled out for the complex. They lay on a slope about
four hundred yards from the fence.

Magic Brown with his big .50-caliber sniper weapon and
forty rounds of armor piercing and HE rounds; Harry
"Horse" Ronson with his H&K machine gun; and Rodolfo
Gonzalez with his Colt M-4A1 with grenade launcher, and
twenty rounds of the 40mm, moved to the west to set up
their diversion.

Everyone had his radio turned on. Murdock called for a
quick radio check. Each man reported with his last name,
except Kat, who used her first.

"Magic, give me a ready one, when you pick your spot.
Keep about twenty yards apart when you start shooting.
Hope you get a shot at the chopper. That might be a good
time to start this party. Let me know when you get a chopper
shot. The bird should come around every half hour."

They left lugging their extra ammo.

Ten minutes later, Murdock heard a ready one in his earpiece. Magic was ready. Murdock had his teams spread out, and ready. Fred Washington, the platoon's second black, would lead the way with his wire cutters, and do a man-sized peel-back on the wire. They knew it wasn't electrified.

Once the fourteen men were through, Washington would temporarily wire the fence closed.

They moved up so they were twenty yards from the fence, and its lights. Murdock had Miguel Fernandez with his H&K PSG1 silenced sniper rifle ready to take out the lights on both sides of the cutting spot. They would do that after Magic had a shot at the chopper.

They all waited.

Ten minutes later, Murdock heard the chopper. He couldn't see it. But Magic could.

"Have target," Magic said in the mike.

A minute later the chopper rose higher, and Magic fired. He worked the bolt, and fired again. He got off three rounds in less than a minute. Now Murdock saw the chopper. It had lifted a hundred feet over the complex. He saw it shudder, then tilt to the right. Another round hit the engine and the whole chopper exploded in one big ball of fire.

At the same time they heard the machine gun rattling away.

A moment later the *karumph* of the 40mm grenades came as Gonzalez lobbed them into the production facility. Alarms sounded. A loud siren went off.

Murdock touched Fernandez's shoulder, and he settled in aiming at the first light, a standard twenty yards from the entrance point. His silenced round knocked it out. He turned the other way, and with two shots blew out that one.

"Go Washington," Murdock said into his lip mike. The black SEAL darted forward and worked on the wire. He cut through the chain-link fence, and soon had it high enough so the first man could squeeze through. More followed as Washington cut more links. By the time he had it four feet high, all the SEALs were inside. He bent the chunk of fence down where it had been, and tied it in place with wire twists.

Murdock spread out his men, and moved toward the central building they needed to capture. He could see armed men running to the west. Good. They waited a moment, then moved forward again until they were just outside the wash of the one-story building's lights.

"Hold," Murdock said in the mike. Each of the SEALs had a personal Motorola communications radio for short distances. Each SEAL had an earpiece and a lip mike. The small transceiver unit fastened to their webbing and gave them instant communications with all seventeen men on the team.

"Keep up the pressure, west guys," Murdock said. He now heard return fire at the muzzle flashes from outside the fence.

Murdock watched the building ahead of them. Lampedusa said it was the right one. Two soldiers came out the door and at once ran to the west. Murdock grinned.

The SEALs knew their jobs. Murdock touched his mike. "We three, let's move." Only three of them would go inside and reduce any opposition, then herd all the civilians together. Murdock, Jaybird, and Les Quinley, with his new H&K G11 sub-gun that fired caseless bullets, charged across the twenty yards to the building and swung open the unlocked door. The three stormed in. Murdock took the right-hand section. He saw two soldiers, and riddled them with half a dozen silent rounds.

Jaybird had the center section of the big building but found no opposition. When Quinley jolted in the door and checked the left-hand side, he saw three soldiers bringing up their guns. He held the trigger back on the G11 and splattered the three Iranians with twenty rounds. They went down without firing a shot.

Already Murdock had run into the room, and herded six of the civilians ahead of him away from the assembly tables. Jaybird did the same and then Quinley pushed six more toward the far corner. They made the civilians lie on the floor.

Murdock hit his mike again. "Franklin, inside."

Franklin rushed in the door a moment later. "Keep these civvies down on their bellies and quiet. Tell them."

Franklin ran up to the eighteen men and ordered them to lie down and be quiet. He said none of them would be hurt.

"Bring in Kat," Murdock said. The door burst open again, and two SEALs ran inside, then Kat came, and then two more SEALs. They had her tool kits. She hurried to the first assembly table, and nodded.

"Two small charges on this one," she said. Joe Douglas pasted the TNAZ block where she told him. He didn't put in timer/detonators. She ran to the next table. This one was more complete. She took her tool kit and began some disassembly.

"This one is going to take more time," she said into her radio.

"We have a defensive perimeter in front outside," Ed DeWitt said on his mike. "Nobody knows we're down here yet. Lots of action up north. Our men still firing, but it's tapering off."

"Longer we're a secret here, the better," Murdock said. He went back to the outside door and checked. He took two of the inside men and put them in front. There were still five SEALs inside. He saw the other outside door and tried it. Locked. He turned a lever and it came open.

Cautiously he looked outside. Six Iranian soldiers stared at the opening door. Murdock brought up his MP-5 submachine gun on 3-round setting, and cut down three of the men with two bursts. One ran. The other two fumbled for their shouldered weapons. He killed them in a second double burst, then sent six rounds after the runner. He stumbled, but kept on going. Murdock called to the five men inside and put them outside along the building as a back door guard. They would have company soon.

Murdock ran to where Kat worked on the third bomb.

"This one is more complete. I need to do some delicate surgery before it gets blown up. You seen anything that looks like it could hold plutonium?"

"Some big lead box?"

"About the size of it."

"Get a rush on here, Kat. We've just been made out the back door. We'll be having company before long."

"If we can find the plutonium, we'll need transportation to move it. Can we steal a truck or at least a jeep somewhere?"

"I'll put my best car thief on it." He touched his mike. "Douglas, we need a truck or a jeep. Take a man with you and try to bring one back. If it's impossible, tell me. Don't get yourself overmatched and killed out there."

"Will do, L-T. I've got Ching with me. We're gone."

"Magic, how is it going?"

"Down to five rounds. Machine gun ammo almost gone. Out of the forties. Should we pull back?"

"You're taking fire, anybody trying to charge you?"

"So far they're just firing from the sides of buildings, and cars. They like lots of protection. We've got a few rocks."

"Move toward the place where the lights went out along the fence when you need to. Longer you can keep them up there, the better it is for us."

"That's a Roger, L-T."

Murdock ran back to Kat. She was sweating. She finished the fourth bomb partial, and looked at the fifth.

"This one is almost ready for the plutonium to be put in. Glad we got here today. Give me ten minutes."

"We might not have ten. Look at number six."

She checked it. "Good plan, this one is a snap." She

showed Al Adams where to put the TNAZ charges on this
one, and ran back to number six.

"Found that plutonium yet?" she asked.

Murdock ran to Franklin, and told him to ask the men in
Farsi where the plutonium was being kept. He did, but
nobody said a word.

He asked the question again. Still silence. He jerked one
of the civilians to his feet and put a Colt carbine's muzzle
against the man's head. Again he asked them. One man
wavered. Franklin moved the carbine, and fired one round
through the thigh of the man he held up. The shot civilian
screamed, and Franklin dropped him to the floor. He jerked
up the man who had seemed about to talk.

"Where?" he asked again. The man shook so hard he
couldn't talk. He pointed. Franklin pushed him in that
direction. He went to the far end of the building, and
showed them a panel on the floor. He caught a ring and
pulled. The six-foot-wide panel lifted up on a counterbal-
ance and a steel box, two feet square, rose on some kind of
an elevator.

Kat ran up and looked at it.

"Heavy as hell," she said. "Steel box that's lead-lined to
hold the plutonium. At least they're protecting it right. Now
we need a truck. Look around for a forklift of some kind."

She ran back to the fifth bomb, which she had to work
more on.

Murdock heard the firing from the rear. A voice came
over the radio.

"L-T, we got a whole shitpot full of Iranians back here
just pissed off to hell. Could use some help."

Murdock ran toward the back door, shoving in a new
magazine. He went through the door low, and felt bullets
whine over his head. He was belly-down behind an old car
of some make. Past it he saw flashes from at least a dozen
weapons.

"Hold fire," he directed in the mike. "Make the bastards

come closer, and get in the light so we don't fire blind. Conserve your ammo. We don't fire blind. Conserve your ammo. We don't have all that much."

The firing continued from the back for a moment, then slackened. Were they going to move forward slowly, or come firing at a run?

"Hey, cowboys, we've got some action out front," Ed DeWitt said. "The jerk in the jeep patrol is driving right up to us. We'll take him out, and try to grab the jeep for Kat. You said you needed transport, right?"

Murdock whispered into his mike. "Yeah, nail the jeep. We also could use three more men back here. The bastards are about to make a charge at us. Get them over here fast. Through the building. Do it now."

24

Wednesday, November 2

2021 hours
Nuclear bomb facility
Chah Bahar, Iran

Three more SEALs charged outside through the rear door, and went prone behind a car and a trailer. Murdock spread them out a little more. Then he saw shadows move into the light. His first 3-round burst from his submachine gun led the way as the SEALs all opened fire.

Ten of the attackers went down in the first barrage; three more turned and ran into the night. Murdock grunted.

"Shouldn't be this easy," he said into the mike. "Keep up the watch. If anybody comes into the light, gun him."

He crawled back to the door, and slipped into the assembly room. Kat had just finished the last partial bomb. All had TNAZ charges on them waiting for the timer/detonators.

Murdock touched his mike. "Ed, what's happening?"

"Two silenced shots just wiped out the driver. We have that jeep. Where do you want it?"

Murdock looked for a truck door. There had to be one. He found it on the back side, just off from where the plutonium box sat. He told Al Adams to open it.

Douglas and Chin had come back to the building when they heard there was a captive jeep. Now the two looked around the big room. On the far side, under a tarp, they found an electric forklift. Douglas crawled on it and hit the switch, and the forklift moved. He checked the panel of instruments again, grinned, and turned the right switch. The rig began to move forward. He steered it around the partial nuclear bombs to the big steel box. It sat on a pallet board.

"Load it," Murdock said. Joe Douglas worked the steel blades of the forklift into the slots of the pallet board, and hit the up switch. The forklift contacted the top of the pallet and strained slowly with the weight. Then it inched upward.

"Damn thing must weigh two tons," Douglas said. He watched it come up, and when it was high enough, he moved the forklift forward.

"We've got company out front," DeWitt said on the radio. Murdock sent three of the SEALs out to help.

The firing began.

Douglas concentrated on getting the steel box over the middle of the back of the jeeplike rig. Then he lowered it gently. The pallet board crushed part of the backseat, then the passenger's seat, as it settled onto the jeep's body. Murdock went to the rig and shook it side to side. The little utility vehicle didn't turn over.

He waved at Douglas. "See if the engine will move the thing. If it will, take it just outside and shut the big door."

Douglas started the jeep, and backed it slowly toward the door. It moved a little faster. "Should work okay," he said.

Murdock nodded, and went to Al Adams. "Put the timer detonators in the charges but don't set any time on them yet. That's the last thing."

He ran to the front door, opened it, and crawled out. DeWitt had his men behind any cover he could find. They had shot out the lights that had bathed the area, and now the whole place was black, except for an occasional muzzle blast from the dark.

Murdock found Ed.

"Must be a batch of them out there, but they aren't firing much. What the hell's going on?"

"Not sure. Hit every muzzle blast you see."

The firing picked up then. A machine gun cut in and drilled a line of nine rounds into the wall of the building over their heads.

"Get on that MG," DeWitt spoke into his mike.

Two MP-5's chattered out six rounds each, and the MG went silent.

"Too damn quiet out there," Murdock said. "They don't want to use any heavy stuff against this building. Their nuclear bombs are inside. They don't want to shoot anything in here that might hurt the bombs. Somebody is holding them back. The minute we leave here, they'll be all over us."

"We'll have to leave soon. You have the plutonium loaded on that little jeep?"

"Ready to go."

The small arms fire picked up then. It was longer range, and the rounds came from down the street. The rounds went parallel with the assembly building. That way they wouldn't hurt anything inside, Murdock decided. He had the men move to better protection. They returned fire, and again the enemy's shooting slowed down, then stopped.

"What the hell are they doing?" DeWitt asked.

Murdock shook his head.

They heard it coming, and couldn't identify it. Sounded like a truck, then a tracked rig.

"Half-track armored personnel carrier," Murdock said. "Where's Magic and his fifty?"

"He's outside the fence," somebody said. "We can use forty-millimeters on this rig."

"Yes, how many grenade launchers we have out here?" Ed asked.

Four men chimed in with affirmative answers. "When he

gets in range, use HE and WP alternately. All four of you fire four rounds each. Get ready, he's coming closer."

The rig had no headlights, to make it harder for them to find it. The first WP helped, spraying the white phosphorous in the street, lighting up the area, and outlining the half-track coming. The second HE found part of the half-track and it veered to the left, then got back on course. A .50-caliber machine gun chattered from the weapons carrier, and the rounds slammed into parked rigs and the side of the building.

"Fernandez, you out here?" DeWitt called on the radio.

"Yes, I'm waiting for a good shot."

Two more 40mm rounds exploded almost at the same time. One hit on the cab, the other the rear of the rig, and it spun around and stalled. It was close enough then that the rest of the men could use their guns on it. Three Iranians fled the injured rig.

"L-T, we've got some trouble back here, side door," Murdock's earpiece told him.

Murdock crawled through the street door and ran across the building to the side door. He'd left four men there. "Trouble?" he asked as he ran.

"Yeah, troops coming up. Can't tell how many. Sounds like a whole damn company."

"Got any WP?"

"I have two," Lampedusa said.

"Put one out in front where you think they are," Murdock said.

A moment later Lampedusa fired the round at fifty yards. It burst in a star pattern of brilliant white fire. For just a second, it outlined a line of troops marching toward them. The fire panicked the men and they broke and ran to the rear.

"The other one, Lam, at a hundred."

He fired it, and the troops kept running.

"Murdock, we've got some new company, sounds like a fucking tank," DeWitt said on the Motorola.

Murdock ran to the front again and bellied out to where DeWitt knelt behind a two-foot-high concrete block wall.

"He stopped. Don't know why." DeWitt said it. A moment later they heard a rumble again and the unmistakable clanking of a tank rolling toward them.

"Great," Murdock said. "At least a tank doesn't have any headlights. The forty mike-mike won't touch a tank. We'd never get close enough out here to throw some TNAZ at him. What the hell, it might be time to cut and run. We're almost done inside. Keep me up to date." Murdock ran back inside, and found Kat. She sat looking at the partly made bombs.

"They didn't do half bad a job," she said. "Another three weeks, and they would be almost ready."

"Sorry to upset their timetable. Can that steel box stand to be tipped over and rolled around?"

She frowned. "In the States I'd say it could. Here, I don't know. Better to treat it like a seven-layer wedding cake—with extreme care."

"Get to the jeep and wait," he said to Kat. He motioned to Al Adams. "Set the timers now for fifteen minutes, and activate them as you go. Do them damn fast, then get out the back door."

He ran to the side door. Nobody was firing. He pulled the four men in and took them to the rear door. "Cover this jeep. Don't let anybody near it. Kat is in it with the plutonium. It's got to take a ride."

Back inside, he called to Franklin, who still watched the Iranians. "Find out if there's any roads down this back side of the facility into the hills."

Franklin asked the men. Most shook their heads. One small man with no teeth lifted his hand. He chattered a minute, then Franklin grinned.

"L-T, he says there's a gate down about two hundred

meters. A service road runs down there and off into the hills a mile or so."

"Good. Bring him with us, then chase the rest of the civilians out the side door over there and tell them to run for their lives. This building is going to blow up."

The civilians went out the door and sprinted away into the darkness. The one with the wounded leg hobbled as quickly as he could behind them.

More firing came from the front. Adams finished setting the timer/detonators.

"We've got thirteen minutes, Skipper," he said.

The three men ran for the front door. At the moment it was quiet out front. They didn't even hear the tank.

"Ed, what's happening?" Murdock asked his Motorola.

"The tank turned off. I keep hearing more troops arriving, but they aren't firing. Can't figure it out."

"Timers set inside. We have eleven minutes. Let's move to the back of the building. We've got the plutonium. Move."

The shadows lifted up, and filtered to the right. Murdock, Adams, and Franklin ran that way. They made it to the back just as a barrage of gunfire opened up on the front of the building where they had been.

The jeep purred quietly. "Move it," Murdock said. They drove away to the rear as quietly as possible. Ten SEALs led the way at a slow trot. The civilian pointed where to drive. They came to a half dozen Iranian soldiers in the darkness, but they ran away without firing a shot.

They had to make a slight move to the left to go around some buildings, and when they did, they came into the glare of searchlights and the tank with its cannon aimed directly at them.

"To the right side," Murdock bellowed. Douglas hit the throttle and raced the little jeep behind a building just as a round from the cannon slammed past them and exploded fifty yards away. The tank lumbered forward. Murdock could see a dozen men behind it.

Murdock called Joe Douglas up with his MG. "Lay down some fire around the corner to bleed those troops off the back of the tank," Murdock said. Douglas pumped out 5-round bursts within twenty seconds.

Murdock dug out a quarter-pound block of TNAZ and pushed in a timer/detonator. "I want two more men up here with TNAZ charges with timers in them, now."

Doc Ellsworth and Ron Holt ran up with their bombs ready.

"When that tank gets in range, we set the timers for ten seconds and throw them for the tank treads. Be sure the set is ten seconds. We don't want any preemies. Get ready, he's almost here."

They were taking some return fire from the men in back of the tank, who had moved to the far side now. The tank nosed toward them, now twenty yards away, but it had no target except a building. Nobody was working the machine gun that must be on top.

The tank clanked and clattered forward. Murdock didn't even try to figure out what kind of a tank it was. It was an old one, but still had a deadly sting, with a 75 to 90mm rifle mounted in it. It came closer. When it was ten yards away, Murdock said, "Now." The three set the timers at ten seconds and threw the bombs.

Murdock's went first and landed just in front of the tank tread. He counted off the seconds. Holt's went next, and hit the tread on top and bounced off. Doc Ellsworth's bomb landed just in front of the side of the tread and bounced on the driving mechanism.

". . . eight, nine, ten," Murdock counted. His bomb under the tread went off. The big machine hadn't quite rolled all the way over the bomb, and it exploded with a shattering roar, lifting the side of the tank a foot off the ground. Two seconds later the bomb beside the tread blew up, and then Doc's TNAZ block on the inside of the tread went off, shattering the track and blowing it off the drivers. It acted as a brake, as the tank kept trying to run forward but only pivoted in a circle around the dead track.

"Move it," Murdock said to his mike. "Run. Douglas get us to the fucking gate."

They took some fire from the stragglers around the tank, but nobody got hit. They went to the side a block past more buildings, then the civilian pointed straight ahead, and they found the gate at the end of a street with no buildings.

Murdock had them on a no-shooting rule. No reason to let the bad guys know where they were.

They made it almost to the gate at the fence when the assembly building blew up. At first it was one jolting explosion, then the rest of the TNAZ went off sympathetically and the sky lighted up like a fresh sun. It billowed upward for ten seconds, then they could hear lumber and pieces of metal falling to the ground.

Murdock shot the lock off the steel gate, and the jeep drove through.

He stopped them a hundred feet down the road, and used the radio. "Magic, where are you guys? Did you fade down the fence to the entry point?"

For a moment he heard nothing. He repeated the words. Then a scratchy voice came through.

"Yeah, we moved along the wire. Haven't seen you spooks. Where the hell are you? Passed our entry point. Gate is still wired shut."

"Keep going the same direction. We're at the east end of the plant, just went through a gate in the wire. Get your SEAL asses down here pronto."

"Like to, L-T, but we got ourselves one huge shitpot full of trouble. About twenty of these hairy-assed Iranians between us and you. They look shit-faced mean after that building blew up. You did good work on it."

"How far are you past the hole in the fence?" Murdock asked.

"Thirty yards, still a quarter mile to where I see the end of the buildings your way."

"How's your ammo supply?"

"Damned near zero. I got two rounds for the fifty, maybe half a belt for the MG, no forties."

"Hang tough, we're coming after you."

Everyone heard the exchange. The troops moved up to Murdock, and waited. "Franklin, Holt, stay here with Douglas and Kat. The rest of you on your horses. We double time until we spot some of the Iranian assholes along the fence."

They trotted, with Lampedusa out front, in a semipatrol formation. Lam led them by thirty yards. It was so dark they couldn't see him. They had moved forward to the fence and along it for fifty yards, toward where they had entered the compound, when Lam hit his mike twice, and they all went to ground. Murdock crawled forward until he found Lam.

"So?"

"Thirty yards ahead. Maybe two dozen camel eaters. They been firing now and then up the pike."

"Move up, no noise," Murdock said in his mike.

Two minutes later the SEALs had spread out in an assault formation, in a line five yards apart.

"Fraggers," Murdock said. Every man had at least two. "Both" he added on the radio. He gave the men a minute to get the hand bombs out of their vest pockets. Then he pulled the pin on his first grenade.

"Now," he said. He threw his grenade forward. He heard some grunts as the other men threw their bombs. The ten fraggers went off in quick succession. They could hear wails of pain and fury ahead of them. They took some fire from the Iranians, but the second throw of grenades silenced those weapons.

"Magic, you guys all A-OK?"

"Right as rain, Boss."

"We're moving up to clean house. Don't shoot at us."

Murdock took the first four men he could see and waved them forward. They had their weapons ready for assault fire as they ran along the uneven Iranian hillside. They saw two Iranians running toward the fence. They let them go. There were no survivors on the playing field.

"Double time, Magic. Get your team up here so we can haul ass. The whole place is going to be charging out here looking for our hides in about ten minutes."

The five SEALs squatted, waiting for their men to arrive. They came three minutes later, two running, one limping badly. Magic had the limp.

Gonzalez carried the big fifty McMillan. Ronson watched Magic.

"Fucking glad to see you shebangers," Magic said. "We stayed in our place about ten minutes too long. We shoulda busted out of there before they got the troops in front of us."

"You hit, big guy?" Murdock asked.

"Just a scratch. I can move. Which way?"

They retraced their steps along the fence, toward the gate at the far end.

"Coming in," Murdock said on the mike, and they teamed up with the rest of the group.

"Now we get this outfit in gear and move down the road. We've got one more job to do."

They hit the downslope almost at once, and Murdock let Douglas turn on the jeep's lights. The road was old, not kept up, made of dirt and filled with runoff gouges and ditches. The going was slow.

After ten minutes, they had left the nuke factory behind and were coming to the first good-sized hill to their left. The road ran directly to what must have been a quarry of some kind.

"Drive it right up to the wall," Murdock said. Kat

scampered out. They had left the civilian at the opened gate, and saw him run back toward the main buildings.

"Get some TNAZ up here," Murdock called. Half the men still carried blocks of the powerful explosive. They brought it up, and Murdock placed it beside, in front of, and behind the jeep, against the heavy rock and dirt of the cliff overhead. He tied the charges together with primer cord, and stood there a moment taking a compass bearing.

"We'll be heading almost due south," he said.

Kat came up and nodded. "Bury the plutonium under hundreds of tons of dirt and rock. Yes, about the best we can hope for. Make sure you use enough explosive."

Murdock put four more quarter-pound chunks on the wall, then moved the people a hundred yards down the gully before he set the timers for ten minutes. He pushed the three timers to on, then jogged down to the rest of the group.

The explosion was larger than the one at the nuke assembly building. The sky lit up again. This time the blast came in the open, and sounded louder than a hundred 105 howitzers going off together. A few rocks flew through the air as far as the SEALs, but none of them was hurt.

"Doc, take a casualty report. Kat and I are going back to check on that explosion. We'll be back in five. Get the troops ready to travel, DeWitt."

They ran up to the still smoking and dusty side of the mountain. The rock slide extended fifty yards on all sides from where they had parked the jeep and its deadly load. There must be a hundred feet of rock and dirt over the plutonium. It could be dug out, but the Iranians would have to be sure that was what was under there. Kat figured they wouldn't bother.

"If they could get that much plutonium, they can get some more. At least we stopped them this time."

They ran back to the other SEALs, put on their gear, and kept moving down the valley.

"We'll get as far away from the place as we can while it's

still dark," Murdock told the men on the Motorola. "Then we'll hole up during the day while they try to find us. Yes, they'll be coming. They don't have the chopper, but they do have a spotter plane, Douglas said. We might ask Magic to shoot it down if they find us.

"I've got a suggestion. We're not going to need those damned Drager rebreathers for a long time. They weigh too much for us land-type SEALs. Let's ditch them here, and travel lighter. We won't worry about name brands now. Our job is to get our asses out of here and to the wet. I figure we have about fifty miles due south to the Gulf of Oman. There's supposed to be a sub out there somewhere waiting for us. Doc, find me."

Murdock heard the men unstrapping the rebreather units and dropping them. They could be tied to the U.S., but right then, Murdock wasn't worried about that. He had a platoon to get over fifty miles of enemy territory. He'd do it any way that he could.

They worked ahead in their usual combat formation with Joe Lampedusa out front, and then First Squad, with Murdock leading.

Doc Ellsworth came up and paced beside Murdock. "We have any casualties?"

"Fernandez took a round in the right arm. Not too bad. I got it treated, and wrapped up. He's fit for service. The sprained ankle hasn't been bothering whoever had it. Sterling got a graze on his shoulder, just a scratch. Band-Aid time.

"Magic is the worst. He has a round in his left thigh. It could have hit the bone, I'm not sure, but I do know the slug didn't come out. In way too deep for me to try to dig out the lead. That gives us three days at the most before he loses the leg. He tells me he can walk. Every step is hurting him. Not sure how much longer he can take it. I gave him two shots of morphine. It'll get worse every hour."

Murdock talked to his mike. "SEALs, we've been lucky

so far. Some nicks and scratches and two bullet wounds. We have fifty miles to go, and when they figure out where we're heading, there will be all kinds of troops in here after us. Iran has over a half million men under arms, a good air force, a few naval ships, and a well-trained and armed army corps. They didn't have much up here at the plant, but you can bet your bottom babushka that they'll be coming after us now with everything they have. Choppers, paratroops, the works. We've got to remain as invisible as possible. No, Magic, you won't be trying to shoot down that spotter plane or any choppers. We're gonna dig a lot of holes on this one."

Murdock pushed the light on his watch.

"It's now 2136. We were on-site too long, but nothing we can do about that now. We have about eight hours of darkness to move our asses. We go at the speed of our weakest man. We didn't tap any kegs of water in there, so let's take it easy on drinking. We may have to make it last for two more days. No water between here and the coast unless somebody is good with a staff against a hard rock."

Murdock heard a few chuckles and figured they were the Bible students.

"Lam, keep us on a due south course unless a valley shows that will keep us out of climbing up and down these damn mountains. We can zigzag a little and make better time, so be it. Now, let's settle down and put in a good six miles an hour. Even if we can average four an hour, that will put us halfway to the bloody Gulf of Oman before daylight."

He dropped back and walked beside Kat.

"How's it going, SEAL lady?"

She grinned. "So far I haven't had to fire a shot. Maybe I'm a little disappointed. The bombs were not even half-done. They won't be able to salvage anything from those blasts to use for new bombs. We've put their program back at least a year."

"Good. Now, about you. When I talked about going the speed of our weakest man, I didn't mean you. Magic Brown has a shot-up leg. He'll slow us down. As long as he's conscious, he'll walk. They'll be coming after us, so don't lose your shooting eye. You'll have plenty of times to test it out before we get wet."

Kat looked at Murdock in the Iranian darkness. He liked the gleam of determination he saw in her eyes.

25

Wednesday, November 2

2100 hours
Nuclear bomb factory
Chah Bahar, Iran

General Reza Ruhollah had been outside his commandeered headquarters at the bomb plant and on his way to where his men reported a firefight was in progress with aggressors. He was furious.

"How the hell did anyone find us?" he had asked his major aide. Then he shook his head. "If they did find us, how did they get through our security? Call out the rest of the military guard. Do it now."

The major scurried away from the staff car where he had been talking to the general through the window. He headed for the nearest building with a phone.

General Ruhollah had just ordered his driver to head for the bomb assembly plant, when the gigantic explosion rocked the whole area and turned the night into a false dawn as one thundering blast roared toward him and then on past with a surging rush of gale-force wind.

"What in hell?" Ruhollah stepped out of the car and stared ahead. Two hundred yards away, flames lit the sky. He bolted back in the car.

"Drive," he shouted. "Get to that fire. Now!"

The driver started the car and drove ahead. A block closer to the fire he had to jog around debris in the road that evidently had been blasted there by the explosion. Half a block from the fire the driver stopped. A truck lay on its side in the road where it had been blown from near the bomb assembly building.

"Far as we can drive, sir," the driver said.

The general pushed open the door and stepped out. A wall of heat hit him and drove him back a step.

"How could this happen?"

He looked around. A half dozen officers had gathered just out of the heat zone. He called to them, and they came over and saluted.

"How bad is the damage?"

"General, sir. The entire assembly plant has been blasted out of existence. We're not sure if it was a malfunction of some of our explosives to be used in the bombs, or something else."

"Explosives in a nuclear bomb?"

"Yes, my General. Ten or twelve powerful ones set in a circle around the device. The mechanism will squirt tritium into the core at the moment the explosives ignite. This generates large quantities of neutrons to boost the fission reaction. That reaction in turn blasts more neutrons into another tritium supply, causing a fusion reaction. We were projecting about four hundred and fifty kilotons for each bomb."

"How could this explosion happen?" General Ruhollah bellowed. "I want a complete investigation. Wasn't there an attack from outside the wire tonight? How did that happen? Did we catch the attackers? Someone told me that there were some lights shot out in one section of the fence. Who did this? Is there a chance that there was some kind of invasion of our facility?"

"Yes, my General. We have had reports of a small enemy

force inside the wire. They killed a large number of our troops, and evidently forced all the civilian workers out of the bomb assembly building. They were military of some kind. The civilians did not recognize any insignia or style of uniform."

"Why wasn't I told about this before now?" General Ruhollah screeched, his face turning red.

"We only now found out. There was an officers party for our commander's birthday, and—"

"Idiots. You'll all be shot, of course. Consider yourself under house arrest. Go now."

The officers saluted. The General didn't bother to return the salute. He edged closer to the flames. They were dying down now. Most of the building was indeed gone. There were only partial walls in places, no roof at all. The concrete floor of the large building seemed to be the only thing left intact.

Gone.

All six of his wonderful nuclear bombs were gone.

He would have to start over. Build a new assembly building. Buy the hard-to-find plutonium and the tritium, and do all of the delicate machine tooling. Again.

He paled then, thinking about the promises he had made to certain of his confidants. Within two months they would have six nuclear bombs. He had promised them that as an absolute, and the last of the huge amount of money had been designated for him.

Could he win them over for more money now that this setback had wiped out any possibility of getting the weapons in the near future? He figured it would take two years, even with the start they had with the facilities, and the experienced men doing the work. Two years. He shivered. Pursuit.

He must find out where the attackers left the facility, and send every man he had chasing after them. Yes, that much he could do. He had two hundred regulars here, well-trained fighting men, some with combat experience.

He hurried back to the car.

"To my headquarters, quickly."

When he walked in, the facility commander and his top three men stood waiting for him.

"General Ruhollah, we were attacked."

"I'm well aware of that. Where did the force come in? Where did it leave the wire? Did they leave any dead behind?"

"General, they came in through a hole they cut in the wire about midway along the west fence. They shot out the lights on both sides, after they launched a diversion attack to the far end of the complex. They shot down our helicopter. We have found where they exited, near the southern end of the wire, where a fence closed off a construction road that led south to the rock quarry."

"Idiots, have you sent troops after them?"

"No, General."

"Send fifty heavily armed guards at once. The best men you have. Is there another helicopter?"

"No, General. We have one at Chah Bahar, but it was ordered to remain there."

"Phone now, get it up here at first light."

The Colonel in charge of the facility had been pointing at officers, and rushing them out of the room for each assignment.

"Now, Colonel, I am horrified at your security arrangements. You have set our program back by at least two years. You will be brought up on charges of high treason. Consider yourself under house arrest. Who is your second in command?"

"Sir, that would be me." A Major stepped forward and saluted.

"You, too, will be up on charges. Depending on how well you clean up the rubble of the assembly building, and reconstruct it, then bring in the required new machinery, equipment, and supplies that are needed, then we will see how severe your penalty will be. Be sure those troops chasing the attackers have orders to kill all of the bastards."

General Ruhollah waved them all out of the room. His aide came in with a fresh pot of special Turkish coffee that he loved. He sat down at the desk and began making plans. All of the troups on the facility would be sent out at first light. They would scour a swath two miles wide. Where would the attackers go?

If they were Arab, they might go east into Pakistan. If they were from the Western whore-mongering nations, they would try to go straight south to the Gulf of Oman and escape to some ship, perhaps even a submarine.

He would send troops both directions. The southern route was the more reasonable. However they were less than thirty miles to Pakistan, and more than fifty miles to the gulf. He would call Tehran at once and order the largest plane that could land at the dirt strip at Chah Bahar to bring in paratroopers. He would fly six more helicopters, gunships with door machine guns. He would alert the MiG jet fighters at Shiraz to fly over the area, watching for any movement on the ground, and to prevent any type of air rescue of the force.

How many men did the raiders use? He had no idea. Fifty men, perhaps less. It was a hit-and-run attack. He could have done it with a dozen good men.

The headache came again, grinding, stabbing, make him shut his eyes and hold his head. He needed relief. How in this boil on the butt of the devil could he find what he needed?

Slowly he sat down and picked up the phone. He had to make the calls, to get the troops and planes coming this direction. Time was the big factor now. He would have to show that he had slaughtered the squads of men who destroyed the nuclear bombs. That was the minimum he would need to do to convince his secret cabal of supporters that he must have more money, that they must make another effort to build their own nuclear bombs. It was the only way that Iran could take its proper place as the major world power that ruled all of the Mid Eastern Arabs. Yes, it must be done.

26

Wednesday, November 2

2236 hours
Hills south of bomb plant
Southern Iran

Murdock moved his SEALs along at six miles an hour for the first quarter mile, then Doc Ellsworth caught up with him.

"Skipper, Magic can't stand the pace. Better cut it down to four mph or we'll be carrying the big guy."

"It's that bad?"

"It is. I'd give him a week of bed rest if I could."

"Stay with him. Have him give the fifty, and the ammo he has left, to somebody else."

"Will do, L-T."

Murdock slowed the pace to what he knew was a mile every fifteen minutes. After another ten minutes he called a halt.

"Check things out. Arrange your gear. Take a quick break. Holt, unpack that radio and let's give it a shot."

Three minutes later, Murdock had his message typed out on the screen. He read it again. "Bankrupt, the word is bankrupt. All is well, coming home. Murdock."

He pushed the send button and the machine encrypted the

message and shot it out in a burst that transmitted for only a tenth of a second. Bankrupt was the code word meaning the plant, and the bombs, had all been totally destroyed.

"Wait for a response?" Holt asked.

"Give them two minutes, then we're moving."

No response came. Murdock had checked his men. Ed DeWitt had done the same. Magic Brown was hurting. He was going to cost them a lot of time before they got wet.

They had heard no response from the nuclear plant. There had been no sound of any troops following them the first half mile. Now they had wound over and around hills, and any sound of pursuit would be hushed.

They marched out again.

Murdock dropped back beside Kat.

"How's it going?"

"Fine. Remember I can out-hike, outrun, out-swim any of your guys. Don't worry about me. I am aware that I haven't fired a shot in anger yet, and I'm still packing this twenty pounds of armament and ammo."

"Hey, maybe it's seven pounds, plus another six for ammo. You're lucky." He paused and watched her in the darkness. "You want to be in a firefight?"

"Not sure, but in the next fifty miles, I'd say it's more than likely that I'll find out. Right?"

"Right. Remember the damned safety." He grinned, and went back to lead the platoon just in back of the scout.

They worked down a slope, and then along a valley for another mile. Murdock checked with Lampedusa. He had a sense about direction, and the best compass in the outfit.

"We're working a little southeast, but I correct every chance I get," Lam said. "This valley looked too damn tempting to pass up."

"I agree. Magic is hurting, that's why we slowed it down. Keep no more than a hundred yards out front."

They hiked on over the barren, rocky hills and gullies, down occasional valleys, and then up slopes again.

Murdock knew they were leaving a trail. Seventeen people couldn't move across this land and not leave a path any child could follow.

They made two more miles.

Murdock thought he heard someone behind them in one long valley. He sent Jaybird Sterling back as a rear guard.

"Just hold here for ten minutes, then come along slowly. If you hear or see anything behind us, shag ass up front, and let us know."

Jaybird nodded and began walking to the rear. Murdock grinned, and went back to the front of the column.

Magic Brown's leg was worse. He walked with a decided limp now and had shucked off all of his equipment, including the combat vest. It was all he could do to keep up at a three-miles-an-hour pace. That meant anyone following them must be gaining.

Murdock turned the problem over in his mind again. Not much they could do to speed up Magic. What they had to do was slow down anyone coming behind them.

He watched the landscape. Lam had them leave a narrow gorge and angle over a sharp hill. Just as they topped it, Murdock had what he wanted. He told Lam to get all the men over the ridgeline, and then hold them. He waited for Jaybird to come.

"Got company all right, L-T. Guess they are about two miles behind us. Can't be sure, but it could be forty or fifty men, maybe more."

"Get Adams up here. Let's have a welcome-home party for our Iranian hosts. Get two of those Claymore mines we brought. Have Adams set them on trip wires about a third of the way up the slope. Put two of them in sequence and aim the blasts to go downhill. Then get your asses back up here."

Murdock told the rest of them the plan and had them spread out along the ridgeline just over the top on the reverse slope. As soon as the mines went off, the whole platoon would fire into the same area, hoping to waste anyone left standing.

Murdock settled down beside Kat. She had her MP-5 up and ready.

"This is good for fifty yards with the silencer," Kat said. "Why don't we take the silencers off? No need for quiet out here."

"Good idea." He sent word on the Motorola to have half the men with MP-5's remove the silencer and put them in their packs.

Murdock checked his watch. It was after 0120. A long time to daylight.

They waited.

For a moment, Murdock caught the sound of equipment jangling. That had to come from the Iranians.

Jaybird and Al Adams rolled over the ridge, and found places along the shooting line.

"All set, L-T," Jaybird reported.

"We all fire when the second Claymore goes off," Murdock said. "Don't wait for me. Fire on that second blast."

Five minutes later they could hear some talk from below.

A cough.

Then someone called out in Farsi.

"Said something about hurry up, too slow," Franklin reported.

Two minutes more.

The Iranian hillside blossomed with a jagged red-and-yellow light and a rolling, cracking explosion as the first Claymore detonated. The flash of light faded in a few seconds, but the shrill cries of pain and desperation echoed up the hill. The sound of the first explosion had almost faded when the second blast tore through the night.

A half second later sixteen weapons fired down the slope. Murdock had his MP-5 set on three rounds and the silencer off. He chattered out six rounds and looked over at Kat.

She held the weapon tightly, stared down the sights, and at last squeezed the trigger. It spat out three rounds. She nodded, moved the muzzle slightly, and fired again. Then Murdock went back to his own weapon and emptied one magazine, before he hit his mike three times, ending the shooting.

"We moving down there?" DeWitt asked.

"No," Murdock said, making up his mind in a nanosecond. "Let's saddle up and get out of here. Lam out front. Come on, move. Some of the survivors might still come after us." The platoon heard the order on their radios, and quickly moved down the hill, away from the slaughter, half expecting some return fire from survivors who would work their way up the hill and fire blindly in revenge.

After a half mile, they figured no one was going to shoot back at them.

"An even bet that they will wait for dawn, and count up their casualties, then try to get their wounded back to the nuke plant," Murdock said on the radio. "Meantime we make tracks until dawn ourselves, then figure out what to do."

Murdock checked on Magic. He was still walking, but his left arm was over Horse Ronson's shoulder.

"Hell, we can keep up with you Boy Scouts," Magic said. But Murdock heard the voice nearly crack. There was none of the usual bluster the big black man was so good at projecting.

They kept walking.

At 0300, Murdock called a break.

Doc changed the bandage on Magic's left leg. He shook his head. It was still bleeding. He put a heavy pressure pad over the wound and wrapped it tightly. The bleeding stopped. He checked his watch. Too soon for another morphine shot.

By the time Doc finished binding up Magic's leg, he had dropped off to sleep. Doc went to Murdock.

"Can we give Magic an hour to sleep? He went out like a baby. He's damn weak, L-T."

"We've got two hours to dawn. He can sleep then. Let him have a half hour, then we get out of here. We've got to find a spot to hole up for the daylight hours."

Murdock had Douglas come up front.

"You said you saw a high-wing Piper Cub–type spotter plane. There wasn't any place I saw near the bomb plant where they could land one. Did it come up from Chah Bahar?"

"My guess is that they have a small dirt strip somewhere in back of the plant. You can land those things on two hundred yards, sometimes less. A bulldozer and two days would scrape out a workable landing field."

"So, it will be in the air at first light. We need to be dug in somewhere. Thanks, Douglas. You and Franklin did an outstanding job going into Tehran. Have to tell me some-time how you got fifteen hundred miles down here."

Douglas waved, and went back to his spot in the Second Squad formation.

They called a halt at 0530. It wasn't dawn yet. Lampedusa had found a craggy little canyon with lots of twists and turns and places where the cloudbursts had sent torrents down the place, carving out holes, sharp edges, and sinks.

"Just like before," Murdock said on the Motorola. "Find yourself a hole and crawl in. Have your camo cloth ready to cover up for the spotter plane. Anybody have any trouble, give a yell."

Murdock watched Kat. She was the first one to pick a spot, settle in a hollow, and pull the camo cloth over her, right up to her eyes. He eased down beside her.

"You get in any rounds back up there?"

"Yep."

"Hit anybody?"

"Don't know. Actually I don't want to know. I fired the damn weapon like I was supposed to." There was a sharpness in her tone. He looked at her but she didn't say anything more.

"Right. You did fine. Some sleep wouldn't hurt." Murdock checked the covers for each of his people. Ed did the same. Murdock said he'd take the first watch of two hours. They'd be in place all day, so some sleep would be good. "If we hear that spotter plane, I'll give some clicks on your Motorola."

He watched the sixteen settle down. Within ten minutes he had trouble remembering who was where. Most of them he couldn't pick out from twenty yards away. He found his own spot where the water had dug out a two-foot-deep gully and squirmed into it. He sat with his back against the end of the hole and watched.

"Murdock," Kat said softly. She was about ten feet away.

"Yes."

"You do good work."

"Thanks, Kat. So do you."

She was quiet then and Murdock turned to watch a small tarantula moving up on a large beetle. It would be no contest once the tarantula got its stinging tail working.

An hour later he heard the first buzz of an airplane motor.

"People, Third Platoon. We have company. A wee aircraft somewhere to the north. Not sure how far away or if he's coming our direction. Just want to be sure you know he's about. DeWitt, take a squad check."

Murdock listened as all seven of his squad members checked in. Murdock did the same for First Squad. They reported in order of march.

"So, everyone's awake, we'll see where our little buddy airplane goes."

It was quiet then. Now and then they could hear a whisper from a soft breeze that missed them in the gully, and the call of an occasional bird. Murdock didn't remember seeing a bird since they had landed in this desolate spot. Must be a desert hawk or a vulture of some kind.

The tarantula struck once, and the stunned beetle turned toward it. The second lash of the tail penetrated the beetle's shell, and a moment later the black bug collapsed on its legs and the tarantula moved up for its meal.

The sound of the plane came closer. Murdock moved lower in his hole and pulled the camo cloth up higher. He wished he had brought some binoculars. Next time.

A moment later the aircraft flew directly over them across the gully, so the pilot or observer would have only a few seconds to look into the ravine.

"Surprise," Murdock said in his mike. "Check your cover, he'll be back. Don't think he can see our foot tracks from even that altitude, but can't be sure. Next time we wipe out our tracks before we hole up."

They waited fifteen minutes and couldn't hear the plane.

"Doubt if he'll be back now," Murdock radioed. "Let's get some sleep."

He looked over at the small animal war. The victor had eaten and left. There was nothing remaining of the big black beetle but the hard shell and two spindly legs.

Survival.

That's what life is all about. Especially for the Third Platoon right now. Survival. His job was to get his men, and Kat, out of Iran without losing anyone.

Survival.

"Murdock?"

It was Kat.

"You don't sound asleep."

"Not nearly. How many men did you say Iran has under arms?"

"Over half a million."

"Oh, damn. And only seventeen of us."

The silence stretched out.

"Logically, it seems that they should be able to throw a couple of thousand troops between us and the coast, stop us cold."

"It would seem so, wouldn't it, Kat?"

"Hey, Lieutenant. I know you and your men are good—hell, the best at this kind of work. But the odds of a thousand to one say there really isn't much you can do."

"Kat, they have to find us before they can stop us."

"After last night's hit on their people, they will damn well know which direction we're headed."

"True, Kat. True. They still have to find us."

Another silence.

"How long before they fly in the reserves? What will it be, paratroopers dropping in on us out of the daytime sky?"

"Probably. And trucked-in troops when we get down far enough that there are a few roads into this barren, desert wilderness."

"Murdock, we practiced that chopper rescue at sea, when we went up the rope ladder. Couldn't they do that on land just as well, or even set down on a gully floor somewhere?"

"Could. But then you have an open overflight of a foreign military force. Plainly an invasion of a sovereign nation. The brass doesn't like to do that sort of thing."

"Remember that old World War Two movie, *They Were Expendable*?"

"I remember the title. We're not in that class. The SEALs never leave one man behind on a battlefield, let alone a whole fucking platoon."

"Sorry, guess I'm thinking too much."

"Never hurts to think, Kat."

"Yeah, maybe. I'm done thinking. I'm gonna snore."

Murdock chuckled. "You do that. I'll never tell."

"Murdock?"

"Sure."

"You said we never leave a man behind. What if a two-hundred-forty-pound man got killed. Say today. How can we carry that man's body out forty miles without compromising the rest of the platoon?"

"Point taken. I buried one SEAL on foreign soil. Last

mission we towed a body through the surf and out to sea for
a submarine pickup. I didn't like either job. I'm going to do
my damnedest to see that I don't have to do either one of
them again."

"But it could happen?"

"Absolutely."

"Good night, Murdock."

"Yeah, dreams of D.C."

Murdock looked over to where Kat lay, but for a moment
couldn't find her. Then the ground moved slightly, her camo
cover. He nodded, and stared down their back trail. They
were on the side of the gully well off the small valley's
floor. He could see over two small ridges they had climbed.

His head snapped to one side as he refocused on one spot
along the back trail. Had he seen a flash of light? He concentrated on the area, and it came again, a flash of sunlight
off something.

Off what? An Iranian soldier's unblued rifle barrel? A
shiny unit metal pin?

He estimated the distance. Not more than two miles.
Could there be a force of Iranian infantry that close to them?
There was no way their tracks directly to this ravine could
be missed by a land unit.

Murdock spoke softly into his mike. "DeWitt, we may
have a problem. Check the back trail. Thought I saw some
sun flashes back there."

"I'm looking," DeWitt said. "So far nothing."

"I'm higher on the ravine," Jaybird said. "Let me give it
a five-minute scan. If they have a unit that close, we just
jumped into a sinkhole of deep shit."

27

Thursday, November 3

0740 hours
Hills south of bomb plant
Southern Iran

Jaybird watched for the flash. It was two or three minutes later when he spoke. "Oh, yeah, I see it again. One odd thing about it, I don't see any movement."

Ed DeWitt chimed in on the Motorola net. "Yeah, I had the same feeling. Either the troops are hunkered down there resting, or it's something not connected to Iranian military."

"Which would be great news for us," Murdock said. He scowled for a minute. "We better know which. Lam, you tuned in?"

"Yes, sir."

"How about a small scouting mission. You can stick to the shadows this early for most of the way. You'll need to get up that second small ridge to check it out."

"On my way. I'll leave my vest here and take my Colt. It's what, about two miles. That's about fifteen minutes each way. I'll try out the Motorola at two miles and see what you receive."

"Go, take care. If it is the Iranians and they come at you, we'll have the fifty out and warmed up."

"That's a Roger, L-T. I'm on my way."

Murdock saw a patch of bare sand twenty yards ahead of him collapse, then Lampedusa lifted out, left the camo cloth, and jogged down the ravine, careful not to step on anybody.

They watched him work along the Iranian hills. Some of the time they couldn't see him in the shadows. The desert cammies blended in well with the barren landscape.

He made it up the first slope, and paused. He couldn't see the flashing from there.

"The flashes keep coming," DeWitt said. "Still looks like the same spot. No movement is a good sign."

Five minutes later, they saw him cresting the second ridge. He flattened out, and seemed to look over the top. The report came in snatches on the Motorola. It was line of sight, which helped.

"Nada . . . see . . . neg . . . On my . . ." He broke off the transmission, and jogged back down the slope, into more shadows.

Fifteen minutes later he was back.

"Some kind of a tin can. It was off our line of march. Maybe one of the prospectors left it there. Bright and shiny with the label torn off. It rolled back and forth between two little ridges, and flashed the sun on most of the moves."

Murdock told them to get back to sleep.

Ed DeWitt said he'd take the watch. He said Franklin would be next up in two hours. Murdock pulled the camo coverup over him and tried to get comfortable. He didn't make it.

"Lieutenant, you might try counting the live Iraqis and the Saudi Arabians that we saved by blowing up those nukes." It was Kat. "Iran would have run roughshod over this part of the world. All they would have to do was drop one bomb to take out a secondary Arab city, and the whole subcontinent would fall right into their laps."

"About what State said in some of their comments. They were dead set on killing the Iranian project. If we make a little noise about it, it could slow down efforts by other Arab states to try the same thing."

"Like Iraq. Yeah, I agree."

Murdock shook his head. "Somehow visions of pretty Arab girls with veils on jumping over a fence don't help me sleep."

"You'll think of something. Good night again, Murdock."

"Yeah, Kat, good dreams to you, too."

Murdock figured he must have nodded off. The next thing he knew his earpiece yelped at him.

"We got trouble, L-T." It was Franklin's voice so it must be after 1000 hours. "That damn spotter plane is coming back. He's been around this area for five minutes, but this time he's coming dead over us going up the gully the long way. Gives him a good look at our little colony here."

"Everyone check your camo cloths, be sure everything is under cover," Murdock said loudly in the mike to be sure to wake everyone.

DeWitt took a squad check, then Murdock did the same. All hands were awake and covered.

Then the light plane swung into place directly over the ravine. There were no tall mountains around it, and the small bird had to be no more than fifty feet over the top of the hill that had spawned the ravine. Murdock marveled at how slow the plane flew, then figured it had a headwind to keep the wing fooled about the stall speed.

The plane seemed to hang in the air almost motionless, then dipped its nose slightly. The engine gunned, and it flew on over the hill above the gully.

"Did he see anything?" DeWitt asked.

"Not fucking much," Ron Holt said.

Lampedusa came on. "Don't be too sure. I hear a chopper."

They were all quiet for a minute.

"Oh, yeah, I've got him coming straight up our gullet. He

can take all the look time he needs to." It was Joe Douglas talking.

"Check those coverups," Murdock said. "Everyone stay undercover, and don't even breathe. He'll be over us in about thirty seconds. Small, chopper, not more than a four-man rig. No more transmissions."

Murdock knew it was highly unlikely that the small chopper would have a scanner-type receiver that could pick up anything broadcast by checking all frequencies a hundred times a minute. But they kept quiet anyway.

Murdock had a slit in the camo cloth over his eyes to watch through. The chopper came straight at them, up the length of the twisting and turning ravine. It was about seventy-five yards long here. Plenty of room for the troops, but also a small area for the chopper to concentrate on. The bird moved slower, then hovered well down the gully.

Murdock worried that it might get so low that it would blow the camo cloth right off his men. Then the chopper did a little dance as a serious updraft caught it and boosted it twenty yards more into the sky.

It came down a little, and still the men inside appeared to concentrate on the spot where Third Platoon had hidden. It moved closer, then had to lift a little to clear the sharp side of the canyon's wall.

Murdock saw the rotor wash from the chopper kick up dust in the canyon. The ship moved higher so the dust wouldn't obscure everything on the ground. A flap of one of the cammo cloths lifted up a moment, then settled back down, covering the SEAL.

Murdock held his breath. The chopper moved forward, up the slope, went past where Murdock and Kat lay, and higher, until it had to surge upward to get over the top of the canyon's slopes.

Then it was gone.

"He will be back," Murdock said in his mike. "Make sure

that all the corners of your hideout camo cloth are secure. We almost had one whip off somebody a moment ago."

As he finished saying it, the helicopter made a return run, working down the slope this time, keeping a little higher so it wouldn't kick up dust, but this also kept the men inside from making a detailed observation of the area.

Murdock eased apart the camo cloth and watched the bird move down the slope. At the bottom it paused, hovering, dropped down to ten feet, and kicked up a storm cloud of dust and dirt, then lifted away, and vanished over the next hill to the north.

"L-T, I don't think he'll be back this time," Doc said. "I should check on Magic."

"Go," Murdock said.

A piece of the desert opened up and folded back, and Doc Ellsworth scurried down ten yards and pulled back another piece of camo cloth. He worked quickly, removing the old bandage, adding some disinfectant, then wrapping the wound again. When he was done, he eased the leg back under the camo cloth, piled sand around the outside of it and hurried back to his own hide hole.

"L-T. Like I told Magic, his leg doesn't look any better. A little more swelling. There's infection inside the wound that I can't get to. That slug has got to come out in thirty-six hours."

"Right, Doc. We'll try to figure something." He checked his watch. It was 1042. Too damn much daylight left. He figured this first day would be the hardest, while they were the closest to the nuke plant.

"Let's get some more sleep," Murdock said. "Who's on watch?"

"I am," Kat said.

Murdock started to protest, then shook his head. "Good, Kat. Stay awake, stay alert to any sound or sight that might get us in trouble. Yell into your mike if that chopper comes back or you see any paratroopers hitting the silk."

"Aye, aye, L-T. I can do that."

Murdock lifted the edge of his camo cloth and looked over at Kat. She had pushed up a little so her face was out of the camo. It gave her a good view of the canyon and the hills beyond and the sky. She was set.

Murdock couldn't go to sleep. The adrenaline still pulsated through his system. It had been close with that chopper. One loose chunk of camo cover and they would have been made. Running in the daylight would have been fatal for them.

At least eight more hours of daylight. What else could go wrong?

"Murdock. Murdock. Wake up, L-T."

Murdock came out of his sleep rubbing his eyes, almost pushing the camo cloth away, then he remembered. "Yes, Kat?"

"Yes. We've got a plane. Bigger one, at least two propellers up high. Seems to be cruising around waiting for some instructions. I've seen it three times now. Must be up four or five thousand feet. Could be more. Not going fast, so it isn't a jet. Sounds like a prop plane."

"I saw it," Les Quinley said. "Must have been the last pass. Kat's right, it's up high, just cruising. My guess is paratroopers. Not more than, maybe, fifteen in a crate like that."

"Figures," Murdock said. "They could fly a plane up here from Chah Bahar. If they have paratroopers there, they could dump them out of anything that flew and had a door to open."

"Sure, but they still need a pinpoint location to drop them," DeWitt chimed in. "That they don't have because the chopper and the spotter plan haven't given them one yet. We're still in the ball game."

"Yeah, but when do we get to bat?" It was Ken Ching.

"We had our first inning ups," Murdock said. "Back there on that hill last night, and we hit a home run. Now we wait for our next shot at batting. Until then it's a waiting game. Not a damn thing we can do until it gets dark."

"Seven more fucking hours!" somebody said.

Murdock checked his watch. 1208. "Who's next on watch?"

"I'll do it," Al Adams said. "Can't sleep on this damn gravel mattress anyway."

"So, the rest of you, get some sleep. It's going to be one hell of a long night once we get in motion."

"Murdock." It was Kat across the way.

He turned away from his lip mike. "Yes, Kat."

"I keep thinking about that damn movie."

"That was another time, another war. Hell, we had over four hundred thousand dead in World War Two. That's the war that movie was about, the Expendables. Couple of dozen more was nothing back then."

"Except for that couple of dozen."

"True." There was a long silent time.

"So we're seventeen," Murdock said. "We have more accidental deaths than that every year in the services. One year the Navy lost almost three hundred men and women dead in auto crashes while off duty."

"Yeah, but you're on duty," Kat said. "I've been thinking about Magic. There is no way he can last three or four days. Not a chance he can walk another, what, forty miles, or more. Hell, Murdock, maybe we are expendable."

"No chance. Shut up that kind of talk. We're all getting out of here, every one of us. Magic included. Now, Lieutenant Kat, I fully expect you to get to sleep. You'll need the rest once we start moving with the darkness."

"Yes, Daddy," she said. He could imagine that sneaky grin of hers.

He snorted and closed his eyes. He figured he'd just rest them a minute.

When he woke up, it was 1640. He let the camo part

briefly and looked around. He couldn't see anybody. Good. He positioned the lip mike.

"Who is on watch?"

"Washington," the answer came back.

"Anything moving?"

"No, sir. No planes or choppers, nothing except one hyper mouse of some kind and a giant tarantula. Each thinks he's going to eat the other one."

Murdock eased back his camo cloth and sat up, resting his back against the sculptured dirt. He took a much folded topographical map of the area from inside his shirt and checked it. He had plotted in the exact location of the plant previously, using the mugger. Now he estimated the distance they had moved south. Was it six or eight miles?

He wanted to know. He took out the mugger. It was the size of a cellular phone and had been in his webbing. He pulled out a small antenna they had adapted for land use, turned on the set, and let it search for the closest four Global Positioning Satellites in high orbit overhead.

Within a few seconds they were locked on and reported his exact location within a plus or minus ten feet. He read the alphanumerical figures on the small screen. They were longitude and latitude. He checked the map again, made a few wavy lines from the borders, and nailed down the position. They were a little over ten miles from the plant. That left forty miles.

Magic, Magic, Magic. He put the mugger away and tried to come up with something that would work. That one small plane, with ten to twenty paratroopers, could blow up into ten or twelve large transports with a hundred paratroops in each one. They could bring in truckloads of infantry when the SEALs got closer to the coast. Damnit, Iran could seal off the coast from them with five thousand troops if they really wanted to.

From everything he had seen so far, somebody wanted to

catch them so bad that he would use every available man and machine that Iran had at its military command.

The watch changed. Murdock was still thinking about what to do when the sun slid behind the mountain to the west and dusk fell.

"Up and at 'em," Murdock said in the mike. "Time to haul ourselves out of here and make some time down the road."

Doc was the first one to Murdock, even before he had his cammo sheet folded and packed.

"Better come and talk to Magic, L-T. He's not good. We're gonna have to do something to keep him with us."

28

Thursday, November 3

1910 hours
Hills south of bomb plant
Southern Iran

"Magic? How bad is he? What do you mean do something to keep him with us?"

"Not fatal, no, he's in good spirits. His damn leg is hurting like crazy. I've overdosed him on morphine as it is. What I think we better do is trash his pistol and K-bar, all of his equipment. Dig a hole for it. He can't carry anything but himself. Somebody else has the fifty and the ammo."

All around them men came out of their holes, dusted off the cammo cloth, and folded it up. Murdock knelt down beside Magic, who sat on the ground.

"Hey, Magic. Shuck out of that combat vest. You don't need to carry that anymore. We'll leave it here for the stupid Iranians. Put it in your hole and have the guys kick it full of dirt from the sides. Nobody will find it for a hundred years. How are you feeling?"

"Hurts like hell, L-T. Got myself fucked up good this time. Holding up the march. Fuck it!"

"No sweat. We're going to get out of here. Dark now, and they can't see us, so we move on down the trail. Another good night of hiking, and we'll be close to the water."

"Try my damnedest, L-T."

Murdock slapped him on the shoulder gently, and went back to his hole. He had his gear on, and his weapon in hand in a minute, and checked around. Nobody could tell that they had been there. Kat stood waiting for him.

"Magic?"

"Not good. We'll be moving at his pace."

Murdock sent Lam out front, then brought up Magic and Ronson in line right behind Kat. Magic had his arm across Ronson's shoulder. Just moving fifty feet was work for Magic. They hiked back down to the small valley, and used it for half a mile before they had to climb another of the never-ending hills.

Murdock figured they were making less than two miles an hour now. Magic was dragging one foot as he moved forward.

Just past 2040, Lam came back and called to Murdock.

"Got some company up front. Don't know where they came from, but they're on a damned picnic. Three big fires, and what must be about twenty small cooking fires. You better take a look."

The moon had come out from behind some clouds, and the outline of a valley fully a quarter of a mile wide showed in the dim light. In the center of it were the fires. Voices floated up from half a mile away. Murdock figured the valley was a mile long. A huge open space in this maze of ridges, canyons, gullies, and mountains.

"Must be a hundred men down there," Murdock said. "Twenty cooking fires and five men to a fire. Too many for us. Can we slip by at the left-hand edge of the valley? It looks like they're slightly toward the right side."

"I'll go take a look. Be a lot easier on Magic if we can. How's he doing?"

"Not the best. As long as he can walk, we move."

The men, and Kat, moved up to the edge of the valley and

waited for Lam. He moved out like a shadow, and was soon lost in the nighttime haze.

Ten minutes later, he came back.

"Yeah, lots of room, as long as we don't talk or rattle. They don't have any security out, no patrols, from what I could tell. I hope they don't surprise us."

Al Adams took Ronson's place, helping Magic and the file move out. They were five yards apart now, in combat mode, just in case a lucky round or fragger came in. That way it could nail only one man.

They moved silently along the open valley. It was smooth and flat, and looked like it might have been a huge lake at one time. They came near the Iranian troops, heard them shouting and laughing, and moved on past without a word.

When they were at the end of the valley, they lifted up and over a slight rise, then Lam had a new bearing for them. Again they angled to the right, and went along a new small valley, then over another low ridge and down a narrow ravine into what might have been a streambed, which lasted for almost a mile. Then it simply vanished.

"Underground," DeWitt said. "The ancient river probably went underground at this point."

They took a break. Magic sat down and Doc looked at his leg. It was swollen more. It had started bleeding again. Doc replaced the bandage and wrapped it. Magic gritted his teeth through it all.

Ken Ching came up and talked to Magic.

"Hey, man, you ever been hypnotized?"

"No, I don't want to run around flapping my arms and crowing like a chicken."

Ken laughed. "Not that show business stuff, the real medical kind of hypnotism."

"Nope, not me. Nobody's gonna dangle a watch in front of me and put me out. I want to know what I'm doing."

Ken shrugged. "Just wondered. Hypnotism is sometimes used to control intense pain."

"Hell, not me."

Ken waved and moved back to his gear. Doc followed him.

"Ching, you can hypnotize people?"

"Sure, been doing it for years. I do myself when I go to the dentist, no Novocain that way."

"Let me work on Magic. If you hypnotized him, the pain would still be there, but he wouldn't feel it?"

"Right. He'd still limp and walk with a lot of trouble, but the pain would be gone."

"I'll get back to you."

They moved out again.

Murdock listened to what Doc had to say about Ken Ching.

"Yes, it works," Murdock said. "But Magic would have to want to be hypnotized before he'd go under. Talk about it to the big guy."

Murdock checked his watch. 2300. They had been on the move for over two hours. Murdock figured they had covered five miles at the most. He wasn't sure how Magic did it. If he went down, their run would be over.

A half hour later, they had managed another small ridge, worked through one more half-mile valley, and climbed up another slope. Doc Ellsworth came back to Murdock.

"Magic says what the fuck, give it a try. Ken says we won't even have to stop walking. He'll do it all with his voice. If you hear some mumbling and grumbling back here, that's what it is."

Murdock sagged back a few steps to listen.

"Magic, you know me. You know I wouldn't do anything to hurt you in any way, right?"

"Yeah, man, right."

"Okay, I'm going to hypnotize you. That just means that you and I will work together to put you in a kind of trance. In this trance you won't do anything that you wouldn't do ordinarily. I can't turn you into a rapist or a robber or anything like that. Do you understand?"

"Yeah, get on with it."

Murdock moved away then, checked with Lam, and they angled to the right this time to keep on their southern route.

When he got back, Doc waited for him.

"Damn that was cool. Magic went under in about a minute. Ken said he was a good subject. For the past five hundred yards, he hasn't groaned once or said anything about pain. He's even walking better. No foot drag, which might have been psychological. He's good for a fast three miles an hour, so we can step it up if you want to."

They did.

Twice before midnight they heard planes flying over. Some were obviously prop-powered and small. Two or three times they heard jets streaking overhead.

"Tomorrow is not going to be an easy twelve hours of daylight," Murdock said.

They took a break at 0100. Magic was talking and joking with the guys around him. Doc checked the leg wound and found no new bleeding.

"Magic, how you doing?" Murdock asked, squatting down beside where the big black man sat.

"Fucking good, L-T. How the hell you doing?"

"I'm gonna make it, Magic. Got to get us wet so we can talk turkey with that fucking submarine."

"Oh, yeah, in the wet this damn leg won't bother me none. It don't want to work right. Doc says I got shot."

"Just a scratch. Don't worry about it."

To one side, Murdock asked Ken Ching how long the trance would last.

"I can reinforce it every three hours. He'll be good until daylight. Then we'll let him pass into a normal sleep."

They ate MRE's there and left twenty minutes later. The next two hours went according to plan. Magic kept up, Miguel Fernandez was now helping him, with his arm over

Miguel's shoulder. They made their six miles and Murdock pulled them up at the side of a high mountain.

Ahead of them a gentle valley opened up that went too far to the east, but they decided they would take it. Just before their short break was over, Lam came back with news.

"I was out front a ways, and I heard some choppers." He pointed down the valley. "Seem to be coming from that direction."

They all looked that way then, and a half mile in front of them they heard large helicopters coming in. Then the choppers snapped on landing lights, making six round islands of light in the wilderness of night.

"Goddamnit to hell," Murdock said. "Lam, get as close as you can and see how many men get off each bird."

Lam left at a sprint, settled down to a trot, and made a quarter of a mile in fast time. He walked forward carefully. At a hundred yards he went flat on the ground. The last chopper had landed and disgorged its troops.

Lam counted twenty-five combat-ready troopers getting off each chopper. Then the birds lifted off, turned off their landing lights, and flew back to the south.

Murdock was surprised by the number of troops on each bird. "That's a hundred and fifty men out there looking for us." He shook his head. "We were making good time. DeWitt and Jaybird, let's talk."

They worked it over for five minutes and all agreed. What was open was the direction. Murdock decided that.

"Okay, platoon, listen up. We're blocked down front. Lam said they were sending out security and what looked like patrols. We can only go around them. We head due east for Pakistan. We're still about ten to twelve miles from it. We'll go east for two miles, then swing south again and maintain that heading. Any questions?"

"Only a hundred and a half?" Gonzalez called out. "Hell, L-T, let's take them. Them ain't bad odds for SEALs."

There were some quiet voices of agreement.

"Now I know that Gonzalez has his insurance paid up," Murdock said. "Okay Lam, lead us out due east."

Kat came up beside Murdock. She had been step for step with the SEALs all the way.

"Maybe we could go all the way into Pakistan. We've had better relations with them than with Iran."

"Their border guards wouldn't ask any questions, Kat. They would shoot us down to get our weapons. No chance we're going across the border. We'll skirt it if we have to, but we'll still be eight to ten miles away. We just jog around this bunch and hope for a better tomorrow."

The landscape changed as they headed east. Here and there they found shrubs and a few trees. In the gullies now were some brush and stunted trees. Murdock hoped they would find some kind of cover like this when daylight came. They could do the hide hole again, but they had been lucky last time. He didn't believe in straining the fates any more than he had to.

Magic Brown was walking better now, and Doc couldn't explain it. He asked Chin.

"The physical pain is still there. The injury is there. But the more he forgets about it, and subjugates it, the better he feels, therefore the better he can walk. Once the trance is gone, the pain will come back like gangbusters. Happened to me the time I had a root canal with hypnosis. The dentist was scared as hell. I told him if I came out of it and started screaming, he could shoot me with a bucket of painkiller."

Dock hesitated. "Chin, with him hypnotized that way, could I go in and hunt for that damned slug?"

"Sure, he won't feel a thing. Do you have the right kind of instruments?"

"Hell no. I've got one probe, a pair of forceps, and a K-bar. About all I have I can use."

"Might do more damage than leaving it alone."

"If it's in there another twenty-four hours, he could lose the leg."

"Hell, give it a try. I'd check with the L-T, though, first. You'll need light or daylight. Either one will be risky for the whole platoon."

Doc talked with Murdock as they hiked along the hills. They were doing more up and down now since the former rivers and any runoff had been going south the way they wanted to go.

Doc explained it to Murdock.

"We'll wait and see about the light. If we find some cover, it might work. If not, we could start a fire or something in a protected spot and line up everyone around it. Let's see closer to morning."

They had made good time the first two miles east, then Lam turned them south again, and they caught a fine valley that made the night march easier.

There were fewer of the shrubs and small trees here, but as they came closer to the coast, Murdock figured there should be more rain, and perhaps more vegetation. They had come another four miles south when Murdock realized it was stopping time. Lam came back with a report that he might have a canyon with some cover. They hiked another ten minutes and just before dawn found it. The brush and trees were no more than three feet tall, but they covered a small canyon ten yards wide and fifty long, as it angled up toward a really large mountain. There must have been some natural runoff here, and any rains would bring down a torrent of fresh water from the catch basin higher up.

Murdock grinned—some good luck at last. The men dug into the tangle of brush and trees and within ten minutes they all had vanished. Murdock pushed in past Kat and found a place he could stretch out. He hit the Motorola.

"I hope all of you are happy with your five-star accommodations. Remember, we're short on water. Ken, see that Magic gets moved into his sleep mode. I have the first watch. The rest of you can eat an MRE or sack out, whichever you want.

"Doc, let's think about that job you might do. It looks possible. You could fix up your area for it later this morning when we check out our actual cover in the daylight."

Lam came on the net. "L-T, I've been seeing some lightning to the north. I don't know how far. That could mean a storm is coming, which would mean rain."

"So, it will cool us off and we can catch some for our canteens," Fernandez said.

"Also it could trigger a flash flood. Know what a wall of water ten feet high and racing along at sixty miles an hour can do to a bunch of campers like us?"

Murdock swore again. "And we're right in the middle of a flood channel for such a torrent if it rains hard in this area. Whoever is on watch, keep an eye on the lightning. That means a spot outside the brush where you're concealed but can see to the north. This might not be the best spot to hide out after all. But we'll stay here until the storm hits to the north or bypasses us. Keep a sharp watch to the north."

29

Friday, November 4

0627 hours
Hills south of bomb plant
Southern Iran

Murdock decided he'd have to get out of the brush so he could see the north and still have some kind of concealment. He passed Kat as he crawled to the side.

"Is it really going to rain?" she asked.

He noted a touch of weariness in her voice.

"Could. Could be trouble. How you holding up?"

"We haven't even done a marathon distance yet. I'm fine. Glad Magic is doing better."

"Yeah, he's the controlling factor on this one. I'll be back in a couple of hours. Get some sleep."

She picked up an MRE. "I think I need some food more than the sleep."

He continued out of the brush to the side, and found a spot where he could see north past a small hill. He settled in below a shrub with lots of gray leaves, and checked north again. A sudden darting lightning bolt daggered down and out of sight behind the hill.

He didn't know enough about the weather patterns in southern Iran to know if the lightning was dry or if it heralded rain. He did know that rain in the desert areas like this one usually came in torrents, suddenly, and in great volume. He remembered eleven hikers in the U.S. desert southwest who were drowned in a sudden flash flood that originated from a rain ten miles away.

It was almost daylight.

Murdock winced when he heard the sound of an aircraft. A jet, probably a fighter, a MiG. It slammed over to the south behind some hills so he never saw it. That meant it was low to the ground. How could you use a Mach one fighter to do a search? It meant that the military was throwing everything they owned into the hunt, whether it would produce results or not.

Something moved to his left. His peripheral vision barely caught it. He turned slowly in that direction, and watched. It was against the hill. The movement came again, and he relaxed. The creature was small and slow, cold-blooded, some kind of a lizard, not more than a foot long. It lifted its head gradually and stared toward him. Did lizards have good eyesight? He figured they didn't. The creature was ten feet away. Its tongue darted out, evidently testing the air for scents. It turned, and waddled away into some brush, evidently satisfied that the strange creature was not a food source or held any danger.

Murdock almost dozed. The temperature rose as the light increased. They would be in the shade until about noon. A big help. He watched the small area behind them that he could see. There were slices of two slopes, and a gully no wider than the one they were in. He was nearly blind from a good observation point of view, but the concealment was worth ten times that drawback.

He looked over the brushy ravine. Nothing showed that seventeen fighters were hidden there.

Murdock hit the mike. "Doc, come and see me. I'm at the edge of the brush."

Doc Ellsworth squirmed out of some overhanging shrubs twenty feet below Murdock, walked up, and sat beside him.

"Magic?"

"Ken will help me. He decided to let Magic sleep for two hours to gain some strength. Then he'll hypnotize him again, and I'll go in and try to dig out the lead."

"I want to be there."

"Right, keep you up to date."

Doc went back to his spot, and Murdock worked on the MRE he dug out of his pack. The main course was macaroni and cheese. Who worked out these menus anyway? He ate what he could of it, buried the rest, and dug out the mugger.

He set up the antenna and took a shot at the four positioning satellites. When the figures showed up on the readout screen, he copied them down on the edge of the map, then plotted them.

They were now well east of where they had been and, from the distance on the map, still twenty-six miles from the coast. Too damn far. How would Magic react after the cutting today? One lucky Iranian bullet could stop his whole platoon dead in the water.

Nothing else happened until his two hours were up. Murdock called Ron Holt to take the next watch. He gave an acknowledgement on the Motorola, and Murdock headed back for his spot inside the brush.

Kat seemed to be sleeping.

He eased down, making as little noise as possible.

"You do this for a living," Kat said.

Murdock grinned. "Hell no, I do it for the amazing high it boots me to. I'm a thrill junkie, didn't you know? There's no war on, so what's a fighting man to do? I'm too chicken to start my own war."

Kat laughed. "Yeah, you say." She watched him in the full daylight now that filtered into the shaded areas under the thin canopy. "What are you going to do when you grow up?" she asked.

"I don't know, Kat. I might learn how to tear apart weapons of mass destruction just for the thrill of it. Why do you risk life and limb just to rip apart nukes?"

"I get this amazing high, like a thousand sexual climaxes all at once. I'm a thrill junkie."

They both chuckled.

"A thousand climaxes?" Murdock said.

"It was a figure of speech."

"Oh, good, otherwise I figure you must have exploded."

"You do have a good imagination, I like that."

"Careful, Dr. Garnet, we still could be expendable."

"Yeah, Murdock, but what a way to go. I figured I was doing mankind a favor by deactivating some nukes. But over here we just saved what I figure is at least a million lives. Iran would have dropped a bomb on some mid-sized Arab city, I'm sure. A million Arabs we saved. Now they're trying to kill us."

"Fortunes of war, Kat. And don't doubt it, this is a war. You ready for a nap? I sure am."

Kat grinned. "Does this mean I'm sleeping with you?"

Murdock laughed. "More like sleeping near me. Remember I still outrank you by date of commission."

"Good night, David."

"Good night, Chet, and you're too young to remember them," Murdock said.

"My dad's first name is Chet. He told me about them."

Murdock thought he'd just got to sleep when his Motorola clicked three times. That would be Doc. He eased away from the sleeping Kat and worked out of the brush, and down where Doc had emerged earlier. He saw Joe Douglas on watch, and crawled in where he saw Doc and Ken Ching.

"Hey, L-T. Ken's got Magic under again. I figure I'll use a tourniquet around his thigh above the wound to try to slow bleeding. I've got two pocket knives and my K-bar. First I'll use the wire probe from my kit, and see if I can find the damn bullet."

Chin held a three-inch hand mirror. He caught a beam of sunlight and bounced it directly on the wound. Doc took a six-inch-long piece of stiff spring steel wire, and gently probed it into the wound. It began bleeding.

He pushed the wire in farther and farther.

"Damn, four inches, and I don't feel a thing." He stopped. "There. I can feel it. Christ, I found the bullet. It's four inches in there." Doc wiped sweat off his forehead. He took the long-handled surgical pliers, which were slender and had an inch-long grasping head on them. He pressed the head of the tool into the wound. It bled more.

Ching soaked up the blood with a white T-shirt.

Doc sweated.

He pushed the forceps in deeper.

Blood spurted. Ching covered it.

"Another damn inch. Am I killing him? Damn, I've never dug into a body this way before."

"Do it, Doc, or he loses the leg," Murdock said.

Doc nodded, and eased the forceps in deeper, then deeper again.

"Touched it," he said, grinning. "Now if I can just get a grip on it." He opened the forceps head and probed more. When he tried to close the pliers, the head slipped off the bullet.

"Damn, missed it. Try again."

Ching used a second T-shirt to soak up the blood that kept running out of Magic's thigh.

Magic stirred in his hypnotic slumber, then relaxed.

Doc positioned the forceps again, opened them, and pressed forward more. When he closed them this time, he laughed softly.

"Got you, sucker!" He began withdrawing the instrument slowly, gripping it so hard his fingers turned white.

He had it halfway out, when a new spout of blood came out beside the forceps.

Ching covered it and nodded.

Doc pulled again, and then with a steady pressure brought the tool out of Magic's thigh, and the inch-long lead slug with it. He dropped both on the ground, put two 4-by-4 gauze pads over the wound, and pressed hard on them with his hand.

Ching slapped him on the back, then mopped Doc's forehead where the sweat ran into his eyes.

"Did it, you ersatz sawbones, you fucking did it." Ching slapped Doc again, and helped wipe up the blood.

"Good work, Doc," Murdock said. "We all owe you a big one. How about a case of your favorite beer?"

"I'll take it the first day we get back to the Grinder," Doc said. They cleaned up the rest of the blood. Doc wiped the wound clean and applied antiseptic around it, then the last of the antibiotic salve he had, and then covered the wound with two more 4-by-4 pads before he wrapped it securely with a heavy bandage.

"Now we let him go from the hypnotic state into a normal sleep, right?" Doc asked.

Ken nodded. "When he wakes up, he's gonna be yelling. Have your morphine shots ready. He should have an MRE, and then we'll put him back under. No reason he has to endure the pain. The hypnotic state is not harmful to him in any way. Be sure to tell him the damn slug is out of his leg. That will help him to get through the pain while he's eating the MRE."

Murdock shook hands with both Doc and Ching, then went back to talk to the lookout. He'd seen lightning three times, all to the north.

While the two looked to the north, they heard a plane coming.

"Bigger than a spotter," Douglas said.

Then they saw it over the hills in front of them. It leveled out at about three thousand feet, and to Murdock's surprise, twelve men tumbled out of the plane, and chutes opened.

"Now, this we didn't need," Murdock said. The men were low enough that they drifted little before dropping into a small valley just ahead.

"Twelve men," Douglas said. "We can take them out easily."

"Yes, if they don't know we're here. They didn't see us, that's for sure. Maybe they're just setting up a blocking position." He stared at the area directly ahead. This gully was one of several that opened into the small valley. It was no more than fifty feet across, and had sharp hills on both sides. A kind of elongated gorge.

From the north came more stabs of lightning, and this time they could hear the rumble of thunder.

Murdock hit the mike. "Everyone, we've just had twelve paratroopers land maybe a mile in front of us in that valley. We've got to stay awake and alert. Be ready to move at a moment's notice. Let's have a squad check. Ed." He waited while the Second Squad checked in. Then he listened as his seven men, and Kat, let him know they were awake.

"Listen up. More lightning, and lots of thunder to the north. We figure it's on this side of the mountain group that this gully fronts. Which means that most of these arroyos around here could be hip-deep in water in a half hour. The sides of our own little canyon here are not too steep to climb. Pick out a route, and a spot at least twenty feet above the floor here, where you are going to dash to when you get the word.

"Lam, I want you to move up the gorge here as far as you can and still maintain radio contact. Maybe five hundred yards. Watch for any flash floods coming our way. If the water is traveling even twenty miles an hour, it will move five hundred yards in a rush. If it comes, you be high on the ridge, and give us all the warning you can."

He let the words soak in for a minute, then continued.

"Douglas. I want you to go high on this ridge to our right, until you can see where those twelve Iranians landed, and tell me what they're doing. If it's a blocking force, they might be setting up a camp. We don't have to tell them that the rains are here, and that they just might be swimming before long. All of these gorges empty into that little valley, and it could develop a wall of water twenty feet high in a matter of minutes. Douglas, go now."

By the time he was through talking, he could hear the platoon members moving around. He ducked in where he had been. Kat was saddled up and ready to move.

"I don't want to swim in this brush," she said.

"Not sure we'd have to. Want to be ready."

The Motorola spoke.

"L-T, I'm about a hundred yards along the gully and working up to the side. It just keeps going. Around this little curve I can see it stretch up here for a mile, with more drainage coming into it. If we get a cloudburst, it'll pour down on you like the Niagara waterfall. I'd say fifty feet off the bottom to be safe. Don't spot any rain yet. Lots more thunder up here and the sky is almost black to the north. I'd say it's moving this way."

"Thanks, Lam. We read you."

He got the rest of his gear together, fitted the pack on his back, and picked up his weapon. Kat was ready to go.

"So, we moving yet?"

"Not until we get some idea it's gonna be wet here," he said.

"Douglas," he said into the mike. "You spot that dirty dozen yet?"

"Not yet. Another fifty feet to the top. Does look nasty to the north. I'd say wet is for sure."

"Roger."

"Doc, how is Magic doing?"

"We woke him and gave him two shots, and he's lucid but hurting. He polished off an MRE, and half of mine. Ching has him back in hypnosis in case we have to move quickly. We're ready. Rest of the guys around here are, too."

They sat there waiting. Murdock checked his watch. It was only a little after 1000. Why did the daytime have to go so damned slow?

"L-T, might have something," the Motorola said.

"Go, Douglas."

"Those twelve guys are camped out in the middle of that valley. Looks more like a walled drainage ditch. Damn cut is twenty feet on each side. They've set up two tents, have a fire going. Can't tell about weapons, but they sure don't look like they expect any trouble. No lookouts I can tell. Fat and happy."

"Good, keep watch on them, and let us know of any change. How far from us are they?"

"My guess, about a mile. Our gorge bends around a forty-five-degree turn. They are maybe two hundred yards below, where it empties into the valley."

"Right. If any of them move this way, bellow at us."

"That's a Roger, sir. I've got all my gear. If you bug out, I'll catch you."

Murdock looked at Kat.

"What's a Ph.D in physics doing out in a rathole like this with sudden death hanging all around you?"

"I'm a thrill junkie, remember? Like somebody else I know."

They both grinned.

"Murdock, I've got some news."

"Lam, go."

"It's raining out there north where I can see. Maybe ten miles up to the tops of the mountains. I'd guess it's raining damn hard. I can't see any runoff yet, but if it comes, I should see it a long time before it gets here. My guess is you should move now. Upslope at least seventy-five feet from the bottom of that brush. No rush, but now is the best time. I've got two hundred feet of elevation here off the bottom."

"Roger that, Lam. Hold your spot, and keep sending us intel."

He looked at Kat. "Now is the time." They pushed through the brush to the side of the gully.

"Okay, platoon, you heard Lam. Let's all move to the right-hand side of the place, looking uphill. That's easiest to climb. We get up there a hundred feet from the brush if we can. Now is the time."

It took them ten minutes to move up on the slope where they wanted to be. There was no brush or growth of any kind up there. They sat beside their gear with cammo cloths spread over them the best they could.

A light wind whipped up.

"Troops in the valley still on a picnic," Douglas said. "Damn, I can smell something cooking down there. I must be downwind from them. Did I hear the water is coming?"

"Not yet, but Lam said it's raining on the mountain. He's watching for a flash flood."

They waited.

"At least they don't have any more air up looking for us," Kat said. "I wonder how many groups of twelve they have out in blocking positions?"

Murdock grinned. "You're starting to sound like a military ma—person." He shook his head. "No way to tell, but I'd guess that they have twenty, twenty-five such groups out, saturating the southern route."

"How can we get around all of them?"

"We take them one at a time." He closed his eyes a little. "If you're a religious person, it might not hurt to do a little praying."

She looked at him, her face serious. "Murdock, we are going to get out of this. I have total and complete trust in your ability, and your special will to live."

"Great. You don't worry about turning up the pressure on me, do you?"

She had started to reply, when the radio chattered in both their ears.

"This is it, L-T. I can see a wave of water heading our way. Must be half a mile away, and roaring downhill like a steam engine with no brakes. No telling how long it'll take to get here. Five minutes, maybe ten. Damn thing is washing away brush and a few trees that must grow up that high. Christ, look at that thing come!"

30

Friday, November 4

1146 hours
Hills south of bomb plant
Southern Iran

Murdock checked his men again. All were well up the slope, a hundred feet from the bottom

"Lam, keep talking to me. How close is the water? How fast is it moving? We're a hundred feet up, is that enough?"

"Damn, sir, I don't know. It's still a quarter of a mile from me. I'm moving up higher. I can see it now sweeping everything in front of it. A wall of water? Well, not really. It keeps tumbling over itself, almost like a breaking wave. But the whole thing must be twenty, maybe twenty-five, feet high. Like a giant breaker that never quite breaks, just keeps rolling forward."

"How fast is it moving, Lam?"

"No idea. A good fast run, fifteen, twenty miles an hour, maybe more. Seems like it's picking up speed as it comes. Strange, though, I've seen floods and things float by. Not here. Just dirty, sandy water. Not even a stick or a tree or a bush. Water ripping at the dirt, roaring along.

"Oh, God, it's almost here. There is a roar, like the ocean. Never heard anything like it. It's right in front of me. Hope

275

to hell you're all high enough. It must reach up fifty feet on the canyon wall here."

"You above it, Lam? You safe?"

"Yeah, unless I fall in. I've never seen a current quite like that."

"Let us know when it comes around the corner you talked about," Murdock said.

"Any minute now, L-T. Now you should be able to see it."

Murdock and the rest of the platoon looked up the canyon, and weren't sure whether to believe their eyes. The water roared around the bend in the gully and headed right for them.

The only thing Murdock could compare it with was pictures of a tidal wave he had seen. The water blasted forward, tearing at the walls of the canyon, tumbling, crashing over itself, sweeping small bushes and brush before it, then pounding them underwater until they could surface far to the rear.

"L-T, it seems to be slowing down a bit up here," Lam reported. "Looks like a big, muddy river with a killer of a current."

"We've got it here now, Lam. We're all up out of the way. The crest is past us now, a hundred yards downstream. Douglas, are those Iranians still having lunch out there?"

"Oh, yeah. Fat and happy. I'd figure they are about three minutes from taking a swim."

Murdock watched the water race past them, and tear down the way until it rounded the bend below and slammed into the small valley with a channel deeply cut from other flash floods.

Douglas came on the Motorola again. "Good god, look at that. I've never seen so much water in a dry river. Must be fifteen feet tall, smashing, crashing, right down the channel. It's within two hundred yards of the Iranian camp.

"Now somebody spots it and yells. The men start racing

for the sides of the channel, but the sides are so steep. Some almost make it, then the soft dirt crumbles and they fall to the bottom.

"Oh, damn. The water hit the camp. Wiped out everything. Men are washing downstream, going under as the water in front rolls and tumbles. One guy got to the top of the dirt side, but the water undercut the piece of land he was on and he dropped in the maelstrom.

"They're all gone. All twelve of them. Nobody can swim in that kind of turbulence, not even with a rebreather."

Lam came back on the radio. "Water is dropping rapidly now, L-T. I'd say it will be all past here in another five minutes. One big wall of water and no backup."

The net went silent for a moment. Murdock watched the raging water storm past them. In a few seconds he could tell the crest had passed, and backwater, with less force and speed, came rolling down the steep incline.

"Lam, work your way back down here. We're going to have to stick to the high ground for a while."

"Roger that, L-T. I'm moving."

"Douglas, see any survivors over there?"

"Not a one, Skipper. I'd say the bodies are a half mile downstream by this time, maybe farther."

"Hold your position. We need to move that way. Platoon, any reason we can't move out?"

"Magic can walk. He's feeling no pain, thanks to Ching. Not sure how mobile he'll be. Figure that out when we hit the flatter ground. I'd guess another three miles per hour."

"We need to find a new hide hole," Murdock said. "Still broad daylight and our old quarters aren't going to dry out for a couple of days. Douglas, you see anything from up there that might give us some cover? We're naked over here."

"Looking south, L-T. Could be another ravine leading out of the valley that is still dry. Can't tell for sure, but the color seems to change inside it. Over maybe two miles."

"We'll try for it."

Five minutes later, Lam walked up, and they moved out over the ridge, picked up Douglas, and Lam headed them for the valley Douglas pointed out. They worked down across a slope studded with rocks and a few bushes, then hit the side of the valley below, but kept to the far fringes of it, out of the path where the flash flood had cut the channel another two feet deeper.

Almost an hour from the top of the ridge, they came to the valley they had figured might have some plant growth for cover. It did, some scrub plants and brush about like the other one. This place was not as thick and the concealment wouldn't be perfect, but Murdock decided it would work.

"Hell of a lot better than being caught out in the open when one of their planes flies over," he said.

Doc came up and talked to Murdock.

"Magic can still walk without dragging that left foot, but he's moving slower than he was. Something is sapping his strength. We'll feed him twice as much as everyone else. Might be some infection inside that leg. If I had a few dozen kinds of antibiotics, I could kill the infection, but don't have any. It's too tricky. Tonight I'd say we'll be doing good if we can make two and a half miles an hour."

"Thanks, Doc. Anybody else hurting?"

"Not that I've heard of. Kat is doing great. She's probably in better physical shape than any of us for stamina. Damn, just thinking about my doing a triathlon gives me the hives."

Murdock went back on the Motorola. "If you haven't eaten your MRE, do it now. I've got first watch. Dig yourself a nice little nest in the leaves and brambles, and watch out for snakes. I'm kidding. Too damn hot out here even for snakes. Watch is for two hours. Washington, you're next. Pick your own victim to follow you."

They settled down in the brush then. Kat waited until Murdock found his spot, then she moved in close to him.

"Hope you don't mind if I'm your roommate," she said.

"Hey, I'm pleased. You're the prettiest SEAL I've ever seen."

"Not much of a compliment, Skipper."

They both grinned.

When they got their resting areas worked out, Murdock waved. "I'm on watch. Be back in two."

He found a place at the side of the ravine where he could have a fair view of their backtrail. The few clouds that had been moving toward them seemed to stall, then some giant, billowing, mushroom clouds built up, thunderheads, but he heard no more thunder. The storm had been stalled, probably by a high-pressure line along here somewhere.

He thought of using the mugger again, but what good would it do? He called up Ron Holt to bring the radio. They set it up on a flat place and picked up the SATCOM satellite in orbit 22,300 miles overhead. Murdock thought about his message. Then he typed it in on the keyboard.

"Stroh. Still 20 miles from wet. More troops moving in. What about alternate pickup by air? Try highest authority. May be a go/no-go option for retrieval. The Expendables."

He read it over again. Should he leave the tag line? He decided to. It would convey the situation. He let Holt encrypt it, then flash it out in a burst of transmission less than a half a second long.

"Thanks, Holt. Get some sleep."

Murdock checked his watch. Nearly 1400. He had another hour of duty. He wasn't hungry. He tapped his canteen. He had emptied the first one, and discarded it. Now his second was almost halfway down. They could use some water.

A half hour later he heard a plane, but it came nowhere near them, it was far to the south. So they must be looking down there or at least dropping in blocking units. He wondered why they hadn't run into another one. Maybe tonight.

Water. The idea crossed his mind. Fresh troops from the

air in a blocking position would have plenty of Iranian water. Worth a try. Maybe tonight.

At 1500 all was quiet. He called Washington softly. The black man came out of the brush, saw Murdock, and moved up.

"Good observation spot, L-T. All quiet?"

"So far. It should be dark in two hours. Roust the camp at that time and we'll figure out what to do."

"Aye, aye, sir."

Murdock headed back for his nest. Kat roused and sat up when he arrived.

"Quiet?"

"Yeah, makes me wonder where they are. Why don't they have choppers out here scouring the place?"

"It's a twenty-square-mile puzzle for them. Where do they start? They know we were at point A with those Claymore mines, but what direction did we take after that? My guess is the military has limited resources on-site yet. They do what they can. Much too limited for a full-scale search and destroy."

"You sound like one of my Annapolis professors."

"Just a trace of my nerves. I do have them, you know."

"Hadn't occurred to me."

"L-T, we've got trouble."

It was Washington. "Like what, Washington?"

"I'd say about fifteen troops, coming up our trail from the north. They're maybe half a mile out. Have one scout out front following our trail, rest behind dispersed."

"Platoon, it's work time," Murdock said sharply on the radio. "Everyone move to the bottom side of the brush, and get yourself a firing position. Break off some growth if you need to. I want Ronson on the machine gun, not the fifty. How many forty-millimeter rounds we have? First Squad, sound off."

Lampedusa had four rounds. Second Squad had three Colts with four rounds each.

"Find a spot and be ready when they reach two hundred yards. Fire on my first shot, two forty mike-mikes, then the Colt. The rest of you stand by. We'll let them get as close as we can. I want that scout close enough so we can smell his breath to suck the others in. I'll take the scout, the rest of you the others. Move."

Kat held her MP-5 and began to work through the brush down the hill. Murdock went behind her. The SEALs lay close together across the twenty-yard mouth of the gully where the last good concealment was.

Murdock found a spot, and broke off three small branches to give him a field of fire. "Silencers off," he said.

Then they waited.

Murdock saw the scout. He moved ahead, knelt, and examined the ground now and then, and moved on forward. He was about seventy-five yards ahead of the main body. Murdock counted sixteen men in the main force, plus one. Seventeen to seventeen.

They waited some more. Murdock looked over to where Kat had bellied down, resting her submachine gun on a low branch. Three magazines were laid out beside her. She looked at him and he saw one eye twitch. He nodded. She tried to smile.

Murdock watched the scout then. The crouched figure was ten yards away from the brush where Murdock sighted in on him, and put three 9mm parabellum rounds from the MP-5 in the Iranian's chest. At once the sixteen other weapons fired. Murdock heard both machine guns, the crack of the 40mm grenade launchers and the spurt fire of the H&K G11 caseless automatic rifle. He shifted his aim at the troops below. Some of them hadn't even hit the dirt yet. He brought down one of them, then looked for the gun flashes. The SEALs fired for three minutes, and followed the trail of two men who lifted up and zigzagged back the way they had come.

Murdock hit the mike three times, and the SEALs ceased

fire. He looked over at Kat. He hadn't thought about her when the shooting began. There was a line of sweat on her forehead. He caught a tear that had rolled down her cheek. He saw that two of her magazines were empty.

"Jaybird, Fernandez, go and make sure."

Fernandez borrowed an MP-5, and he and Jaybird ran down the slight rise to where the Iranians lay. They heard half a dozen shots, then six more.

"Weapons, ammo, water?" Jaybird asked on the radio.

"Water," Murdock said. The two men scurried around the bodies, and then ran back to the brush. Each one carried six canteens.

Jaybird found Murdock. "Could have been a scouting patrol. Not sure. They looked like seasoned men. No kids among them. My guess they weren't paratroopers."

"Might be a larger force behind them?" Murdock asked.

"It's an assumption," Jaybird said. "Which means I'd just as soon get the hell out of Dodge City."

"Yeah, distribute the canteens. Pour and fill. If they can drink it, we can drink it." He touched his radio mike.

"Platoon, good shooting. We have any casualties?" Nobody said a word. "Good. Two or three got away, so now they'll know for damn sure where we are. It'll be dark in half an hour. We're going to hit the trail again, and head due east. Maybe we can mess up their logistics somehow."

Murdock looked over at Kat. Her head was down on her arms.

"Hey Kat, you all right? You hit?"

He moved her way. She held up her hand. "No, I'm not wounded. I just killed at least one man, and it's going to take me a moment or two to get used to the idea. I've never even killed a mouse before in my whole life. Now, I . . . I shot that man."

"Kat, he was shooting at you. The only reason he came out here was to kill us, to kill you."

"Yes, I know that." She looked at him then, and wiped

away the tears. "Let me live with it for a few minutes." She sat up. "When do we load our empty magazines?"

Murdock grinned. She was thinking ahead. She'd be all right.

They left ten minutes later, just after 1600. They walked on rocky ledges whenever they could. They had the last man in the line brush out their tracks with a blanket from one of the dead Iranians. They moved in single file to make detection harder. It was still broad daylight and that bothered them all.

The total plan was to vanish from the site of the killing field and leave no trail. If they could keep that up for two or three miles due east, they could buy a lot of time before the Iranians found them again.

Magic had fired his sniper rifle, the H&K PSG1. Ching was near him but wasn't certain if he had come out of the hypnotic spell or not. Magic had trained to fire the weapon. He would do so on command in or out of hypnotism. A quarter of a mile into the march, Magic bellowed in pain and called to Ching. Five minutes later as they marched, Ching had put Magic into his hypnotic trance again, and he swung along at a three-miles-an-hour pace.

In the ten minutes of calm after the firefight, Doc had checked Magic's leg. It had bled a little but not much. Doc was amazed at the guts and stamina Magic was now showing.

At 1730, Murdock called a halt. It was almost dark. He put their east trek at three miles. He talked with Lam.

"Should throw them off the trail. Anyway they can't start to track us until daylight. We can be to hell and gone before then."

"South again. We may hit the wet yet."

"How far you guess we are from the gulf, L-T?"

"Seventeen, eighteen miles. But I've got a hunch when we come to within ten miles of it, we'll run into hundreds, maybe thousands, of troops. By now it's a matter of national pride that they nail us. We've just set back their plans for total control of this whole subcontinent by two or three years. They've got to find us, or maybe get thrown out of power."

Murdock called Ron Holt up. He had the SATCOM set up and turned on by the time Murdock had his message ready. "Stroh. Lull in action. Magic still critical. Need immediate response. What's with the extraction? Murdock."

They sent the message and waited. Murdock figured he'd give Stroh a half hour to reply. To his surprise, he came back in less than ten minutes.

The decoded message came over the small screen.

"Murdock. Top Dog considering. Iran has told the world. They blame everyone. Needed tools ready in Gulf. Would have to be a night action. Contact me in twelve hours. Stroh."

"So?" Kat asked.

"The President is still considering lifting us out of here with a Navy chopper supported by Tomcat fighters. It would be at night."

"Yeah, heavy. The U.S. invading a sovereign nation. Even at night. If one of the birds went down, there would be international shit hitting the fan, right?"

"True. So we keep moving. Let's saddle up, men. Remember, the only easy day was yesterday."

Kat shot him a quick glance. "You guys actually say that."

Murdock waved, and they moved forward due south through the dark Iranian night. There was no valley here. They trailed over a slant of sandy desert mountain, and down the other side to a ravine. It headed south. They took it.

Twenty minutes later they heard a call from Lam. "Hold," came over the radios. Murdock hurried ahead to where Lam lay on the crest of a ridge.

"Another blocking group. In a damn fine place. This is a

kind of pass with high ridges we can't climb on both sides. We go through here or we backtrack about five miles."

"Move up," Murdock said on the Motorola.

Jaybird looked over the ridge at the small encampment of soldiers. "Probably parachute guys," he said. "I'd figure maybe twenty at the most. One big fire, and four cooking fires. They must have arrived late in the day."

The ravine they were in was forty yards wide.

"No question, we take them out," Murdock said. "Even if it gives away our position. Nothing else we can do.

"Ed, take your squad down the left-hand side. Stop out about seventy-five yards. I'll bring First Squad in on the right at the same distance. We'll get a little cross fire that way. Sooner the better. Ed, give me two clicks when you're in position."

Jaybird stayed with Magic Brown as they moved down the hundred yards along the gentle downslope toward the camp. Kat walked along beside Murdock. He touched her shoulder.

"You all right?" he whispered.

She held up three full magazines and nodded.

But Kat wasn't sure. She had fired blindly last time, aiming only the first time, and had seen the man she aimed at take three rounds and get smashed to the rear. Could she do it again? Could she aim at a human being and cause his death? She gripped the MP-5, hating it for a minute, but knowing this was why she did all of the training. What if she let an enemy man stay alive long enough to kill Murdock or Jaybird? She had to do it. She had to fire at the men down there. She had to.

What bothered her, as they moved up on the target, was if she could actually kill another human being . . . again.

31

Friday, November 4

0820 hours
Nuclear bomb plant
Hills north of Chah Bahar, Iran

General Reza Ruhollah stared at the colonel who had commanded this facility until the heathens attacked it. General Ruhollah was in no mood to tolerate traitors.

"Colonel, I relieved you of your command here. I restricted you to your quarters. What are you doing in my office?"

"I must protest, General Ruhollah. My men have been subjected to your illegal orders. My guard troops have been sent into the field without proper rations. You have ordered my subordinates to rebuild the assembly plant, but have given them no resources."

"Colonel, I'm telling you one more time to keep your mouth shut. Not one more word."

"I still must protest, General Ruhollah. My men have been slaughtered at the hands of a well-equipped military force. I ask that adequate protection be given . . ." The Colonel stopped.

General Ruhollah lifted a German-made machine pistol

and fired six rounds into the Colonel's chest. He slammed backward, hit the wall, slid down, and died as he lay on the floor, his eyes still wide in total disbelief.

Two aides rushed into the room.

"Get this trash out of my office and clean up the mess. I have to call for more troops. Quickly now."

General Ruhollah went back to his desk. He picked up the phone and was soon asking for more reinforcements from Shiraz and Bandar-e Bushehr.

"You can have two thousand troops here within eight hours," he stormed on the phone. "I don't need authorization from Tehran. I'm ordering you to send those troops to Chah Bahar this morning, and have them here before dark. Get them moving, combat-ready, with three days of ammunition and rations. Move them now."

He hung up and made another call similar in nature to the Army Commander at Bandar-e 'Abbas, which was much closer. He demanded the troops be on hand by four that afternoon. When he hung up, an aide came in the room.

"General, there is an aircraft landing at the small field. It may be the Army Supreme Commander. It is the same kind of two-engine turboprop plane he usually uses."

"Thank you, Major. Meet him, and see that he's brought here at once with all normal courtesy."

The General sat back and smiled. He would show his one superior in the Iranian Army the damage, his moves so far, and his plans for stopping the attacking force before it could reach the coast.

He would have nearly a thousand troops on hand before dark. They would be deployed at the end of every road leading into the mountains around Chah Bahar. He would throw in as blocking units all he could find. He would continue to drop in twelve-man paratroop teams to block all normal avenues south. He would use the jets from Bandar-e 'Abbas to search for and harass any movement they heard about.

The enemy force was still a mystery. It had wiped out all

but three men on the first patrol he sent out. Twenty-seven men dead, two of the escapees wounded. It was a potent force he was following. He must do everything he could to stop it.

He was sure that General Shahr would agree. The devils must be hunted down, and slaughtered, then their nationality broadcast to the world as invaders and murderers of the lowest order. It had to be a Western power, but which one? Perhaps it was Israel; they were tricky and deadly.

He heard a car pull up outside his office and stood, straightened his tie, and brushed off his uniform. He looked at the wall and floor where the Colonel had fallen. All signs of the blood had been cleaned up.

As the door opened, he stood and snapped a salute.

"General Shahr, good morning. If I had known you were coming, I would have had a fitting welcome for you."

General Shahr was short and heavy. He wore five stars on his shoulders, and a scowl on his face.

"This nuclear plant, this bomb making—why didn't I know anything about it?"

"My General, I was simply following orders of our honored President and some of his highest advisors. I am only their active tool to get the project completed."

"And you have failed miserably. Even now I understand you draw in our troops to find the attackers. Why can't our half million troops track down this band of saboteurs you estimated at no more than twenty?"

"They are professionals, General. Deadly, deceptive, experts at concealment. We will find them. By nightfall we will have them blocked off from the sea. They can't go through Pakistan. We will close the circle and slaughter them to a man."

"You will have no more part in the battle, Ruhollah."

He froze in place when he heard his superior disregard his title and use only his name. It was a sign that all was not well.

"You have deceived your superiors, you have conspired behind my back to seize this power and, with it, control Iran and all of the peninsula, and most of Islam. For that you are a traitor to Iran, and you must pay the price."

General Shahr took a revolver from his waistband and shot General Ruhollah twice in the chest. Ruhollah slumped to the floor, both hands holding the holes in his chest. He looked up at his commanding officer and started to say something.

General Shahr shot him in the head, and General Ruhollah slammed to the floor, blood pooling beside his head and running down to the stars of his rank on his shoulder.

General Shahr nodded, called in his men to remove the body, then settled down to the situation map on the wall, and began making phone calls.

Ruhollah was an idiot to think he could get away with this. He had been monitored all the way. As soon as the project was a success, Ruhollah would have been eliminated, and the Army would have taken the credit. He would have ousted the President, and overruled the Ayatollah, and he, General Shahr, would have ruled two-thirds of the Arab world with his bombs, and the threat of his bombs.

Now they were set back at least two years, and he knew they would be monitored closely by the foreign powers. Still it could be done with total secrecy, and with an underground facility. He had plans for it already.

He turned back to the map. If he were a military force running for safety, exactly where would he go after heading south? Continue on that way, divert to the east and slip through the porous border with Pakistan, or sit, and wait for some kind of an air rescue? Any of the three were possible. He reached for the phone to check on the nearby bases and see if they had been alerted. It would be a busy afternoon.

32

Friday, November 4

1920 hours
Hills south of bomb plant
Southern Iran

Five minutes after they parted, Murdock had his squad in position. Magic insisted that he get back his sniper rifle to use in the attack. Murdock let him have it. He put Kat next to him, and then the rest of his squad in a rough line aimed at the dozen troopers about seventy-five yards away. It was fully dark now.

Murdock waited. Moments later he heard two *tsks* on the earpiece. DeWitt had his SEALs ready.

Murdock looked quickly at Kat. She had her submachine gun up and ready. He took a deep breath, aimed at the man standing in front of the big fire, and jolted off three rounds.

At once the whole platoon opened up.

Kat hesitated. Could she do it again? Then she triggered off three rounds. They were high. She brought the muzzle down and fired again into the sudden churning mass of men. There was screaming, men looking for their weapons, men dying. She shut her eyes for a minute, heard firing beside her and opened them, and fired again on 3-round bursts until her magazine went dry. She ripped it out, put another one in, charged a round, and aimed back at the men below.

Suddenly she heard firing from behind her. She saw three dark shapes running at them from the rear. She whirled, brought up her weapon, and triggered nine rounds at the three shadows. One screamed and dove to the ground. Another fell dead without a word; the third turned and ran back the way he had come.

Murdock looked behind him. He saw one of the dark shadows crawling away. He put a 3-round burst into him, then looked at Kat.

She nodded, swung her weapon back to the front, and kept firing.

Murdock checked the scene carefully. There was no more return fire from the troopers below.

"Think we did it," DeWitt said on the radio.

"Yeah, cease fire," Murdock said. "Ed, send in two men to check them out."

Murdock lifted off the dirt and ran to the rear where he found the two Iranians. Both were dead. He hurried back to their line.

Ahead at the small Iranian camp, he heard two shots, then all was silent.

Kat stared at him. "Those shots?"

"We have to make sure the enemy are all dead. We don't take prisoners or leave wounded."

Kat flinched. Her face surged into a scowl. "Isn't that . . . Isn't that a little cold, brutal?"

"Absolutely. We're not here to play games or give credits for the enemy's bravery. It's simply kill or be killed. The way you reacted just a minute ago. You saw the three coming when the rest of us didn't. You reacted. You saved at least three of our lives right here."

"Clear front," the radio said in their ears.

The SEALs moved down and surveyed the wreckage. There was little they could use. The ammo didn't fit, and they didn't want to pack along any additional weapons. Their canteens were still full.

"No one escaped down here?" Murdock asked.

DeWitt shook his head. "What was that firing to the rear?"

"Three surprised us from behind. Two are down, and one got away."

"So we better shag ass out of here," DeWitt said.

"Yeah, let's move," Murdock said.

They walked away down the slope of the small pass, and Murdock moved back beside Kat.

"So?"

"I'm alive. That's the main purpose now—to stay alive. It's like when you can't breathe, nothing else really matters. Like now. If we don't survive, none of my high and mighty principles mean a pile of shit, to drop into the SEAL vernacular."

"True. We survive, then we figure out about living. It can be a tough road."

"We'll make it."

"Good work back there. If they'd been better shots, we'd be digging two or three graves right about now."

"Didn't think you left anyone behind."

"Sometimes, depends. Here we would have had to. We couldn't carry out even one body."

"Hate to mention it but you forgot to ask for a casualty report," Kat said.

Murdock frowned. "Yeah, we didn't take much return fire. Some, I guess." He clicked his mike. "Hey, casualty report. Sound off if anybody got hit."

For a moment there was no sound on the radio, then one small voice came on.

"Yeah, Doc might take a look at my arm. It doesn't seem to be working right."

Murdock moved over beside Kat. "Why in hell didn't you say so?"

"You didn't ask. Hell, a SEAL can fight over a little

pain." She grinned in the darkness and hoped Murdock could see it.

Doc came storming up.

Murdock called a halt. He asked for Holt, and had him set up the SATCOM.

"How bad is it, Doc?" Murdock asked.

"I'm gonna have to amputate," Doc said, sounding relieved.

"You try it and I'll use up my full magazine on you," Kat said.

They both chuckled.

"One slug cut through about an inch of Kat's forearm," Doc said. "Missed the bone. Kat will hurt like hell for a week or so, then will have a war wound to brag about. Oh, yeah, it will leave a battle scar and everything."

"SATCOM is ready, L-T," Holt said.

Murdock knew his message. He typed it in. "Stroh. How about a pickup? Can receive you now. Answer me, we're running out of time and ammo. Murdock."

As soon as they switched to receive, the small screen lit up. The message was short.

"Murdock. Possible. Contact us in two hours. Have your exact coordinates and time of day there."

Murdock snapped off the set. "We contact them again at exactly twenty-one-forty-two. Doc, you got your patient bandaged?"

"Ready to rock and roll. Hear she saved the fucking day back here."

"True. You almost had a lot of work to do. Let's get out of here at three miles an hour. Go, Lam."

They hiked again through the Iranian hill country darkness.

Twice they heard jets overhead. Once a propeller-driven plane sounded to the south but faded out.

Murdock heard the next sound a half hour later. It was a chopper and headed their way.

"Big bird coming," he said. "Possible that the guy who got away back there had a radio. If he did, they must know about where we are."

The chopper came closer, scouring the ravine to the left. They saw the powerful searchlight. It turned the ground into daylight for a circle of twenty yards.

"Scatter," Murdock said. "Try to find a rock to curl around and use your cammo cloth. He's gonna work this gully for damn sure. Magic, can you use that fifty?"

"Fucking A, L-T. Armor piercing?"

"Give it a five-round try if he comes within two hundred yards of us. No, wait for a hundred yards. You can't miss at that range."

"You got it, Skipper."

Ronson had been carrying the fifty and the ammo. He loaded five rounds of the armor-piercing types and handed the weapon to Magic. He hunkered down behind a two-foot rock and rested the weapon over the top.

"Come on, sweetheart," Magic said. "Come and let papa give you a shot or two."

Chin watched him, and looked over at Doc. "Hell, I don't know if he's still under or not. Could be pure adrenaline, a nervous high. He doesn't even seem to know he's got a shot-up leg."

"Hope it lasts," Doc said.

They had spread out to be fifteen yards apart. Murdock watched the bird with its long arm of light probing the canyon. Soon the pilot or observer was satisfied, and the bird angled toward the next gully, the one they had been hiking up.

"Stay low and don't move a muscle," Murdock said.

"Never fear, the Magic man is here," Brown chortled.

The big chopper swung closer. At two hundred yards it picked up the gully, changed course, and began working up it, no faster than a slow walk. It gave the crew plenty of time to watch below. It was over a hundred feet in the air so the rotor wash made no dust problem on the ground.

"Closer, you son of a bitch," Magic whispered into the mike.

They waited. It kept working uphill toward them. It would be a hundred yards from Murdock when the light touched the first of the men in Second Platoon, more than that distance from Magic.

"Your guns are free, Magic," Murdock said. "Fire at will."

Just as the chopper swung over the rock Ed DeWitt had claimed, Magic fired. The round slammed through the cabin of the chopper. Before the bird could make any move, Magic had worked the lever and chambered a new round and fired. This one thundered into the engine compartment. At once black smoke poured from the bird.

Magic fired again. The armor-piercing round exploded inside the machine somewhere and it angled sharply to the left. The rotor went on freewheeling when the power stopped. The craft righted itself, then plunged straight to the ground a hundred feet below.

"Go clean it up," Murdock said. "On me, my squad." The first squad ran downhill toward where the chopper hit the ground with a loud explosion and fire. They ran to within fifty feet of the burning wreckage but couldn't get any closer.

"Work the perimeter and look for survivors," Murdock ordered in the Motorola. They found none.

Five minutes later, the fire had burned itself down to a few flames and a lot of smoke.

"Clear front," Murdock said. "Let's get away from this bonfire."

Lam met them when they rejoined the platoon. "South? L-T?"

"Right. No way we can fool anyone about where we are now. As soon as that chopper's radio went out, there must have been two or three more birds heading this way. We make some tracks. Some concealment would be nice from the lights the new birds must have. See what we can find."

They hiked again. This time Magic insisted on carrying the fifty. Ronson didn't tell him he still had ten rounds in one big magazine for the fifty.

Murdock watched his timepiece. They made good time for the first hour. It was 2100. In forty-two minutes they would contact Uncle Sugar, and hope for good news.

Murdock eased to the rear and walked beside Kat.

"How's it going?"

"Good. I'm good."

"Really?"

"I'm surviving, after all. We'll see. First survive, then take a shot at getting a life, right?"

"Yeah. The arm?"

"I got some ibuprofen from Doc. Four of the suckers. Taking the burn out of it. I'll make it. Is Uncle going to pop for a chopper for us?"

"Hard to tell. At least the President is in on it. If I tell them you're wounded, it should be a cinch."

"Don't you dare, Murdock. I mean it. Don't say a word about me."

"You got it. First Squad owes you one, SEAL. You remember that."

They hiked for another half hour and Murdock stopped them against a steep hill with a lot of moon shadows. Holt had the SATCOM set up before Murdock asked him.

He worked the mugger and got their coordinates, which he wrote down on the edge of his map. He used a small mouth-held flashlight to be sure he got the figures right. Then he keyed the screen. His message.

"Murdock has his ears on."

He snapped it to receive, and seconds later the screen showed a response.

"We have a go on chopper. It has lifted off its birdhouse

already and is on the way. Two F-14's will fly cover at time of pickup. ETA when you give us your exact coordinates. Use two red flares on the ground to mark your LZ. Make it as level a spot as possible. Coordinates. The Seahawk will give you three strobe flashes, then three more for identification as it comes in."

Murdock typed in the coordinates from the mugger, had Holt double-check them to be sure, then zapped out the burst of transmission.

They waited with the set on receive. It was five minutes before the screen came to life.

"Murdock. ETA your site 2240. Use two red flares to mark LZ. Any hostile action?"

"No hostiles now. Will use green flares on any hostiles. May be three hundred yards off coordinates for level LZ. Waiting."

Murdock looked at the silent set. Done. "Fold it up, let's find an LZ."

As soon as he heard the problem, Lam took off on a run. He was back before Murdock got the platoon moving.

"L-T, out here to the left about four hundred yards we have a valley of sorts. Level spot a hundred yards square."

"Let's move it there," Murdock said. "Keep your eyes and ears open. We don't want to be surprised this close to home."

They hiked to the spot, and Murdock gave the two red flares to Jaybird to light, and throw when they heard the friendly bird and saw the three white strobe flashes.

"Perimeter defense," Murdock said. "We watch everywhere, all the time for the next fifty minutes or so. Holt, be ready to switch to receive on the Miltac frequency so we can talk with the Seahawk and maybe the F-fourteens. Let's move."

"That chopper we shot down," Kat said from ten yards to his right, "will they send in some more right away?"

"I would. Try to get us here before we slip away again. It

depends how good the guy who got by us is, and how good he is on coordinates."

They waited.

Twenty minutes later, Murdock felt easier about it. A quick landing, sprint to the big open door. Pile in seventeen bodies and a brisk takeoff.

It didn't work out that way.

Twenty minutes before the Seahawk was due, three big choppers came in from the north. They spotlighted two of the platoon and dropped down two hundred yards away. Doors clanged and Murdock could just feel the troops rushing out.

"Magic, your big one is free. Everyone fire at those choppers. Now, keep it high so we don't hit any friendlies."

The guns opened up, the ones that could reach out two hundred yards. The MGs chattered. Magic got in one lucky round on one of the dark choppers and it mushroomed into flames. That backlighted twenty Iranian troopers charging toward them. Half of them went down on the first volley. That slowed them.

A moment later three more choppers came in due south of the platoon.

"Damnit, fucking damnit to hell," Murdock bellowed. "Half of you hit each side. Hold up on the short guns."

Before they had warmed up on the second trio of enemy helicopters and their troops, Holt was on the Motorola.

"Skipper, I've got two Tomcats two minutes away. They suggest we hit those chopper guys with some green flares."

"Roger that. Who is closest to each side with the flares?" He got responses, and thirty seconds later, they shot out the rifle flares at the enemy choppers.

Almost before the first one exploded with a green light, an angry bird from the sky swooped down and laced the Iranian chopper area with fifty rounds of 20mm cannon fire. A second Iran helicopter exploded in flames.

The second green flare hit the southern force and soon the

second Tomcat slammed in on target and got away seventy-five to a hundred rounds of cannon fire before he pulled up and went around for another pass.

In four minutes the Tomcats had made four passes at each of the enemy contingents. Two more choppers caught fire, and there was little return fire from the Iranians.

Holt hit his lip mike again. "L-T, I have a Seahawk coming in. Suggest we light the red flares."

"Do it," Murdock barked.

He saw the flares burst into color just as the Tomcats made another pass, blasting the remnants of the Iranian forces into deadly fragments.

The big Seahawk settled to ground inside the two red flares.

"Magic and Kat first," Murdock said loudly in his mike to get over the chopper sound. "Go, you two, now go, everyone else right behind. This ain't no waiting game we've got here."

33

Friday, November 4

2244 hours
Landing zone in hills
Near Chah Bahar, Iran

Murdock watched as Magic and Kat both ran to the open door of the Seahawk while the rotors whirled. They jumped on board. Murdock heard firing from behind him. He turned and sprayed the area with the rest of his magazine, then ran for the chopper with the last of the SEALs. He had almost made it to the door when he saw Kat lean out with her MP-5, and shoot off a full magazine of rounds in one burst.

The rounds went well over his head and toward where there had been more muzzle flashes behind them.

Murdock pulled himself into the Seahawk.

"DeWitt, do we have a count?"

"You're the last, Murdock. All seventeen SEALs present and accounted for."

A crewman slammed the door shut, and the chopper pulled up like it was on a spring, jumping into the air and slanting away from the groundfire.

Murdock looked around in the dim light of the chopper. "Anybody get hit in that last exchange?"

"Oh, yeah," a voice said.

301

"Washington?" DeWitt asked.

" 'Fraid so, L-T. Caught one in the shoulder, I was almost in the fucking door. Two feet away from getting home free. Kat there pounded out about sixty rounds just then and I figured she pushed them crackers' heads down."

Doc Ellsworth was by Washington's side a moment later. He pulled off the cammy shirt and looked at the wound. The Navy crew chief brought a flashlight.

"Oh, yeah, Washington, you bought a good one. Hit the bone and didn't come out. We'll let the real Navy doctors on the carrier take care of it." He bandaged it up and slipped the shirt back in place except for the sleeve. Doc gave him three pain pills. "You take it easy. We'll have you in sick bay inside of an hour."

"How's Magic?" Murdock asked the medic.

"Don't know. He hasn't complained. Magic? Where the hell are you?"

They stared around the cramped inside of the Seahawk.

"Hey, he's over here," Kat said. "Looks like he's passed out."

Twenty minutes later they were nearing the big aircraft carrier in the Persian Gulf. It had steamed down close to Dubayy of the United Arab Emirates to cut down on flying time.

Magic had come around once, grinned, waved at them, and drifted off to sleep.

"He's been running on empty for the past day and a half," Doc said. "Living on guts and hope. That leg wound really drained him, then he kept hiking along with the rest of us. There's got to be a ton of infection in that leg."

"We'll land in fifteen minutes," the crew chief told them.

A half hour later, on board the USS *Monroe CVN 81*, Murdock and DeWitt saw their people into sick bay. Kat got quick treatment. They took Washington into surgery to dig out the slug. Magic was another matter.

"Massive infection," a Navy surgeon said. "He's lucky to be alive. Another twenty-four hours and it would have eaten him up. Good work getting that bullet out. We'll go after the infection with antibiotics. He should be up and around in a month."

"When can he fly back to Balboa Naval Hospital?" Murdock asked.

"Two days, Lieutenant. Not before."

Murdock went for a telephone chat with Don Stroh, then had the biggest steak the mess could provide.

An hour later, Murdock was in his quarters when a knock came on the door. He opened it. Kat stood there looking washed and combed in a clean pair of cammies, with her railroad tracks on her collar.

"You keep those bars of rank with you all the time?" Murdock asked.

"Hey, you said to. May I come in?"

He stepped back, and she went in and sat on a chair.

"So, we made it, we survived," Kat said.

"Now we start thinking about having a life, again."

"I've been wondering about that. I think I'm through tearing nukes apart. As beneficial as it might be. I've always liked research."

"You shouldn't have any trouble finding a spot. Maybe at M.I.T. or Cal Tech."

"No, I don't want that much pressure. Lower expectations, lower stress, more time to have a life."

"Good thinking. Hey, I'd like to give you a medal, Kat, but I can't do that. You probably saved my life out there, but it's all one big, dark secret."

"I know. I can tell some civilian what I did, but then I'd have to kill him. I know."

"Any regrets?"

"Well, I'm not sure I wanted to find out how it felt to kill another human being. Three, in fact, maybe more."

"How does it feel, Kat?"

"Part of it damn good, especially those two bushwhackers who came up behind us. I cried after the first one. But then the old bugaboo about surviving came to the fore, and I had to cope with that. Survive first, get a life afterwards."

"You'll do fine, Kat."

"What about you?"

"I have another part of my life waiting for me in Washington, D.C."

"That would be Ardith Manchester, beautiful lawyer type."

"You knew that all along?"

"Sure, I research more than physics when I take on a job."

The phone on the desk rang. Kat shrugged, lifted it off the set, and gave him the handset.

"Yes, sir."

"Murdock. Stroh. I've had half that damn carrier force trying to find Kat. Any idea where she is? Somebody here wants to talk to her."

"I think I could find her. Just a minute." He handed Kat the phone. "It's for you."

Kat took the handset. "Yes, this is Katherine Garnet."

"May I call you Kat?" the booming voice came.

She frowned. "Yes, of course."

"Don Stroh here has been telling me what a great job you did becoming a SEAL for a week. We're all proud of you here at the White House."

"The White House?"

The voice on the other end chuckled. "Don didn't tell you. This is President Mason, and I want you to be sure to stop over and see the First Lady and me as soon as you get to Washington. Have Murdock bring you. I need to talk to him as well. Just wanted to offer my congratulations. You might have prevented World War Three, or at least some disastrous fighting among the Arab states. You rest up now. Don says you're due to fly home in two days."

"Yes, and thank you. Thank you very much, Mr. President."

"Don't mention it. You get that arm healed up now, y'hear?"

"Yes, sir." The line went dead and Kat hung up the phone, a strange smile growing on her face.

"The President," she said.

Murdock grinned. "I guessed as much. Hell, won't be any getting along with you now for the next three days."

"Shut up, Murdock, and buy me a Coke. Shouldn't you be checking on the troops or something. I thought us SEALs took care of our own."

"Just about to do that. Most of them should be sleeping by now. Let's go check them out."

Tuesday, November 8
1040 hours
Third Platoon HQ
Coronado, California

Four days later, Murdock stretched out in his office chair and relaxed. Magic Brown was safely tucked away in Balboa Naval Hospital in San Diego. The doctors were surprised how the infection had spread, and repeated how lucky he had been not to lose the leg. The evaluation was that he would need a month of bed rest, massive medications, then two weeks of rehab before he could start to work out with the platoon again.

Fred Washington's shoulder was on the mend. The bullet had done no damage to his shoulder bones and he'd be good as new in three weeks.

Kat had been treated at Balboa and released. She had taken a commercial nonstop flight from San Diego's Lindbergh Field the next morning. Murdock had her phone number and would contact her when he got to D.C. in a week or so.

He was helping Jaybird get the men on week-long passes, and the squad room was half-empty.

When the phone rang, he let it go four times, then figured Jaybird wasn't around.

"Yes, Third Platoon."

"Made it back, I hear."

"Stroh, don't you ever sleep?"

"It's the middle of the day. Just wanted to say hi."

"Hi, Stroh."

"Oh, the President is as happy as a mud turtle in a hen house. Says the Iranians are mad as hell, but can't figure out who to blame. They couldn't nail down whose jets or chopper invaded their sovereign airspace and soil, but they won't openly admit they were working on nuclear bombs. Our experts say they can't get anything built now for at least three years. Everyone will watch what they sell to Iran that could be used in a nuke."

"Good. Tell the President to remember me when I go up for my next stripe."

"You, full Commander? Then they wouldn't let you go out to play with the dangerous toys."

"Sure they would. I've seen some three-stripers in the field."

"Not much anymore. At least not working your special gig. Hey, I was just wondering what you know about the New Russian Navy."

"Not a damned thing, and I don't want to know. I've got a month's leave coming and I'm taking it. As a wise person told me in the middle of that country over there. 'First we survive, then we find a life.' I'm going to take a shot at finding a life. And Stroh. Don't call me. You'll probably know where I am, but unless the President has a serious health problem, or the moon spins out of orbit, don't call me."

"Yeah, sure, big guy. Like always. You stop by and see

me when you're in D.C., and say hello to that sweet little
girl, Ardith."

"Good-bye, Don."

"Good-bye, Murdock."

Tuesday, November 15
1400 hours
Surfside Motel
Cannon Beach, Oregon

Ed DeWitt had been back from Iran for over a week now.
For the last four days he hadn't even thought about the
SEALs. It was new territory for him. He had taken a
two-week leave. He and Milly were on what they called a
pre-honeymoon. They drove up the long California coast
toward Oregon, stopping at every small town and village.
They shopped, and ate all sorts of unusual foods, bartered
with the natives, and chilled out on the scenery and good
company.

Now they lay on lounges watching the Pacific pound
against the shore at Cannon Beach, Oregon. The sun had
just rimmed the horizon and sparkled a hundred shades of
pink, deep reds, and purples into the generous spread of
Oregon clouds.

"I may never go back," DeWitt said, sipping a cold beer.

Milly grinned. "Says who? We've got one more week. In
about five days you'll get up and scan the international
headlines. You'll call the quarter deck once a day to see
what's going on in Third Platoon. You'll worry about how
Fred Washington's shoulder is healing."

She sipped at her beer. "Hey, Ed. I wouldn't want it any
other way. If you didn't do those things, you wouldn't be
you. I fell in love with the real you. In spite of all the
damned drawbacks—the danger, the outrageous things they
ask you guys to do—I guess I wouldn't have that any other
way as well."

"Woman, you make a lot of sense. Now rub my back."

She did. "I had the idea to rub you somewhere else."

"Not out here."

They hadn't talked about Kat. Milly kept rubbing his back, then massaged his shoulders.

"Tell me about Kat. How did she do?"

"Like one of the guys, honest. She was a lady, who killed at least three of them. She probably saved the lives of one or two of Murdock's squad when three guys came up behind them. She heard them, turned, and cut down two of them with her submachine gun. The third one ran."

"That's enough. I don't want you to tell me so much you'll have to kill me. I'm glad she did well. Terribly happy that she didn't mess up and somebody else got killed. End of talk."

She stood and caught his hand. "Now, inside where there's a little privacy. I have something else I want to talk with you about. Body talk I guess you'd call it."

Ed DeWitt grinned. "Yeah, let's call it that."

SOMETHING EXPLODED
IN THE SKY...

...something metallic, something swirling, something from hell. Four dark beasts filled the southeastern horizon like the lions of the apocalypse. The reflection of morning light off the sand splayed like blood across their wings...

Startled from the half-daze of the monotonous watch, the sentry grabbed his rifle and flung himself against the sand-filled bags at the front of the trench. It took a moment for his brain to register the fact that the planes were coming from the south and not the north—they were friends, not foes. The thick canisters of death slung beneath their wings were not meant for him.

"What the hell are those," he asked his companion as the planes roared over their positions.

The other soldier laughed. "You never saw A-10 Warthogs before?"

"They're on our side?"

"You better pray to God they are."